THE MORNING AFTER

Suzanne Forster

JOVE BOOKS, NEW YORK

THE MORNING AFTER

A Jove Book / published by arrangement with
the author

PRINTING HISTORY
Jove edition / April 2000

All rights reserved.
Copyright © 2000 by Suzanne Forster.
Cover illustration by Franco Accornero.
This book may not be reproduced in whole or part,
by mimeograph or any other means, without permission.
For information address: The Berkley Publishing Group,
a division of Penguin Putnam Inc.,
375 Hudson Street, New York, New York 10014.

The Penguin Putnam Inc. World Wide Web site address is
http://www.penguinputnam.com

ISBN: 0-515-12800-7

A JOVE BOOK®
Jove Books are published by The Berkley Publishing Group,
a division of Penguin Putnam Inc.,
375 Hudson Street, New York, New York 10014.
JOVE and the "J" design
are trademarks belonging to Penguin Putnam Inc.

PRINTED IN THE UNITED STATES OF AMERICA

10 9 8 7 6 5 4 3 2 1

O N E

&

"Good night, Princess, don't forget me."

Whispered words. His hushed, smoky voice swirled in Temple Banning's head as she awakened one morning to totally unfamiliar surroundings. It was the most sumptuous hotel suite she'd ever seen, but she had no idea how she got there.

Or who the man was.

She was lying in a canopy bed, surrounded by Chantilly lace and fresh-cut flowers. There was a magnum of champagne in a silver urn next to the bed and a room-service cart, covered in white linen and set with fine china. Silver bowls and tiered trays were laden with sweets, lump caviar, and other exotic tidbits. Two crystal flutes of champagne sat untouched, the bubbles now gone flat.

Temple would have thought she was dreaming, except that her dreams had never been this good. This was too lavish. Too perfect.

She sat up carefully, not wanting to disturb anything, including the rose petals fluttering on the bed like blushing butterflies. A lilac-sprigged coverlet concealed her from the waist down, but not the bodice of her white plissé night-gown or the delicate straps that had drifted down her arms.

Her breathing quickened. Panic stirred her as she searched her memory, and visually scanned the room, but still had no idea what she was doing there. The last thing she remembered was the nightly routine of going to bed in the apartment that had been provided by the company when they brought her out here. It was March fifth, another date-less Friday evening. And now, according to the digital display on the suite's clock radio, the next morning.

The suite was quiet. Temple decided to find out if she was alone, but as she drew back the coverlet, she saw the dia-mond on her finger. Surrounded by sapphires in the antique white-gold setting, the marquise-cut stone was stunning, ex-actly the sort of thing she would have picked out for herself.

"Donald?" No one answered when she called out the name of her former fiancé. For a moment she wondered if she'd suffered some kind of lapse and let herself be talked into marrying him, simply because he wanted that so badly.

What was going on here?

Temple was an expert at putting others first. Until re-cently it had been a way of life. But on her last birthday she'd turned thirty—and made some difficult choices. She'd said no to Donald, very gently, and yes to the dream job that had brought her out here to Ventura, California.

If she *was* in Ventura. Beyond the bedroom, tucked away in a daydreamer's alcove, there was a sitting room with wraparound window seats, rich cherrywood surfaces, and Tiffany lamps. She could see gardens beyond, lush with pink foxglove, climbing roses, a wisteria-draped arbor. All lovely, but none of it familiar.

Temple drew on a matching plissé robe for a look around. This was not her lingerie. She'd never seen it before, but it felt like cool air flowing against her skin. So did the matching mules she slipped on her feet. They made her feel light and floaty as she walked across the room. It was almost as if she'd had a dizzy spell and couldn't catch her balance.

The empire wedding dress draped over an antique settee wasn't at all familiar. Nor was the bridal bouquet of lilies and snowdrops or the lacy blue garter. She picked up a veil, and a cloud of In Love Again filled the air. It was her favorite perfume.

But none of those things commanded her attention like the piece of paper lying on the occasional table. It was a marriage license with her name at the top and her signature at the bottom. His name was there, too, in bold print: Michael St. Gerard. But it was no more familiar than the room or the wedding ensemble. She didn't know this man.

Don't forget me. That voice. Those words. How could she forget someone she'd never met?

What she did remember, as if it were a dream, was the shadow touch of a man's hands, the lightning touch of his lips. She remembered heartbeats pattering like rain, the sweet riot of surprise . . .

Temple had barely settled the veil on her tousled auburn tresses when she encountered herself in the mirror. She looked a little tipsy, her eyes dark and tenderly questing for something, her mouth lush, surprised, and just the tiniest bit slack. A tendril of hair had caught in her eyelashes. Another had attached itself to the dampness of her throat. She didn't wear her hair this way; long and curly. She usually pinned it up. Even the color in her face was high.

She could have been one of those women who'd drunk too much and found herself in a lonely motel one morning with some man she hardly knew, married on a dare. Only she wasn't in a motel. This was a luxurious honeymoon suite, and there was no man in evidence.

She began to laugh, it was all so bewildering. She couldn't

imagine who would play such an elaborate practical joke on her, even Denny Paxton, her arch-competitor at the ad agency. She hadn't been in California two months, and she didn't know anybody well enough for that. But what else could it be?

"Good morning, Mrs. St. Gerard." A feminine voice chirped softly in Temple's ear as she picked up the phone in the suite.

Temple had swooped the moment it rang, hoping it would be someone who could tell her what was going on. The phone was one of those antique French handsets. Temple had to hold it at both ends to get the mouthpiece lined up, but the woman didn't wait for her.

"This is the concierge," she said over Temple's half-hearted attempt to explain that she wasn't Mrs. Anyone.

"Are you enjoying your stay so far?" she asked. "Is there anything you'd like this morning? Your husband asked us to check."

"My husband?"

"Yes, he's terribly sorry he was called away so abruptly. It was the middle of the night, and he didn't want to wake you. He said there was an emergency in the overseas operation that could take a few days to clear up. But he wanted to make sure you had whatever you needed. Can we send up some breakfast, Mrs. St. Gerard? Our warm raisin brioche is delicious. Coffee? Fresh champagne?"

This was not the call Temple had been hoping for.

"No, thank you," she said. "Nothing." The phone was already halfway to the cradle, and she was more than halfway to being completely confused. "Wait!" she cried. "The man, did you see him leave?"

"Man?"

"Yes, Donald, my . . . husband. He's five ten, medium build, brown hair, and silver wire-rim glasses."

"Donald? I thought his name was Michael." The clerk laughed merrily. "No, I didn't see him. I'm the day person, but I can tell you one thing, Mrs. St. Gerard . . . whatever his name might be, you're a very lucky woman."

Now Temple did hang up the phone. Her confusion was complete.

"What in the world?" She gasped out soft laughter and sank onto the bed, taking in her luxe surroundings all over again. Who would do a thing like this? Temple couldn't imagine. When she'd made the move from Houston, she'd left everything that was familiar behind. This was perhaps the first time in her relatively uneventful life that she'd known what she wanted and dared to declare herself. Dared to say it out loud.

Maybe she shouldn't have been surprised that no one supported her. Donald thought she'd gone crazy. How could she even consider a job in another city? Relocation was out of the question. After struggling through medical school and his residency at Houston General, he'd borrowed heavily to pay off his debts and to set up a general practice office. Besides, he didn't like California. Too much sun, too much skin. And he was adamantly against the idea of Temple's taking an apartment and commuting.

Temple understood Donald's predicament better than anyone. She knew how hard he'd worked because she'd been there, up until all hours with him, night after night, helping him write papers and cram for tests. She'd had to back-burner her travel agency job, even though she was the advertising director and loved her work. But when suddenly opportunity dropped the golden apple in Temple's lap, it was quite an eye-opener.

Perhaps for the first time, she saw how others viewed her, and it was a sobering experience, especially since these were the people who were supposed to want the best for her. To

Donald she'd become the equivalent of a life-support system. He needed her there when things got rough and he couldn't function on his own. He'd become accustomed to his regular shots of oxygen, but he couldn't see that she might need some support and encouragement, too. That she might have talents crying out to be expressed.

Her fiancé's lack of insight was a bitter disappointment. But it was Temple's little sister who broke her heart. Ivy Banning was a Grimm's fairy tale heroine with her oval pixie's face, braided laurel wreath of golden hair, and brilliant knack for ferreting out the culprit in every new Mrs. Jeffries's mystery novel. At twenty-one, Ivy was well past the age of consent, but she'd always seemed happiest when she could spend her days baby-sitting and her evenings reading or donating her time at the local library, reshelving books. In truth she was a shy and lonely young woman, whom Temple had probably persisted in thinking of as a child.

Naturally Ivy had taken the news of her sister's job opportunity badly. Ten years ago they'd lost both their parents to a virus the couple contracted while traveling in Africa, and it had fallen to Temple to raise Ivy, as well as sheperd her through the devastating experience. Even for sisters their bond was an unusually close one, and Temple had expected Ivy to be upset. She hadn't expected her quiet little sister to barricade herself in her room and stage a hunger strike.

That was when Temple realized that she'd done too much, loved too much, and worst, needed to be needed. Too much. She'd had a hand in training both her fiancé and her sister to be selfish, and it broke her heart.

All of this had eventually brought Temple to the decision that split open the cocoon and released the butterfly. But it wasn't her thirtieth birthday, it was her life. *The one she hadn't lived.* She loved Donald tenderly and Ivy to distraction, but not enough to give up what remained of that life.

This was more than a job beckoning to her, it represented a new start, a future. Hers.

As gently as she could she told Donald she couldn't marry him. And that same night at dinner she painstakingly explained to Ivy why she wanted to put their deceased parents' home on the market. . . .

Rose petals fluttered as Temple's thoughts returned to the present. She left the canopy bed and walked to the occasional table. The document that lay there had the chill of authenticity. It said she was the wife of Michael St. Gerard. But the only Michael she knew worked at the farmers' market, behind the produce counter, selling vine-ripened tomatoes, fresh arugula, and the Greek olive oil she loved.

She turned to the room and struggled to remember how she'd come to be there, but there weren't any steps to retrace. It was all a blank. Maybe she'd been transported by aliens. Or maybe she'd won some kind of contest and this was the prize. A fantasy wedding and honeymoon, and they'd awarded it even though there was no man in her life. If that was the case she ought to relax and enjoy it. It would all be over soon enough. And what was the likelihood of it ever happening again?

But there was a man. Unless she'd dreamed it, someone had been in the room with her. He'd kissed and touched her, called her princess, and—she could still feel the weight of his body, the steam of his breath. The thrilling force. She could feel his desire to possess her, the urgency of it.

He had touched her, kissed her—

What else had he done? And why had his voice sounded vaguely familiar?

Her hand dropped to her stomach. Something stirred inside her, shivered and tightened in her depths. She could feel it radiate out to her fingertips. Her body was alive with memories, but her mind recalled nothing. It seemed as if her senses wanted to confess all, every detail of what had happened to her last night in a stranger's arms. But their signals were a language her brain didn't understand.

It was true that she'd lived a relatively sheltered life until recently. The things she hadn't done were probably taken for granted by most women her age, but that didn't account for the fact that she couldn't remember. She didn't use drugs, she never drank to excess, despite the empty bottle of champagne. And nothing else made any sense . . . unless it had something to do with the virus she contracted in Zaire, the same one that had taken both her parents.

Her mother and father had been struck down while trying to help famine victims in Africa, and Temple had flown there to bring them back to the States. But when she arrived they were already gone, victims themselves of a devastating outbreak that had killed hundreds.

Temple had found herself quarantined in a hospital ward with terminal patients whose bodies and minds were being ravaged, and it was one of the most harrowing experiences of her life. She was locked in a death trap, barely able to communicate with the medical staff, most of whom were sick, too. And worse, she was stunned by the loss of her seemingly indestructible parents.

Her mother and father had always been the quintessential flower children—free spirits, yet deeply dedicated to their causes. For as long as Temple could remember, they'd traveled the globe on one mission of mercy or another. And even if they had sometimes neglected their own small brood in their zeal to save the earth's children from starvation, they were good people, with a fire in their hearts to make a difference.

Temple still found it hard to believe that a microscopic blip had ended their lives and their dreams. But Agent Z190 had turned out to be a ruthless killer, resistant to any known antibiotic at the time. It attacked the respiratory system first, and if the viral pneumonia it created didn't kill its human host, the agent went systemic and attacked virtually every organ, including the brain.

Most of the victims in Temple's ward had suffered severe memory loss and dementia, similar to the advanced effects of Alzheimer's. Temple's case had been something of a miracle, according to the Centers for Disease Control in Atlanta. She'd escaped with a mild form of the pneumonia and no neurological symptoms. There had been hazy patches since then and sleep that felt unusually deep, but nothing like losing several hours of her life. *Nothing like this*, she thought. And she'd always attributed those episodes to overwork or lack of exercise.

It might be a good idea to call the CDC, she told herself, and speak with the woman who'd investigated the outbreak in Zaire. She'd been a doctor as well as an epidemic intelligence services officer, and she'd spent hours interviewing Temple in Zaire, and then again after Temple was medivaced back to the States, where she was subjected to another quarantine and more testing.

What was the woman's name? Temple struggled to remember. Susan Gilchrist? It terrified her to think that the virus might have been dormant until now, and that stress or some other factor had reactivated it. She had no idea what she'd done or had been done to her since Friday evening.

The shivering inside her turned icy. She needed to get dressed and get out of this place immediately.

The phone rang again as Temple was searching the closet for her clothes. It was the same sunny-voiced desk clerk. Mr. St. Gerard had also arranged for transportation whenever she was ready to leave, the woman announced. All Mrs. St. Gerard had to do was call down, and a limo would be waiting out front.

"That won't be necessary," Temple said, realizing as she hung up that she hadn't thanked the woman. That was how rattled she was. She'd been known to thank meter maids

when they gave her a ticket. She would find some other way
to get home, a taxi.

But not an hour later she was seated stiffly in the back of
a silver stretch Mercedes, gliding up the 405 freeway, and
headed for her apartment in Ventura. Just as the clerk had
promised, the limo was sitting in the driveway, idling when
Temple came down, and the driver had approached her as if
he knew her.

She'd told him she wasn't Mrs. St. Gerard, that he'd mis-
taken her for someone else. But he'd acted as if he didn't understand her and had responded in a language that sounded
like French. He'd been impossible to refuse the way he'd
gallantly taken her hand and helped her into the limo. And
then he'd swept her luggage into the trunk, elegant Louis
Vuitton bags she'd never seen before.

Clothes she'd never seen before for that matter. None of
her own things had been in the closet or the bags. She'd
found a trousseau of beautiful and costly designer wear in
her size, and the outfit she'd slipped into had fit like a
glove. The label said TSE, and the black cashmere pants
and shell were beautiful. There'd been a matching cardigan
to keep her warm, but it was the underwear that had awakened her senses like nothing else. It had fit like a second
skin, literally, like flesh against her body, the velvety palm
of a hand . . . cupping her.

Temple resisted the urge to squirm. That was the sensation
she felt, and it had made her supremely uncomfortable. She
would have gone without panties, except that she couldn't
decide which was the lesser evil.

The limo was a revelation, too. The interior was dove
gray leather, and the sound system was playing the CD she'd
loved in college, Michael Bolton's first release, *Hunger*. On
the console nearest her there was a chilled silver container
of fresh strawberries, another of heavy whipped cream, a

split of champagne, and a crystal bowl of M&M's, her favorite candy.

It had to be Donald, she realized. No one else knew she'd once had a secret thing for Michael Bolton. Apparently he'd decided to remind her with a grand gesture what she was missing by not marrying him. But it was so unlike him to be this impetuous. If he'd struck it rich, it couldn't have been at his medical practice. Last she knew he was still heavily in debt.

She looked longingly at the strawberries, aware that she was starving. She took the biggest one she could find, swiped it through the whipped cream, but failed miserably to get the huge thing in her mouth. Laughing, she licked the whipped cream off her lips and noticed the driver glancing at her in the rearview mirror. More laughter bubbled up as he smiled and nodded at her.

Had Donald won the lottery?

TWO

God love a cardboard box, Temple thought. The miserable things were stacked all over her apartment, still unpacked from her trip out west, but she was actually glad to see them when she walked in the front door. At least that hadn't changed. It was home sweet Home Depot around here.

Leaving things undone had never been Temple's style, but she'd never been a creative director, either, in charge of her own account and responsible for the team effort. At work she'd been forced to embrace the joys of Post-it notes, executive decisions, and delegating. At home there wasn't anybody to delegate *to*, and she couldn't seem to squeak out a second to get herself properly settled. But for once none of the disarray bothered her. She could have kissed the cardboard towers.

She gently patted the nearest one, which happened to be several crates of her parents' travel mementos.

"Nice boxes," she said.

While the limo driver brought in her luggage, Temple did

a quick visual inspection of the living room, dining room, and kitchen, and was greatly relieved to see that nothing appeared to have changed. There were no magnums of champagne chilling on the coffee table or designer wedding dresses draped over the furniture. Just the normal chaos.

The driver refused her tip, gallantly, of course. Perhaps he thought she needed the money more than he did, given the condition of her place.

Once he'd gone she went to the bedroom to unpack her luggage, but only got as far as opening the garment bags and taking out a couple of the outfits. She didn't know what to do with the clothes! They were exquisite pieces—a silvery white Gucci sheath with a voile overskirt, and a mauve Armani pantsuit, but they weren't hers, and it made her head hurt trying to figure out where they'd come from.

She abandoned them on the bed and went back to the living room, vowing to put the confusion out of her mind long enough to relax and enjoy being home again. She kicked off her scuffed black suede loafers which, along with her purse, seemed to be the only personal items that had made it through the trip with her.

If shoes could talk, she thought.

Falling into the nearest chair, she gave silent thanks for the privacy and safety of her own space. She loved her "ocean-close" apartment. It was a spacious, airy enclave done in sunny whites and warm mapley woods, with a light-drenched atrium courtyard off the dining room that she grandly called the conservatory. That was her favorite room, but she enjoyed the living room, too, with its distressed marble fireplace and dazzling skylights. One day when she had the time and the money, she would accent the entire place in stripes.

Not prison stripes, except perhaps for the guest bath, which might be fun. She wanted regimental stripes and flags of state, the deep reds and greens of a sovereign banner or the smart tans and black of an Italian couturier. Straight lines were neat, orderly, and reassuring. When the environment was right, her mind was freed.

But right now her mind was tired. She could have fallen asleep in the chair if it weren't for her rumbling stomach. As far as she knew she hadn't eaten since some time the day before, and she was famished. Across the room, in her little white sparkler of a kitchen, the refrigerator beckoned. She rose to her feet and headed that way on an odd wave of light-headedness. She'd felt the same way in the suite, slightly tipsy, when she tried to walk.

This meant a trip to the doctor, she told herself. And she couldn't forget to call the CDC, either. She was haunted by the thought that it was the virus, but the possibility that she might have been drugged had occurred to her, too. There wasn't any of the lethargy or hangover she would have associated with that. Of course the amnesia alone was reason enough to get a checkup.

The refrigerator door became Temple's anchor as she peered at what was inside. The interior glowed like a shrine, even though the light was blocked by several bottles of ridiculously expensive champagne and an assortment of gourmet fare. Where had the food come from? The refrigerator had been nearly bare when she'd walked in from work on Friday.

In fact, she'd been making herself a grocery list when Shirley, the apartment's grandmotherly manager, had appeared with a thermos of piping hot chocolate and some teriyaki chicken wings. Shirley was always clucking about Temple's weight and bringing her care packages, which Temple was honestly grateful for, even though the menu could be a little offbeat at times. Mostly she liked the clucking, because at five feet four and a solid hundred twenty pounds, Temple didn't consider herself underfed.

Now Temple swung the door shut and went through the

rest of the apartment again, carefully this time. Cancelled theater tickets were tacked to the bulletin board that hung next to the refrigerator, but she couldn't remember going to the performance. There was also a reminder note in her own handwriting to call Michael, which didn't make any sense unless it was the name on the marriage license. There was no one in her immediate circle named Michael.

Fighting dizziness, she hurried to her bedroom, where she discovered a man's shirt and slacks, hanging in her closet. The garments were hand-tailored and, according to the label, purchased from a Saville Row shop in London.

That was all she found, but it was enough.

Someone was tapping at her front door, she realized, moments later. By that time Temple was standing at the breakfast bar that divided her kitchen and dining room. Her first impulse was to call 911, but she was too stunned to move quickly. And then a soft "Yoo-hoo?" told her she was safe. It was Shirley.

"Come in!"

The manager opened the door and poked her head in just enough so that her natural platinum pixie cut and gold-rimmed half-glasses were visible. The reflection from the conservatory windows hid her eyes, but Temple could see the pucker of concern in her brows.

"Did you see that cruise ship of a limo out front?" she asked. "That was something, wasn't it."

Temple didn't know how to respond. Shirley must not have seen her get out of the limo, and Temple didn't want to alarm the older woman by pouring out her fears. It was such a bizarre story anyway.

"Shirley, did you see or hear anything odd last night?" she asked. "I was gone, and I think someone's been in my apartment."

Shirley stepped into the room and glanced around. Her darting eyes were the same Prussian blue as the billowy nylon exercise outfits she lived in, and she looked to be in remarkably good shape, although Temple had never actually seen her exercise.

"Mind if I have a look?" she said, giving the doorknob a jiggle. She inspected the deadbolt, then walked over to the sliding-glass doors that opened onto the terrace and knelt to check the lever lock in the frame. She was serious now, in her apartment manager mode, and this was part of her domain.

"You think someone broke in?" She rose, tapped the glass pane, stepped back, and looked up at the skylights. "Were the doors or windows open? Is anything missing?"

Temple dutifully answered her questions and followed her around. She didn't feel up to dealing with the police anyway, and why bother with Shirley there. Nevertheless, it was a little awkward when they got to the bedroom and Temple had to produce a man's shirt and slacks.

"I don't know where they came from," she admitted.

Shirley looked over the garments without actually touching them. She would have made a good detective, Temple thought.

"What about all this?" she asked, referring to the Louis Vuitton luggage and the designer clothes draped across the bed.

"They showed up in the hotel room where I was staying," Temple said. "I don't know how they got there." Shirley blinked over her half-glasses. She peered at Temple. "Any possibility they're from Mr. Saville Row? The guy in your closet?"

Temple's shrug said yes, there was. At this point nothing would have surprised her, but she was still reluctant to tell Shirley the whole story. She wanted some time alone to try to put the pieces together. It was just that she had no idea what puzzle she was working on.

Somewhere in the apartment unit a door slammed, shaking the walls, and it began to snow in Temple's bedroom. Plaster flaked lazily from a crack in the ceiling that Temple had been meaning to tell Shirley about.

It drifted into the older woman's hair and speckled the toffee-colored carpet around her feet with white. But Shirley was no longer interested in the challenges of solving crimes or even apartment managing. All she could see was the silvery white cloud of a dress on the bed.

She walked to it and fingered the voile skirt as if she were imagining herself in it, dancing to Hoagy Carmichael's *Stardust*, swirling and twirling in the Avalon ballroom on Catalina Island.

"You don't remember the man who gave you all this?" she said in a tone that sounded nothing like the irrepressible Shirley. It was far too soft and wistful. "It must have cost a fortune, Temple. How easy could he be to forget?"

Temple had no idea who he was, only the vague notion that somehow, somewhere she'd heard that smoky voice before. But there wasn't a chance to say anything. Shirley had already whisked up the dress and turned to the dresser mirror where Temple stood. Temple got a whiff of sweet clove gum and Vaseline Intensive Care lotion as the older woman held the outfit up and looked at herself, but the stars in her eyes were as bright as any teenager's. She was off into a Cinderella story of her own making. She even executed a little spin.

"Don't get me wrong," she said with a moist, earthy chuckle. "You don't have to tell me who he is if you don't want to. I understand about personal space, or whatever they're calling it these days. But this mystery guy of yours could break into my apartment any ol' time. You are one very lucky girl."

Temple's smile may have matched Shirley's for wistfulness. Where had she heard that before? However, she could see the makings of a problem as she watched the other woman sway to imaginary music. It was not going to be easy to make people believe she knew nothing about Michael St. Gerard.

Ventura was a male city in terms of its geography. The stubborn, rugged, and muscular strip of land that lay due north of Los Angeles was known for its artisans and its beautifully weathered coastline. And the masculinity spilled over into its commerce as well. There was agriculture, there was whale-watching, fishing, and shrimp-boating.

Rough trade. Guy stuff.

Certainly no one had ever accused Ventura of being a mecca for advertising agencies that specialized in cosmetics. Of the locals who'd heard of Blue Sky, most thought it was some kind of restaurant. Naturally the agency's mission was to change all that, and it was off to a solid start. They'd been open for business less than a year, but their list of name clients was growing. And those clients' success was its own testimonial.

People were starting to say that Blue Sky made things happen, and Temple was proud to be a part of the buzz. She looked forward to her job the way others anticipated a dream vacation. Holidays were supposed to be the great escape, but this was hers.

Work was something of a guilty pleasure for Temple. She'd had to break an engagement, painfully sever the umbilical cord with her sister, and forge a new independence in order to be where she was. She'd also tried to leave behind the compulsion that had dominated her life—putting others first.

Fortunately it was working. The last time she'd spoken with Ivy she'd been overjoyed to hear that her sister had enrolled at a local college back home in Houston. "Social Ecology" was the major she'd chosen, but Temple would have congratulated her if it had been "White Collar Crime."

Ivy was starting to forge her own independence, and Temple was terribly proud. She wanted her little sister to be as happy as she was.

Temple still couldn't believe how she'd fallen into the job at Blue Sky. There'd been a full-page ad in the local Houston newspaper. She'd opened the jobs section one Sunday morning, and there it was. NEW AD AGENCY SEEKS CREATIVE DIRECTOR, ART DIRECTORS, AND COPYWRITERS. She'd done all the PR and promotions for the travel agency, including their website. She had a modest portfolio, and her résumé was ready to go. Expecting nothing, not even an acknowledgment of her submission, she sent the material.

The following week the agency's president called, an exuberant woman named Sonia David, who offered to fly Temple out for an interview. Temple was dumbfounded. She was thrilled. She said yes to the offer. Yes to herself. And once there, she heard that most awe-inspiring of sounds, the cosmic click that says this is going to be a perfect fit. This is right.

She'd loved Sonia, and apparently Sonia had loved her, because there'd been a job offer waiting in the tray of her fax machine when she got home. They'd sent it while she was in flight, and they'd offered her not a copywriting position, but a creative directorship. The package included a car, an expense account, and a salary that was more than twice what she made at the travel agency.

Temple was certain they'd made a mistake. The letter was supposed to go to someone else. She faxed her acceptance the same day and waited for the other shoe to drop.

What she got instead was a contract. They'd sweetened the deal. They were giving her an apartment and relocation expenses as well. Temple could hardly believe her good fortune.

What happened when something was too good?

That question insinuated itself in her thoughts like a cat

curling up in a dark corner for a nap. It snoozed there throughout her time at Blue Sky, waking occasionally to stretch and have a look around. And on one of those occasions it spotted what looked like the enemy, a dog with its nose to the ground.

Denny Paxton was already in a senior position when Temple came aboard, and he was also the logical choice for her job. Temple worried about jealousy and resentment, but Denny had turned out to be too competitive to waste time on petty emotions. If he couldn't be the biggest star, then his goal was to be the brightest one, and perhaps to show the agency they'd made a mistake in passing him over.

With that the cat had yawned and nodded off again, and Temple had gone about her business. But along the way she'd learned that she could count on it stirring just when things were moving along perfectly, *especially* then. The other most likely time was when she stepped into the elevator every morning.

This Monday morning was no exception.

The agency had the top two floors of Ventura's only high-rise, and Temple was on the fourteenth floor. She either took the lift or climbed the stairs, but with the load of materials she carried around, it would have been easier scaling Everest.

The elevator seemed haunted this morning. Temple told herself it was nothing more than a carryover from the weekend, but she'd always been uneasy in small, enclosed spaces and as a child had dreamed of falling down wells and getting trapped in dark, suffocating confines.

She braved the box anyway, but with the question of "what happens . . ." so strongly in her mind that it felt as if she should escape before the doors closed and take the stairs instead. She would have if Blue Sky's president hadn't stepped in behind her.

Sonia smiled brightly, hit buttons to the two top floors,

and before the elevator had begun to move, the transforma-
tion was complete. The box was now a protective bubble,
ascending to the heights. Blue Sky's leader radiated opti-
mism and serenity. No elevator was going to act up with her
aboard.

Temple relaxed on that count. There was another niggling
concern, but she assigned it to the sheer force of Sonia's personality. Temple had always thought of herself as reasonably attractive and had been told she had an ethereal quality,
which was quite a compliment given how little she'd done
with her looks until recently.

She'd brightened up since leaving Houston, including
growing out her brunette tresses and having them woven
with warm auburn highlights. But attractiveness was relative, especially in the presence of a diva, and Sonia David
qualified. Compared to her ironed raven pageboy and moist
dark eyes even burnished auburn waves and cloudy-day
gray eyes seemed rather plain.

Was that why Sonia had fixed her with a curious stare?

The two women exchanged pleasantries, then briefly discussed Temple's assignment to launch the media campaign
for a new men's cologne by Fabrici, an Italian designer. And
then it got awkward. Sonia continued to stare at Temple as if
she were waiting for her to say something. Temple had no
idea what that might be, and had already begun to wonder if
there was cappuccino foam on her lips or toilet paper stuck
somewhere.

She adjusted the shoulder strap of her bulging briefcase
and glanced down to see if her blouse was buttoned.

Finally she asked, "Is something wrong?"

Sonia cocked her head, and her eyes took on the penetrating quality she was known for. "I was about to ask you that.
I don't want to pry but—you cut the honeymoon short?"

"Honeymoon . . . short?"

"Yes, you weren't supposed to be back until next week.

You had a room at the Montmarte, and then you and Michael were flying to Paris."

Michael? Paris? Temple didn't know what to say.

The two women stared at each other while the elevator shuddered and the doors opened again. It was one of the account teams that piled in. They were going out for coffee and croissants. Fortunately several of them desperately needed to talk to Sonia, and a line formed.

When the fourteenth floor arrived, Temple slipped out unnoticed and headed for her office. She should have taken the stairs.

Asking around to see if she'd told any of her coworkers she was getting married was not an option. She was too new on the job to risk looking that flaky. Instead Temple sat in her impressive corner office, with her "Welcome Aboard" gifts, a Montblanc pen, a cut-glass desk plaque, and a cloisonne laser pointer, and pretended to be working on the Fabrici account.

She had the door shut, and had asked her assistant, Jody, to hold any calls that weren't urgent. But none of this was good. Blue Sky had an open-door policy. The agency believed strongly in camaraderie and teamwork. Temple believed in it, too, but she couldn't bluff her way through any more congratulations. Nor did she want to get trapped on any more elevators.

She'd already put in a call to Donald, made an appointment to see a gynecologist, and left a message for Dr. Susan Gilchrist at the Centers for Disease Control in Atlanta, explaining that she needed to talk to her about the virus she'd caught in Zaire. She didn't know what else to do at the moment.

The phone buzzed so loudly it made Temple jump. She pushed a button, thinking maybe this was one of her calls. "Yes?"

"I'm going to lunch." Jody's voice rang over the intercom. "Want me to bring you something back?"

"Food?" Temple hadn't realized it was that late, or that she was ravenously hungry until that moment. Strange that the thought of eating was somehow repellant.

"Yes, food!" Jody laughed. "I was thinking about Wok City. Maybe Mongolian chicken?"

"Oh, God." It was Temple's favorite, too, but she could hardly imagine it today. The last time she couldn't eat was in seventh grade when she had a mad crush on her life science teacher.

"No, thanks, Jody, work to do. I'll grab something later." Like an Alka Seltzer, she thought.

The next noise Temple heard was a tap on her door.

She glanced at her watch and sat back, preparing herself. Only fifteen minutes had passed, so it couldn't be Jody. The blotter she'd been making notes on was polka-dotted with doodles of flowery flow chart symbols and a man's name. Michael. She'd written it in nearly as many different ways as there were script. This was bizarre. She was writing his name as if he were an intimate.

The tapping became more insistent. "Temple? You having hot sex with the window washer or something?"

Temple recognized the voice and smiled. "Come on in," she called out. Annette Dalton was the only coworker she'd had time to develop a close relationship with at Blue Sky. Temple didn't necessarily tell her everything, but they were approaching that stage, and she was pleased to hear a friendly voice.

"Wwwwellllll?" The door swung open and Annette stood on the threshold, her hands on her hips.

She had a way of stringing words out until you could hang clothes on them. Temple beckoned her into the office. She'd already decided what to say if there were any more questions about her honeymoon. She'd come down with something—a bug—and she still wasn't herself. That would get her through the next couple of days and buy her some time to find out what was going on.

"Some of us actually work around here," Temple quipped, ripping off her blotter sheet and crumpling it. "Pull up a chair. I'm ready for a break."

But Temple had forgotten that Annette rarely bothered with chairs. Her coworker was petite, tireless, and generally thought to be the agency's more prolific member, idea-wise. She was also one of its more eccentric, preferring bright stretchy capris, tight blouses and multicolored nail polish to Temple's single-breasted blazer and slacks look.

Temple kept waiting for the honeymoon question, but Annette never asked. Sprawled on the floor on her side, she seemed completely involved in bringing Temple up to date on the office gossip. Apparently a couple of the copywriters were having an affair, and their very own president was said to be dating a plastic surgeon who'd done so may stars' faces, he was a celebrity himself.

Temple rose and walked past Annette to the window, a large corner one that nearly spanned the room in both directions. She loved her window.

"Interesting," she said, though she hadn't heard a word since she got up. She was transfixed by the stream of anonymous foot traffic on the sidewalk across the street, and wondering if there was a man in the crowd named Michael, who actually knew what had happened to her this weekend.

At some point she realized her friend had stopped talking.

Temple turned and saw Annette studying her. The sharp silence reminded Temple of her elevator ride, but this time she was the one to break it. She gave out an audible sigh, then walked over and sank down on the floor next to her. It was either the sigh or the look on Temple's face that prompted Annette to bend toward her and touch her arm. At any rate that was when Temple knew she was going to tell her.

"Annette, bear with me because this is going to sound strange. Did you and I ever talk about what I was doing this weekend? Did I say anything about attending a wedding?"

Annette looked perplexed. "Whose wedding?"

"My own."

Annette gasped out laughter but didn't speak. Each silence Temple had endured today seemed shorter and more explosive. Why did it feel as if they were only going to get worse?

"Something happened to me this weekend that I don't understand—"

Temple's voice broke, and Annette took her hand. "What is it? Temple? You're scaring me."

Temple quickly relayed the bizarre story, as much as she knew of what had happened that weekend. She tried to convey it in a calm, rational tone, concerned that Annette would think she really had gone crazy. Temple was beginning to wonder about that herself. But if she was hoping her friend could clear things up, she was doomed to disappointment. As it turned out, Annette knew nothing about any wedding or honeymoon plans, and was as bewildered as Temple.

Annette was the only one that Temple would have confided in, and it was hard to believe that she knew nothing. Temple didn't understand what that meant. She didn't understand at all. How could the others know and Annette not? She quizzed her friend, asking her to think back. Was there ever at any time mention of wedding plans, a trip to Paris, or a man named Michael?

"No." Annette didn't even have to think about it. "How could I have forgotten something as juicy as that? But I did wonder why you seemed a little secretive about your plans for this weekend," she admitted. "Normally you tell me when you've got something going on."

"I didn't *have* anything going on," Temple protested. "There weren't any plans to be secretive about. I was going to stay home and work, the way I always do."

Now Annette was busy rifling through one of the coin purse–like bags she always had hanging around her neck. After a moment she produced a snapshot of Temple and a striking man with long dark hair and an equally dark mustache. Temple had never seen him before.

"I thought maybe you were going to be with him," she said.

Temple took the snapshot. She and the man were standing side by side, and there was a mirrored bar behind them. The light was hazy and shadowed, possibly a restaurant setting, which made it difficult to pick out details. But Temple could see contours, enough to discern that the man was stunning, just the slightest bit sinister, and if she were inclined to fantasize, exactly the type she would have fantasized about.

"Who is he?" she asked.

"You don't know? You two acted like long-lost friends."

"Friends? I've never seen him before."

"Temple, *of course* you have. You met him week before last. We were over at Tortilla Flats after work, celebrating my birthday, remember? There must have been a dozen of us."

Tortilla Flats was a local watering hole, and Temple remembered the party, but not the man. "What was I doing with him?" she asked. "Was he part of the group?"

"I never saw him before." Annette was on her knees now. "You went over to the bar to get another pitcher of margaritas, and the next thing I knew, you and this guy were talking to each other. Several people were snapping pictures at that party. I don't know who took this one. . . ."

Temple nodded, but she'd barely heard what Annette said. She simply couldn't imagine herself doing any of the things her friend had just mentioned. It wasn't Temple Banning's style at all. But so much was different in her life now, and she was aware of a personality change since coming to Blue Sky. She wasn't the dutiful fiancée or the substitute mother anymore. The atmosphere at an ad agency was more open and freewheeling, without the normal boundaries and the structure of her former situation. She'd had to loosen up. The creative energy demanded it. She even laughed differently, with more earth in it.

And maybe she'd actually done what Annette was suggesting—mosey up to a bar for margaritas and strike up a conversation with a perfect stranger—but it was hard to believe. As she stared at the dark-haired man, Temple realized that her hand was moving. The picture was fluttering in her fingers, but no matter which way it went, the effect was the same. He had the kind of eyes that followed you everywhere, like paintings of saints or religious figures. These were eyes you couldn't escape.

THREE

"Michael St. Gerard?" Temple sounded out of breath as she said his name. She could hear her own voice caught in the hush of the mouthpiece. It was part expectation, part exhaustion. It was dread. And hope.

She crossed her fingers.

She'd lost track of how many calls she'd made that evening. There weren't any St. Gerards in the Ventura County directory, but she'd found several in each of the various L.A. phone books. And she'd just gone through all of them but one. This one.

Please let it be him, she thought.

"Michael?" The gruff male voice at the other end of the line sounded skeptical. "You sure about that?"

"Yes, I'm calling for Michael St. Gerard. Is this him?"

Laughter exploded in Temple's ear, followed by the clunk of a dropped receiver. She heard the man muttering something that sounded like "No way in hell," and then he bellowed "Yo, Mike! There's some weird chick on the phone. She must be weird if she wants to talk to *you*, man."

The next utterance Temple heard was the wobbly scrape and squeak of male adolescence.

"Yeah? Who's this?"

A teenager? He didn't sound much more than twelve or thirteen. Temple ticked her head back and forth, signaling Annette, who was lying across the end of the bed, crossing off names in the phone book. She had one hand slapped to her forehead, holding her bangs out of her eyes, and her short spiky black ponytail stuck up like tail feathers.

"Sorry, wrong Michael," Temple said, hoping he wasn't going to get ragged too badly by the other guy, who was probably an older brother.

She hung up the telephone and fell back against a pile of throw pillows she'd picked up at a white sale. They were toffee-and-white striped, and went perfectly with her flounced spread and window curtains. But she would probably have bought them no matter what color the stripes were.

Temple inspected some imaginary cobwebs above the bedroom door frame, studiously avoiding her friend's expression. Annette's head was cocked and I-told-you-so was written all over her face.

"What did you expect?" she chided. "You're assuming he lives around here, you're assuming he's listed."

"I know, I know, but I had to try."

"You need a detective," Annette insisted. "You're not going to find a guy who can afford designer clothes and limos in the phone book."

They were in Temple's bedroom, holed up like two strategists in a war room. Temple was sitting cross-legged, the phone in her lap and her skirt hiked up to her thighs. She hadn't bothered to change after work. She'd been anxious to get her search under way, and had dragged her friend along for moral support, luring her with promises of the champagne and goodies in the fridge. The organic shiitake mushrooms had done the trick.

Annette, whose religion was low-fat, and who solemnly believed Victoria's Secret's "City" catalog was the answer to business casual, was wearing slim black capris in liquid matte jersey and a hot-pink jewel-neck sweater. She'd hung her boxy black cardigan on the doorknob.

"I've got a couple more cards up my sleeve," Temple said. The idea of a detective didn't appeal to her, although she hadn't examined why.

"You may have cards, but you don't have time to play them," Annette pointed out. "You should never have let Sonia know you were back. She wants us to start conferencing the Fabrici cologne account tomorrow, and by Friday she wants to hear pitches. You're the team leader, and this is your first big account, Temple."

The knots in Temple's stomach had formed a rope ladder. Annette had missed her calling. Give her a bullhorn and a rickety van, and she could drive around predicting the end of the world. Big account, indeed. Temple had been entrusted with Blue Sky's largest client to date, and if anything went wrong it was more than her position at stake, it was the company's profitability, their reputation.

The expectations were sky-high. Fabrici was huge, and Blue Sky stood to pick up a much larger chunk of their business if they came up with a winning campaign. That was why the expectations had to be met, even exceeded. They'd picked her to carry it off, and she wanted to do them proud.

But that was only a part of it. She had a personal duty to fulfill, as well as a dream. She'd hurt people in order to take the job. She'd disrupted lives, and even though it was quite possible that Ivy and Donald were better off because of her decision, Temple needed reassurance that her "birds" could fly and that no permanent damage had been done. She also wanted to know that she'd made the right choice for herself. What a relief to be able to say that it had all been worth it.

"What do you think?" Annette asked. "I know someone who's good. I could call him for you."

Temple looked up, startled. "What? A detective?"

"Duh," her friend said softly.

It would have been easier to say yes, turn the problem over to someone else, a professional, and get on with her life. But Temple's sense of privacy had already been violated. And she wasn't comfortable with the idea of bringing in some stranger to rummage through her personal life. Nobody could give her back the lost time, not even a detective. But he could make the whole experience seem sordid—

Temple hesitated, surprised at where her thoughts were taking her. Annette would probably have told her she'd attached some sort of romantic significance to the weekend. That was ridiculous, of course, but it did feel as if the experience was too intimate to share with a cynical, case-hardened professional.

Certain memories from that night seemed strangely fragile and in need of some kind of protection, even if she didn't completely understand why that should be true. It was scary to lose twelve hours of your life. But to wake up with all the trappings of a fantasy wedding, with a hauntingly sensual voice in your head, saying things you could never have imagined a man saying to you, that was an uncanny experience.

It would have embarrassed her to admit that she'd daydreamed about such things as a very young girl, before the world had intruded and told her none of that could happen to a mousy little drudge like her. She was blessed with neither extraordinary beauty nor talent, which meant that

dream careers, and certainly dream men, were out of her
reach.

Crazy, but it almost felt as if she'd been given a chance to
beat those odds. The perfect career was hers to lose. And the
perfect mate? That still seemed a long shot, but somebody—
she was reluctant to call him anything so corny as a mystery
man, but that was what came to mind—had given her a
glimpse of what the ultimate wedding night could be like.
And maybe there was a part of her that would rather not
know what had really happened in the honeymoon suite than
to have that tainted.

The truth was she didn't know exactly how she felt. She
hadn't sorted it all out yet. Mostly because it just didn't
seem real, none of it. But she would be fine. She just needed
a little time to get herself oriented. Once her life was back to
normal, things would start to make sense.

"Let me think about it," Temple said, more to appease Annette than anything else.

She slid off the bed and went to the beautiful old serpentine chest that held her foldables and underwear. Her parents
had had it shipped back from a trip to the Orient, and eventually they'd given it to Temple when they saw how dili-
gently she'd worked to restore the black lacquer finish and
handpainted flowers and leaves. A large whorled nautilus
shell sat on the chest in a mirrored tray, along with Temple's
watch and various pieces of jewelry.

The shell was perfect enough to have come from a curio
shop, but Ivy had found it on the shores of Virginia Beach, a
memento of the only vacation trip the Banning family had
ever taken together. Ironic that with world travelers for parents, the two Banning girls had rarely gone anywhere. In
some sense they'd raised each other in the old ramshackle
farmhouse that housed their parents' treasures from all over
the globe. The rickety old museum was their security, their
roots.

Eventually Ivy had given the shell to Temple as a gift because Temple could hear what no one else did when they held the pearlescent chambers to their ear. Not the roar of the ocean or the drama of the elements, Temple had heard someone whispering to her. A distant voice, but listen as she might—and she did, often falling asleep with the shell at her ear—she couldn't understand what the voice was saying.

Finally she realized, in the profound way that children do, that she didn't understand because she wasn't ready to know. She'd also taken it on faith, the way only a child can, that someday the voice would come closer, and she would be able to hear what the nautilus was trying to tell her. Someday, one day, she would be ready.

"Thought enough yet?" Annette prodded.

Temple laughed. "Not nearly."

She picked up the shell and held it to her ear.

"Temple? It's a Dr. Donald Kent to speak to you."

Finally. Temple had been leaving messages for her ex-fiancé for the last two days and was getting worried that he hadn't called back.

She dropped the purple Rollerball back into the box of colored pens she'd been using to draw word association bubbles on a large sketch pad. It was a creativity exercise designed to help break mental logjams, and Temple had one on the men's cologne account.

"Thanks, Jody, I'll take it," she said, considering the speakerphone's blinking red light. She needed to talk to Donald, but she was naturally apprehensive. They'd only spoken a few times since she moved to Ventura, and the calls had mostly to do with selling the Banning place. At Donald's recommendation she'd used his real estate agent, but there'd been problems with escrow.

The calls had ended badly each time. Donald had gone

from being hurt and embittered to trying to talk "sense" into Temple. And in his quiet way he was extremely persuasive. She had been awash in guilt by the time they hung up, and had vowed to change agents so that she wouldn't have to call again, but each time something had forced her hand. Just as this situation had, she realized.

The red light flashed in her periphery. Temple picked up the phone and forced brightness into her voice. "Donald, how are you? Thanks for calling back."

"To what do I owe the honor?"

She got the sarcasm. It had a blunt force, despite his modulated tone. No time for regrets today, she told herself, but disappointment welled anyway. She kept hoping he would let go, and feeling responsible that he hadn't. Obviously she hadn't let go yet, either, not completely.

"There's a problem," she told him. "This is not going to be easy to explain, so bear with me."

Her elbows dug into the pulpy pad she'd been drawing on. It felt as if she were trying to convince him of the authenticity of an alien abduction as she described what had happened to her. But to his credit he listened quietly, letting her tell him every bewildering detail, including her vague recollection that a man had spoken to her and the things she'd found in her apartment.

She ended her story on faint breath . . . and to total silence. He must be calling from work because she could hear someone talking in the background, probably the receptionist or his medical assistant. She knew he'd had difficulty getting his practice going, but maybe things were turning around.

"Donald?"

"I don't know what to say, Temple."

"Just tell me you don't think I'm crazy."

"Of course I don't think you're crazy." He hesitated, clearly choosing his words. "But you're obviously under some significant stress. You don't have any experience with high-pressure jobs and fast-lane lifestyles."

"Donald, I'm not living a fast-lane lifestyle, and this isn't stress-related, believe me. I'm sorry to be dumping this on you, but I had to call and talk to you about it—"

"Temple." He cut her off in a firm voice. "You can call me anytime, about anything, you know that. You don't need an excuse."

He thought she was cracking up, or inventing some crazy reason to call him. She drew a deep breath. This wasn't what she needed. She wasn't going to get what she needed from him, which was probably reassurance that the whole thing was a prank.

"Just tell me whether or not you had anything to do with it," she implored.

"You're asking if I assumed a fake name, drugged you, kidnapped you, and married you while you were unconscious?"

She heard his disbelief and should have thought to reassure him that she wasn't accusing him of anything. It was just that she'd never planned a wedding with anyone other than him, so he was the first person that had come to mind. The only person.

But her focus had been snared by something else, by that one word. "Drugged me? Do you think that's what happened?"

She fished out the pen and began tapping the pad with it. Within seconds there were purple specks all over the paper. It looked like a connect-the-dots puzzle.

"That would explain the amnesia," she said, "but I've been thinking about the virus I caught in Zaire. You remember."

Donald had been in medical school at the time, but he'd flown out to Maryland, where Temple was being treated at Ft. Detrick, the U.S. Army's Institute of Infectious Diseases, after being transferred there from Zaire. He'd discussed her case at length with Dr. Gilchrist, who'd flown in from Atlanta, and some of the other researchers, hoping to glean whatever information he could about the situation, at which point Dr. Gilchrist had taken him into her confidence and informed him that Agent Z190 was one of the deadliest viruses yet discovered, and Temple's was a unique case.

The doctor had made it clear there was no need to panic. The outbreak in Zaire had been contained and the odds of one ever occurring in the States was extremely small. She'd patiently explained to Donald that the "Z" stood for Zaire, the number one indicated it was the original strain of the virus and number ninety indicated the year of the outbreak.

She'd also explained that Temple would be held at Fort Detrick only until she was completely clear of the infection. Gilchrist herself had taken the blood and tissue samples they needed for analysis, and the Atlanta Center's technicians were already working around the clock in their Biosafety Level 4 lab to isolate the virus, which was just the first step of many in developing a vaccine. Ultimately they hoped to sequence the virus's proteins and produce an antibody response. But meanwhile if they could discover why Temple had developed antibodies and survived when so many hadn't, they would be that much closer to their goal.

Much of the Zaire ordeal was a blur in Temple's mind, but she remembered quite clearly Dr. Gilchrist telling her that someone had pulled some strings to get her out of there and back to the States. "It wasn't our people," she'd informed Temple. "You were medivaced into Dulles by a private team, who contacted our emergency mobile unit and had you brought to Fort Detrick. Lucky break, too. That Zaire situation was a cesspool. You could have survived the virus and died from a nasty staph infection."

Temple had never learned who was responsible, even though Donald had made inquiries through his network of medical contacts. But right now she was more concerned about Z190 than phantom rescue units.

"Donald, when the virus went systemic, the central nervous system was affected, remember? Some of the victims hallucinated and totally lost touch. They didn't know where they were."

"But yours never went systemic, Temple. You had a mild case of pneumonia at most."

"Yes, and weakness, dizziness—" Just like she'd been having lately. "What if something's wrong? What if the virus has been dormant all this time? What if something's triggered it?"

She was talking too fast. Panic was stealing her breath, and she knew how this must sound to him.

"Temple, something is wrong," he said softly. "You need to see a doctor."

"Oh, I'm going to," she assured him. "I have a call in to Dr. Gilchrist to ask about the amnesia. I also made an appointment with a gynecologist. I was due for a Pap anyway."

"No, Temple, I meant me. I'm a doctor."

She took a mental step back, aware that he was asking the impossible, and wondering why he didn't understand it.

I can't do that, Donald. I can't give back the golden apple. You of all people should know about the sacrifices one makes for the opportunity of a lifetime. You made them. And required them of everyone around you.

But, of course, he didn't understand. This wasn't his opportunity.

Temple stared at the wild splatter of dots she'd created and thought if she had a million years, she might be able to

see order within the chaos. It was right there, she knew.
There was a pattern, a mysterious, yet obvious pattern, if she
only had the distance to see it. There was a pattern to everything. But perhaps that took a God's-eye view.

In the background of her thoughts, she heard Donald's
voice, soft and insistent. "Now, Temple. Come home now,
before it's too late."

FOUR

No rest for a virus hunter, Dr. Susan Gilchrist thought ironically, tossing her briefcase on the two-drawer file cabinet next to her desk. She slipped off her gray wool blazer and hung it on the back of her office chair, then figuratively rolled up her sleeves.

She hadn't been back from lunch five minutes and she was already faced with a dozen messages, according to the digital display on her phone, half as many faxes, and undoubtedly a bursting E-mail queue. She normally worked through lunch when she was here in her office at CDC's Atlanta headquarters. But today she'd had an interview with a CNN reporter about an Asian flu prediction the Center had fluffed.

Actually it was Susan herself who'd fluffed the prediction, possibly in her "eagerness to think the atypical strain was some new and menacing pandemic," her boss had kidded. At least Susan had been able to counter the reporter with the Center's excellent track record and to remind him how they'd solved Legionnaires', localized the Lassa fever virus, and swiftly identified the lethality of Ebola, to name just a few.

Now she was doing several things at once—listening to her messages, taking notes, skimming her faxes, *and* unwrapping the mint she'd brought back from lunch—when a faint tapping sound told her someone was on her doorstep.

Spotted and chased up a tree, she thought.

In this case it was her favorite lab technician, Brian Rice, who was hovering, probably with news of some amino acid sequence he'd been trying to analyze. The young microbiologist had only been with the Special Pathogens Branch a few months, but he was eager to make his mark, and Susan liked that in a new hire. She'd been accused of being too ambitious herself, but that drive had earned her several rungs on the ladder. She'd been named section chief of Disease Assessment, and there was talk of another promotion, whereas most of her accusers had done little more than finish their two-year stint as intelligence officers and move on.

"Just scoped the blood samples that came in from the fast-food place in Poughkeepsie." Brian sighed. "Plain old salmonella."

"Nothing exciting there." Susan gave him a wink and went about her work. "Better luck next time."

"I'm considering a virus dance," he announced, his tone reflective. "You know, the way they used to do rain dances? You jump around, sing off-key real loud, and the gods shower you with pestilence to shut you up. Maybe they'll send me my very own Ebola, think?"

Susan did not respond except to cock an eyebrow. That was Brian's cue that she was otherwise engaged, and when she glanced up, the doorway was empty. She got up and quickly shut the door, then returned to her desk and picked up the phone. She always retrieved voice mail first, despite all the new high-tech ways to communicate. It was her the-

ory that people still went to the phone when it was urgent.
They wanted that voice-to-voice contact with another
human being, even if it was just a recorded message.

She hit the speaker-phone button and let the messages
play. The reaction to her live TV interview was already coming in, but that was to be expected. Health was big news
these days in the wake of AIDS, cloned sheep, and designer
babies.

She was perusing faxes, sorting mail, and only half-
listening when an urgent male voice caught her attention.
An internist at a Southern California HMO had called to report what appeared to be a virus of unknown origins. He'd
already notified the county epidemiologist, but had been
told their manpower was tied up with a hepatitis scare. The
internist was worried because this new virus, if that's what it
was, appeared to be highly infectious and deadly. One of the
patients, possibly the index, seemed to have stabilized, but
another patient had already died, and a third was gravely ill.
He wanted some help from CDC.

"Here it is," Susan said under her breath.

She stopped writing and simply listened as the internist
described the symptoms, emphasizing that the virus appeared to incubate in hours and be fatal in days. Susan
didn't move. She wrote nothing. There was no need to take
down the information. She already knew everything he was
going to say.

The next few messages were routine, but the last one was
a concerned female voice that Susan immediately recognized. The caller took pains to remind Susan who she was—
as if Susan could have forgotten—and to leave a home
number where she could be reached.

Temple Banning, Susan thought, the poster girl of Z190.

How perfect was this? After ten years it was finally all
coming together, and this time she was going to walk away
with the prize. The first thing she had to do was call the in-

ternist and tell him to isolate the victims immediately, institute barrier nursing, and put a gag order on any hospital employees involved with their care. No one was to talk to the press or allow them in the building. She also made it clear he wasn't to release the patients' medical records to anyone, even health care practitioners.

As for getting to Southern California, she would take some personal time and make her own arrangements so as not to alert anyone in the branch. That way she wouldn't have to notify the CDC duty officer that she was leaving for L.A. Once she'd cleared up the mess on her desk and done some delegating of tasks, she was on her way.

She tapped out Temple Banning's number and got a canned message about Temple not being able to get to the phone. Susan would wait then. She was only going to speak with Temple herself. It wouldn't be smart at this stage to leave a voice mail trail.

After a moment she settled back and heard the chair groan plaintively, probably because the springs were unused to that angle. She rarely rested. And smiled even less. But she was doing both now. It had all begun with Temple Banning. Perhaps it was going to end with her, too.

Shortcuts, what a handy little concept that was. Temple had always thought of life as a series of hurdles that had to be negotiated perfectly before you could get to the finish line. Knock one over and you were out of the race. It was only since Blue Sky that she'd discovered you could not only knock over hurdles, you could dart around them and even completely ignore them, in which case, they often seemed to vaporize as if they'd never been there.

Not everything had to be done the hard way, she'd realized, and some things didn't have to be done at all, which was exactly the tack she'd taken with the honeymoon night. Shortly after her conversation with Donald, she'd decided to ignore the incident in the hope that it would vaporize, and strangely enough, it had.

There'd been no more lapses of memory, no more mysterious objects appearing in her apartment or comments from anyone at work about her unexpected return. It simply hadn't come up again, plus all her attempts to solve the mystery of Michael St. Gerard had led nowhere.

The marriage license that had declared her his wife was in limbo as it turned out. It would take weeks to authenticate, according to the county clerk's office. That hadn't surprised Temple either, but the ring had. It was real. An appraiser had valued it at nearly thirty-five thousand dollars, leaving Temple in a quandary. She'd opened a safety deposit box at her bank and stored it there, but that was only a temporary solution, she knew, until she could find the rightful owner.

Even so, Temple's routine had returned to normal for the most part. And that was exactly where she needed it to be as the male cologne project threatened to take over her life. The team met every morning to brainstorm ideas, and their sessions sometimes ran on into the night. One untested creative director, an art director, two copywriters, an intern, and Denny Paxton, the accounts exec, with possibly the fate of the company resting in their hands. They juggled ideas like bowling pins, struggling to come up with the perfect way to "sell a smell" to an oblivious market, the millennium male.

Tonight they'd worked until ten and nobody could think coherently anymore, but they still hadn't come up with a brainchild that was strong enough to pitch to Sonia, in Temple's opinion. It was midnight now, the session was set for nine the next morning in Sonia's office, and that felt as close to failure as Temple ever wanted to be.

She set her alarm for six and then noticed the message light on the phone machine. She was too tired for any eleventh-hour ideas from Annette, but hit the button anyway, then kicked off her loafers. There were only two messages

recorded, and as soon as the first one began to play, Temple
stopped undressing and sat on the bed. She had one arm out
of her silk blouse and her skirt unzipped. It was as far as she
got.

It was the nurse practitioner from the doctor's office
where she'd gone for a checkup the day before, a precau-
tionary move after the night at the Montmarte. The results of
her tests were in, the nurse said. They'd found no trace of either semen or STDs, although she was recommending that
Temple take an iron supplement because her levels were a
little low. And because the blood test they'd run had proved
positive.

Almost as an afterthought the nurse added that Temple
was pregnant and should make a follow-up appointment to
talk about prenatal care.

The next message began to play, but Temple couldn't hear
it. The nearly indecipherable male voice sounded as if it
were coming from another planet, the far end of the universe. She could make out only a word or two, but something about the message told her it was urgent, a plea from a
man with an accent that sounded vaguely French.

She hit the REPEAT button and turned the machine's volume on high. But it wasn't the machine. It was her. She was
in shock. She could hardly hear.

"Temple, this is Michael," he said. "I couldn't contact you
until now, but please know that I'm thinking about you
every moment, and that I'd never expose you to danger. I'd
sacrifice myself first. That's why I had to disappear. There
are people who want me silenced, and I'm afraid they'll try
to get to me through you. I'm going to give you a name, and
I want you to contact this man if you have the slightest fear
for your safety. He was in military intelligence, and he'll
help you. I'm trying to protect you, Temple, please understand that. And forgive me, if you can."

The name he gave her was Mark Challis, but the number

was more than she could manage. She hadn't fully grasped the first message. Pregnant? No, that wasn't possible. There had to be some mistake. And this man who claimed he was Michael St. Gerard, if that's what he was claiming. He must have her confused with someone else. That's all it could be, a series of crazy mistakes and misunderstandings.

Temple was too exhausted to panic, too exhausted to cry, though a part of her wished that she could have done something that normal. She lay down on the bed, half-in, half-out of her clothing, and fell asleep that way, grateful it wasn't necessary to think anymore, about anything.

"You're hiring a detective?" Annette glanced up from the ladies' room sink, where she was washing her hands, and caught Temple's reflection in the mirror. "When did you decide that?"

Her voice dropped to a whisper. "You look like hell, Temple. Are you okay?"

Temple knelt to peer under the stalls and make sure they were alone before she spoke. She'd run into Annette in the agency rest room on her way to her office. It was just seven-thirty, and early for the rest of the staff, but she didn't want to take any chances.

She did look like hell. Annette's surprise was reflected in the glass, but all Temple could see was her own shadowed, sunken eyes and drawn mouth. She'd slept badly and there was no energy for anything but getting it out.

"There was a message on my machine from a man who said he was Michael," she told Annette. "It had to have been the one on the marriage certificate, because he apologized for disappearing on me. He said someone was after him, wanted to silence him—"

She hesitated, knowing how it sounded. "He said he was afraid for my safety."

Annette yanked some paper towels from the dispenser

and turned toward Temple, drying her hands. "So that's why you want to hire a private eye? Because someone's after you?"

"No, because I'm pregnant."

Annette's green eyes became piercing. She crumpled the paper towels and got rid of them in the receptacle. "You've seen a doctor then? Is this Michael guy—is he the father?"

Temple's briefcase strap was cutting into her shoulder. She let it drop to the floor with a thud. "Is he the father?" she said faintly. "How would I know? I can't remember a thing that happened that night. That's why I need a detective."

It was a moment before Annette said anything. She seemed to be thinking through what Temple had just told her, and Temple was grateful for that much. She couldn't think at all.

Annette slowly turned in a circle, exactly where she stood.

Temple had seen this before. Her friend was processing, and she needed some movement to put things together, much as most people would pace.

Annette stopped with her back to Temple, then came all the way around. "Come with me," she said abruptly. She was already heading to the rest-room door and beckoning for Temple to follow.

In the seconds it took Temple to get her briefcase, Annette had disappeared through the door. Fortunately Temple knew her way through the maze of cubicles and hallways, but she was impressed with how quickly Annette had negotiated them. When she came upon her friend's cubbyhole, Annette was down on her knees, going through the bottom drawer of a file cabinet.

"Remember I told you I knew someone," she said.

"Annette, I can barely remember my own name these days. What are you talking about?" But Temple's gentle sarcasm was completely wasted. Annette was too busy rifling to have heard anything she said.

"I offered to give you the name of a good detective." She was still hunting through the folders, which didn't seem to be in any particular order, certainly not alphabetical.

"Oh, that, yes—"

"But you didn't want to go there, remember? Hang on, there's a file here somewhere from when I used to work at the newspaper. Oh, wait—here!"

Annette pulled out a manila folder and slammed the cabinet door shut. Temple shushed her, not wanting to attract attention. Someone could have come in since they had.

Fortunately Annette was now absorbed in leafing through the contents of the folder, which seemed to be made up of old newspaper clippings. After a moment she pulled one out, skimmed it, and smiled.

"This is it," she said. "His name is Mark Challis. When I knew him, he was like . . . legendary or something."

Suddenly Temple was light-headed. There was only one visitor chair in Annette's office, and luckily it was nearby.

"Mark Challis? Are you sure? I think that's him, Annette. The man who called me mentioned an investigator, and that name sounds familiar. Military intelligence?"

"Oh, my God," Annette breathed. Silently she handed Temple the article.

Temple read through the yellowed piece, which looked as if it had been hastily cut out of the paper. It described Challis as a former agent for the Defense Intelligence Agency's Office of Strategic Service, and said he'd gone freelance and become a sought-after troubleshooter for multinational corporations. The work he did was described as diverse, high-level, and high-risk.

Temple was halfway through the article before she realized that Annette herself had written it. Again Temple was impressed. The analysis she'd done of his personality was fascinating. It was based on a study of dangerous occupations, and it described Challis as having a cobra temperament, which was said to be typical of risk-takers. Cobras were defined as individuals whose vital signs dropped as danger rose. They actually grew calmer in risky situations.

Temple was clearly not a cobra temperament. By the time she'd finished reading, her heart was pounding with some emotion she didn't understand. "You said you knew him? Is he really like this?"

Annette's eyes danced with smile. "I did the piece while I was *dating* him. All right, only a couple of times, but do you believe it? The man is something else, Temple."

She struggled not to giggle. "I worked for the *L.A. Daily News* back then, and somehow I convinced him to let me do an interview. He revealed almost nothing, to be honest. Much of the article is speculation."

Still on her knees, she studied Temple intently. "Mark Challis is the best, but you need to understand that he's a full-fledged spook, my gentle friend. Prepare yourself."

The thought was chilling to Temple. She had no experience with anyone in that world. Even everyday law enforcement was out of her realm. Temple Banning had never had a speeding ticket. But what were her options? It was imperative that she talk to Challis himself, as he could have information about "Michael."

Annette was already looking through the phone book. "Challis isn't listed," she said, "but I've got some contacts. I think I can track him down."

"It's all right. I've got his number from the message 'Michael' left." The walls swayed and the floor tilted as Temple stood up.

Annette dropped the book and leaped to steady her. "Are you all right?"

"Dizzy spell. It'll pass in a minute."

Temple didn't move until the room had stopped and she

could focus in on Annette. "There's something you have to do for me," she said. "You have to get the team an extension on the pitch meeting. Talk to Sonia, tell her I'm sick, whatever you want, but there's no way I can do it this morning."

Annette looked skeptical, but Temple couldn't let her say no. "Just do it, Annette, please. Cover me, all right? I need more time."

FIVE

❧

Mark Challis's headquarters had no name, logo, or designation of any kind on the door. But it was housed in a dramatic downtown L.A. tower with a view of the Pacific. Temple found it only because Challis's male assistant, who spoke just one decibel above a whisper, had given her careful directions to the building and the floor.

He'd ended by saying, "Walk toward the black glass doors at the end of the hall. You'll see."

And Temple did. She saw the doors, she saw herself, and as unlikely as it seemed, she saw what a mystic in an altered state might have called a microcosm of the universe. The black glass had the effect of reflecting your image and drawing you into it at the same time, a magnetic pull that increased as you neared. You couldn't not see the doors. You couldn't not walk toward them. And then there was that point at which everything melded, at which you stepped into yourself, and ceased to exist. Or became whole.

He had a corner office, too.

It made hers look like a changing booth.

Temple had to smile as she made the inevitable comparisons. She'd thought nothing could compare with her corner, but his was three times the size, probably a quarter of the length of the building, and a breathtaking combination of glass and jutting steel.

A Japanese print hung on the wall behind his inlay mahogany desk and banker's chair. There was a spray of white orchids on the credenza. And music playing that she couldn't place. It was a lovely, eerie melody that held her attention but completely eluded her.

The assistant had escorted her into Mr. Challis's office and asked if she wanted anything, some lemongrass tea? Mr. Challis was on his way, he'd said. Temple had told him she was fine, and made it a point to thank him and Mr. Challis for opening the office on a Saturday. With a slight bow of his head, the solemn young man had left her alone. Left her to wonder how much the office reflected the other man she was about to meet and reveal the intimate details of her life to.

It would have been easy to dismiss his domain as a cold place, as cold and forbidding as the blue ocean outside. But like the black glass doors, there was depth and movement in the gleaming patterns. The flowers weren't cold. The music wasn't cold. It was haunting.

"Ms. Banning?"

He'd come in the door behind her. Temple rose on a wave of light-headedness. It was that way all the time now. She was reluctant to turn and make herself even dizzier, which meant he had to walk to her chair, come around, and face her as he extended his hand.

It was perhaps not the way he usually met people. It might even have appeared to be a ploy on her part.

"Mark Challis?"

"How can I help?" he asked.

His hand was firm and subtly commanding. Much

warmer than hers. And powerful enough to whisk a woman out of harm's way, she imagined. Or bring a man to his knees.

She hoped it wasn't the other way around.

Temple felt a quiver of sensation deep in her belly. It was as quick and primitive as fear, yet exquisitely complex, she sensed. She might even have shuddered if there hadn't been so many conflicting impressions.

She didn't know quite what to make of him. At first glance he looked more like a successful CEO than an ex-intelligence officer. He was tall, over six feet, with dark wavy hair, a muscular build, and a fleeting smile. Calling him handsome would have been too easy. But she didn't have another word to describe the lean, austere features and the diamond-cut of his jaw. Or the impact of his dark shirt and tie.

Arresting, certainly. But that hardly did it justice. Severe, yet sensual. Hard-edged elegance. None of those things worked, and Temple was a person who liked things to work. She'd never been at ease with shades, nuances, and ambiguity.

"Please," he said. "Sit down. Make yourself comfortable."

She did, happy to end the balancing act.

He walked to the windows and settled himself against the credenza, near the flowers. They made an unlikely pairing, Mark Challis and the orchids.

He was still staring at her. And Temple felt as if the air she was breathing had edges. Annette had captured him in the article. There was a glimmer of something in his countenance, in his eyes. An inner stillness, she thought. Diffuse yet focused, and not unlike a cobra.

That was it. That satisfied her for a moment.

She apologized for cutting into his weekend, then told

him she needed to locate someone. "It's a rather bizarre story."

He appeared to be looking out the window as she described what had happened, starting with that Friday night and bringing the strange chain of events up to the present. She left out some of the highly personal details, but she did tell him about the pregnancy, and her conviction that the lab had made a mistake.

He didn't react. Nor did he seem to be listening. But she sensed that he was taking everything in and even drawing conclusions in some mysterious way that investigators do, moving game pieces in his head.

The music she'd noticed earlier filtered through her thoughts as she told her story. It had begun to sound familiar, but she couldn't place it.

He was still absorbed with the world outside his window when she finished. "And why did you come to me?" he asked at last.

"Because Michael St. Gerard urged me to in his phone message. It sounded as if he knew you."

He turned to look at her, and Temple felt the sensation again. At the very base of her being, something shivered.

She had the distinct feeling that they were on totally different planes as she feathered her hair back from her eyes and waited for his reaction to her story. But he didn't appear to have any interest in what she'd told him. Not at the moment. None, she realized.

"Should I tell you what I know about you?" he asked.

Their eyes clashed. Alarm had brightened hers.

She didn't answer. If she had it would have been "No, please don't." Simply because. A threatened woman didn't need a better answer.

"I know that you're new in this area," he said. "That you haven't adjusted to the pace or the pollution, that you're overly polite and probably go out of your way to avoid confrontation."

"Overly polite?" No, *please* don't. Had she said it aloud?

He shrugged out of his suit jacket and dropped it over the back of his chair, as if he were getting down to business.

"Your clothing doesn't fit—I should say, specifically your bra doesn't fit. It's one of those lacy underwire things, and there's wad of M&M's making a nasty mess in your briefcase."

A pinching sensation nipped at Temple's ribs as she breathed. It *was* her bra. How did he know about that? She glanced at her briefcase, which was sitting in the chair next to her. It was open, but surely not enough that he could see inside.

He smiled, and read her mind.

"I'm an investigator," he said. "I've made a study of body language, speech patterns, face and voice reading, even jury selection criteria. It's my job."

And what a hit he'd be on the talk show circuit, she thought sardonically. "My body language told you there were M&M's in my bag?"

"That . . . and the fact that you've been on videotape since you got out of your car."

A television screen descended, blocking one of the windows. It appeared to be floating in space, and on it, Temple was pulling her car, a Buick Le Sabre with Texas plates, into a slot in the building's parking lot. She got out, adjusted the belt of her slacks, tweaked her too-tight bra, and visibly started when a city bus backfired.

"I am not overly polite," she said under her breath.

"No? Then why did you apologize to that bush?"

He pointed to the screen.

Now she was in the building's lobby, glancing at her watch and walking toward the elevator. She bumped a potted plant and dropped her briefcase on the floor, spilling its contents, which included a bag of M&M's. Most people would have rescued the case first, but Temple steadied the plant as she might have a person. What she said to it couldn't be heard, but it was an obvious expression of concern. She even went so far as to set straight a couple of leaves and pat a branch.

"That isn't a bush," she said tightly. "It's a diffenbachia *tree*."

"So I'm right? You did apologize?"

Temple gathered up her briefcase and rose from the chair. "Are you going to help me, Mr. Challis?"

Go out of your way to avoid *this* confrontation, she thought.

He left the credenza and walked to his desk. "No, actually I'm not."

"Excuse me? What did you say?"

"I can't help you. Sorry you had to make the trip for nothing."

He wasn't sorry. There wasn't a flicker of regret in his expression as he sat in his chair and began to sift through the papers on his desk. Apparently this was his way of letting her know they were done. "Mr. Challis?"

He looked up without moving his head. There was a warning in his eyes that actually frightened her.

"I *can't* help you, Ms. Banning," he said.

"Would you at least tell me why?" she persisted.

"I don't know anyone named Michael St. Gerard, and I don't take on individual cases. Even if I did, yours is out of my league. It's straight out of the tabloids. And that's what you were going to tell me next, right? That you were abducted by your stepfather and you're carrying his love child?"

He was making fun of her. Temple's voice snagged on some hidden emotional reef when she tried to talk.

"What I told you is true, all of it." It actually sounded like she might cry, and that was unthinkable. Her body must be awash in hormones, swamped. What else could explain the whiplash emotions? And what kind of insensitive beast was he to speak like this to someone in her situation?

But if her reaction was inappropriate, his was worse. She averted her eyes and brushed away the moistness with her fingertips, trying to get to the single tear before he noticed. But when she glanced up, he was watching her with what could only be called a neutral expression. Apparently he didn't care that he'd made her cry.

"Yes, I am polite, Mr. Challis. So shoot me. Because if I had a gun, I'd be very tempted to use it on your secret surveillance camera. And if I were *you*, I'd duck. How polite does that sound?"

With that she snatched up her briefcase from the chair, glaring at him as she hooked it over her shoulder. She must have been moving at a pretty good clip by the time she got to the doors of his office, because the case swung out and hit the brass handles. Nothing broke, but the noise it made was awful. She did not apologize.

The doors of the elevator glided shut behind Temple with a heavy swish. She turned to grasp the handrail and exhaled, releasing what tension she could. If there hadn't been twenty-plus stories, she would have taken the steps. All she wanted was to get out of the building as quickly as possible, get to her car and maybe lay a strip of rubber as she peeled out of the parking lot. She was that upset.

She couldn't imagine why he let her tell him that whole ridiculous story, and then refused to take her case. It felt as if he were toying with her, especially when he gave her the reason. She had little doubt that men like him were involved in ruthless power games and took great pleasure in playing them. The cobra temperament probably excelled at that sort of thing. The cold exercise of power.

She told herself it would be fine. There must be a dozen detectives in the area with strong credentials. She would hire someone else.

That decided, she turned—

And saw the man standing in the elevator with her.

The wall slapped her shoulders as she came up against it. Her gasp whistled like steam.

Mark Challis. He must have slipped in behind her. She hadn't heard him. All she could see was the menacing size of him. And the question that shadowed his expression.

He was holding something out.

"Is this yours?" he asked. "I found it on the floor of my office."

It was her nautilus shell. She'd put it in her briefcase this morning, probably foolishly thinking it might convey some kind of protection, like a charm, or help her find her way through the quagmire her life was becoming.

Temple took it from him with shaking hands.

"It's beautiful," he said. "I wouldn't have taken you for a shell collector."

She dropped it in her bag, surprised at how surgically accurate he was about her, camera or no camera. She cut him off when he tried to apologize. "I'm fine."

The wall panel lit up at NINETEEN, then EIGHTEEN. Temple felt as if she'd been in the elevator forever, but they weren't even close to the ground. Never again, she thought. I don't care how many flights I have to climb.

"I have a lunch appointment," he told her.

She stared at the panel, silent, willing the car to move faster. This was a first for her, blowing someone off. She'd never done it before, and it was almost painful, although she didn't know why. She never planned to see him again anyway.

The floors flashed by. They were better than halfway down when he told her to press STOP.

"Why?" The lights flickered, but Temple couldn't find the button.

"Something's wrong."

They reached SEVEN and all the floors lit up at once. The elevator shuddered hard, and Temple clutched the railing as an alarm shrilled. A red light began to flash. And the floor dropped out from under her.

The elevator was falling!

Challis grabbed her and pulled her away from the panel.

"Hang on to me!" he said. "There's an emergency brake. It will stop us, but we may hit hard."

The car became a landslide of light and noise and shuddering suction. Temple closed her eyes, anticipating the collision. He'd locked his arm around her waist as if he could break their fall with his body.

"Lean into me and relax!" he shouted over the noise.

The car rattled, a wood shack in the wind. It slowed and jerked and sighed. Temple could hear the screech of grinding brakes, the burning friction. She thought they were safe and asked Challis, but all he did was gather her closer and brace himself against the railing. Were they going to crash? She let out a gasp as he locked her tight and lifted her off the floor.

The impact rocketed upward to her skull. She could feel the jarring pressure in her head, but then it was over. He had absorbed most of the impact, and even more miraculously, he kept them both from being tossed around like flotsam. Temple didn't know how that was possible, other than sheer gut strength.

She was still clinging to him when the doors creaked opened. They'd stopped short of ground level, a few feet up from the mezzanine floor. She could see a security guard running toward them and a row of curious bystanders, who'd apparently been waiting for the elevator.

"Are you all right?" Challis asked her. He hadn't released

her yet, but he'd tilted back to look at her, and the concern in his eyes was evident.

"I think so."

"I don't." He jumped down from the elevator and held his arms out for her.

"What are you doing?"

"We're taking you to a doctor," he announced with finality. "You said you could be pregnant."

The gathering crowd made it look like a scene from a Hollywood movie. Temple was embarrassed, but too shaken to put up an argument. She dropped to her knees, reached out for him, and was tugged into the bracing strength of his arms.

She had been right about his hands. They could whisk you out of harm's way.

Challis turned to protect her as he began to shoulder his way through the gathering crowd. He directed the hawkers to disperse, and was polite but firm as he put off the security guard, who knew him by name, with a promise to brief him about the accident later. Temple was impressed with his command of the situation. But for her part, it felt terribly awkward being carried around that way, head bobbing, limbs dangling, people staring. At least she'd worn slacks.

He fully intended to carry her through the lobby and probably out to his car, she realized. And finally she had to put her arms around his neck to anchor herself.

"I really think I can walk," she whispered to him.

"I'm sure you can," he whispered back. "But why bother when you can ride."

"Congratulations!" Dr. Dan Llewelyn's fatherly beam of a smile included both Temple and Challis, though he directed the words to Temple. "You're exactly where you should be for this early in your term. You have a healthy baby on the way."

Clearly he expected them to be more pleased about the news. He'd also taken it for granted that they were a couple. And Temple hadn't corrected his mistake. She could barely fathom the confirmation of her pregnancy. She'd been in denial until this moment, she realized, hoping it was a mistake and that her life might return to normal.

But that was not to be. Her life was about to change drastically. And she couldn't begin to imagine all the ways. Right now she was struggling to imagine the next nine months.

She'd been examined by the doctor privately, and though she'd provided him with the necessary medical history, she hadn't shared all the gruesome details of her situation, reasoning that he only needed to know about the elevator accident and her concern that she might be pregnant.

He'd done the usual pelvic, followed it up with an ultrasound and taken several vials of blood. He'd recommend vitamins and iron supplements, then given her samples. After all that, he'd called Challis into the room and shown the two of them a videocassette that discussed the changes in a woman's body during pregnancy. It had even weighed the pros and cons of sex at various stages, to Temple's dismay. And now all three of them were in Llewelyn's office, discussing "their" baby, hers and Challis's.

Challis hadn't bothered to correct the doctor's impression that they were a couple, either, although it was clear by the way the two men had greeted each other on a first-name basis that they were acquaintances. The doctor had also refused to charge them a fee, saying that he and Challis's father went "way back."

Temple was numb. Possibly Challis was being gallant by not revealing that they weren't a couple. Maybe he did didn't want to embarrass either one of them. She didn't know how to make sense of it other than that. She didn't want to try. All she wanted was to get back to her box-filled apartment where she could be alone.

But that was not to be, either. When they left the doctor's office at long last, Mark Challis insisted on taking her home. He didn't want her driving after what she'd been through, and he'd already arranged for a flat-bed wrecker to pick up her car and deliver it to her apartment building.

"You didn't have to do this," she told him once they were on their way. "I could have taken a taxi from the doctor's office."

"A taxi to Ventura would have cost a hundred bucks" was his only comment.

She hadn't thought about the cost, but he was right, of course. Ventura was an hour north of L.A., in good traffic.

If it hadn't seemed like an intrusion, she would have thanked him. But he'd gone silent again, his eyes on the road, his hand resting easily on the wheel of the black BMW.

Temple studied the extraordinary length of his fingers and the width of his hand across the back, from thumb to curled little finger. She'd felt the power of his grip, but there was more than physical strength in those contours. His light olive skin had a sensuous quality that was made almost erotic by a sprinkling of dark silt. And the way his palm curved the wheel stirred a familiar sensation in Temple's depths.

She wondered if he was the kind of man who had manicures. He dressed elegantly enough, and the watch on his wrist looked like a very expensive Phillipe Patek. But she suspected not. He didn't seem indulgent in that way. If she were to guess she would have said he was spare in his habits, even ascetic. She didn't know why. He just struck her that way.

He glanced in her direction and smiled faintly at her expression.

"Is it my driving?" he asked.

"You drive just fine." She returned his smile. "But you seem deep in thought."

"I am," he admitted. "There's something I need to tell you, and I'm not sure this is the best time, but if I'm right, it can't wait."

She slid back in the seat. "What is it?"

"There's a chance it wasn't an accident."

"What? The elevator?" It was the first thing that came to her mind. "Someone was trying to hurt you?"

"No, Temple." His tone was soft, grave. "It wasn't me they were after. I never use that elevator. I have a private one in my office."

"Who then?" She stared at him, refusing to go where he was taking her. There were only two people in that elevator, and if it wasn't an accident and it wasn't him, then—

They were on the freeway, but he took an exit and then wheeled off the road, into the deserted parking lot of a grocery store.

"Is there anyone who would want to hurt you?" he asked her as he cut the car's engine.

"No!"

"What about the phone message? Didn't the man who called warn you there might be danger?"

"Michael St. Gerard?" She conceded that much. "He said they might try to get to him through me."

"But he didn't say how. Or suggest that they would go to these extremes. It takes some planning to rig elevator cables to break."

Fear stabbed at Temple. "Is that what you think happened, that they were rigged to break?"

His silence frightened her terribly.

"I don't know," she said. "I don't know what St. Gerard meant. I don't even know who he is. Or who *they* are."

He regarded her soberly, as if coming to some kind of decision. Finally he pried her hands loose from her briefcase and took them in his. It startled her. This was the last thing she could have expected of Mark Challis, but he knew exactly what he was doing.

He clasped her hands so firmly they couldn't shake. She could feel the strength and quiet certainty that emanated from him, and her shock was replaced by a rush of warmth. It felt as if he were flowing into her through the connection their hands had made. Transfusing her . . . and within moments she began to breathe as he did. Calmly. Evenly.

"I can't take on the case," he said, "but I will try to find out who St. Gerard is for you, all right? I can do that much. Meanwhile, it might not be a bad idea to check into a hotel for tonight, rather than go home."

"A hotel? Is that necessary?"

His hands tightened possessively. "Under the circumstances, it's erring on the side of caution. And if you were my client, I would insist. There wouldn't be any argument about this."

Temple felt as if she were battling an overpowering current, that's how forceful he was, just in his tone. "I'm not a client," she reminded him. Gingerly. She didn't want him to take back his offer.

"Is there anyone you can stay with?"

She wasn't open to that, either, but she nodded and pretended to consider it. Maybe she was a bit set in her ways, but she'd paid a huge price for her independence. And the thought of having her life taken over in this way, even for the best of reasons, was not something she looked forward to.

"A friend?" he pressed.

Temple's first thought was Annette. Her coworker already knew about the situation, and Temple hoped they were close enough that she could ask for this kind of help. In fact, Annette had sent her to Challis, which struck Temple as coincidental, but probably only because she was so shaken. Fear could make you grasp at anything to explain it away. She would ask her friend for help, if it came to that, but only she could decide when to take that kind of action. No one else could do it for her, not even Mark Challis.

"There is someone," she said. "But I can get myself there. And I'll need to go home first for my things."

"You will do it?" he asked.

She nodded, aware that it was easier to agree with him than argue. This was not a man you wanted to have a confrontation with, whether you were the type that avoided them or not.

She didn't know whether to be relieved or disappointed when he took his hands away. It felt as if she'd been taken off a heart-lung machine. That's how powerful his presence was. She sensed that he was still there, focused on her in the silent, absorbing way he had of studying things, but suddenly she was feeling terribly exposed and didn't want him to see that.

She rearranged herself and glanced up with a quick, dismissive smile. "I'll be fine," she assured him. "Just fine."

SIX

◦◦◦

Mark Challis had an investigative staff of thirty, a research team of more than half that many, and subcontractors across the continent. His reach was global. It had to be. His work involved safeguarding against speculative attack and hostile takeovers, asset protection, threat assessment, security risks, and a number of the other highly sensitive "intelligence" services that large corporations required.

His agency had a policy against individual clients because Mark knew from his own experience that the work got too personal and messy. Nobody cared when corporations blew the hell out of each other. It was an accepted part of doing business, even applauded. When people took aim at each other, blood was shed. The body count rose. Revenge had a ricochet effect that took out anything in its path, including investigators.

But despite his convictions, the morning after the incident with Temple Banning, Mark met with one of his most promising new investigators and asked him to see what he could find on Michael St. Gerard. At this stage Mark was curious more than anything else. Curious enough to bend company policy and break his own rules.

He had many ways of judging people. One was by the effect they had on his pulse rate. And hers had been interesting. Not faster. Harder. His pulse hadn't quickened. It had slowed, thickened, dropped low in his chest. Like an anvil, he'd thought, when he'd taken hold of her hands. She must have felt the impact because it had reverberated all through him.

When his heart slowed down, his mind sped up. For as long as he could remember it had been that way, a biological anomaly that defied the experts. He'd been tested by the military. They didn't know what to make of it, but they had recognized it as a survival skill worthy of the most cunning predators.

And Mark had used it to search and destroy when that was the only recourse, to survive, to seal himself off. He had lived his life on the periphery, and not only because of his work. The edge was a place where his mind worked and his heart took cover. It was the safest place for a man who had walked through the fires of hell and knew they had nothing to do with physical death.

This morning he'd come up in the private elevator, then gone out the side door of his office and taken the back way to the investigators' bay. Still on the periphery. Skirting life. Skirting death. Still there, in limbo.

Now as he returned to his own exceedingly quiet work space, he realized that he had mishandled Temple Banning. He should have insisted she find a safe haven for the night. He was virtually certain she hadn't, and that she wasn't taking him, or any of this, seriously. Such a mistake, he thought. People's first reaction to trouble was denial. Some of them stayed in that state so long they died of it.

The ability to rationalize, reconcile, and avoid reality had always fascinated him. What puzzled him was the reason. He'd boiled it down to apathy or fear. Most of the country lived in a rosy everything-was-going-to-be-all-right state of mind, whereas he lived on the cusp of vigilance, the cusp of disaster. The question was: Where did Temple Banning live?

There was a stack of research reports waiting for him on his desk. The agency had several cases in progress, and he liked to be kept up-to-date. He took off his jacket, a black leather Andrew Marc that would have cost him a month's salary when he was in the military, pulled the shoulders together, and dropped it over the back of a chair. He then pushed up the sleeves of his white crew neck sweater and gave his shoulders a ritual flex.

His wardrobe was expensive because that was what his clients wore. It was important that he "blend" and not draw unnecessary attention to himself. But he liked space, too, plenty of working room, for his body as well as his mind.

Settled in his chair, he turned and gazed out the window, but his focus drew inward. This was another ritual he'd come to enjoy, observing his own thoughts. The goal was to listen to the mind's conflict, the beliefs and opinions that fought each other. The psyche was a battlefield, and if you grew quiet you could hear it. The reason, he'd learned in his study of the martial arts, was lack of self-knowledge. Until you knew yourself completely, you would always be in conflict.

And when a man was at war with himself, he was weak.

This morning it took only a few seconds for Mark's mind to grow quiet. Over the years he had come to know exactly who he was, which allowed him to achieve the effect readily, just by tuning in to the flow of air through his nostrils. It was the well he went to for renewal, and probably the source of his mental strength.

When he was done he continued to look out the window, aware of the clouds and the occasional seagull. Finally he turned back to his desk and set about his work. He checked his E-mail first and forwarded much of it to his assistant to handle. There was some correspondence that required his personal attention and an attached file sent by one of his researchers. The correspondence could wait, he decided.

The file turned out to be a newspaper clipping. A woman had reported a bizarre assault to the police, and the researcher had noted that it was the third such case that month. He'd also pointed out that while none of the women had any memory of the incident, they'd each been abducted, drugged, and based on medical exams, subjected to a gynecological procedure, which wasn't described.

Additional evidence that the assaults might be serially connected came from the women's accounts. All three had reported having temporary amnesia, a condition the article described as "retrograde." And they'd each visited a walk-in clinic in recent weeks, but they'd gone for different reasons, and their ages varied widely.

Mark made a note to contact his source at LAPD and request copies of the police reports. The victims' medical records would be the mother lode, if he could get them, but that was a long shot. Finally he jotted down the similarity to Temple Banning's situation—i.e., the amnesia—and along with it, a reminder to check out her exfiancé. Mark wasn't going to share any of this with his investigator just yet. He wanted to see what the new man would turn up on St. Gerard. It would be a good test of his abilities.

Once he'd gone through the rest of the material, Mark settled back to reflect. He'd already concluded that the assaults were serially connected and that someone out there was either playing doctor or God. But that was an easy guess. Those were the power games that fueled most secret heterosexual male fantasies and made every straight guy in the country a suspect, although few would ever act on the impulses in a criminal way, *unless* there was a hang-up with women. Mark had some experience with both roles because of his medical training in the military. Playing God was less dangerous to the patient, he'd found.

Ironic that as he mused on the case what caught his eye was the videocassette on prenatal care that Temple Banning had left on his car seat, probably intentionally. He'd dropped it in his out box this morning, intending to get it back to her at some point.

She'd been damn uncomfortable in the doctor's office, the pregnant party, sandwiched between two men she didn't know, and forced to watch a half-naked woman blithely describe the intimate changes her body was going through. Even Mark had thought it was pretty explicit for an instructional video, but probably necessary, considering the subject matter.

They'd watched the woman's breasts change and her belly swell. It had even described the increased blood flow to those areas, the way skin could flush for no reason and certain membranes could engorge. And of course Mark was thinking about the woman next to him, who showed not the slightest sign of pregnancy in her slender body. And, of course, he felt some stirrings of curiosity . . . some deep stirrings.

He could feel them now. His heart rate was up a little, an aberration for him, and heat was crawling up the back of his neck toward his hairline. Apparently blood was flowing and certain membranes were engorging. It wouldn't take much, he thought, aware of the sharpening sensations. And the turmoil.

He closed his eyes, determined to clear the radar of interference, and saw her there on a screen that had been perfectly blank moments ago. She could have been describing the intimate changes in her body or rising out of her chair to confront him in his office, to dress him down, storm out the door, and make everything he said about her a lie. He wasn't sure. But his mind wasn't quiet anymore.

"Ivy in't here right now, Ms. Bannin'. She went off to the amusement park with a group from one of her classes."

Temple started to say that was impossible. Her little sister never went to amusement parks. Besides, this was the night she and Ivy were supposed to have a phone date. They usually talked around seven on Saturday evenings. This twang-talking housemother on the other end of the line must have it wrong.

Temple wanted to say all of that, but she was afraid it might send Ivy into paroxysms of embarrassment to have her big sister making a fuss. So she asked the woman to let Ivy know she'd called, thanked her, and set the mobile phone down with a sigh.

Temple had sunk into her favorite chair almost the moment she walked in the door from her ordeal with Mark Challis. She hadn't showered and changed, hadn't eaten, hadn't done anything but fall back, let out a moan of relief, and then called her sister.

But Ivy off with a crowd of kids? Temple should have been thrilled her little sister was making friends. She wanted only good things for Ivy. With all her heart she wanted that, but this was a milestone Temple wasn't totally prepared for. It made her stop and reflect.

Nothing was ever going to be the same again, she realized, and the shock of it crashed over her like a wave. Every aspect of Temple's life had changed, including her relationship with Ivy, who had needed her for everything, it seemed, even to breathe. But no more.

It was all gone, her sister, her parents, her past, her future with Donald. Her role as caretaker. All of it, gone or transformed into something unfamiliar. She had wanted freedom, but she'd never imagined it would feel like this.

When she got up from the chair, it was slowly. She didn't want to set off the dizziness again, but it was time to do something—reclaim control. She would take a shower, have a snack, go to bed. Anything she could do would help, even if it was just to get out of the chair.

But she only made it as far as the kitchen.

The fluorescent lights were too bright when she turned them on. They tipped the floor beneath her feet and made her reach for the wall to steady herself. She couldn't pretend this was going to be okay. She didn't have the heart for it, especially if it meant lying to herself. This apartment, her refuge, felt as alien to her as the honeymoon suite had. It was no longer home, if it ever had been. The walls were bare, the boxes unpacked. It was a way station on some unknown road, and that awareness made her feel so terribly alone.

But she wasn't alone . . .

She touched her stomach and tears welled in her eyes.

A baby, dear God, what was she going to do?

The chair she'd left was miles away, so she sank down on the floor instead, the cold tiles of the kitchen, knowing her legs wouldn't support her. She didn't know how to deal with the rigors of pregnancy and the responsibilities of a child when her life was in utter turmoil. And even if it hadn't been, she'd decided against the Mommy Track, if that was what they were still calling it.

It felt as if her life, her home, even her body, were not her own. If she'd ever needed her family, it was now. Someone close, someone who cared. Ivy was the logical one, the *only* one, and maybe that was why Temple had been crushed not to reach her. But she couldn't tell Ivy what happened. It would frighten her to death.

There was some terrible irony in knowing she couldn't

have told any of her family, not even her parents if they were alive. That wasn't the way the Banning family did things. Temple didn't fall apart. She was the glue. Now she wondered if there'd ever been a time when her parents had wished she would turn to them and ask for their help or counsel. She never had. She couldn't break out of the prison of strength and helpfulness she'd built for herself.

Temple bowed her head, and as she closed her eyes, she heard his voice, cautioning her, gently trying to make her understand the danger she was in. *There's something I need to tell you, and I'm not sure this is the best time. . . . There's a chance it wasn't an accident.* That should have frightened her more than it did, because if Mark Challis was right, someone was trying to kill her, and she had no idea why. She had no enemies that she knew of. She'd never done anything to intentionally hurt anyone.

That was why none of this made sense and why it couldn't be happening to her, Temple Banning. She didn't understand what she'd done, what sin she'd committed, to bring such wrath down upon her head.

"Why?" she whispered aloud. "Why me?"

Susan Gilchrist knelt at the open door of the courtesy bar in her hotel room and searched the contents for something to drink, preferably ice-cold, preferably good and strong. She'd had a long, miserable day, and tomorrow wasn't looking any better.

She'd spent the morning with the HMO chief of staff, who brought her up-to-date on the conditions of the three patients, including their treatment modalities and test results. He also introduced her to the members of the medical staff who'd worked on the cases, including the internist who'd called Susan in Atlanta.

Fortunately they'd done a reasonably good job of quickly isolating the patients in an unused wing of the building, and they'd instituted full barrier nursing. But Susan was disturbed that some of the hospital staff weren't wearing protective gear. She ordered everyone on the floor to don face masks and those working directly with the patients to suit up in gowns, caps, booties, and gloves.

They hadn't determined what the disease was, she discovered, but they knew what it wasn't, which was most everything. Nearly every test they'd done was negative, and the others weren't definitive. In fact, Susan could have told them what they were dealing with, but she didn't want panic in the ranks. And it wouldn't have been smart to commit herself before the CDC tests were in.

With that in mind she'd had blood drawn, urine specimens collected, and rushed them, along with throat swabs, to Atlanta. She'd sent everything to the attention of Brian Rice, and her first order of duty tonight, after she'd finished off at least a split of something, was to call and alert him it was coming. She didn't want the samples to fall into any other hands, or for him to report his results to anyone other than her.

"Nothing but Chardonnay," she observed, gingerly pulling a small bottle from the loaded fridge. She butchered the cork in her impatience to get it out, then poured herself a cloudy tumblerful, and kicked off her shoes. The king-size bed looked so inviting, she piled up several pillows and stretched out fully clothed.

With a sigh she set down the glass and fished her tiny Motorola Startac from the pocket of her jacket. She wouldn't be able to relax until she'd left word with Brian.

She'd expected to leave a message on his machine, and it surprised her when he answered the phone. He often worked late at the containment lab, but she hadn't expected him to be there at—she glanced at her watch—one A.M. Normally she would have checked to see if there was a problem, but he didn't offer to explain, and all she could think about was her own situation.

"I've got a special favor to ask," she told him. She quickly briefed him about the samples and told him what she thought they were dealing with.

"Christ, Susan, a recurrence of Agent Z190?"

"It's all right," she assured him. "Everything's under control here. The HMO is observing isolation procedures, and there haven't been any new cases since the last one, which was three days ago. Given how quickly the virus incubates, I think it's already contained."

"God, I hope so. Z190 could wipe out the population of L.A. in about a heartbeat, including the tourists, like yourself."

He was right, of course, and the thought was unnerving. She took a drink of the wine and held the cool glass to her feverish cheek. Lord, she was warm. Stress, probably, but when she got off the phone, she would have to check the air-conditioning.

"Relax, Brian. I'm on the job, okay? Just don't broadcast that I'm here. I'll explain why later, and call me as soon as you've isolated the virus."

"Sure, but that could take awhile the way Z190 mutates. I can't make any promises. You may be back before I've got anything. By the way, when will you be back?"

"You were close with that tourist thing. I'm taking some personal days when I finish up here, but I'll be in touch. And you can reach me anytime. You've got my cell phone number."

"Just three cases?" he asked, clearly still curious about the virus. "Is one of them the index?"

He was asking her if she knew who the primary case was, the one who passed the virus on to the other two.

"I'm on top of it," she said, hoping to fend off any more questions. "Only one of the surviving patients was strong enough to be interviewed today, so I've still got some investigating to do."

In fact she knew exactly who the index was, but she was keeping the woman's true identity under wraps for reasons of her own. Her investigation so far had revealed some interesting complications, including a love triangle between the three cases. One of them was a graduate student who'd passed the virus to her professor, with whom she was having an affair. He'd then taken it home to his beloved wife. And there was one other piece of information that would have brought the news media out in droves, had they knows it. The grad student was one of the three Amnesia Assault victims.

Dr. Susan Gilchrist, bright star of the CDC's Special Pathogens Branch, had plenty of reason to keep a tight lid on this one.

After she and Brian had said their good-byes, she finished off the wine, then picked up the cell phone and tapped out Temple Banning's home phone number, as she had done several times in the last two days. The message machine came on, and Susan snapped the phone case shut. Where the hell was the woman?

She tossed the cell on the bed and looked at her empty wine glass longingly. She'd had to lie to Brian tonight, but not about the situation at the HMO. This was much more grievous than that. She'd told him *everything* was under control.

Annette Dalton dropped her bombshell somberly, hesitating between sips of the warm spiced cider she'd made for herself and Temple. Her gaze was tilted down, but her lashes came up as she spoke, giving the appearance of a woman about to divulge an important state secret.

"Did I ever tell you that I hold the Ventura County record for having attended the most performances of *Phantom*?"

"Never," Temple said with equal gravity. "How many is that?"

"Seventy-three, counting the Davis Gaines and the Norman Large performances, but not counting the times that Norman filled in for Michael Crawford.

"I have his shorts," she said proudly.

"Norman's?"

"Michael's!" Her head lifted with a quick little smile. "I know a stagehand," she explained, hazel eyes twinkling.

"You're sure they're Michael's?"

"*Of course.* They were swiped right out of his clothes hamper."

"Dirty shorts?"

"Oh, I hope so. Temmmmmmmpull, it's Michael Crawford!"

Annette winked and Temple felt a little queasy.

Both women were snuggled on either end of Annette's couch, covered in chenille throws and savoring the cider and the warmth of her small fireplace. It was the one unstandard feature in an otherwise fairly standard southern California apartment. White stucco walls, closet-size kitchens with breakfast bars and pile carpeting. Noisy air conditioners shoehorned into the wall.

Temple had decided it was Annette's personal touches that made the place livable. Her friend was a romance nut. She had a nearly complete collection of Frank Sinatra's early singles on vinyl and a video assortment of "tortured love stories" that ranged from *Last of the Mohicans* to *Swamp Thing.*

But her tour de force was an autographed life-size Phantom cutout that stood next to the fireplace. It was why Temple wouldn't have dreamed of questioning Annette's claim about the authenticity of Michael Crawford's briefs. Temple knew "serious fan" when she saw it.

The fire flickered and flowed, roaring softly.

Ol' Blue Eyes flowed, too, delivering a rendition of "My Foolish Heart."

Temple let go a contented sigh that sounded as if it had been locked up forever, yearning to escape. She felt safe in this place.

"This is nice, Annette, thank you for inviting me."

She'd pulled Annette aside that morning at work and told her about the elevator incident. Annette's response had been to insist that Temple come over that very night. She'd also given her a key to the apartment and told her to stay as long as she wanted.

It had touched Temple deeply, and made her realize that she wasn't alone, that sometimes friends were closer than family. Or at least their expectations were different, and liberating in this case. Annette was perfectly willing to take charge and tell Temple what to do, for her own good, the role Temple had always played.

It felt warm to be bossed around, comforting like the fire. Even now Annette was watching her with an eagle eye.

"You okay?" she asked. "You're smiling."

"Smiling is good, silly." Temple laughed and leaned over to select a red M&M from the giant-size bag sprawled on the coffee table. The candy was her contribution to the cozy evening.

Annette watched with curiosity as Temple popped the glossy red disk in her mouth and proceeded to suck off the sugar coating in its entirety before she bit into the rich chocolate filling. It was a ritual of delayed gratification that could have been the metaphor for Temple's life.

"Whoa," Annette exclaimed softly. "Don't you ever want to scoop up a handful of those things and just crunch down? Don't you ever get that urge? "

"Yeah," Temple admitted, "I do."

"Well . . . ?"

"I can't. I just can't."

"Of course you can, silly!" Annette took it upon herself to demonstrate. She sorted through the bag, picked out a dozen or so, mixing the colors with abandon, shoveled them into her mouth, and bit down with a grin.

"D'lishus," she said.

All Temple could think about was how excessive that was, how wasteful, and how divine that messy mouthful of chocolate must taste. She couldn't even imagine such self-indulgence. It just wasn't her.

"How about a movie?" Annette suggested when she'd consumed her bounty and licked a dab of chocolate from her lips. "I just got *Hope Floats*. Or how about some Sinatra?"

Temple cocked her head. "Isn't that Sinatra singing?"

"Wake up, girl, that's the Velvet Fog, Mel Torme. In a minute he's going to sing 'Moon River.'"

"I thought 'Moon River' was Andy Williams."

Annette gave Temple a look that said she was hopeless. She'd already unearthed herself from the blanket and gone to her "entertainment center," which amounted to a Victrola-like turntable, balanced on top of a CD player, both of which sat on a heavily listing cabinet, propped by paperback books.

Temple didn't like to look at the thing.

"*A Summer Place!*" Annette crowed, rifling through a stack of videos. "I *love* this movie. Massive angst. It's the one where Sandra Dee and Troy Donahue can't keep their hands off each other, and she gets pregnant, and they cry all the time because they're so much in love, but they go for this illegal abortion, and—oh."

She glanced around at Temple, apparently just realizing what she'd said. "Sorry."

That was when Temple understood why Annette had been so breezy and chatty all evening. She was trying to distract her. "It's all right. I'd rather talk about it, if you're okay with that. I think I need to."

"Absolutely." Annette sat on the floor where she was, shivered, and pulled her Princess Diana T-shirt over her knees. "I'll shut up and listen. Do me good."

Temple tossed her the throw, then settled back, wondering where to start.

"I keep thinking about the irony of my ending up married and pregnant by some phantom husband after I broke my engagement and left home to take this job. It feels like a cosmic joke."

"It would, only I'm not sure the cosmos is that warped."

Temple nodded. "Sometimes I think I'm losing my mind."

Annette gave her an earnest stare. "You can't remember anything that happened that night? Nothing?"

"I know how crazy that sounds, but it's true. The last thing I remember was sitting in my apartment eating chicken wings. When I opened my eyes, it was Saturday morning."

They'd already gone over this. Temple had told Annette about the man's voice and the music, both of which could as easily have been a dream as not. Other than that there was nothing, certainly nothing substantial. Temple hadn't had any flashbacks the way amnesiacs were supposed to.

"At least Mark Challis has offered to help find Michael," Temple said. "But meanwhile, I don't know what to do about this pregnancy. I vowed never to make the mistake my parents did and have children I wasn't prepared to care for."

Annette freed her knees from the T-shirt and sat forward, leaning over her crossed legs. "I can tell you what I'd do if it were me, but you're not me, Temple. You need to give yourself plenty of time with a decision like this, and the good news is you don't have to do anything tonight. Your job is to relax and take care of yourself."

She executed a catlike stretch and spirited the bag of M&M's off the table. "And maybe do a little thinking about the Fabrici account, hmmm? Sonia cornered me today and wanted to know when we were going to be ready. I can't put her off any longer, Temple."

It hadn't occurred to Temple that she would make any decisions about her personal life tonight, although she had wanted to come closer to knowing her own mind and heart on the subject of single motherhood. But maybe it made sense to go about her life for a while, let things return to normal, if that was possible. When you didn't try to force a decision, one sometimes came to you. The right one, she hoped.

Annette had popped a red M&M in her mouth and she was sucking on it experimentally.

"I think we're going to nail Fabrici," Temple said. "I've got a red-hot idea for their new men's cologne. It just came to me, you know, one of those gifts from the gods of advertising."

"Red-hot? Tell me about it!"

"Not yet, it's still embryonic, you should excuse the expression. I need a little more daydream time." A lot, she amended, but why scare Annette, too.

And, in fact, Temple did have an idea, but it was less than embryonic. It was more the swimming sperm stage. And it had been inspired by Mark Challis. If anything worthwhile had come out of her meeting with him, it was her fixation with his striking features, his inborn sense of style, and those beautiful serpentine eyes. The man had a presence that brought key words to mind like *quiet power*.

A man who could hold you quietly in his power, she thought.

When she got up tomorrow, she would do some right-brain stuff. She would get out her sketch pad and her colored pens, and maybe, just maybe she could do something with that.

SEVEN

Stairs or elevator? That was a no-brainer, Temple thought as she hitched up her loaded briefcase and headed for the stairs. She would have rappelled the side of the building before getting on another elevator.

It was late, nearly seven P.M., and the halls of the fourteenth floor were empty. It looked as if she was the last one to leave, and a deserted stairway probably wasn't the safest place for a woman alone. But safety wasn't high on Temple's list of concerns that night. Her mind was still in the conference room, where the Fabrici team had been working on the men's cologne account.

Temple had kept her own brainchild under wraps in order to see what the other members had to offer. They'd batted around several ideas but needed to narrow it down to one as quickly as possible, and nothing had seemed to stick. As team leader, she'd learned to watch for synergy—the peculiar vibe that occurred when the members began to play off each other's input, triggering chain-reaction responses.

Nothing had come close today, and she'd been about to spring her idea on them, when Denny Paxton suggested they try a "Banned in Boston" concept. It was his theory that women should protest the cologne because it was an unfair weapon in the battle between the sexes. The other members picked up on it immediately and began throwing out slogans. With mixed feelings, Temple realized he'd hit on something.

It had been edgy with Denny since the beginning. He was thirtyish, attractive in the rather typical Madison Avenue "suit" fashion, fast-on-his-feet, and most of all a charmer, who was used to getting his way with people. But he hadn't gotten Temple's job, despite his experience and seniority, and there was tension. Their styles clashed. Denny was surface friendly, but aggressive, a closer. More than once since Temple came aboard, he'd faked her out by stealing the ball and running with it, which left her to try and figure out how to get it back.

It had happened again today, she realized.

Maybe she *was* too damn polite, but she wanted the Fabrici account badly. That, and the obvious need to demonstrate some leadership skills, had forced her to be open to Denny's idea. There was also the strong possibility that his idea had more mainstream appeal than hers, so she'd kept hers on hold, and reminded herself that it would have received some resistance anyway. The images she had in mind *were* a bit risqué, although sometimes that was what it took.

She must still have been deep in thought when she reached the basement where her car was parked. She was probably looking at the floor, because as she turned to go to her assigned stall, she stepped blindly into the path of a huge, vibrating object. She hadn't seen the idling car sitting there and couldn't stop in time to avoid it. Her shin hit first, and then she pitched forward across the hood.

She caught herself with her hands. But she could feel the

heat and the deep churning of a big engine before she sprang back. It was a black BMW with windows as menacingly dark as the car. Opaque glass concealed the driver.

Panic gripped Temple as she stumbled over something on the floor. A briefcase. It was hers, but she didn't remember dropping it. She wasn't even sure this was the right garage. Nothing looked familiar.

The BMW's door swung open. She would have run, but the driver was out of the car and walking toward her already. She stepped back, certain that it was Mark Challis. But then not certain of that, either.

"Are you all right?" he asked.

He was wearing a casual jacket of creamy chamois leather, a black crew-neck sweater, and narrow-leg jeans. It wasn't the look she associated with him, and in the watery light of the garage, his entire countenance seemed different. His features were shadowed in an unusual way. Faintly demonic, actually. Long gothic lines that could have been rendered by a Flemish master. And yet everything was bewitchingly tip-tilted, even his eyes. The effect was quite stunning.

What was it about his face? she asked herself. You couldn't take your eyes off him, but you also couldn't pinpoint what it was that made you stare. There were secrets hidden in his expression that encouraged you to search closer, an optical illusion that might resolve itself if you looked long enough.

He returned her stare, and she touched her mouth, wondering if she had on any lipstick. "What are you doing here?" she asked.

"*Are* you all right?"

His tone of authority brought a nod of confirmation.

"I'm not hurt, if that's what you mean." She hadn't stopped thinking about how she looked since he appeared, she realized, wondering if her upswept hair had straggled free from its claw clip and if her mascara had run.

The briefcase lay by her feet. She picked it up without taking her eyes off him. Briefcases were shields, weapons. She didn't carry a purse, so hers was heavily packed with work materials, makeup, and the marketing books she'd been reading. It would do some damage if swung.

"I have some information for you," he said.

"Information?" She searched her memory. "About Michael St. Gerard? What is it?"

"There are conditions."

Ah, conditions. He wasn't exactly undressing her with his eyes, so she assumed he meant money. "How much?"

"You come right to the point." His tone was faintly appreciative. "It will cost you an evening."

"You want . . . an evening?"

"I want tonight. I'll give you the information if you have dinner with me."

She cocked her head, crossed her arms, and perhaps even smiled at him. "I think they call that blackmail in most of the fifty states."

"You'll like this place," he assured her. "It's a winery with a renowned French chef, a five-star restaurant, and a cognac crème brûlée to make your knees buckle."

"They call *that* bribery."

She held her ground, even as he moved past her to the passenger door of the car and opened it.

"They'll serve dinner in the vineyards if you request it," he went on, "beneath garlands of rice-paper lanterns and arbors loaded down with grapevines. And best of all, we'll be undisturbed. It's safe, isolated, secure."

"I'm not dressed for a five-star restaurant." She tipped the lapel of her blazer as proof, wishing she had a more sophisticated wardrobe. She was so busy at work she'd become dependent on the jackets and slacks of her travel-agency days.

But Challis had gone silent. The elevators were about fifty feet behind him. He glanced around as if he knew one of them was about to open. When it did, and the building's receptionist came out, Temple acknowledged the smiling older woman with a wave.

Challis remained silent and intent until the intruder had pulled her car out and driven away from the garage, and then he turned back to Temple.

"Ask me," he said, looking her over with an X-ray sweep of his dark eyes. "You're perfect."

Temple was still back at the elevator. And totally unprepared for Challis's gaze to drop to her ankle boots and begin its upward slide. This was no once-over. This was the visual equivalent of a pat-down for weapons. No cavity inspection? she marveled.

"We're going to be outside," he explained in a neutral tone. "You'll need that jacket."

Had she said yes yet?

He was like the doctor who'd examined her, she realized. Physicians routinely crossed boundaries of personal privacy in order to do their work. Obviously investigators did, too. But if Challis thought nothing of invading her privacy in that way, what else could she expect?

His car was her answer. The seat belts buckled automatically as soon as the doors were shut, and the sound the locks made as they sealed told Temple this was no ordinary BMW. A remote-control device sat on the console. Probably not for a garage door, she decided.

She pointed to it. "What's that?"

"It starts the car from a distance, then sweeps for bombs."

"Really?" She countered with a quip, perhaps to cover her uneasiness. "Is there a device in the trunk that spews out nails?"

He'd already pulled the car out of the garage, and he was heading toward the freeway on-ramp. It was dark outside, but the fluorescent streetlights revealed his expression as he glanced her way.

"We haven't used nails in a while," he explained dryly. "But there are blinder lights concealed above the rearview window, and the vehicle is self-contained, with a one-hour oxygen supply in case of chemical attack."

It was more than Temple wanted to know. That people could have a need for these devices outside of James Bond movies was disturbing. That someone like her might have need of them was inconceivable. Up until recently she'd lived what most people would call an uneventful life. It was all she'd ever expected to live, which made this experience—riding in a bomb-proof car with a P.I. who was investigating her own phantom wedding—too bizarre to contemplate.

"You're quiet," he observed after a while.

"Just thinking how much I love crème brûlée" was her soft response.

"Tell me about the missing twelve hours."

"I've done that," Temple insisted.

"Tell me what you left out. The one thing you neglected to mention. What was it?"

"There were several things." She hadn't mentioned the music, the food, or the champagne. There was the peignoir set, the empire wedding dress and veil, the blue garter.

"A million little details," she said evasively.

"Yes, but there's only one small little detail you're avoiding, one that matters."

What Temple found difficult to avoid was his gaze. Even when she wasn't looking at him. Her fingers entwined the delicate coffee cup she was holding, and as she brought it to her mouth, she could feel him there, in the steam coming off the coffee and moistening her lips. In the silk blouse that lifted with her breathing. That was how closely watched she was.

He was in the back of her throat, where the muscles quivered when she tried to speak.

If only the waitress would bring their dessert.

"Temple . . . talk to me."

"Someone was there," she blurted. "In the room with me. In the bed. It wasn't a dream. He kissed me."

"But you think it was more than that, don't you. That he made love to you."

"If he did," she confided to her crumpled linen napkin, "it would have been the first time."

"You're—"

Heat flooded her throat as she looked up. "I am. Or was."

He seemed stunned, and it was exactly the reaction she expected. She hadn't told either doctor, but the first one had checked her for evidence of rape and not found any, including semen. And since she'd been wearing tampons for years, there was no evidence of her virginity, either.

"You weren't intimate with your fiancé?" There was a husky hesitance in his voice. "Forgive me, but these are the kinds of things I have to ask."

"It wasn't like that with Donald." She wasn't sure how to explain. "We'd known each other since high school. There was never any romance in the way you're thinking, just an understanding that we would always be together."

"Then I'm doubly sorry about the Montmarte," he said after a moment. "It can't have been what you wanted for the first time."

"Actually . . ."

She thought about it and met his questioning gaze with a faint smile. "It was exactly what I would have wanted for the first time. Only not under such nightmarish circumstances."

"Of course."

"Of course," she echoed.

He picked up his coffee cup, and she took it as a sign that

they'd covered the subject. But just as he had to ask the tough questions, she had to answer this one.

"Like most women," she told him, "I've had my share of romantic fantasies, maybe more than most because Donald and I chose to wait. And I probably shouldn't admit this because I know how it's going to sound, Mr. Challis—"

"Mark," he urged.

"Mark—" She hesitated, drawing on a scarce resource. She had so little experience baring her soul. "In a strange surreal way, Montmarte was the most romantic thing that's ever happened to me."

She looked him straight in the eye. "Pathetic, huh? What's happened since, now there's a nightmare. But that one night, it was—" Her voice thickened, and she broke off, embarrassed. It was quite remarkable, she thought, remembering the whispers and the yearning, the sweet surprise.

"A dream," she said.

"Everyone's entitled to dream, even a surreal one."

It had begun to feel awkward again, and they both retreated to their coffee. Temple was wondering if she should have told him about the virginity. She didn't regret it for herself. It was time to tell someone, although she did wonder about her choice of a near stranger when even Donald hadn't known. They'd never discussed it, she and Donald, although he had probably taken it for granted.

Interesting that Mark Challis hadn't taken any such thing for granted. He'd been rocked by her news, and she didn't know what that meant.

Temple was aware of something else as she sat across the table from him. If the hotel had been the most romantic experience of her life, this was the second. There were fairy lanterns of rice paper swinging above their heads and heavy bunches of grapes drooping from the vines. Somewhere in the vineyards, a string quartet was playing. Maybe that explained her mellow mood. Or was it the moonlight, filtering through the leaves and sprinkling their table with lace?

It was hard to imagine that any kind of nightmare could touch her here. And that was the irony. Despite the conflict Mark Challis stirred within her, despite even the powerful enigma he exuded, he made her feel safe when she was in his presence. She couldn't imagine a situation he couldn't handle or a challenge he wasn't equal to, including her. Tonight he actually had her remembering what it was like to be near an attractive man, to feel the inner stirrings and sparks.

Tonight she had told him something that no one else knew.

The crème brûlée arrived at last, and Temple was happy to have something other than sex to concentrate on. The dessert was mouthwatering, and she made it a point to tell Mark so, exclaiming over the rich, satiny texture and the crackly brown sugar topping. Her appetizer, a terrine of foie gras, had been delicious, as had the sturgeon, encrusted in porcino mushrooms, but she'd been too nervous to eat much. This she intended to enjoy, if only to keep thoughts of her dinner partner at bay.

"You were serious about loving that stuff, weren't you," was Mark's only comment.

Temple was savoring it the way a kid would an ice-cream cone, coaxing it along with slow, languorous licks and creamy suction, making it last as long as possible, the way she did the M&M's. But as she spooned the last of the mixture into her mouth, she also coated her upper lip with it.

"Where's my napkin?" she murmured, searching her lap.

Challis gave her his, possibly for the express purpose of watching her clean herself up. He could have been watching a beautiful woman do a striptease. He'd been that intent through the dessert course, and now his darkening male interest drew Temple's breath to the back of her throat.

She had drunk no wine that night because of her condition, but she could almost smell ripening grapes in the air, could almost taste them, tart and fruity in her mouth. It made her tongue sting sweetly. Her mouth juice up. She swallowed the wetness and felt it secrete again, a hot little pool of spiced liquor. This was crazy. The cords of her throat were so tight she couldn't swallow. In another moment she would be drooling.

His napkin saved the day.

"You do have a knack for losing things," he said. "Napkins, shells, hours of your life . . . and this."

His chamois jacket was hanging over the back of his chair. He reached inside and drew out a cassette. Temple immediately recognized it as the one from the doctor's office, where she and Mark had been held hostage to every excruciating detail of the mother-to-be's highly fertile, highly sensitized anatomy.

Apparently the experience had been excruciating only for her, if the smile on his face was any indication.

She took the cassette and dropped it in her bag with faint thanks. At least he'd reminded her that she herself was pregnant. And married. And that he was her private investigator. That should make things less confusing.

"We came here to talk about Michael St. Gerard," she said. "Why haven't we done that?"

"You might not want to know," he cautioned.

"Of course I want to know." She'd expected him to tell her the moment they arrived, but he'd put her off with the excuse that he needed more information from her first.

"What is it that you're avoiding telling *me*?" she asked. Turnabout seemed fair play in this case.

"I don't have any good news," he said.

The string quartet had stopped playing, and the sudden silence felt as hollow as Temple's chest. His tone made it sound like a death sentence. "Tell me anyway. It couldn't be worse than not knowing."

He took a drink of his wine. He swirled the glass and lowered his gaze. "The elevator was tampered with, as I feared. The marriage license is valid, as I feared. And Michael St. Gerard is nowhere to be found."

"As you feared?" He nodded, and she fell back in her chair, weak. The feeling of helplessness flooded her. "What does it all mean?"

"In my professional opinion? Someone is setting you up. For what, I don't know."

"What should I do?" She sat forward, unaware that she was gripping the tablecloth until he touched her curled fingers.

"What you should *not* do," he said, "is panic. That will accomplish nothing except to make it more difficult to work with you."

She didn't know whether to respond to the warmth of his hands or the coolness of his tone. "Work with me? Does that mean you're taking my case, Mr. Challis?"

He didn't answer other than to say, "Tell me about the illness that took your parents' lives, the one you survived."

In a tight voice she told him about her trip to Zaire, not knowing that her parents were already gone and that an entire hospital ward had been wiped out before they could get the virus contained. She'd been stricken, too. She'd been quarantined in Zaire, and then held for observation and tested exhaustively after being transferred to Fort Detrick, but despite all their efforts, they'd never come up with the answer to how she'd survived.

Temple's greatest concern had been for her little sister. Ivy had not only lost her parents, she was left to work through the shock and grief alone. There was an aunt in a neighboring city who could care for her, but no big sister to hold her and ease her adolescent heartbreak. No "Tempo" to braid Ivy's golden hair and loop it around her head like a laurel wreath.

The two of them had never been separated, and even though Temple had felt burdened by her caretaker role at times, she loved her little sister. She'd petitioned every day that she be allowed to go home, not for herself, but for Ivy.

"It must have been hell," he said, sitting back in his chair. "You were close to your parents, of course?"

Temple met his steady gaze and held it. She'd answered her last question for Mark Challis. "So, are you taking my case?"

"Maybe." He nodded. "There are conditions."

Their waiter had glanced at them several times, Temple noticed, probably wondering whether he should approach the couple, who one moment were gazing warmly into each other's eyes and the next, firing icicles. Temple thought he was wise to stay away.

"And what would those conditions be?"

"You have this thing about independence, about freedom. And while I can appreciate the ideal, it can't be indulged any longer. Not if you expect me to keep you safe."

"Who said anything about safe?" She'd only thought it, thank God. "All I want is for you to find Michael St. Gerard and end this craziness."

"And I don't work like that. When I take on a client with security concerns, it becomes my responsibility to see that they keep breathing, that their heart keeps beating every second of every moment they're under my care. You can't be any different, Temple. If you don't give me complete control, I can't work with you."

The wrought-iron chair made a terrible scraping sound as she stood up. "Complete control?"

"Or I can't work with you."

"But I'm not in that kind of danger."

"What you're *in* is denial. You've been warned that you could be in danger, and there's already been one attempt on your life."

All she could do was shake her head.

"Make up your mind, Temple. Say yes, and from now until this is over, I'm your guardian angel. I protect you, teach you, hear your confessions, and eventually, I will even stare back at you from the mirror. I become you. That's how I keep you alive.

"Say no and I'm gone."

Temple felt as if she were being smothered. It was his total certainty that confused her and boxed her in. If there were no absolutes in this world, no one had told Mark Challis. She couldn't pretend to be certain of anything except that she couldn't do it. He was asking her to give up too much, to place her life in his hands, and she didn't know how to do that. She'd always been the responsible one. How did she now turn that role over to him? It was her identity.

"What's it going to be?"

He rose from the chair and she waved him back. "Not yet," she said. "I need some time."

"There is no time. I'll get the car."

"No!" She sucked down a breath. "No, don't get the car." Tears welled up for no reason that she could understand. "No, I'm not leaving with you. And no, I don't need a protector. I've been taking care of myself for years."

Say no, and I'm gone.

She whispered it. "No."

"Why is it that girls kiss with their eyes shut and boys with their eyes open?"

"Ivy?" Temple tipped the phone receiver back and looked at it. "What boy? Whose eyes are we talking about?"

This was the first time Temple had heard of any such thing in her young sister's life. Ivy seemed to be adjusting to college life with a vengeance. Temple herself had just walked in the door from the dinner with Mark Challis and heard her phone ringing. She knew it couldn't be him, looking to compromise, but that hadn't stopped her from the fleeting hope. Instead it was her little sister, in an unusually chatty mood.

"I think it's because men are visual," Ivy stated blithely. "And it stimulates them to watch what they're doing."

"Ivy? What are they teaching you at that school?"

Temple heard the tone of her own voice and realized she'd been sucked directly into the Church Lady mode. *Ivy isn't ready for a relationship. She's too young. She doesn't understand boys. She needs to concentrate·on her studies, get a degree—*

"It's an experiment for my social ecology lab," Ivy explained. "A random sample of men will be kissed under controlled circumstances to provide evidence that the open-eye phenomena exists, and then I'll test my theory of arousal by—"

Theory of arousal? "Ivy, who designed this experiment?"

"Me," she said proudly. "Cool, huh?"

"Cool. Very cool. Who's doing the kissing?"

Temple was in her kitchen, squatting down inside the open refrigerator door and sorting through her meager provisions. She'd thrown all the gourmet stuff out, and now she had a craving for something, but didn't know what it was.

"I haven't figured that out yet," Ivy said. "I suppose it could be me, but then objectivity might be difficult."

"I should say. You're only twenty—"

"Twenty-one! And I've never been kissed, Temple. Even you have to agree that sucks."

Was Ivy *really* twenty-one? For some reason Temple persisted in thinking of her sister as a gangly, slightly morose, very brainy child. But she had to give that up. Ivy needed this chance, and Temple's wisest move would be to get out of her way. Young women weren't supposed to live their lives for others and then suddenly awaken in their thirties, realizing they had no identity except as someone's devoted daughter. Or sister.

Temple tucked the phone under her chin. She'd spotted some chunky peanut butter in a screw-top jar, but it was going to take two hands to get it open.

"Ivy, you know you can always call me, even at work," she said. "Just holler at my voice mail, and I'll get right back to you."

"Sure. You tell me that every time we talk."

"I do?" I just want her to know I'm here, Temple thought. She has to be able to reach me. I don't want to disappear on her the way our parents did.

Temple grunted from the brute force of her efforts with the jar. She didn't have a spoon, either, but that was why God had made fingers.

"Tempo, are you all right?"

No, Ivy, I'm pregnant. And I have no idea who, how, or why.

"I'm fine," Temple said, tapping the lid against the ceramic tile at her feet. There was more than one way to open a peanut butter jar. "Just stressed. We're trying to finish up this men's cologne campaign."

"How about 'Men who wear Fabrici kiss with their eyes shut'?"

Temple laughed. "Cool. Very cool."

"Are we unpacked yet?" Ivy asked.

Temple couldn't see the boxes stacked against the far wall in the living room, so it was easy to pretend they weren't there. "Don't be a smart-ass, Ivy. Of course I am."

"Not."

"Smart-ass," Temple mumbled. She wanted peanut butter, but not enough to crack her ceramic tile. She set the jar aside and began to search anew. Maybe something salty.

"Ivy, I'm your big sister. Is it time for us to have that talk about boys and sex and . . . oh, God, what else? Birth control?"

"Don't be ri*dic*ulous. You told me when I was twelve. And besides, I'm a social ecology major."

Her sister could probably have brought her up to speed on her own pregnancy, Temple realized, wondering where'd she been when Ivy had crossed that line into adulthood. She hadn't noticed it happening, and now there was little she could do but hope that whatever guidance she'd offered over the years would see her sister through.

"Ivy, promise me one thing, okay? Just this one little thing. Don't get that beautiful blond hair cut off and dye it green."

"You don't like green hair?"

"I don't like hair I can't braid."

Her sister's sniff was contemptuous. It told Temple that if she was trying to tug on Ivy's heartstrings or make her nostalgic for the old days, it wasn't going to happen. She had well and truly cut the cord.

"Never mind," Temple said bravely. "You do whatever you want to with that gorgeous head of hair. Shave it if that suits you."

"Tempo, I'm going to be *fine,*" Ivy said pleadingly.

"I know, baby, I know. Just give me a minute to get used to the idea."

After they'd hung up, Temple shut the refrigerator door and turned to face the boxes Ivy was talking about. They contained books, knicknacks, some inexpensive art, and the treasures her parents had collected in their travels. Temple had become the curator of the family museum, and she had no idea what to do with all of it now, but she couldn't bring herself to put it in storage.

She couldn't bring herself to unpack it, either. As she stared at the boxes, she didn't know what her reluctance meant except that this place, this apartment that she had once loved and coveted as a symbol of her freedom, didn't feel like her home. And putting knicknacks around wouldn't solve that.

The phone rang and she grabbed it up, hoping, praying, it was Mark Challis, ready to compromise. Desperate to compromise.

"Hello?"

"Tempo, you were serious about my hair, right? Because I wasn't going to tell you, but the girls here gave me a makeover the other day, and it's not green or anything. I guess you could say it's black . . . and magenta."

"Ivy, no!"

EIGHT

"All's fair in love and war, *unless* you're using All's Fair!" Denny Paxton waggled a spray bottle of the cologne in the air, then pretended to spritz it under the arms of his khaki suit jacket. A thatch of reddish-brown hair fell onto his forehead and was dispatched with a shake of his head. Look, Ma! No hands, he seemed to be saying.

The smattering of nervous laughter was encouragement from his team members, who'd gathered in Sonia David's office that morning for the pitch meeting. And a tense meeting it was. The one person they needed to impress was their president. But she sat at her desk, impassive, tapping her own Montblanc and occasionally tucking a raven straggler into her sleek French knot.

"All's Fair is the ultimate weapon in the battle between the sexes," Denny went on, flashing his own ultimate weapon, a July Fourth sparkler of a grin. "One whiff and the ladies, they are going to drop like flies, gentlemen. Be glad All's Fair *isn't*."

Temple stood a little away from the rest of them, behind the circle of couches where the team was sitting. It gave her the advantage of observing without being observed, like a spy satellite. Absently she tore off a piece of her poppyseed bagel, then thought better of eating it. She'd been doing that all morning and had accumulated a small peninsula of crumbs on the napkin next to her water glass. She would have to remember to dispose of the mess later and not to grab the napkin to blot anything.

Sonia did not look happy, and as team leader, Temple was responsible for her happiness. Temple had put Denny on notice that his angle might antagonize women and that Sonia fell into that grouping. Now it looked as if Temple should have been more assertive in her feedback. Maybe overruled him altogether.

"There is *nothing* fair about All's Fair," Denny continued.

"I should buy that for my boyfriend's birthday?" Sonia cut in incredulously. "So he can make other women drop like flies?"

Shit, Temple thought. Shit.

Sonia had addressed the question to Denny, but she was looking at Temple now, who couldn't argue because it was exactly her concern. Women bought the cologne for the men in their lives—their husbands, boyfriends, brothers, sons, bosses. Women bought everything, even the beer for *Monday Night Football*. Someday the marketing mavens were going to embrace that cosmic reality and take over the planet.

Meanwhile, she should have discussed this more thoroughly with her team. She should have insisted, but they'd been desperate for an idea, and she'd been reluctant to pitch hers because it might have looked as if she were trying to sabotage Denny's.

"Humor would take the edge off," Temple suggested.

"Right," Denny chimed in. "Especially with a great comic

actor. Someone nonthreatening like Robin Williams or Billy Crystal."

"Why not both of them?" Annette Dalton popped up. "A fly dropping competition? Could be hilarious?"

"The cologne attracts flies?" The president's tone had gone from incredulous to cold. "That's the hook?"

"Only figuratively," Annette said. "I meant women, of course."

"You're quite sure the public will make that figurative leap from flies to women?"

"We'll find another angle." Temple was emphatic. "I like the name, All's Fair."

"I don't," Sonia said, standing. "I think we need another name *and* another idea. I do hope you can pull one out of the hat, because the Fabrici brass will be here tomorrow, and if we don't get this contract—well, let's *get* this contract."

Her tone was arch. "Back to the drawing board, boys and girls?"

The idea wasn't even worth discussing in her mind, Temple realized. It had no merit whatsoever. She should have seen that and averted this disaster. Fabrici was too big an account to worry about massaging team members' egos. Concerns about ruffling Denny's feathers had clouded her judgment and allowed her to go with a concept she knew was flawed.

The group was rising heavily from the couches, dispirited. The visitors had been crushed by the home team, and they were off to the locker room.

Denny was already at the door when Temple called out, "Wait! We haven't pitched Speak Softly yet."

The president gave her a skeptical look. Temple's team slowly came around, equally skeptical. Only Annette had a spark of hope in her eyes.

"Our ace in the hole, yes?" Temple said, speaking to Annette and silently pleading for her support.

"Uh . . . absolutely," Annette said, nodding. "Speak Softly. A killer idea. Just killer. Why don't you pitch that idea, Temple."

At this point everyone was standing, and it was too much to hope that they would all return to their seats and give Temple the floor. There had been an execution. Something had died, an idea. And none of her team members had the heart to face the firing squad again. Even if they had, how could they be expected to take a blind risk. They'd never heard of Speak Softly until this moment.

Temple brushed imaginary bagel specks from her designated "pitch" outfit, a slimming gray pinstripe pantsuit, and walked to the side windows. If she didn't have a receptive audience, at least she would have the Santa Monica mountains as her backdrop.

"Speak Softly," she said. "Roosevelt's legendary advise to mankind. 'Speak Softly and carry a big stick,' to be precise."

"A big stick?" Denny chortled under his breath.

"Exactly." Temple challenged him with a look. He hadn't moved from the door, but he was postured defensively, his mouth tight with anger. She was afraid he would sway them all against her before she had a chance.

"Before you say the imagery is too obvious, let me clarify." She turned to Sonia. "Let me tell you why it's not obvious, why it's not only subtle, but exactly the imagery we want to convey to a culture that has misplaced its boldness, its daring, its noble hunter instinct."

Okay it was a little corny, but Temple had been distracted lately. There hadn't been enough time to prepare. Fortunately she felt a kinship with the concept, and had from the first. The rightness of it would have to carry her.

"Ask anyone how humans communicate, and they will say 'through words.'" She paused for effect. "But that isn't true, and everyone here knows it. We're in the communica-

tions business, but only twenty-five percent of human com-
munication is actually verbal. The rest is body language,
imagery, sounds, even intuition. And it's been that way
throughout time."

The coolness coming off the windows penetrated the
back of Temple's jacket. She couldn't suppress a little
shiver, which, oddly, had the effect of fixing their attention
on her.

"So please, consider that carefully," she said. "Consider
the innate power of Jungian archetypes and primitive sym-
bolism before you reject the idea I'm offering.

"*Speak softly. Carry a big stick.* What are we doing when
we employ this imagery? We're harking back to our tribal
history, to early man with a club. We're ennobling the original hunter-warriors, when man's instincts were pure and he
killed only to survive."

Temple hesitated, aware that Sonia had stopped tapping
her pen and the room had gone quiet.

"Those pure instincts live in modern man today," she
said, "but they're thwarted. He can only express them in so-
cially acceptable and *totally* unsatisfying ways. Men no
longer need to hunt to survive, but they still have the instinct."

She held up the spray bottle. "This cologne, Speak Softly,
speaks to that impulse. It—"

"It's the big stick!" Annette cut in.

Temple braced herself for the laughter. She would never
have phrased it that way, but in fact, that was the angle she
was going for. Annette had totally stolen her thunder, in a
way that only Annette could do. And maybe that was a good
thing, but clearly no one knew what to say. Even Sonia appeared to have no input. Yet.

But Annette wasn't frozen. She was off and running.

"I'm on this," she said, wheeling toward the other members as if they were in a no-holds-barred brainstorming

session. "I'm so on this! Let's say we've got a guy in a tux, a real babe. And what if his big stick starts out as a wooden club, then morphs to a golf club, and then maybe a baseball bat or a rifle, even a composer's baton. We've got the noble hunter thing, and we're covering all the other bases."

"Not a rifle," Sonia said.

"*Not* a rifle," Temple agreed, exalting at those three beautiful words. They told her she had what she wanted. Sonia had offered a suggestion, which meant she was mulling the idea. It had merit. Maybe she even liked it.

Sonia sat down at her desk and jotted some notes on the pad. "I like the tux. There's something elegant about a tux, but dangerous, too, which is how we would want this cologne to be perceived."

"Elegant menace," someone offered.

"Silent, but deadly," another suggested.

The cobra, Temple wanted to say, with thanks to Mark Challis, wherever he was. The idea had been born in her attempts to read and understand the elusive investigator. Obviously she'd been searching for the secret to his personal brand of magnetism. A man who could hold you quietly in his power, she thought.

Within seconds the fuse had been lit and the team was crackling like a string of Lady Finger firecrackers. They were fighting to be heard. Ironically, Temple was forgotten in all the excitement, which was fine with her.

She was a little unsteady, but light enough to float as she walked back to the credenza where she'd been standing. Her throat was dry and she reached for the glass of water she'd left there. But the ice shifted and water slopped over the rim as she took a sip.

Temple grabbed the napkin to blot her mouth—and watched poppyseed bagel droppings explode in a mushroom

cloud. They were everywhere, all over her slimming pin-
stripes. And she was too happy to care.

No one would ever have called it Sin City. There were as
many churches per capita as any other metropolis of its size,
Goodwill, the Salvation Army, and Girl Scouts of America
all had branches there. But if you were in the mood to raise
a little celebratory hell on a work-week night, then Ventura
offered some interesting choices.

There were discos, diners, bistros, and bars. The Boom-
pah Bistro was famous for its blackened electric eel and its
polka band. Ciaobella offered a four-star assortment of
Northern Italian dishes. But of all of the eateries and
nightspots, the Last Virgin Roadhouse was the newest and
hottest, hands down.

Its bar menu boasted salmon-avocado wraps, lightly lu-
bricated with extra-virgin olive oil and stuffed with healthy
broccosprouts. And its buckskin-clad young male waiters
were reputed to be as innocent as newborn colts. If one were
to ask they would tell you that it was a prerequisite for the
job, along with drug testing.

Temple couldn't have spoken to the virginity thing, of
course, but in her experience, the waiters were extraordinarily attentive, always making sure water glasses were filled
and napkins were properly placed across the lap. Good at
tossing Caesars and flambéing desserts, too.

But despite all that, she and Annette both swore the reason they liked the place had *nothing* to do with the service. It was the roadhouse ambience, the bluesy combo
that played Monday through Thursday, and the superb
food.

Tonight they'd come by to celebrate that afternoon's
meeting with Fabrici cosmetics. Fabrici's extremely picky
marketing vice president had liked the Speak Softly concept. He wanted a few modifications, but he had liked it,

and that meant it was Blue Sky's deal to lose. Barring an unforeseen disaster, they were about to be awarded one of their biggest contracts ever, and it was Temple's idea they'd bought.

What did happen when something was too good to be true? she wondered.

"This calls for caviar and champagne," Annette said, perusing the menu.

"Annette, friend of my bosom—" Temple gently pointed out that there were sixty different kinds of beer on the menu, and not one bottle of champagne. "I'm drinking for two anyway," she said, "so it's decaffeinated iced tea for me. How about we share an order of salmon wraps and maybe barbequed chicken quesadillas?"

Annette nodded her agreement as she excused herself to go to the rest room, leaving Temple to contemplate the roadhouse's ambience. It was meant to be a replica of the early West variety, but the sawdust on the hardwood floor was only for show. The high-backed booths were fashioned of golden maple, elegantly cushioned, and curtained in cabbage roses.

A waiter appeared to take their order, and then Temple got comfortable, feeling rather decadent as she settled herself against the back wall and stretched her legs out on the bench. It was that kind of place, trendy, but very casual. And she was more than ready to shed the tension of the last few days. The pressure was off for now, she and her team had actually caught the brass ring, which was unbelievable. A dream of dreams. And, impossible as it would have seemed just days ago, some parts of her life were beginning to feel as if they were back on track again.

Her work routine had returned to normal. She was putting in her usual twelve- to fifteen-hour days. There hadn't been any more threats on her life or messages from strange men, and she included Mark Challis in that category. She still had to decide whether to pursue the investigation, but she could always contact another P.I. Of course, there was the pregnancy. She was postponing her decision about that until she could catch her breath. But even the idea of being pregnant didn't seem quite so alien and overwhelming.

She was just glad to have her life back.

Annette slipped back into the booth with a grin that creased her elfin face all the way up to her ink-jet eyebrows. "We kicked *butt* today," she said.

Temple whipped the laser pointer from her purse, hit pulse mode, and waved it like a sparkler. "Big ol' butt," she said, laughing in a throaty way that wasn't like her.

Jarrod, their waiter, appeared with their drinks, an order of overstuffed salmon wraps, some dipping sauce, and two plates.

Annette dug into her food without apologies, expertly negotiating a bursting wrap while Temple watched and sipped her tea. She was almost too tired to eat, and in the past, she wouldn't have bothered. Her favorite brand of dieting had been to skip meals, but that would have to stop, she imagined. It wasn't only her welfare she had to be concerned with now.

Suddenly the dining room was pungent with the rich smells of mesquite grilled chicken and barbeque sauce. The air was laden, and Temple drew in a fragrant breath, savoring it as Jarrod appeared with a platter of quesadilla oozing with melted cheese. He set it grandly in the middle of their table.

Temple's appetite made a quick recovery. She arranged herself at the table while Jarrod snapped open her napkin and placed it on her lap. He then served up generous portions for each of them, and discreetly asked if they needed anything else before he left. The only thing Temple needed was another order of quesadilla. She could have eaten the entire thing herself.

She had an oozing triangle to her mouth when Annette made a strange sound. "Tastes funny," she said, grabbing her napkin and covering her mouth. She held up her hand as if signaling Temple to wait.

Temple was almost too ravenous to stop, but she pulled back to look at the food. Nothing appeared to be wrong, but when she brought it to her nose, she caught a whiff of something deadly. Deadly to her. She forked through the quesadilla on the plate, releasing wafts of the telltale odor.

Temple shoved the plate away from her, horrified. "There's soy sauce in the quesadilla. It's saturated with it."

"Soy sauce?"

Annette didn't understand the problem, and Temple was trembling too hard to explain. She was violently allergic to soy sauce. Even one bite could have sent her into anaphylactic shock and been fatal. The allergy stemmed from her ordeal in Zaire, where she'd had an adverse reaction to one of the antibiotics she was given to ward off infection. Even now certain foods could trigger the same response, and each time she was exposed, the risk of a deadly reaction increased.

"My God," Annette whispered, "are you all right?"

Temple nodded, but she was badly shaken.

They gathered their things to leave, and when the waiter arrived with the bill, Annette questioned him about the food. He seemed genuinely bewildered and explained that the quesadilla wasn't normally made with soy sauce. But he could do little more than apologize and offer to take it off the bill.

"We never serve it that way," he said as Annette and Temple left. "I don't know what happened."

It was a chilly night, and Annette insisted that Temple wait inside the portico while she got the car. They'd come in

Temple's Buick, but Annette was adamant that she knew how to drive a Le Sabre, and that she would chauffeur them back to Temple's place and fix her something to eat.

Temple acquiesced gratefully. She needed a moment to talk herself out of the paranoia that had taken hold. The soy sauce was a coincidence. It had to be. Some cook got his ingredients confused and doused the quesadilla instead of the stir fry. That's all it was.

She shuddered, and told herself it was the weather or her fatigue, anything but the fear that was creeping into the heat of her bloodstream and turning it cold. The portico was like a breezeway, channeling currents of chilly March air, and her suit jacket wasn't warm enough. She yanked the lapels together and wondered where Annette was. It had been at least fifteen minutes. She probably couldn't get the car started, Temple thought, despite her cockiness.

Temple decided to go rescue her. Huddling inside her jacket, she walked around the side of the building and approached the lot. Every space was full, but they'd arrived early and snagged the preferred spot by the delivery entrance, away from the other cars. Temple gave up a quick smile as the engine purred to life and the tail lights snapped on. She'd been about to give her friend a bad time.

She held her jacket close and ducked her head against the wind, running toward the car. She wanted to catch Annette before she pulled out. But as Temple drew near, she heard a sharp pop, like a tire blowing out. Suddenly her Le Sabre was engulfed in flames, and there was a strange roaring in Temple's ears.

She knew it was dangerous, she knew something horrible had happened, but she continued running, running and screaming until the explosion knocked her to the ground and drowned her out.

NINE

"Ma'am! Can you see me? *Ma'am?*"

She couldn't see anything. The sky was blackness and flames. But the apocalyptic sound never left her ears. It roared like a beast, a fiery behemoth, and the earth trembled. She could see nothing, smell nothing, feel nothing. None of her other senses worked, but she could hear that sound, the end of the world.

"Ma'am, please! Talk to me! Do you know your name?"

Someone was calling to her, but his entreaties were lost in the fury. He was somewhere beyond the black inferno that enveloped her. And even if she'd understood what he wanted from her, there wasn't any way to get the words out. Breathing was agony.. Her nostrils drew on fire. And now there was a smell filtering into her consciousness. No, a stench. A thick, choking stench.

Something terrible had happened, but what?

"Hold still, ma'am! Don't move. There's been an accident."

Her car! Annette! It came to her instantly.

Temple felt the force of someone's hands on her shoulders, a massive weight holding her down. "Annette?" she croaked.

"Ma'am? Your name is Annette?"

"No—" She struggled, but the force bore down. It felt like stakes and ropes, pinioning her to the ground.

"Hold still! The paramedics are on their way."

She fell back, exhausted. The black cloud still clung to her, but gradually an image began to take shape in front of her eyes. A man was bent over her, his face smudged and filthy, his teeth bared in a grimace. He was the one holding her down, but despite his frightening appearance, Temple understood that he was there to help her.

She tried to focus, but her eyes burned as if they'd been scorched. They'd been open all the time, she realized, wondering how that could be possible. *She'd been staring at him, but she hadn't seen him.*

"What happened?" she got out.

"How many fingers?" he wanted to know, holding up two.

"Please tell me what hap—"

"Shhh." He hushed her. "You need to lie still until we can get you checked out. Can you remember your name?"

"Temple . . . Temple Banning."

"Good, now stay with me, Temple. I need some information."

He asked where she lived and other questions, the kind he might have posed to a lost child. He wanted to know if she could count to ten backward. At some point she realized that he was a fireman. And that there were others, hordes of them. Firemen and policemen. The parking lot was crowded with people, with howling sirens and flashing lights. There was a TV crew and a roped-off section of bystanders. Everyone was shouting to be heard.

"Stay with me, ma'am."

Temple tried, but the images fuzzed, and her lids drooped. There was too much noise. It pounded at her. And her eyes felt as if they'd been pricked with stinging nettles.

She washed in and out of awareness. Fingers probed the pulse in her throat. Someone was checking her vital signs and moving her limbs. Sharp little lights shined into her eyes. And the next thing she knew she was being helped to her feet, only this was a different man, older and not nearly so fierce.

Dizzily she saw that her car had been demolished, and the shock of it brought her back.

"Annette?" she whispered. "Annette!"

She searched the Le Sabre's smoldering carcass with her eyes, terrified of what she might see. The enormity of it would not allow her to believe that her friend had been caught in the explosion, but there was no way to fend off the horror that was seeping into her thoughts. The evidence sprang at her from every corner. It jolted her numbed senses.

The stench she'd smelled was burnt upholstery. It was molten metal and gaseous fumes. The air was black with floating cinders, and everything was covered with a gritty layer of soot, including her. It smelled of destruction, this place. It smelled of death.

Temple clutched herself, too numb to feel the pain as her fingernails dug into the flesh of her arms. She turned in a circle, looking for her friend. Looking for someone to help her. Please! The paramedic who'd lifted her to her feet wasn't there. Neither was the fireman.

"What happened to Annette?" she implored.

She might as well have been invisible. No one seemed to hear her. They rushed around her as if she weren't there. Dizzily she pivoted again, and reached out to stop someone, but whomever she touched caught her by the arms and moved her out of the way. Someone else shouted at her to stay by the "unit."

But Temple didn't know where the unit was. She didn't know where anything was for a second, not even the pavement beneath her feet. What was happening? How could this be happening?

She continued turning in a circle until someone called out her name. She couldn't make out who it was as he strode toward her, but he pulled her into his arms and held her, held her so tightly she couldn't move, couldn't turn anymore. . . .

Couldn't spin helplessly.

"Temple, for God's sake," he said.

It was Mark Challis who'd come to her in the midst of all the chaos, and he was embracing her like a man might a loved one he'd nearly lost. Temple could feel the shaking power of his grip, but she didn't understand it.

"I'm all right," she told him, laughing at how absurd that sounded. She might never be all right again. Her car had just been blown apart. And her friend—

"I can't find Annette," she whispered.

"She's in good hands. It's you I'm concerned about."

Temple wanted to know about her friend, but he wouldn't let her talk. He pulled off his overcoat and wrapped it around her.

"Come here," he said, searching her grimy, shattered features. His jaw went tight with concern. And then he drew her back into his arms again, and she reeled at the shock of his sheltering warmth.

Tears welled. Sadness burned. Was this what safety felt like? Was she the only woman alive who didn't know what it was like to feel protected?

"What are you doing here?" she asked him.

"Annette called me from the restaurant. She was worried about you. She told me you were served something that could have been deadly if you'd eaten it."

Temple muffled a sob in the curve of his shoulder. "She went to get my car, Mark, and I don't know what happened to her. No one will tell me."

"It's all right," he said, but his attempts to quiet her only frightened her more.

"What happened to her? Is she really all right?" Temple drew back and stared at him searchingly.

His face was shadowed, dark with regret. "Yes, she's fine."

No, Annette wasn't fine. Everything about him, his features, his voice, told her that Annette wasn't fine, that some terrible thing had happened.

"Tell me the truth," she insisted.

"It isn't good, Temple. Sometimes the truth isn't good."

She rocked sideways and caught herself. She was totally off balance. The world was spinning again, and it felt as if everything inside her had gone limp. Her legs were failing. They wouldn't hold her.

"We're getting you out of here," he said.

He picked her up and began to walk through the crowd, carrying her in his arms and yelling at people to get out of the way. No one was going to block Mark Challis's path, including the policeman who saw him and shouted at him to stop.

"Hey!" the officer called. "Where are you going with her? I need to ask her some questions."

"You can contact me," Mark said. He fished in his overcoat pocket and handed the man his card. "She's my wife, and she's pregnant. If I don't get her out of here, she's going to lose this baby."

Apparently the officer backed off, because Mark kept right on going. Temple had no idea where he was taking her, but she collapsed in his arms with a shaky sound. Within moments he'd reached his car and had her settled in the passenger seat with a fur throw over her legs. Then he put her

briefcase in beside her, and Temple realized he'd salvaged it
from the accident. She felt tremendous relief at seeing it.
This was her work, her life. And at the moment it seemed to
represent everything she had.

His door opened next and he was beside her, starting up
the car. Temple didn't ask where they were going. She just
closed her eyes and surrendered to the inevitable, and if that
meant she was surrendering to the man, as well as to his
terms and conditions, then so be it. She couldn't fight anymore. She didn't even have the strength to be frightened.

But as he drove away, one thought rose in her mind like a
star that appears on the horizon. Appears out of nowhere. It
flared so brightly it blotted out all of her other concerns,
even the anguish of not knowing about Annette.

She's my wife, he'd said.

The sky outside Mark Challis's office was as black as if the
windowpanes had been painted with India ink. There was no
evidence of a world outside. All light seemed to have been
extinguished. The towering skyscrapers were dark. There
were no low-flying planes. Even the stars had blinked out.
Challis's lamp-lit room could have been balanced on the
point of an axis, spinning slowly in deep space.

It was that dark, that cold.

Temple drew her legs onto the couch where she was sitting and tucked the fur throw under them. She'd heard that
cliché about the blood running cold in your veins, but like
most people, she'd never taken it literally. Body tempera-
tures didn't drop to freezing. It wasn't possible, any more
than the core of your being could crystallize like ice.

But it felt cold enough, dark enough.

Sitting in the shadows of his office, she knew it must be
late, dead of night. He'd carried her up in the elevator, over
her weak protests, and deposited her on a slippery leather
couch that nearly spanned the long side of the big room. It

sat opposite his desk, where his darkly elegant head was bent over the phone. Haloed by incandescent lamplight, Mark Challis was making calls that involved setting up a secure place for her to stay.

Temple must have slipped back into a state of denial, because she couldn't believe any of it. She was going along with his plans because she didn't know what else to do. It seemed like her only option. *She didn't want anyone else to be hurt.*

A soft strain of violin music filtered through her thoughts. The melody could barely be heard over the low conversation Challis was having, but it was a lovely piece, reminiscent of the one she'd heard here before. Temple still couldn't place it, but with a slight breath, she gave herself over to its trills and spirals for a moment, letting her mind glide with the lilting glissandos, and hoping it could coax her back from the cold.

Finally he hung up the phone and turned to her.

Even now, with her spirit so shattered, she couldn't not stare at him. The room was lit by a recessed panel that ran the length of the windows and cast a strange glow. But she was instantly, and perhaps even helplessly, caught in the enigma of his features. The optical illusion that was Mark Challis.

If she'd been in a different state of mind, she would have avoided his direct gaze, but tonight she was a shipwreck survivor, tossed by high seas. What could she do but grasp at any line that was thrown her? Her friend was gravely injured, or worse, and Temple didn't know which way to turn. She was in dire need of help, and that's what he was offering.

"Should I have gone to the police?" she asked him, wondering why she hadn't. "Told them everything? About St. Gerard, I mean—"

"You still could," he said. "If you have a death wish.

They'll question you, send you home, and put you on the bottom of their docket. You'll be a case number, a buried file. They won't give you the protection you need. It's doubtful they'll even believe you."

Gut instinct told her he was right.

"Tell me what I have to do, then," she said.

"That's easy. You have to disappear."

"Disappear? But my job—"

"No *buts,* Temple. This is where I take over, and you know what my conditions are. Total control. You have no rights, not even your God-given constitutional ones. Your life is mine."

His tone was neutral. The blunt force of his message was carried by the way he turned his head and gazed at her. But Temple had already made her decision. There was just one thing she wanted.

"Before I go anywhere with you," she said, "I have to know what happened to Annette."

The breath he took was visible. Barely breathing herself, she said, "She didn't make it, did she?"

"The paramedics wouldn't confirm it, except to her next of kin. But I don't think so, Temple. I'm sorry."

His voice was harsh with regret. Annette had been a friend of his, too, Temple realized, but she could feel no sympathy at that moment, only desolation. Witnessing his sorrow was a blow to her defenses. The icy shield shifted. It splintered, and she was pierced by pain. By grief. For Annette, the vibrant friend who had always come to her aid. For Temple's own helplessness and guilt. Grief that felt like fire.

"I was meant to die," she said. "Not Annette."

Challis shot up. He left the credenza rocking and his shadow soared upward.

Temple was too weighed down by emotion to react. But she saw him in the periphery of her vision, looming and angry.

"What happened to Annette was a senseless tragedy, Temple. *It doesn't have to happen to you.*" His voice was brutally hard. "Or the baby. There's another life to consider, for God's sake."

"Yes," she said numbly.

"I can protect you. No one else needs to be hurt."

"No one," she agreed.

Somehow, miraculously, the fracture inside her had already begun to seal off, and she was going numb again. Soon she would be cold through and through. Meanwhile she could feel nothing except a lead weight pressing on her breastbone. It was small, the size of a paper dollar, only heavy. Cold and heavy. And it sank all the way to her heart.

"Good, then it's settled," Mark said. "I have a few more calls to make."

He returned to his desk, and Temple did her best to relax. She rested her head and stared at the ceiling, listening to the music. Why did it seem like the same piece was playing over and over? And why didn't she recognize it? The melody was eerily familiar. She wasn't a classical music buff, but this had to be something she knew.

She closed her eyes, captured by the haunting notes. Softly she hummed the tune . . . and heard a man's voice whispering in the distance. *Good night, Princess. Don't forget me.* Who was he? And where had she heard that voice before?

Her heart leaped to wild rhythm, and the music crescendoed in her head as if someone had turned up the sound system. It was the same song that was lingering in her head when she woke up in the honeymoon suite. The same song. The longer she listened, the more certain she was.

That night was not an illusion.

The music was real.

And so was the man.

She could be pregnant by that man.

Temple blinked open her eyes and stared at Mark, who was absorbed in what he was doing.

She was touched by an icy frisson, by a creeping sense of disbelief. It couldn't have been him that night. No, it couldn't! But her mind seized on the thought, and her instincts told her not to let him take her anywhere. She could scarcely consider the possibility that she might be overreacting. Or that she was overwrought because of what she'd been through.

"I'm filthy," she said abruptly. "I have to clean up."

He glanced up as she threw off the blanket. If he needed any proof, all he had to do was look at her dirt-streaked face and grimy clothing. "Is there a bathroom nearby?" she asked.

"You can use mine."

He pointed to a doorway on the opposite wall, but Temple shook her head. "I need a ladies' room. There are things in there, products you wouldn't have."

Even pregnant women spotted occasionally and had to wear pads. She hoped that was how he would interpret her request. Mark stared at her a moment, and she thought he was going to refuse her.

"Down the hall on your right," he said. "I'll be done here in fifteen minutes. Be sure you're back by then."

She picked up her briefcase and nearly staggered under the weight of it. As she walked to the door, her heart was wild. Was he really going to let her go?

TEN

❧

"Right there!" Temple cried, pointing. "Pull in there."

The taxi driver wheeled the car around, narrowly negotiating the driveway of Temple's apartment building.

"I'm over there on the corner," she said as he pulled into the motor court that occupied the center of the Versailles-like structure. The lot was filled to capacity, so he came to a stop in front of her place and double-parked.

A searching glance out the rear window reassured Temple that they weren't being followed, and the sparse traffic told her that her watch might be accurate. It said three-fifteen in the morning. The taxi ride from downtown L.A. had run close to an hour, but that couldn't account for the lateness. She'd totally lost track of time since the explosion and had no idea how long she'd been unconscious in the parking lot.

"Would you wait for me, please?" she asked the driver. "I'll be right back."

She grabbed her briefcase and opened the door. But that was as far as she got. From the confines of the car, she stared at the entrance to her ground-floor apartment and wondered if it was safe. This was her own home, and she wasn't sure if she dared go in. Everything she owned was in there. But it felt as if she'd been invaded on every front, and this was her last refuge, which made it all the more vulnerable.

"Lady? You okay?" the driver asked.

She nodded and forced herself to get out. "I won't be long," she called back to him. "Please wait."

The walk to her door was an exercise in courage. If she hadn't been concerned about being pursued, she might not have made it. She fitted the door key in the lock and braced herself, expecting anything, even to be blown apart. A cat was meowing somewhere nearby. That was the only sound she heard as she twisted the handle and opened the door.

No explosion. She was still alive. But relief was fleeting. The pressure crept up a notch as she stepped inside.

The small table lamp in the hallway was on, just as she'd left it. Nothing looked amiss as she headed for the bedroom, but she didn't have time to go through the place. There wasn't time to do anything except strip off her grimy pantsuit, clean up as best she could, pack a bag, and go.

Moments later she was in a pair of plain gray sweats with a warm zippered jacket, and her Nikes. She had her duffel bag stuffed with jeans and sweaters, her favorite shoes—a well-worn pair of black suede loafers—her bathroom gear, the vitamins that were part of the prenatal package Dr. Llewelyn had given her, and even her briefcase.

There were still pockets to be zipped and Velcro flaps to secure. But she stopped for a moment to listen, wondering if her apartment was always this silent. The gentle rush of forced-air heating blew overhead, but otherwise it was quiet. Too quiet. She could still hear music playing in her head.

"Oh, God," she whispered. Her heart twisted as she noticed the nautilus shell on her bookshelf. If there'd been a moment to spare, Temple would have held its mother-of-pearl chambers to her ear. The last time she'd done that, there'd been a different quality to the whispering words. She couldn't tell if they were warning or beckoning to her.

She slipped the shell in her jacket pocket, aware that she'd forgotten something else, underwear. The top drawer was tricky. The slider was broken, and if you pulled it too far, it would dump the contents all over the floor. She inched it as far as she could and began to pick through the panties and cotton tanks she often wore in place of bras.

A white paper triangle peeked from beneath her nightgowns. An envelope corner, she realized. Gingerly she lifted the gowns and saw a small packet of notes, probably not more than a half-dozen. They were written on fine linen stationery and tied with a white velvet ribbon. Temple had no idea what they were, but as she picked them up, she caught a whiff of the same fragrance that had permeated the honeymoon suite. In Love Again.

Her throat burned with an unreleased gasp.

The packet hit the carpet and broke apart, fluttering the notes like a white linen fan. She knelt, rushing to read them. They were all addressed to "Princess." Each professed the writer's ardent love, and his longing to be with her. And they were all signed with the initial M.

Who else could they be from but Michael St. Gerard?

"Where to, miss?"

Temple threw her duffle into the backseat of the taxi and climbed in behind it. "A Greyhound bus station," she told the driver. "I don't care which one. Whatever's closest."

"Sure, lady, anything you say."

He spoke with the resignation of a man who'd seen one too many crazy fares and had opted out of the caring business. Temple's reaction was a pang of envy. What she wouldn't have given for that kind of stoicism. It still felt like cold terror, rather than blood running through her veins.

Her mind couldn't quite grasp what was happening as real, but her body was in full, wild flight. Her chest tightened with each breath, and her muscles hadn't realized it was safe to stop sprinting. They sparked restlessly, urging her to move.

It felt as if she were trying to escape her own fear as much as to escape Mark Challis. And her only solution was to get on a bus and ride to wherever it was going. From there she'd get on another one. And another. She wanted to keep moving, for as long as it took to understand.

She searched the street as the taxi driver pulled back onto it. In her state of mind any set of headlights looked suspicious.

"Thank God," she murmured as a car that had been behind them turned off onto a side street. What she failed to notice were the eyes studying her in the rearview mirror as she scrutinized the road.

It reminded Temple of the chapel of a church. There were glowing windows down each side, a long, narrow center aisle. There was even a guiding spirit at the front, encased in his pulpit of frosted glass. But better than any of that, it was dark inside and nearly empty, the perfect refuge for a soul seeking respite.

Only the reek of diesel oil, hanging in the air like an old curtain, and the constant thrumming motion, belied the images in Temple's head. Maybe it was exhaustion, or her need to feel safe, that made her think of the Greyhound bus as a sanctuary. What better place to escape the ravages of life than a church.

She was alone on the ride, except for one other passenger, an older man near the front, who appeared to be sleeping. Temple had seen him as she boarded, stared at him for a moment, curious about the black knit sailor's cap he wore, and then she'd put him out of her mind.

Right now her one thought was to weave an impenetrable cocoon around herself, to find a place inside her where no one else could reach. She had to stop running, start breathing.

When I work with a client it's my responsibility to see that they keep breathing, that their heart keeps beating every second of every moment they're under my care. . . .

Mark Challis's terms and conditions.

"Who in God's name was he?" she heard herself murmuring. He called himself a protector, but the image that loomed in Temple's mind was of a predator. It was him she was running from, she realized. He was her only known assailant.

She dug the nautilus from her pocket, catching a whiff of its briny essence as she cupped it to her ear. The soft crashing had always soothed her, but tonight she was grasping at straws, searching for answers. It was probably wishful thinking to imagine that the shell had something to tell her, but the notion had been with her since childhood, when magical solutions were very much a part of her life.

Her father and mother had been free spirits and progressive thinkers, always in search of some new and beguiling truth. They'd encouraged daydreaming and magical thinking. It was only later that Temple had come to reject those things as frivolous. By then her parents had begun to seem rootless and irresponsible, and Temple had taken over the family caretaker role. She'd had to be the steady, practical one, who'd held two jobs since grade school to supplement the meager family income and make sure she and her sister didn't go without the necessities of life. Because of that, the dreamer inside her had died.

A sense of sadness eddied as Temple realized how much she mourned the loss. Still. She gazed at the shell and an odd thought occurred to her. There was a moment when the whispering had sounded almost like a mother hushing her child, telling her that everything would be all right. "Shhhhh now, baby, don't be afraid. Shhhhh . . ."

What Temple wouldn't have given to hear those words.

"Santa Barbara station," the driver announced. "For those continuing on, there's a snack bar and concession—"

His message jolted Temple out of her reverie. They were stopping already? She had no idea where to hide. She dropped the shell in her pocket and glanced around to see if there was any kind of emergency exit. What assailed her next was a mental image of the bus being hijacked by men in black ski masks with automatic weapons. Or one man with anthracite for eyes and the cunning of a cobra.

The very things that had drawn her to Mark Challis now seemed frightening and sinister. Temple had built a wall of denial around her, but it was cracking under the pressure. Any delay, any obstacle, posed a threat.

She didn't move as they rolled into the station, and neither did the other passenger. Once they'd parked, the driver rose and excused himself with a reminder that they would depart in twenty minutes. He might as well have said forever. As he disappeared down the boarding steps, Temple fixed her eyes on the door of the bus, trying not to imagine what could happen in such a vast, unmanageable length of time.

Elevators could plummet, food could be poisoned, cars could be blown up . . . and women could be impregnated against their will. Anything and everything that was terrible could happen in twenty minutes.

She stared at the door until its empty space dominated her thoughts. It was an unguarded entrance that invited some form of disaster. It felt as if she were trapped, with no way out. She could have abandoned the bus and taken another one, but leaving seemed risky, too. She prayed no one would walk up those boarding steps, and her heart ticked out the seconds to safety. Maybe she could run out the clock if she just concentrated hard enough.

A shadow flashed by one of the windows, and Temple lurched around. She sank down in the seat, peering at the doorway in the wild hope that it was a customer on his way into the terminal. *That it had nothing to do with her.* Several moments passed, and she began to allow herself to hope again. Maybe it was another false alarm. She began to breathe.

Whoever it was, he must be gone, she told herself. It would only have taken a minute or two for someone to come around and enter the bus. She settled back in the seat, her heart slowing . . . but in the quiet that overtook her, she heard it clearly.

Footsteps. Someone was climbing the stairs.

A dark form appeared in the doorway, and Temple pressed back against the seat. She couldn't tell if he was real or if her overtaxed mind had created the very thing she feared. But the sight of him made her stifle a cry.

All she could see was the deadly purpose that drove him and the cold serpent's stare. He looked like a viper in human form, and it was so stark an image that Temple couldn't tell who had actually climbed the steps. But someone had come aboard, she realized. A man.

"Next stop, Stockton," he called out.

She fell back in the seat, limp. Tears nipped at her lids, but the sound that caught in her throat was laughter. It was only their driver who'd come aboard, the good shepherd of this vagabond church. Temple Banning had been given another reprieve. She began to shake, but it was from relief more than fear. The possibility that she might actually escape left her weak with anticipation.

The bus struck out for its next destination, and Temple sagged against the seat. She'd been rigid to the point of cracking, and now every muscle was tingling and useless.

Her hands wouldn't stop trembling. Worse, she had only the vaguest idea where she was going or what she was going to do.

Exhausted as she was, she had to come up with some kind of a plan. Wherever she happened to be in the morning, she would call Blue Sky and report in sick. She would also try to find out what had happened to Annette, but even the thought brought her sadness, because Temple was almost certain what she would hear. Mark Challis had already tried to give her the bad news.

Annette hadn't made it. Her friend had died in the explosion, and the weight of Temple's breath felt as if it could crush her chest. She couldn't comprehend how any of this could have happened, except that it had to be a tragic mistake. The only possibility that rang true was that she, Temple, had been confused with someone else. And even that didn't explain Mark Challis's involvement, whatever it was. She had no idea how he fit in, unless he had her confused, too.

She closed her eyes, hoping for sleep, but her mind was still plagued with dark and frightening images, and her fatigue was too profound to block them. She had no choice but to let the haunting events of the last few weeks float in her head. With a taut sigh, she surrendered to everything that threatened to engulf her, the drowning music of the bus's journey, the smell of gasoline fumes. And, as she finally drifted off, to the beckoning whisper of the ocean waves.

Temple was jolted out of her exhaustion by a rattling blast. Vibrations shook the bus like gale winds. Her heart was racing wildly as she opened her eyes. The bus was still dark, but it felt as if they'd stopped. And yet the chair beneath her was trying to throw her to the floor.

"What's happening?" She sprang up and banged her head on the overhead compartments.

At the sound of her voice, the passenger who'd been sitting up front the entire trip rose and turned to face her. Only he wasn't wearing a sailor's cap now, and he wasn't an old man. His dark hair fell nearly to his shoulders and his gaze had the grounding capacity of an electrical discharge.

Instantly Temple's world was sharp with detail. Every color she saw was vibrant, every angle and contour her eyes encountered cut into her senses. Hours ago, when her car exploded, she couldn't see. Now that was all she could do. See. Her other senses were too stunned. She couldn't hear, couldn't smell or touch. She had already tried closing her eyes, but there was no way to block him out. The other passenger on the bus was Mark Challis.

ELEVEN

There was no way to escape him. She was trapped. Only one other time in her life had Temple been physically confined. When she was quarantined. Then she had feared for her little sister's welfare. Now she feared for her own.

Challis approached her slowly, advancing down the aisle as if he were prepared to do the worst, whatever was necessary to regain control. Of her.

She pulled herself forward and cast about, looking for help, knowing it was useless. The driver had disappeared. She was alone on the bus, and the odds against escaping Challis twice were astronomical.

The rumbling train she'd heard was a helicopter. She could see it through the windows. Powerful blades whipped the darkness, thrashing it into a storm that bent double the trees and bushes. Its engines vibrated the earth. And Mark Challis never once took his eyes off her.

She'd thought of him as a man who could hold you with his eyes, but that was a grievous understatement. She had already begun to feel the effect of his paralyzing force by the time he stopped opposite her seat. She searched his features, trying to gauge the danger, but as always, they were unreadable.

"Why did you run, Temple?"

"I was frightened."

"That's it? You were frightened."

"It seemed like enough reason at the time." If she gave any thought to telling him the truth, that it was the music she heard in his office, she reconsidered when she realized how crazy that would sound. In truth she had nothing on which to base her suspicions of him, she realized. Nothing other than a dim memory of some strange melody.

"Frightened of what?" he asked. "Not me, surely."

"Yes, you," she flared. "Of course you! Who gave you the right to come after me like this? I'm surprised you didn't net me like a cornered animal."

"I would have," he said.

And she believed him. "Well, you've wasted your time. I'm not going back with you."

His tone was low, compellingly reasonable. "You're going with me, because to do otherwise would be insane."

He sat down in the seat next to her, forcing her to press closer to the wall. His proximity made her feel as if she *had* been cornered. Earlier she had asked herself if he was protector or predator. Now her heart leaped to answer that question.

"Temple, if I could find you, they can," he said. "And if they find you, they'll kill you."

"How do I know that you won't!"

He met her startled gaze and held it so long she began to feel herself going quiet inside. It was a strange, emptying experience, as if she'd run the rapids and now she was drifting toward a calm, still pool.

It amazed her that he could have this effect on her, especially when it was him she'd fled. She'd responded in a similar way the day of the elevator accident. It had felt as if he were transfusing her through the warmth of his hands, and within moments she had begun to breathe as he did. Calmly. Evenly.

"If it was me who wanted you dead," he told her, "you wouldn't be here to ask the question. Think about it. There's been plenty of opportunity."

"What *do* you want, then? Why are you going to these lengths?"

"I don't know," he said softly. The question seemed to have caught him off guard. And his hesitation said that he really didn't know. "Maybe because you're a friend of Annette's, and one senseless tragedy is enough. Or maybe it goes deeper than that."

He stared into her eyes, her heart. "What if this is about you? What if I just don't want you to die?"

Temple's throat grew warm, aching as if something had caught there. She heard him clear his throat, and wondered if he felt it, too. She would have given anything to know what was going on inside Mark Challis, and if he was even capable of the emotion she saw in him. She didn't know what to call it but tenderness, and it always touched into her own vulnerable feelings. But she couldn't succumb to them now.

"It's going to take a leap of faith," he told her. "But you must know what's at stake, Temple. It's not just your life on the line."

When she still didn't answer, he took a deep breath. "Temple, don't be foolish. You can't go on like this. There comes a time when you have to trust someone."

She looked up at him, wondering if that was insight or a lucky guess on his part. She struggled with trust over the smallest things. It was pointless to depend on anyone but yourself. She'd learned that over the years, just as she'd learned that the very people you should be able to trust and turn to for help wouldn't be there if you did. Who had ever taken care of Temple Banning but Temple Banning? And now he was suggesting she abandon the one belief that had kept her safe. Her belief in herself.

It was true that she had no idea how to protect herself. She didn't even know what she was dealing with. Someone wanted her dead, but they hadn't bothered to tell her why. And she couldn't begin to guess the reasons. Her mind was haunted with faceless phantoms and unanswerable questions. But right now one of them stood out like lightning against the storm. One unanswerable question: When there was so much at stake, was it foolish to take a risk? Or foolish not to?

The sense of peace Temple felt at first light was extraordinary. She didn't know how to explain it. Dawn was breaking over the California coastline. Magical dawn. A pink pastel mist clung to the shore. The horizon was a line of radiant amber light, and the Channel Islands were strung like irregular pearls on an ocean of dark blue velvet.

The helicopter approached the islands from the north—San Miguel, Santa Rosa, Santa Cruz, Anacapa. These were the four northern isles believed to have been linked a million years ago and connected to the California mainland by a land bridge that was part of the Santa Monica mountain range. The closest, Anacapa, was just twenty miles from Ventura itself. And farther south there were four more, the largest of which was Santa Catalina.

The longer Temple stared at the scene below, the more the islands looked like shells, a charm bracelet of nautilus shells, arranged like stepping stones to the shore, and all of them whispering of unexplored life. Beckoning, she thought, aware of how fanciful she sounded. But they did seem to be beckoning.

Three of the islands they were approaching belonged to the National Land Grant. Only Santa Cruz was partially owned by a private family. Temple had thought that was where they were heading. But clearly not. The chopper pilot flew past Anacapa and banked west toward a slightly larger land mass just beyond the chain.

She was familiar with the area because of her travel agency experience, but she hadn't realized there was another island. This one was truly a verdant paradise, undoubtedly drenched by pounding winter rains and the shy new spring. There were black cliffs, mossy green valleys, and soaring cloud vistas. Blue hillsides were swept with soft green grass and blanketed with red and orange flowers.

"It's called Peregrine Island," Mark said. "You'll see why when we land."

He was sitting beside her in the passenger seat of the helicopter, and she was aware that he'd been watching her throughout the short trip from the mainland. Probably expecting her to change her mind and leap from the noisy beast. He would have been surprised to know what she was actually thinking. If she'd been a person who believed in signs, she would have said that the breathtaking view had confirmed her decision to come with him. She'd never witnessed such serene beauty.

It wasn't that there hadn't been an impulsive quality to her decision. It was more emotional than rational, and yet it had also felt right. The turning point had come when she realized that she'd never relied on anyone other than herself, and how sad that was, how empty. She hadn't allowed herself to need, to trust. It hadn't been possible the way she grew up. But it was possible now.

Mark's advice had the ring of truth. There did come a time when you had to trust someone, even if it meant putting your life in his hands. Especially then. She told herself that was true and needed to believe it.

"Hang on. We're coming in." He pointed toward an asphalt circle on the ground. "There's the helipad."

What surprised Temple as they circled to land was the lineup awaiting them on the ground. It looked like a military honor guard, without the flags or uniforms. She couldn't tell whether or not they were armed, but the half-dozen or so men were very official in stance. There was even a jeep with a driver.

Mark had told her he used the island as a secure refuge for his high-risk clients. Temple wasn't sure what she expected, but she hadn't seen any obvious signs of security measures, other than the men awaiting them, and a satellite dish or two she'd noticed as they flew in.

Mark shot from the seat without warning. He startled Temple by opening the sliding door, leaping out of the helicopter and turning to help her. The landing had been so smooth, she hadn't realized they were on the ground. She reached for his hands, but he caught her by the waist to lift her down.

Temple saw it coming, but there was nothing she could do. They were going to be thrown against each other. Her own unsteadiness was the cause. She gripped his shoulders, but it didn't help. All she could do was suck in a breath and hold on as he lifted her out of the cabin with the ease of a male dancer partnering her in a ballet.

If Temple had had a rating scale, this sensation would have soared to a ten. She was aware of the friction of his clothing as she slid down his body, the rustle of his distressed leather jacket and the way her fleecy top snagged on his belt buckle. She could also feel the corded musculature of his thighs. Why wasn't she surprised that he had a powerful build? It went hand-in-glove with what he did for a living.

More alarming was the possibility that he could feel every twitch and quiver of her body. Her ankle joints were loose, her pulse flighty. Gingerly she freed herself from his belt and tilted backward. She expected to see the same flush of surprise that she was feeling. But when she looked up, he was already intent on guiding her toward the jeep.

The wind whipped her hair and clothing as they crossed the helipad. Mark draped her shoulders with his jacket, and when they got to the jeep, he excused the young man behind the wheel, saying that he would drive her to the house himself. There was no saluting, although Temple half-expected it. The two men did exchange faint smiles, seeming to share the kind of secret knowledge that males instinctively possess about females in their midst, especially females deemed to be in need of protection.

Once Temple had safely strapped herself in the passenger seat, Mark went to speak briefly with a lean, deeply lined older man, who looked like he might be the senior member of the group, perhaps the chief of security.

Again Temple detected a kind of code language in the men's exchange. There were few words, but a great deal of information imparted, she suspected. What I wouldn't give to speak that language, she thought, wondering if Mark intended to tell her what he had planned.

Moments later they were underway, Temple hanging on to the handstrap as Mark negotiated the bumps and ruts of a well-worn paved road that, according to him, ran the perimeter of the island. With evident pride he filled her in on Peregrine's history during the course of the short trip.

It was named, he told her, for the falcons that were first imported from China in the mid-1800s by a Frenchman who purchased the island for the purpose of wine-making and hunting. He created a small fiefdom, bringing in French and Italian laborers to build his "castle" and work the vineyards. He also stocked the island with enough buffalo, wild board, and deer to draw hunters from all over the world.

"The vineyards failed to thrive in the cool, wet climate," Mark explained. "And the Frenchman eventually grew tired of his hunting retreat. It fell into my family's hands when he abandoned it for livelier pursuits. My great-grandfather turned it into a wildlife preserve. And now I've transformed it into a compound for clients who require high levels of security."

"How secure is the island?" Temple asked.

"I'm a consultant to foreign governments, as well as the U.S. military," Mark informed her dryly. "The Pentagon should be as secure as this island."

"But I don't see anything," she said, looking around searchingly. Some of the Channel Islands were fairly barren, but sea mists and moisture-laden winds had turned parts of Catalina, Santa Rosa, and this one into near rain forests of flora and fauna. There were rolling hills and valleys, blanketed with rich greenery and vividly rainbowed with early-blooming wildflowers. The trees were alive with birds, and the road was alive with tiny, furry things that darted back and forth in advance of the jeep.

Temple was enchanted by them until Mark touched her arm and pointed up. In the dense blue heavens above, the hawks he'd spoken of soared and drifted, carried by powerful air currents. It was a breathtaking sight, and one Temple wouldn't soon forget. She'd never been to the Mediterranean, but this place reminded her of the lush islands she'd written about during her travel agency days.

"If you could see the security," Mark pointed out, "it wouldn't be secure."

He steered the conversation back to the island, and Temple realized that it was going to be all business with Mark Challis. She was going to be treated like one of his clients, as if there'd never been anything between them. Her fingers curled around the handstrap and tightened, despite the smooth stretch of road they were on. Staring out at the scenery, she wondered why she was thinking that there had ever *been* anything between them.

It surprised her that she could react so strongly. The emotion felt fiery, too strong for disappointment, and yet, what else could it be? It made her wonder what was going on with her as much as with him. Fortunately, she caught sight of something out of the corner of her eye that distracted her. Contained within a chain-link fence and camouflaged by a stand of island oaks were several radar towers with monitors that looked like small, oddly shaped satellite dishes. She knew very little about such things, but she'd come across terms like microwave, motion, and infrared detectors in the occasional technothriller she'd read, and it seemed that she might be looking at something along that order.

This paradise, Temple reminded herself, was also a fortress.

A fortress and quite possibly a fiefdom still, Temple decided. She could hardly believe it, but there was another lineup waiting for them as Mark pulled the jeep into the crescent-shaped driveway of an enormous ivy-draped stone estate. Temple marveled as he came around the car to let her out. The place he called home looked more like a hunting lodge than a house, which made her wonder if this was the original Frenchman's "castle."

A small group of men and women were assembled in front of the massive oak doors. Temple took them to be the household staff by their friendly demeanor. It wasn't at all military, nor was the affection with which Mark introduced his gardener, his handyman, his cook, and finally, his housekeeper, June, a wisp of a woman with tilted eyes, graying hair, and an imperious air about her.

June was an exception to the general mood of welcome. She barely touched Temple's offered hand and was curt to the point of being impolite. But it wasn't her manner that gave Temple pause. There was something familiar about the housekeeper's chilly gaze. They couldn't have met before. June lived on this tiny island, and Temple was originally from Houston. The odds were infinitesimal. Still, there was something.

If Mark noticed June's behavior, he didn't give Temple time to dwell on it. He took her by the arm and led her into the castle. Just as she suspected, it had been built for the former owner, who had called it Peregrine Hall, according to Mark. Later the place had been remodeled and renamed Wings by his family.

"There are four wings branching from the main one," he told her as they walked through the foyer. "From the air it gives the house the appearance of flight."

"It's magnificent," Temple told him, admiring the octagonal foyer's muraled walls and jade chandelier. It led into a main hall with vaulted ceilings that immediately brought to mind the great cathedrals. The floor was a still sea of black and white marble with the reflective surface of mirrors. Here the chandeliers had tiers of white crystal, suspended in more pale jade, and the wall's lighted niches housed an art collection of museum quality, Temple was sure.

She was generous in her praise, and Challis seemed pleased. "Most of our guests aren't here by choice," he said, "so we do our best to make them comfortable."

He gestured for the housekeeper. "You'd probably like to get settled yourself. June will be happy to help, and now, if you'll excuse me, I have some business that can't wait any longer."

"Don't let me keep you," Temple said. "But there's no need to inconvenience June. I can manage. Just point me in the right direction."

"Don't be silly." June's chin snapped up, cutting off all

protests. "You'll only get yourself lost. You're staying in the mill cottage out back. I'll take you there."

Temple was trying hard not to take the housekeeper's attitude personally. She wanted to think it wasn't just Temple Banning who'd been singled out. She wanted to think June had a grudge against all humankind. Not that much of a stretch, actually.

"You'll love the cottage," Mark said to Temple. "It's a converted millhouse built by my forebears, and back in those days its wheel provided the only power on the island."

"Really? I can't wait to see it."

"Come along!" June called back. The housekeeper had already signaled the handyman to pick up Temple's duffel, and the two of them were off at a good clip.

Temple gave Mark a wan smile and dutifully set off, playing follow the leader down a tunnel-like hallway that was paneled in oak, lushly dark, and seemingly endless. Invisible beams from the graceful vaulted ceiling lit drawings and photographs of the island in its various stages of development.

Temple wanted to stop and look, but risked losing sight of June. The hallway led next to a dazzlingly bright room that smelled of fresh, damp soil and peat moss. It was domed by latticed windowpanes that cascaded like a waterfall to the blue tiled floor. Emerald ferns drooped from tiered baskets, and Kentia palms as tall as trees arched toward the light.

This was a real conservatory, Temple thought. Even as she rushed through it, and without seeing the rest of the house, she knew that if she lived in Wings, the conservatory would be her respite, her favorite of all places. She'd always loved the smell of foresty, growing things and the serenity of nature, but had never found time for anything beyond the small atrium in her apartment.

The room's glass doors opened onto an observation deck

with a stunning view of the coast. Temple's eyes hadn't adjusted to the light, but she glimpsed the vast Pacific on one side, mountains on the other, and promised herself that she would find time to explore all of this later. June and the handyman were already crossing a weathered bridge that spanned a tumbling, stream, flecked with silver, and on the far side was the sweetest little wooden cabin Temple had ever seen.

It didn't look to be more than two or three rooms with a cozy thatched roof, a flagstone foundation and chimney, complete with a covered porch whose railings were laden with flower boxes. A mossy wooden millwheel churned in a creek that meandered from the back of the cottage and emptied into the larger stream in the front.

June and the handyman were inside by the time Temple got there, busying themselves with last-minute touches. Temple took a look around, delighted with the airy, sunlit interior and the ceiling's natural wooden beams. There was a quaint little dollhouse of a sitting room with a stone fireplace, ivy-sprigged curtains, and a shiny brass daybed that would undoubtedly serve for sleeping. There was also an adjoining bathroom with a claw-footed tub, and the kitchen was bordered by a breakfast bar.

June was arranging some freshly cut flowers in a milk pitcher, which she'd placed on a rustic white pine writing desk. Temple's duffel bag was on a cedar chest at the end of the daybed, and the handyman was piling logs on the fireplace grate.

"Can I help you with anything?" June asked Temple. "Draw a bath?"

"Oh, a bath! That would be lovely, thank you."

As June nodded and left the room, the handyman asked Temple if she'd like him to start a fire. It was chilly enough, Temple decided, and it would be relaxing to nap by the fire after her bath.

"Thank you—" She smiled at him, realizing she couldn't remember his name. He looked like a friendly sort. His round, flushed face and roomy denim overalls made her think of Mr. Green Jeans.

"Eddie, ma'am. Eddie Baker, and you're sure enough welcome."

A short time later the fire was crackling, the bathtub was brimming with steamy, scented water, and Temple was blissfully alone. Eddie had departed with a shy wave of his hand, and June with a brusque reminder that lunch would be served at one.

The feeling that washed over Temple as she began to undress for her bath was indescribable, a seven or eight on that inner scale. She'd never felt such exhaustion, but it wasn't wholly bad. There was a sigh of relief involved, and even though she was afraid to give in to it entirely, she felt peaceful as well as tired.

It seemed as if she might have made the right decision in coming to the island, and that in itself was a huge relief. Her intuition was sending her signals that she could be safe here. And she wanted to believe it was true.

She pulled her sweater over her head and hung it on a wall hook. As she stepped back, she noticed a flash of movement in the corner of her eye. A freestanding mirror peeked out from behind the bathroom door. She'd caught her own reflection.

She continued undressing, aware of the process in a different way. By the time she was down to her panties, she'd begun to wonder about the pregnancy and the physical changes taking place in her body. She opened the door a crack, enough to see that her breasts looked a little fuller.

She wanted to see more.

TWELVE

Mark was well aware that the guest cottage gave the illusion of total privacy. Yet in reality it was anything but. Hidden in the rustic exposed beams of the ceiling in each of its three rooms were tiny security cameras, recording images at eight frames a second and transmitting them to a desktop computer.

He stood across the room from the computer, as if enough distance made it less a violation that he was watching her every move. He was angled against the wall of bookcases, leaning into one shoulder, his arms folded across his chest. Fortunately the shadows masked his expression. No doubt he resembled some dark enemy of the natural order of things.

He felt like that, dark and disorderly. A voyeur. A violator. Not that he had any choice, really. Or would have chosen differently if he had.

The book-lined room that served as his office whispered with efficient noises, the faint swish of an atomic clock's precision second hand, the low electronic drone of his desktop. Mark didn't register any of it, not even the occasional rise and fall of his own breathing. Nothing could compete with her deafening presence.

The island's security was designed to protect the perimeter of the island from external threats. Mark used technology calibrated to detect boats and planes, not to spy on the clients under his care. He'd never wired his own house or offices, although on occasion he'd found it necessary to keep clients under surveillance for their own protection. But that was different. They'd been informed. And he'd looked but not watched. Now he was watching.

The object of his attention had already slipped out of her gray sweatsuit, and she was looking herself over in the mirror behind the bathroom door. Her panties were the high-cut cotton type, and she wore a clingy tank T-shirt rather than a bra. But what had captured him was what she was doing.

She was delicately inspecting her body in the glass, as if searching for signs of her condition. She lifted the tee and drew down the panties just enough to peer at her belly. Then she turned to the side for another view and smoothed the soft curves with her fingers, looking for any indication of swelling.

Finally she straightened, lithe and long. And cupped a breast.

Mark felt the back of his neck tighten.

She was weighing, measuring. It wasn't sexual to her, but no man could watch this without being affected. For that moment he was caught, a conductor receiving direct current, and the powerful charge expressed itself in his body. Feeling flowed through him, unblocked. Seeking. Searching for something that didn't exist anymore. It shocked him. The urgency. God.

At last he wrenched himself away and by doing so, put

her in danger. This was a mission and a crucial one. He had to watch, no matter what the hell it did to him.

Amazing that one half-dressed, newly pregnant virgin could have that effect. He'd faced armed death with less reaction. His pulse rate had spiked when she'd begun her self-examination, and it was a piercing sensation to a man who'd reduced his range of expression to a narrow bandwidth. Normally, even in the most dangerous of circumstances, his heart rate barely registered.

"Flatlined," his doctor had once joked, but Mark knew the survival value of that. And even if his profession hadn't called for it, he preferred it.

He'd never trusted the mercurial nature of what most people thought of as normal emotions. Love and hate, joy and sorrow, those "normal" feelings could rain devastation on a life. They had left his in shards. And sitting on the cabinet opposite his desk was the reason—a mounted Malay lacewing butterfly.

The exquisitely fragile wings had always made him think of flowers in flight. Its crimson petals were actually fringed by a delicate gossamer lace pattern in snowdrop white. Some people might have found it ironic that he associated the butterfly with death and destruction. Mark found it ironic they didn't, considering the violence routinely done to such beauty in the name of preserving it. For him the lacewing was a constant, torturous reminder of what could happen when your life spun out of control.

It also reminded him daily, hourly, why he continued to despise the man who fathered him, despite the fact that Jonathan Challis was now dying. Mark couldn't look at the butterfly without being reminded of what Jonathan had tried to preserve at any cost, and what Mark himself had destroyed, trying to set it free.

Who was the monster? he wondered.

He turned to the wall of bookcases behind him. They

were originally from an eighteenth-century cloister in France and numbered among the priceless pieces his family had salvaged from the original "castle." He'd never been more aware of their history, or of his own.

His father was a man of iron will. He and Mark had clashed early, and repeatedly. He'd wanted his oldest son to take over the software industry that he'd built from the dwindling family coffers, and Mark had thrown himself into it, improving on everything Jonathan had done and taking the business to its current worth in the tens of billions.

But it wasn't *his* business, *his* vision. Stunning as his father's achievements had been, they weren't Mark's, and because of that, it was an empty victory. Every man needed to leave his own footprints in the sand, and perhaps Mark more than most, although he had often wondered whether that had more to do with his mother's unusual lineage than with his father's persona. At any rate, when Mark had finally rebelled and followed his heart, it had set off a chain reaction of painful events that had left the Challis family in shambles.

Emotion had proved to be lethal in his case, more dangerous than any armed enemy could be. And ironically, the more tender the emotion the more damage it could do. Anger didn't hurt. Love did. Desire did. If the gods had deemed that there was just one thing Mark Challis could control in life, it would have been those emotions, regardless of the price he had to pay.

Moments later, when he turned back and looked at the computer screen, his subject had stepped into the tub and sunk in the steamy water up to her neck. She was totally concealed. All he could see was her flushed face and her dark, butterfly lashes as her lids drifted shut . . . and maybe he was glad.

• • •

Susan Gilchrist was still wet from her shower when she heard something that made her whirl toward the bathroom door in confusion. She grabbed a towel off the rack, wrapped it around her, and was still tucking in the ends as she rushed into the other room and turned up the volume on the TV.

A commentator was describing an accident, and Susan thought she'd heard Temple Banning's name mentioned. The noise of the shower had drowned out everything prior to that, and unfortunately Susan had missed the entire segment. She'd arrived just in time to see the channel's female anchor reappear with a sum-up.

"The police tell us that the actual owner of the vehicle is now considered to be missing," the anchor said. "They're looking for a thirty-year-old advertising executive named Temple Banning."

A picture of Temple flashed briefly on the screen, and Susan stood there, dripping on the hotel carpet.

Disappeared? What the hell was going on?

The sound that caught in her throat was abject disbelief. If this was true and Temple Banning really had disappeared, then everything Susan had done so far had backfired.

She walked the length of the room and back, taking a couple of deep breaths to calm herself. It wasn't in her nature to panic. Her first observed autopsy had been a grade-school kid whose internal organs had ruptured from a massive E. coli infection. The other students had gagged and been sick, but Susan hadn't blinked. Afterward the pathologist had remarked that she must have been born with the nerves of a safecracker.

It was that same nerve that had brought her to this point. But there wasn't any choice now. She was going to have to call in reinforcements.

• • •

Every man had a secret room inside him where he indulged the dark mysteries of his heart. Thoughts and desires he could tell no one because they would have judged him, just as he would have judged them for their secrets, human nature being what it was—fearful, intolerant, and inescapable.

People judged each other cruelly. Eddie Baker had realized that at a very young age. He'd also understood that it was the source of all loneliness. It forced men into hiding. And even though having such a hiding place brought great guilty pleasure, nothing could ease the soul-loneliness of never being able to share who you were.

But Eddie had discovered a way to push the worst of it away for a while. He'd found another way to connect. He'd created a real room, a lair where he could indulge the mysteries without fear of being discovered, or shamed. The island had several old, abandoned buildings, but the foundry best suited his purposes. He'd walled off a side room, engineered a virtually invisible entrance. And gone there every chance he could.

He was there now. Surrounded by his secrets, by his collection of mysteries, all of them begged, bought, or stolen. He'd never had a wife, never had children. These were his babies, his *girls*, and they did bring him great guilty pleasure.

As he'd grown his collection, he'd begun arranging them according to their special characteristics, but overall he just loved the supple grace of their curves, the shiny lips, and the heady, smoky fragrances they gave off when they were hot. God, if they weren't just like females, he thought now, gazing at the six-by-six glass display case he'd constructed, and struggling not to laugh. He could never make up his mind which one of them he liked best.

There was Carol, of course. He was aware of her litheness as he lightly played his fingers over her contours, admiring her sleek lines. Maybe what he liked best about her was the way she seemed poised like a ballerina on one, endless limb, if she was tilting just right. But he also loved that lacy little skirt she wore. What did they call those things? Tutus?

He was tempted to pick her up, but he let his attention drift to Amanda next. Last thing he needed was a jealous woman on his hands. He smothered another chuckle. He didn't want anyone who might be wandering around outside to hear the fuss. No, he did not want that.

Amanda was big and busty, lots of brass and sass. All woman, that one. Maybe a little too loud when she mouthed off, but he'd always found it in his heart to forgive her. Hell, she was decked out with the prettiest set of thirty-eights he'd yet to come across, enough to fill out a man's hands just so. Wore her skirts short, too.

His girls were all special to Eddie, but if he had a favorite, it was the newcomer. He'd come by her just last week, and he still got a charge out of gazing at her long mahogany mane and pert, open mouth. And then there was that sweet little switch that made her jump when he touched it. God, he loved the feel of her as she rested against his shoulder. He could have danced with this little beauty all night long.

He hadn't named her, though. It had to be perfect, her name, just right, and nothing had come to him yet.

"Sometimes you have to wait," he told himself as he stepped back from the gun case. "Wait until it comes to you."

The beep of his pager startled him, and brought a frown. The world could intrude on him anywhere, he realized, no matter how well hidden he was. He hated that. The only other place that gave him any sense of peace was the estate's vast gardens. He was happy when they let him work on the flowers, but it wasn't like this. Not the same.

His reflection bounced back at him from the dusty glass case, confirming that something was wrong. His smile echoed the same dread that twisted deep in his gut. Every once in a while he was able to grasp the power of his dark mysteries, and it always shocked him. His girls *were* just like women. Shiny and beautiful, but lethal if mishandled. He didn't like the idea of using them to hurt anyone. He didn't like that idea at all.

His pager beeped again, alerting him that it was urgent.

As he left the room a moment later, the one thing he did not look at was the flesh-and-blood woman. Her picture lay on his table, the place where he cleaned his prize possessions. But he couldn't look at her anymore. Her sadness cut through him.

Tiny red eyes glared at her from the darkness, and the hot, burning orbs brought macabre images to mind. Vampire bats, hanging in the rafters. Rodents, slithering through cracks in the walls.

That was all Temple could see when she opened her own eyes. Bright red ones, staring back at her. She sat up, disoriented. It was a moment before she realized the fire had burned down to embers. Not eyes. They were coals. A few more moments passed before she knew where she was.

"The sitting room," she said, looking around. The only dying light came from the fireplace, but she could make out the small room and its quaint furnishings. She could also make out her own bare legs. She'd forgotten to bring a nightgown, but there was a men's white dress shirt in the cabin closet, along with some other clothes that were probably loaners for guests who hadn't had time to pack. The one gown she'd found had seemed daringly sheer, and since the shirt was roomy enough for several people, she'd gone with that.

She tugged it down, covering her legs, and became aware of a soft pattering noise. It sounded like it was raining outside, and then she remembered the creek and the millwheel. There was a little waterfall right outside her window.

She'd curled up on the daybed for a nap after her bath. That was the last thing she remembered, but by the look of things, she'd had a good, long rest. The window curtains were open, and it was dark enough outside to be the middle of the night. There was a clock on the fireplace mantel, but she couldn't see the hands.

Over the smoldering ashes of the fire, she caught the scent of something yeasty and delicious. There appeared to be a tray on the trunk coffee table that wasn't there when she went to sleep. Her empty stomach rumbled noisily as she swung her feet off the daybed and perused the crusty baguettes and cheeses, an assortment of fruit and sweet breads. There was also a pitcher of fresh lemonade that gave up the essence of ambrosia.

Temple was ravenous. She couldn't remember the last time she'd eaten, unless it was the roadhouse, but she hadn't touched the salmon wraps, and then they'd brought the tainted dish. Now she couldn't stop herself. This food could have been laced with cyanide, and she would have eaten it. She ripped a large chunk from the bread and sliced a creamy wedge of brie.

There was no other way to appease her rumbling stomach but to stuff it with mouthful after heavenly mouthful, and within moments half the cheese and bread were gone. She was eating too fast, but that couldn't be helped. Food had never tasted this good. When she'd eased the worst of the hunger pangs, she turned to the pitcher and poured herself a tall glass of lemonade. The ice had melted, but the flavor was as sweetly piquant and fruity as if the lemons had just been squeezed.

She drank deeply, quenching her thirst.

Finally, when she could think about something other than staving off starvation, she picked up a cluster of tart red grapes and settled back to savor them. It wasn't until she discarded the plucked stem that she noticed a folded note propped against the bud vase on the tray.

It was engraved with the initials M and C.

Temple's heart actually fluttered as she picked it up. She never knew what to expect from Mark Challis, she realized, least of all surprises like this. The note expressed regret at not seeing her at lunch or dinner and suggested that she join him on a tour of the island the next morning.

"Might be a good idea to get familiar with the area," he'd written.

Which could imply she was going to be there awhile.

"We'll see about that." Her hushed words could barely be heard over the sound of crumpling paper. Her stomach had begun to churn again, but this had nothing to do with hunger. She was starting to understand the predicament she was in. She was a virtual prisoner on the island, if Mark decided to keep her here. There was no way to leave, short of swimming, and even if that were possible, she could never do it. She hadn't taken to the water as a kid.

A loud creak issued from the porch outside.

Temple rose from the bed, preparing herself for a knock at the door. Had he knocked when he brought the food? she wondered. She glanced down at the shirt she was wearing and realized that he must have come in the room while she was sleeping.

If this was his "your life is mine" mode, it wasn't going to work for her. She'd agreed to his rules, but that had been in a moment of duress, and now they were going to have to find some form of compromise. Even if his overriding concern had been that she not go hungry, he shouldn't have walked in while she was sleeping. It didn't matter that he owned the place and considered himself some kind of bodyguard. This was her space now, and he really should respect that.

She hurried to the door and opened it, ready to confront

him. But there was no one there. She hadn't imagined the creaking, but old houses made noise. It could have been the wood planks and shakes. That didn't change the fact that she was losing control of her life. Had already lost it, to be exact.

She didn't know what day it was, what time it was. Somewhere along the way her watch had stopped running. She had no idea where the money was coming from to pay for his "secure refuge," but she doubted very much that Mark Challis's services came cheap.

When she'd worked for the travel agency, she'd made up flyers, trumpeting the wonders of island vacations. "Is there an island getaway in your future?" she'd asked, never bothering to answer that question for herself. Of course there wasn't. Temple Banning didn't travel. She didn't have adventures with the single exception of Zaire, and that was hardly a getaway.

She shut the door and locked it from the inside, wondering what it meant that there was nothing more than a chain lock on the door of a house that was supposed to be secure against everything, including terrorists. There was nothing else she could do tonight, she realized. But first thing tomorrow she was going to pose these questions to Mr. Challis. And then she was going to make some phone calls and get her life back on track.

THIRTEEN

Luck was with Temple the next morning. No one in the main house seemed to be up when she slipped in the observation deck entrance, which told her it must be very early. The housekeeper hadn't struck her as the type to sleep in.

A beautiful old Persian carpet muffled her steps as she proceeded down the long hallway in search of a telephone. The kitchen was probably a good bet, but she wanted the privacy of an office, where there was less chance she'd be interrupted.

The corridor took her to the enormous entrance hall, a cathedral that once again stole her breath with its miles of black and white Carrera marble, jade chandeliers, and blue porcelain torchieres. At the deep end was a Baroque arch that framed the sunken living room. Off the hall to one side were the library and formal dining room, so it seemed likely that the office she was looking for might be on the other side.

And what an office she found.

This has to be his domain, she thought, trying to take in the scope of the room she'd come upon. Hidden away in the farthest wing of the ground floor, it was totally different from his sleek suite of rooms in the city. Every wall was a richly carved bookcase that stretched from floor to ceiling. The windows were deep-set seats, upholstered in damask. In one corner, there was a freestanding Oriental screen, in another a fireplace, surrounded by emerald foliage in huge cloisonné pots.

It was stately, serene, and timeless. She really could have been in another century, in a castle on a cliff. If he had modern equipment, it was hidden in the mahogany cabinets. The only exceptions she could see were the computer that sat on his antique writing desk and the mobile phone.

Temple's plan was to call her boss, explain what happened, and ask for a leave of absence, beg for one, if necessary. Given the Fabrici contract, she might have a chance of succeeding. She hadn't heard from Dr. Gilchrist, either, and she would have to call Ivy and tell her she'd be away for a while. She would use business as the reason, although she didn't like the idea of concealing the truth from her sister.

Ivy was the only person she felt deeply connected to in this world. As far as she knew, they had never lied to each other, she and her sister. With vagabonds for parents, they'd needed to depend on each other, and honesty had been their mainstay.

Now it felt as if Temple had to shut Ivy out when in fact she needed her most, and that hurt. But the truth would only frighten her, and Temple wouldn't have known what to tell her anyway. What mattered was that Ivy know how to contact her and that they stay in touch.

Probably Temple should have gone straight to the phone and made her calls. And maybe she would have if the room hadn't already worked some kind of spell on her. It had a certain compelling ambience, much like the conservatory. Honestly, nearly every room in the house seemed to speak to her, enticing her to stay, to drink in its essence and perhaps discover something.

About herself? she wondered. But that wasn't clear. Nothing was clear. It wasn't possible to explain feelings that were so vague and ephemeral. They would sound silly, yet something inside her responded, and pulled so insistently she was forced to acknowledge them.

She'd always wondered about the paths people chose in life, especially in her parents' case. They had seemed to fall into their nomadic lifestyle so naturally it was almost as if the path had chosen them. Temple had felt that way about her job at Blue Sky, and now she was wondering if houses could choose people, too. Because if that were the case, this one seemed to have chosen her. She could feel her soul opening up to this place.

She took another moment to look around and explore the room. There was a celestial globe near the bookcases by his desk and an atomic clock on the fireplace mantel. Everywhere she looked there was something to absorb her, but her eyes were drawn next to a colorful object encased in a small glass dome.

As she neared the cabinet across from his desk and saw that it was a butterfly, her stomach turned over. Caught in full flight, it looked fragile, yet vibrantly alive. She'd never seen anything like it. The delicate wings were exotically patterned and lacy edged. It could have been a swatch of the finest embroidery. But it was beauty wasted on Temple. Her insides were churning. She could barely bear to think of such an exquisite thing reduced to a sightless, soulless trophy.

There was also a collection of old books on the cabinet, held fast by brass lions. She swiftly turned her attention to them, and to the wall above them, which was hung with awards and commendations, all engraved to Mark Challis for his skill in the martial arts.

Temple pulled out one of the books and opened it, surprised at the yellowed, curling pages and ornate script. It appeared to be a very old text on martial arts, and possibly a Japanese translation. The hand-sketched pictures were of men in stances that Temple associated with karate, although she had no idea what discipline it actually was.

All the books were about martial arts, she realized. She studied the spines and drew out one called *Innate Power*. It was a newer publication and written in English, but less about positions than philosophy.

"Whenever you consciously try to rule your life in any way," it said, "your intuition will remain silent."

It was almost indecipherably mystical, but Temple read on, fascinated. " 'Mind like the moon,' " she murmured. " 'Mind like water.' "

She wanted to know what that meant, but the tap of footsteps interrupted her. She thought they were headed her way and strained to hear them. Unsure, she stepped back, then moved into the shadows by the screen, thinking she could slip behind it if she had to. As she stood there, poised, she saw the book. She'd left it lying open on the cabinet!

Mark Challis entered the room before she could decide what to do. Not daring to breathe, she pressed back against the screen and watched him proceed to his desk. She expected him to sit down and go through some papers or pick up the telephone, in which case she could try to sneak out without being seen. Instead, he remained standing as he turned the computer on.

The monitor lit up, flipping from screen to screen as he hit different keys and typed out instructions. Oddly he never did sit down, which kept Temple poised for disaster. He could so easily turn at any second and see her there.

But he was absorbed by the monitor as it flashed a picture of a room that looked sharply familiar to Temple. Challis clicked a mouse and different views of the area appeared—the daybed, the fireplace, the trunk coffee table, and the flowers on the writing desk. It was the cottage where she was staying, she realized. These were pictures of the millhouse, but why was he looking at them?

He brought up views of every room, including the bathroom. And gradually she began to realize that these were not photographs of the cottage. A new shot appeared on the screen every few seconds. He was manipulating a live camera, or perhaps several of them. He had the cottage under surveillance, and the system was hidden in the very ceiling beams she had admired.

Apparently he'd been watching her all along, and she could only imagine what he'd seen. The thought gave her chills. It made her ill. She couldn't say he hadn't warned her, but she would never have believed it would go this far. If this was what he thought he had to do to protect her, then who was going to protect her from him? Even worse was the possibility that he might be trying to justify some secret perversion. She couldn't bring herself to imagine that he actually liked spying on women while they undressed.

A series of chimes echoed throughout the house, and Challis responded by shutting the computer down. A moment later he'd left the room, perhaps to answer the door, and Temple was alone. But far from safe. Far from calm.

Somehow she had to figure out how to get out of the house without being detected. Even if she only got as far as the cottage, it would give her some time to think how to confront him. He could watch her with surveillance cameras, but he couldn't read her mind.

"Miss Banning?"

Temple was crossing the entrance hall moments later when she heard the housekeeper call out her name. June was standing at the door to the formal dining room, wafts of delicious steam drifting from the platter she held in her hands.

"You must have heard the breakfast chimes," she said, with a surprisingly cordial smile. "I've set the big table and prepared my special mushroom cassoulet in your honor."

June seemed to have taken it for granted that Temple had come over for breakfast, and Temple knew it was smarter to play along than to try to explain what she was actually doing there.

"Thank you." She forced an answering smile, although breakfast was the last thing she wanted right now, especially if she was going to be sharing the cassoulet with Mark Challis. Her linen painter's blouse and faded Levi's weren't exactly the appropriate attire for a formal dining room, but Temple didn't see how she could refuse at this point. She didn't have much choice but to tough it out, everything considered.

To the manor born, she told herself as she breezed past June and entered the dining room. She nodded at Mark Challis as if she breakfasted at grand tables like this one on a regular basis. At least twenty feet long, it could have been hand-carved from the trunk of a massive oak. It was probably the most beautiful piece of furniture Temple had ever seen. And that was just the table. The chairs were works of art. The place settings and crystal were fringed in gold. And the shimmering lancet window behind Challis made the head of the table look like a celestial throne.

Temple went immediately to the opposite end before realizing there was no place setting there. The only other one was right next to Challis. Convenient for talking, she thought sardonically.

"Good morning," he said as she dutifully took her seat at his right hand. "Did you sleep well?"

You should know, she thought. You must have been watching me toss and turn, among other things. She wondered what the odds were that he *hadn't* been glued to the screen while she was getting ready for her bath. Quite a show she'd put on for the private investigator's edification. Almost as good as the video they'd been forced to view.

Damn him, she thought as heat flashed up the back of her neck and fanned out across her scalp. It even burned the lobes of her ears.

Fortunately, June created a distraction by serving the bubbling mushroom dish and pouring coffee which she assured Temple was decaffeinated. When the housekeeper was done, Temple took a few uneasy bites, and realized she couldn't eat until she'd resolved some things.

"I need to make some phone calls," she said. "My boss, my sister, my apartment manager." Dr. Gilchrist, she thought, aware that the call would take more explaining than she wanted to do. "And to be honest, I don't care if it breaches security. I'm in danger of losing my job, and Ivy has to know where I am so she can contact me—"

She held up a hand to silence him, in case he had any thought of interrupting her. "I also want to know what your services are costing me. I'm not wealthy. I doubt if I'd ever qualify for a loan."

"Nothing," he said, bringing her tirade to a close. "My services are costing you nothing. A deposit was made to my account last week that more than covers my fee."

"A deposit?"

"Yes, ten thousand dollars. I received an anonymous E-mail, telling me the money was to be used to ensure your safety, and when I checked my account, it was there."

"Who did it?" She stared at Mark. "Him? Michael St. Gerard?"

"Apparently he wants you safe."

So that was it, Temple thought. She had no clue as to St. Gerard's motive, but this made her wonder about Mark's. She would have thought he had plenty of money.

"As for your office," he went on. "I've already contacted them and arranged for you to be on medical leave for the rest of the month. It was no problem. They hardly needed to be told you were in danger once the story hit the papers."

Temple wanted to protest, but he'd left her at a loss. Maybe she ought to be grateful he was doing his job, but the extent to which he was invading her life was appalling.

"And, of course, you can call your sister and your apartment manager," he said. "I have a secure phone you can use. We'll take care of that at your convenience."

He picked up the thermal carafe and warmed up her coffee. "You need to eat, Temple," he cautioned, but stopped short of adding the obvious, that she was eating for two.

"Which reminds me," he said, "I'm having Dan Llewelyn flown out to the island to check on you and make sure everything's all right."

Temple couldn't speak. He'd just answered all her concerns, at least all the ones she could think of, and some before she could even voice them. If that was supposed to reassure her, it didn't. She wasn't used to having her every need anticipated. Or any need, for that matter. That had always been her job in life, and having the roles reversed on her was unnerving. At moments like this she didn't know what frightened her more, him, or the threats on her life.

She would never get used to having someone think for her, breathe for her. She didn't know how to give up that much control.

She put her fork down and steepled her hands, pressing

her fingertips to her mouth. Maybe it was that or the trembling that told him something was wrong.

"I told you how it would be," he said quietly. "You knew what my conditions were when you agreed to come here. There are things I will have to do to protect you that will feel like violations, Temple. Neither one of us has any choice in that. It's the nature of the beast."

The beast being. . . ?

She looked at him, stared hard at him, wanting to tell him that she knew what he was doing, knew about the cameras, but something held her back. Once she did they would both have to acknowledge what he'd seen, and then it would be out there, open for discussion. This might be all business to him, but it wasn't to her. She couldn't handle being that exposed right now. It was possible she might come to grips with the physical nakedness, but nothing more. The emotional nakedness she would feel was beyond her imagining.

She began to pick at her breakfast again, aware that he was still studying her. Her sense of outrage eased a little as she sorted through the cheese and egg mixture, absently looking for chunks of mushroom. Logic told her that everything he said was true. She had been warned. It had never occurred to her that *she* would be under surveillance, but it hadn't occurred to her that she would have to lie to her sister, either. Life wasn't neat or clean that way. Sometimes people were forced to do bad things for good reasons, and apparently that included Temple herself.

She couldn't taste the cassoulet, but got some of it down for the very reason he suggested. She was eating for two, although apparently, she was still in some denial about that. She didn't feel the slightest bit pregnant, except for the queasiness, and who wouldn't be queasy in her situation. She continued to wonder if it was a mistake, and if Dr.

Gilchrist would tell her it was simply a mild recurrence of the virus.

They ate in silence until she ended it with an abrupt statement. "You invited me on a tour."

"I did, but if you don't feel like going—"

"Oh, but I do," she said emphatically. "I want to go."

He looked a little perplexed, and she found that extraordinarily gratifying. She had wrested the cloak of mystery away from him, and she wasn't giving it back without a fight. He didn't need to know that in the last fifteen minutes it had begun to seem vital to know more about the island she was a virtual prisoner on. And everything she could possibly find out about him, her prison guard.

"The weather's a little iffy. We might want to wait a day or two," he suggested.

But Temple wasn't having any of that. "I'm going on the tour," she said softly, "with or without you."

"Could we stop?" Temple called out over the roaring noise of the jeep. "Please!"

Mark glanced over at her. "You okay?"

She shook her head, certain she must be chartreuse by now. "Carsick!"

They'd reached the northeastern side of the island after about a half-hour on a roughly paved road. It paralleled a ridge of majestic cliffs, and although Temple couldn't see over the side, she knew it must be a sheer drop, and the mere thought made her dizzy.

Mark pulled over, letting the engine idle as he came around to help her down. Temple was unsteady enough to be grateful for the aid, but once she was on the ground, she eased away from him. She didn't want a repeat of the helicopter episode.

"Do you want to sit down?" he asked. "I've got a fold-up chair in the back."

"I'm queasy," she said with a certain amount of irony, "*not* at death's door. I'd like to walk."

She started toward the cliffs, but he caught her by the arm and gently tugged her back. "Wait a minute," he said firmly. "I'll turn off the engine and come with you. The cliffs are steep, and it's easy to lose your balance."

She'd just caught a glimpse of some jutting reefs offshore when suddenly he was back and taking her by the elbow.

"Why are you treating me like an invalid?" she asked him as they made their way through the rocks and underbrush. The winds were brisk, but they carried the primal smells of salt and plankton, and Temple drank them in. Somehow she had known the sea air would help.

"You said you had morning sickness."

"I said I was *car*sick."

"Same thing."

"No, it isn't," she insisted. "One is caused by motion, the other is caused by—"

"By what?" he asked.

"Pregnancy," she said through gritted teeth.

She tried to get around him, but he blocked the way. "Why was that so hard to say, Temple?"

"I thought we were taking a walk," she snapped.

"You know what?" He moved again to stop her. "You could make my job a lot easier. You could quit denying what's happened to you, including the pregnancy."

"And you could back off," she said, "and let me deal with my 'condition' in my own way, thank you."

She pushed around him and he let her go this time.

She was annoyed with him, to be sure, but the moment she got to the ledge, she turned around and grabbed his hand, glad he'd followed her.

"Oh, my God," she whispered. She'd never seen such a dizzying drop. They were perhaps thirty feet high. But it wasn't the cliffs. It was the ocean. The water was so crystal clear, she could see forever. Fathoms. Leagues. Or however they measured ocean depth.

"What are those, fish?" she asked. She was pointing to a bright orange school that Mark explained were girabaldis, California's state fish.

"And those are calico bass," he said, drawing her attention to several vibrant amber and black clusters. "The yellow and gold tentacles are actually kelp, and the green stuff on the bottom is eel grass."

"How deep is the water?" she asked.

"The visibility is about eighty feet."

Temple was still marveling at the sight when he pointed out that the wind had picked up and clouds had begun to roil in from the west.

"We should get going," he said. "It looks like rain, and the jeep doesn't have a top."

Temple shivered, but she was reluctant to leave. This ocean seemed willing to reveal all its secrets to her, everything the nautilus shell was holding back. Maybe it would tell her what it was whispering.

"Look, Mark!" Temple pointed to the reefs beyond the kelp beds. Hidden in the fluttering boas of green and gold was the decaying hull and mast of a small boat. Apparently a sailboat of some kind had crashed on the reefs.

"What is that? A sunken boat?" She turned to Mark and what she saw frightened her. The skin had pulled taut over the bones of his face, and his expression had changed to one of grim death.

"What is it?" she asked.

The sky went dark as she stared at him, and the wind turned bitterly cold.

"What's wrong?" she whispered, becoming aware that he couldn't hear her. It began to rain, but still he wouldn't move. He seemed horrified at the sight of the boat.

The sky lit up with a jagged branch of chain lightning.

Thunder cracked and the sprinkle turned into a downpour. The rain actually hurt it was pounding so hard, but Temple couldn't get him to move. The wind was gusting so powerfully, she was afraid they would be blown off the cliffs.

"Mark?" she cried. "It's pouring. We have to get out of the storm. Mark? *Please!*"

FOURTEEN

"Look out!" Temple cried.

A tree branch cartwheeled past them, driven by the wind. Lightning struck again, with such force the smell of ozone rose like steam.

Mark's head whipped around. He looked right at her, stared at her sharply, and this time he saw her. His features flared with recognition, and he flew into action.

"Jesus—" He dragged her into his arms to shelter her. "Let's get you out of here."

The storm was so severe it was a struggle to get to the car. The wind raged, blinding Temple. She couldn't see, couldn't walk against the block wall of its force, even with Mark's help.

"Hang on to me!"

He bent over double, and Temple braced herself as he picked her up. His strength was astounding. He had arms like stanchions. His muscles cut into her they were so hard. But the wind and rain were ferocious. She didn't know how he was able to carry her when it took all her strength just to hang on.

The storm did its best to rip them apart. Temple had never felt such rending force, even in the tornadoes down South. She sealed her body to his, burrowing like an animal, and when her arms began to ache, she ringed them tighter.

She heard a snarl of rage and knew it was him, in a battle against the elements. His body shuddered violently, and his arms nearly crushed her as he stumbled.

Dear God, they weren't going to make it.

"Hang on," he got out.

She nodded, knowing he couldn't hear her whisper, *"I will."*

But her strength was beginning to ebb. The terrain was rough, and the storm furious. He tripped again, and Temple was gripped by fear. He was blinded. Whatever forces strived to tear them apart were winning.

"Put me down," she pleaded. "Let me walk."

She shouted at him, but he couldn't hear her. He kept on going, heading doggedly into the storm. But there was something different about the way he moved now. He'd bowed his head and gone utterly silent. The snarling noises had stopped. He seemed barely to be breathing. It was as if he'd transformed into some force stronger than the wind. She could feel the change in him. He was moving easier now, as naturally as if the storm were at his heels, almost running with her in his arms.

Temple's face was hidden in his jacket, but she was aware that the rain had stopped battering at them like fists. Suddenly it was calm, like a boat entering a protected harbor.

She didn't realize he hadn't carried her to the car until her feet touched something solid. His jaw was set in a grimace as he put her down on the floor of a stone building. It was tiny, the size of a closet, and there was no door. The gale was howling around them, but it couldn't penetrate the walls.

They'd beaten it. They'd won. Temple's shudder of relief bent her forward.

He saw the emotion and pulled her close. "Are you okay?" he asked.

She couldn't stop shivering. "What is this place?"

"It's a stone lean-to made by the early Indian settlers. Their version of a storm cellar, but above ground."

"We're lucky it was here. What a gale."

"A westerly," he said, still fighting to catch his breath. "They blow up this time of year, but they don't last long."

She was soaked through to the skin and shaking uncontrollably. He'd given her a lightweight jacket for the trip, but it wasn't waterproof and as he helped her get out of it, the sodden condition of her linen blouse was obvious to both of them.

"You're going to need something dry." He shucked his own jacket and pulled a cableknit fisherman's sweater over his head. "Here—"

The sweater was fresh from the heat of his body, and she reveled in its warmth. But as she clutched it to her chest, another shudder racked her, and this one was painful.

"It won't do you any good unless you get out of that blouse first," he told her.

She was too chilled to protest, but her fingers weren't steady enough to get the buttons undone. She fumbled and gave up in frustration.

"Should I look the other way?" he asked.

"No, I want you to do it."

"Do what?"

"Unbutton my blouse." She met his gaze and saw the mix of emotions. He was searching her face, hotly curious, but Temple wasn't in the mood to mince words. "What's wrong? It's not as if you haven't seen me naked."

Now he was tilting back, all dark, suspicious eyes. "What do you mean?"

"Well, you have, right?" She wanted him to say it, admit it. But he wouldn't. And she didn't have the strength to out-wait him. Her teeth had begun to chatter. She grabbed for the sweater, but he yanked it back.

"You said I'd seen you naked, Temple. What did you mean?"

"Dammit, Mark!"

"Come here," he half-growled. He yanked her close, tipped up her chin, and began to work on the first button. The wet material was a challenge, even for him. The tiny buttons were locked like gems in settings, but finally he had the top one free.

The second was even more stubborn, and by the third button he'd reached her breasts. "Hell, this could take forever. Maybe you should slip the sweater on over your blouse."

"You're the one who told me to take it off!"

"All right," he said, his voice going strangely harsh. "I'll get you out of this blouse, but first, let's get one thing clear. I *have* seen what's under it. I won't apologize for that be-cause it's my job, but I will apologize for not telling you."

"Why didn't you tell me?"

"I don't know."

She stared at him in surprise. That was quite an admission for The Man With All the Answers, especially the way he was towering above her and glowering at her, his hair black with rain and wildly blown.

She was aware of the hot throb in her voice as she said, "Are you going to stop?"

"Watching you? Not a chance."

If he wanted her to believe it was his sworn duty to keep her under surveillance around the clock, and that's the only reason he was doing it, he wasn't terribly convincing. The huskiness in his voice made Temple feel as if she couldn't breathe.

Nor could she look at him. Their eyes were too hot. There

was too much electricity between them. And worse, her nemesis had returned—that terrible little quiver in the pit of her stomach. But it was more than that, it was an indiscernible cry for help from within, and somehow Temple had no idea how to answer it.

"All right, let's get this done, dammit." He rubbed his hands as if to warm them and make them more accurate, a bomb-squad veteran.

Temple stepped back and took herself out of his range. Now she couldn't let him do it! Another button and he would have exposed her bra. But that wasn't the problem. She didn't care what he saw at this point. She just couldn't bear what was happening inside her.

"Now what's wrong?" he asked.

Everything about this situation was wrong. And whatever was wrong with her, specifically, she wished to God it would stop. The electricity, the quivers, the cries from within, all of it. Nothing about that related to the Temple Banning she knew and understood, from the storm outside to the storm inside. *She didn't like being pregnant.* Not if it was going to make her this sappy and emotional.

"Just give me the sweater," she said.

But his shoulders had come up and his head had come down. She could almost hear the hot breath that shot through his nostrils.

"Shut your eyes," he said.

"Why?"

"Just do it. *Now.*"

Her lids closed, and she felt him grip the placket and rip. The indomitable little mother-of-pearl buttons exploded like popcorn. They flew every which way. She heard fabric tear and wondered if the blouse was salvageable. But mostly she was glad he didn't peel the garment from her body like skin. Instead he dropped his sweater over her head and pulled it down to her chin, leaving her a tent under which to finish the job.

"You're on your own," he said, clearing his throat of its scratchiness.

"Yeah, thanks," she replied, tossing the sodden fabric on the floor. Talk about a mess, she thought, meaning more than the wet clothes. It was one thing for him to be watching her from a distance, with what was undoubtedly a certain amount of professional detachment. It was quite another for him to undress her in this tiny space, where emotion was swirling around them like the storm outside. It was impossible, and they'd both realized it, him sooner than she. What Temple didn't understand was why. What was this storm between her and Mark Challis?

Maybe her eyes asked that question, but he didn't answer it. He was all business again as he draped his jacket around her, and then went about picking up the wet clothes. It was just as if nothing had happened, and Temple didn't know what to make of that, unless he was feeling the way she was. She ought to have been grateful, of course, but that was never the way it worked.

She walked to the shelter's opening and looked out. The rain had nearly stopped, and the wind was dying down. The storm was over, and she felt disappointment and confusion.

"You were right about the westerly," she said.

He moved past her and ventured outside. The horizon was clearing of clouds, and there was even a hint of a rainbow. "I think it's safe to start back now." He turned to her. "If you're up to the drive."

Temple assured him she was. She might be a rehab candidate emotionally, but at least she was warm and dry and, more important, standing on her own.

As it turned out the jeep was not that far away. If they'd continued down the road fifty more feet and rounded a gentle curve, she would have seen their stone shelter, standing near a hodgepodge of gnarled pine trees.

It took a little work to get the jeep seaworthy again. The storm had littered it with debris and the bucket seats were full of water, but Temple was glad to be distracted. There was so much she didn't understand, and this crisis had only added to the turmoil that was her life. She insisted on helping him bail water, and afterward, while he finished clearing debris, she dried the seats with rags he kept in the trunk.

By the time they were done, and the car was ready to go, the sun was peeking through the clouds, and the rainbow was in full arc. Temple, who didn't believe in signs, was nevertheless, emboldened. She gave in to her curiosity and asked what seemed like a very dangerous question.

"Do you know whose boat crashed on the reef?"

He looked up and all but slammed into her with his eyes. It felt as if the wind had whipped up again, and Temple had been hit by a gale-force gust. The block wall of the westerly had not been as impenetrable as this man, she thought.

She said nothing more. The question was as dead as if she'd never asked it. They stood across the car from each other, separated by a small, but seemingly unbridgeable space. He looked so icy and imperturbable, so back in charge, he might as well have been miles away, she thought.

The trip back was equally quiet, which left Temple's mind free to get annoyingly noisy. She really didn't want to dwell on what had just happened. She had more than enough on her own plate, but her jangled nerves wouldn't leave it alone. There were many questions she wanted to ask, but given what had happened, only one that seemed safe.

She waited until they were close to the house to ask it.

"Something happened while you were carrying me," she said. "I didn't think we were going to make it, but you seemed to get a second wind."

"It's an Aikido principle," he said, seeming to know exactly what she meant. "When you know you can't win, the key is to stop fighting and embrace your opponent, which in this case was the storm. If you embrace him without hatred, you can use his energy."

"Really?"

"The only thought on my mind when the storm hit was making sure you were safe. I forgot all about that principle, but it does work."

Temple wanted to hear more about his need to make her safe, but she already knew where that path led. He would not say what she wanted to hear. He would answer her as if he were the investigator and she were his client. And, of course, that was true. She was.

"Check out our hills," he said, pointing toward a fiery range of peaks in the distance.

Where Temple was from they would have called them mountains, but she was impressed with the carpet of brilliant orange flowers that blanketed the slopes. She'd never seen anything quite so vibrant. It was bright enough to be seen from the mainland, she was sure.

"Sea dahlias," he said, anticipating her question about the flowers. "They only bloom like this in early spring. In the fall they lose their leaves and turn into gnarled black skeletons. It's an eerie sight to see the mountains transformed into a forest of witches' fingers."

"I imagine it is," she said, still entranced by the fiery display. "But right now I can't decide what's more beautiful, those mountains, the lush green canyons, or the sea cliffs we just came from."

Everywhere she looked there were meadows of wildflowers, clusters of trees, and rolling valleys that seemed swallowed by dark ravines. Here and there little wells of water oozed out of the ground, forming streamlets that fed the greenery. She'd also caught glimpses of wildlife darting about.

"What you're looking at is the interior of the island," he said, nodding toward a gorge that looked verdant enough to be a rain forest. "It's beautiful, but that's the one area you should avoid."

"Why is that?"

"Let's just say it's for security reasons." He gave her a penetrating look, as if he wanted her to respond.

"No problem," she said. "Consider it avoided."

By the time they'd rounded the point and the house had come into sight, Temple was thinking how much the island reminded her of him. Like the proud, isolated body of land, he seemed a force unto himself, solitary and shaped from harsh circumstances. He wasn't dependent on anyone, frightened of anything. His strength seemed to come from some inner source. She admired that, and wondered how much of it came from his martial-arts training.

"Can anyone learn Aikido?" she asked. "Because I think I'd like to."

"Are you sure?" He looked at her, frowning as she nodded. "Aikido isn't about combat. It's not a way of fighting. It's a way of life. It will change you."

Something quickened inside Temple. Perhaps she was responding to the quiet authority in his voice. It almost sounded like a warning. Or maybe she wanted what he was offering, change. "I'm sure."

"All right, then," he said. "I'm going into the city today. I have an appointment at the office. But we can start tonight, when I get back."

And meanwhile, she wondered, would he be watching her at any point? On the glowing landscape of his computer screen? For her own protection, of course. And if he was, would he be as totally in command of himself as he appeared to be at this moment? She wanted to think not, but something told her a man like Mark Challis had crossover tracks for emotions. He had the ability to switch lines with the ease of a train conductor.

What a gift, she thought, to be able to switch off the fine trembling that was still alive inside her.

An update on Michael St. Gerard awaited Mark when he arrived at his office that afternoon. According to the new investigator, St. Gerard was not in the system. All standard inquiries had led to a dead end. He'd used a credit card at the Montmarte, but that was the first and only time the card had been activated. The man didn't exist, and Mark wasn't surprised.

Paul, his assistant of nearly a dozen years, had just brewed a fresh pot of lemongrass tea in the infuser and brought him a cup. He blew the steam off the top and took a careful sip. It was scalding, hot enough to burn the taste buds. But Mark had become addicted to its bittersweet flavor and relaxing effects. Lemongrass could quiet and sharpen the mind at the same time, unless you drank too much, of course, and then it became a hallucinogen.

But there was more information in the update, and Mark set the tea down to cool. His investigator had done a background check on Dr. Donald Kent, Temple's ex-fiancé, and the most interesting reference had to do with the doctor's whereabouts when the attacks on the "Amnesia Assault" victims, as the press was calling them, took place.

Kent was in Southern California at a medical conference when the first assault was committed. And he was in Vegas at an ob-gyn seminar just prior to the second. His whereabouts at the time of the third hadn't been verified. But Kent was not an ob-gyn, Mark noted, although he probably had to deliver babies in his general practice.

Mark picked up the phone and tapped out the investigator's extension. He got voice mail and left instructions for him to initiate a deep background check on St. Gerard and continue the investigation of Kent, including his finances. There were indications that Kent was heavily in debt.

When Mark had finished with the instructions, he turned to his laptop and brought up his E-mail. He only had a few minutes before his appointment arrived, not enough time to go through everything in his queue. He quickly scanned the addresses and opened a letter with an attached file from one of his subcontractors, a retired homicide detective with active law-enforcement contacts.

What Mark pulled up on the screen was a pirated copy of the Ventura Police Department's Scientific Investigation Division report. It confirmed that no fingerprints were found on Temple's car, and the explosives were wired into the ignition.

Mark settled back in his chair and picked up his mug, holding it near enough to his mouth to draw on the fragrant steam. He studied the report, curious at his reaction. He should have felt something, but he didn't. He was as detached as if it had happened to someone else's car. It could have been a case he knew nothing about, a statistic. Maybe that should have reassured him. This morning he'd lost it for a moment or two. Foolish mistakes like that could get someone killed.

He rose and walked to the windows, the mug resting in his curled fingers, burning the tips. He stared out at the bright, hazy cityscape, but his focus was inward. His thoughts were still on the explosion, still detached. He was familiar with just about every type of homicide known to man. But in his opinion this was the perfect way to kill. Whoever expected to turn the key of his car and die? There was no way to safeguard against it.

"Mr. Challis, Ms. Diane Bradley is here."

It was his assistant on the intercom. "Send her in, Paul," he said, reluctant to relinquish this odd, quiet mood he was in. By the time he got to his chair, an attractive fortyish woman had entered his office.

"Come in and sit down." He beckoned her to the chair that faced his desk, noting her tailored pantsuit and precisely cut brunette bob. It fell toward her face and swung when she walked. For the most part, she looked like any other reasonably conservative, college-educated working woman who might have a job in the building.

"Anything I can get you?" he asked as she sat down. "Coffee? Tea?" He held up his steaming cup. "It's hot."

"No, thanks." Her smile was etched with worry. She didn't want tea and sympathy. Like so many of the people who walked through his door, she wanted to get right to the point.

He already knew who she was—one of the three women assaulted in the most bizarre serial crime wave he could remember in a long time. But he'd only read the newspaper accounts, and he wanted the details in her own words. Her phrasing and body language would tell him a lot, probably more than she would.

She needed little encouragement. Within moments, she'd spilled it all out.

"I'm not a kook like the police have implied, Mr. Challis," she told him. "I'm a systems analyst, a divorced mother of two, and I didn't make this story up. It happened to me."

He tried feeding back to her what she'd told him. "Someone abducted you, drugged you, and perhaps even performed some kind of medical procedure on you, but you recall nothing?"

"That's right. I know how it sounds, but it's true. And according to the doctor who examined me afterward, whoever did it may have used a speculum and taken some vaginal tissue, perhaps for a biopsy."

She was not just defensive, she was concise and specific about it. That was good. Crazy people weren't.

"Are you pregnant?" he asked.

She looked startled. "I have two grown children in college," she informed him. "In fact I was at a women's clinic just the week before the assault. I'd missed a couple of periods, but I'm not involved with anyone, so I knew I couldn't be pregnant. Turns out I'm premenopausal. They put me on hormones."

She told him which clinic, readily answered the rest of his questions, and then asked if he would take her case. It was only when he hesitated that she became rattled.

"Mr. Challis, how can I convince you to help me? I was told you were the best, but that you rarely took on individual clients."

"That's true, Ms. Bradley, I don't—"

She nearly rose from the chair. "Wait, hear me out. I'm certain the police are on the wrong track, and I want to know who attacked me and why. Someone drugged and violated me. He robbed me of my mind, my memory, and my very will to defend myself. But the worst of it is that no one believes me."

"I do, Ms. Bradley," he assured her in a quiet voice. "I believe you."

There was something about the assault victim who sat opposite him that made him think of another woman in his life, the lovely, brown-eyed mother he lost as a teenager. Maybe it was the dark, shiny hair and the graceful tilt of Diane Bradley's eyes, dulled as they were by worry. He imagined they were bright when she wasn't besieged by fears. He wondered if his mother's had ever been bright.

"Will you take my case, then?" she asked.

He told her he would, and she sprang out of the chair, as if to embrace him. Something stopped her, perhaps his sudden distant expression. He didn't get close to his clients. Emotional involvement of any kind was never a good policy, and he'd already made that mistake once today.

"Thank you," she said, clutching her hands and obviously close to tears.

He walked her out to Paul's area, so his assistant could explain the agency's policies and procedures. People who needed investigators were rarely in a good place in their lives, and Mark relied heavily on Paul's nurturing abilities to deal with their emotional distress. Paul was terrific at reassuring the clients, especially after Mark had unnerved them.

Once he was back in his office, he went through everything he'd been sent by research on the case. The three victims appeared dissimilar in almost every way, except their gender and their claims of temporary amnesia. They ranged from an eighteen-year-old English major to Mark's client at forty-six. And because of the discrepancies, the police had ruled out the possibility that they were linked.

He picked up his tea and settled back to think. By this time the mug had cooled, but the infusion was still warm and richly perfumed with lemongrass. As he drank the tea and contemplated the case, he realized that he agreed with his new client. The police were on the wrong track. Mark was appalled at their lack of imagination.

FIFTEEN

Temple had been waiting for this moment. Finally she had the entire house to herself. June had retired to her room after lunch, perhaps to read. Temple couldn't imagine the prickly little housekeeper letting her guard down long enough to nap. But at least she was out of the way, and the rest of the staff were off somewhere, probably busy with their various chores.

It felt strange not to be busy herself. Her frantic schedule at Blue Sky had made time a precious commodity. Nearly every waking moment had been consumed by work. She wondered if her team had been assigned a new account and how they were doing. Denny Paxton was the obvious choice to run things while she was gone, and Temple had mixed feelings about that. Interesting that her situation couldn't have worked out better for him than if he'd engineered it himself.

Temple caught her own frown in one of the hallway mirrors. She couldn't imagine anyone going to all that trouble just to get her out of the way, even Paxton. She hadn't yet spoken to anyone at work. The explosion and Annette's death were too fresh in her mind. And maybe it was naive, but she still held to the theory that she'd been confused with someone else, and when Mark got to the truth, she could return to a normal life, and her job.

Meanwhile she'd called Ivy and explained that she'd been given an account requiring travel, but would be in touch regularly. She'd left a similar message for Shirley, and one for Dr. Susan Gilchrist, who was on assignment herself, doing field work, according to the receptionist at the Centers for Disease Control. Temple had left the last two her home number and told them she would be calling there to pick up messages.

The simple act of leaving messages was reassuring, she'd realized as she'd hung up the phone, but it had also brought home how isolated she was, and how at loose ends. She couldn't remember being faced with such a vast amount of unstructured time, certainly not under circumstances like these.

Even now she wasn't quite sure where to start her explorations in the huge house. She'd changed into jeans and a wool cardigan after the storm that morning. But the air seemed to carry a chill, so she snugged the sweater around her and pulled the sleeves to her wrists. A shiver brought goose bumps. She wouldn't have felt warm with a parka, she realized, but it had little to do with the weather. This was about curiosity and perhaps some trepidation.

Still, she enjoyed the wanderings of her imagination as she explored rooms that brought the past alive. The house was a nearly exact replica of a restored seventeenth-century castle, with a fireplace as the focal point of almost every room. The main drawing room's blaze was enclosed in an engraved crystal screen and topped by a mantel of imported

English mahogany. But the library's magnificent stone open-hearth fire was Temple's favorite.

Today the oozing logs burned rich and apricot-yellow, as succulent as ripening fruit in a bowl. She enjoyed the crackling warmth and the plumes of apple-scented smoke as she wandered through the bookshelves, admiring the leather-bound first editions. When she'd browsed her fill, she returned to the main hall to have a look at the art collection displayed in its low-lit niches. There were classical figures, Italian urns and Japanese cloisonné vases.

Caught in a late-afternoon lull, the house might have seemed hushed to anyone else, but Temple was just beginning to realize that she had always been able to hear, or was it sense, what others couldn't, like the voice inside the shell.

Yesterday in the conservatory there'd been the feeling that she was supposed to be there. The room had seemed to reach out and touch her. But this was different. Today it felt as if the house were watching her . . . and waiting for something. It was all around her, a vibration in the air, like music the ear couldn't quite register. There was a sense of expectancy, but she wasn't causing it. She was responding.

She'd meant to avoid the dining room where they had breakfast, but the door was closed, and curiosity got the best of her. She entered to sun slanting through the windows at an angle that sheened the long table and turned it into a slice of gold. It brought to mind the morning she'd been seated at his elbow, and easily within touching distance of him. Vividly brought it to mind. She could almost hear echoes of their conversation and feel the sharpening tension.

She didn't linger in the room. She didn't like the conflict that rose inside her, or the feelings she wanted very much to avoid. She could remember thinking once that she had special receptors for his voice, but it was more than that, she realized. It was his presence, even in the lack of it, his essence. Now the awareness was so strong it was electrical, painful.

"No," she said under her breath.

No, it was not possible that she was getting involved—not with a man like him, and not in a mess like this. He was a cobra. He had no emotion. And she had nothing but. A quaking titmouse. He would have her for lunch. He'd almost had her for breakfast. Besides, the situation was already hopelessly complicated and to make it worse would be reckless. She didn't act in that manner. She wasn't reckless.

Temple lectured herself with the conviction of a woman who'd been both self-sufficient and self-reliant for better than half of her thirty years. She was *not* getting involved. And if that wasn't true, she would make it true. She might be at the mercy of her hormones. She might even be trapped on an island with him, but that didn't make her incapable of rational decisions about her life choices and he wasn't going to be one of them.

Limestone tiles scraped beneath her feet as she turned and refocused on her mission to scope out the house. This was not a travel agency's fabulous island adventure. She was here because someone was trying to kill her. If she could keep her mind on the physical danger she was in, she might have a chance of escaping the emotional.

Her immediate choices were the front parlor, the kitchen, or the butler's pantry, but the main drawing room was directly in front of her, and none of the other rooms interested her the way it did.

The Baroque arches that fanned above her head had a Moorish quality. They formed a gateway as she descended a short flight of stairs to a spacious sunken chamber. The pink marble fireplace at one end was graced by palms, Oriental screens, and conversation pieces. At the other end a grand piano sat on a pedestal, presiding over a circle of woven cane chairs. And in between spanned a wall of French doors.

She was struck by the room's quiet majesty, but a sound made her stop at the bottom of the stairs. She hesitated, listening. This time she *had* heard something. It wasn't her imagination. It resembled the chimes that announced breakfast, except that these were lower, soft, and melodic. She wondered if it was music. She couldn't tell where it was coming from, but intuition drew her across the room, toward the French doors.

Throughout the house, the doors were framed with leaded-glass panels, the most beautiful of which were right here in this room. They led to a brick terrace, bordered by fruit trees and flowers, and looming above the gardens was a medieval clock tower, several stories tall, each floor ringed by paladian windows with small square panes.

Temple crossed the terrace, fascinated by the octagonal structure. She'd been curious about it since she noticed it from the helicopter when they flew in. But the house, with all of its wide-spread wings, was something of a maze, and if it hadn't been for the music, she might never have found her way here.

The tower didn't seem to be structurally connected to the house, but she couldn't see an outside entrance either. It appeared to be all windows, but the panes were clouded over. Temple couldn't tell if it was dust or some kind of frosting process as she moved from window to window, scratching lightly on the panes. She was trying to form a peekhole when she heard a creak and felt something give.

The window she'd just touched was actually a door.

It parted a sliver, then opened wider when she applied more pressure. Temple's heart changed rhythm as she peered inside. The interior resembled a small rotunda. It was empty of furniture, except for a great white iron staircase and a maze of tubular piping that looked more like a ventilation system than plumbing.

The room was surprisingly clean for what appeared to be an abandoned structure. Surgically clean, Temple thought as she stepped inside. How odd. The floors were laid with luminous white tile, and the walls were lined with a translucent material that gave the windows their frosted effect.

This could be the stairway to heaven, Temple thought ironically. What had she stumbled upon?

She moved closer and glanced up the first flight, thinking she'd heard the music again. Celestial bells? Or perhaps it was someone whispering. It did sound like soft voices coming from above. She heard a sigh, a moan, a rush of indrawn breath. And then another moan, so low it was barely discernible.

Dear God, she thought. Someone was up there, making noises and doing something that sounded . . . intimate. She shouldn't be eavesdropping, but some horrible fascination held her in place. The moaning was so low and guttural it was hard not to imagine two lovers trysting in a tower room. Hard not to imagine hot flesh-colored bodies and ice-white sheets.

She went very still, waiting, telling herself to go. And then suddenly everything was quiet again, and her curiosity mounted. She was torn, certain she ought to leave. But finally, after several seconds of indecision, she began to make her way up the steps, thinking she might have misinterpreted the sounds. Someone could be injured.

The first landing took her to another flight, where the width of the stairway narrowed and the rake steepened. It wasn't a traditional spiral staircase, but Temple felt a little dizzy, perhaps because of her condition. She held on to the railing to steady herself. But before she'd taken the next step, a shadow fell across her path.

"What are you doing here?" a voice gasped.

Temple nearly tumbled over backward. She lost her grip on the railing and snagged a balustrade to hold herself. She couldn't see anything but the blinding white steps in front of her, but she'd caught a glimpse of someone on the landing above her, a terrifying figure in dark robes.

"What are you doing here? Answer me!"

Temple couldn't answer. She couldn't breathe, but she recognized the small, shrill voice. It was June, the housekeeper. She had flown at Temple out of nowhere, like a rabid bat, and when Temple was finally able to look up, she understood why she'd been frightened. Hovering just above her, June looked demented. Her mouth snarled with anger, her eyes were hot and wild.

"What's wrong?" Temple asked.

"This tower is condemned," the housekeeper warned. "You should not be here. The stairs aren't safe."

Temple didn't understand. She couldn't stop shaking. "But you're standing on them."

"I weigh nothing, and I know my way around. It's not safe. I'm telling you, the stairs *won't* hold you."

Temple thought better of arguing in the face of June's piercing stare. She simply nodded and began to make her way back down.

"You must never come here again!" June called after her.

Temple picked up the pace, anxious to escape, but her silence seemed to provoke the other woman. When she didn't answer, June's pitch rose to a near scream.

"You should not have come to this island! It isn't safe. There are poisonous serpents everywhere. Do you understand me? Snakes!"

"Snakes?" What was she talking about? Temple turned, but the question locked up in her throat. This crazy old woman with the gleaming yellow eyes was the snake, she thought. Never in her life had she seen such venom as was dripping from the tiny, wiry features above her. Before Temple could look away, June emitted a low hiss of rage that frightened Temple to her core and sent her flying down the steps.

• • •

"Oh, Eddie, it's you! I thought it was Mr. Challis."

"Sorry, ma'am." The handyman shuffled in the doorway of Mark's office. "Didn't mean to frighten you."

"It's all right." Temple gave him a reassuring smile. She'd been waiting for Mark in his office, and she'd glanced up to see Eddie peeking in from the hallway. The handyman looked as startled as she was, and Temple was afraid he might bolt.

"Do you know where Mr. Challis is?" she asked. "I heard the helicopter come in awhile ago. We had an appointment this evening."

"Well, ma'am," Eddie said. "I think he's still down in the basement."

"Basement?" Temple hadn't known there was one. "What's he doing there?"

"I wouldn't know, ma'am." Eddie's voice faded as he inched away from the door.

"Wait," Temple called to him. But by the time she got to the doorway, there was nothing left of the handyman but the faint fragrance of roses. He must have been working in the gardens that day, she realized. But the darkness of the hallway had swallowed him up.

She peered into the gloom, hands on her hips and shaking her head. Someone needed to speak to Mark about his household staff. June had frightened her badly today, and all she wanted Eddie to do was let Mark know she was waiting. Apparently she would have to do that herself, but she had no idea where the basement was.

The clock on the fireplace mantel said it wasn't quite six yet. Perhaps not officially evening, but she was anxious to hear if Mark had learned anything about Michael St. Gerard, or about what happened the night her car exploded.

Temple's thoughts turned inevitably to Annette, and the familiar sadness that gripped her was tinged with guilt and frustration. Her friend had died and there was nothing Temple could do about it. Nothing except this, *hide*.

That sense of helplessness was one of the reasons Temple hadn't allowed herself to dwell on the tragedy. It was like a chronic, untreatable injury. The inability to fix it seemed to contribute to the pain. But as she thought about that night now—and let her mind move backward to the other incidents—she wondered about the coincidence of Annette's having been there.

Her friend was the only connection Temple could see in all of this. She'd had the snapshot of the man who could be Michael, she knew Mark Challis, and she'd been with Temple during two of the three attempts on her life. But the last one had taken Annette's life, Temple acknowledged, which probably meant that it *was* coincidental.

Or that someone had wanted to be rid of her, too—

Gooseflesh rippled Temple's arms. The hall was drafty. The whole damn house was drafty. She'd dressed lightly on purpose, in workout shorts and a tee, in case the Aikido lesson Mark had promised involved some martial-arts moves. But the cold wasn't to blame. She simply couldn't go where her thoughts were taking her. It was still beyond her ability to comprehend anything so terrifying as someone wanting to kill her, much less one of her friends. It couldn't be that. There had to be some other explanation, *one that made sense.*

"The basement," she said, orienting herself.

She hadn't noticed any stairways to lower floors earlier today, but she did remember a little alcove in the corridor that led to the observation deck. They'd passed it when June was leading the way to the guest cottage.

Fortunately it only took her moments to get back there, but it wasn't stairs that were tucked away in the alcove. It was an elevator car. The old-fashioned lift had a lever handle and iron grillwork that disappeared in its accordion folds

when you opened the door. It didn't look at all safe, but
Temple boarded anyway, bolted the door, and cranked the
handle in the direction that said DOWN.

It was a slow, jolting trip, and the bar wouldn't budge
when the car finally hit bottom. For a moment Temple
thought the door was jammed, but when she turned around,
she saw that the other side was grillwork, too.

This was the exit, she realized, startled.

Beyond the loops and scrolls was one of the loveliest
sights she'd ever seen. A subterranean swimming pool,
made of turquoise marble and jeweled mosaics. The pavilion that housed the pool was bathed in a nocturnal blue
glow. Peering out from the car, she could see a colonnaded
lounging area at the far end, with chaises, low tables, and
chairs. At the end closest to her was statuary that made her
think of a Roman basilica.

She rolled back the door and stepped out, aware of how
still the water was. Not a ripple in its Olympian length. The
air was cool, but the steam coming off the surface told her
the pool was heated. She gazed in wonder at the alabaster
statues and the celestial mural painted on the ceiling.

Just the day before she'd been taken with the crazy notion
that she was giving up her soul to this house. Now she was
beginning to understand how that could be possible. It was
paradise. The cool blue silence was as calming as a dream of
water.

She was still caught up in the feeling when a sharp crack
sounded. It ricocheted around the pavilion with such speed,
Temple couldn't tell where it had come from. She thought it
was a gun. Or a diver hitting the water like a bullet. But it
was exactly the opposite, she realized.

A swimmer had come up from the depths. He broke the
surface the way a geyser blows under pressure.

Temple saw it happen. Unless she was still dreaming.

She watched him come out of the water with his arms at

his sides, then rise up, catch the rim of the pool and heave his entire body out of the water. A guttural sound forced out of him as he propelled himself into the air and landed on his feet in a cloud of steam.

Water sluiced down his torso, covering him like a hot, shimmering veil. Temple couldn't take her eyes away. Nothing specific could be seen in the way of body parts, but she had the instant impression that he was naked. *Naked.*

What she could see was contour, the gleaming limbs that had driven him through the water, the long arms and legs, the wedge of shoulder and waist. All of that was discernible through the veil. And it should have been enough to tell her that she was dealing with a man in his natural state. But some subliminal awareness in her brain urgently wanted to fill in the blanks.

It was a moment before she realized that the water had stopped sluicing and the steam had cooled. Before she realized that he'd seen her and was staring at her as if he were waiting for her to speak.

"Lost?" he asked when she said nothing.

"Not anymore."

"Maybe you should be."

His voice echoed strangely in the pavilion. It sounded unreal, but Temple knew she wasn't dreaming now. None of this was a dream. She couldn't be that lucky.

"I need to talk to you," she said, composing her voice. "It's urgent."

"Urgent? In that case, talk to me."

"Here?" Her quick head shake came off as a shiver.

"Are you cold?"

"No! But you must be freezing." She glanced down and let out a despairing sigh. "Or not."

The blanks had been filled in to overflowing. And she couldn't do this. She couldn't have a serious conversation with a naked man.

To his credit he never openly smiled, but she caught the flicker of irony in his expression as he registered her reaction. If he felt awkward, he did a good job of concealing it as he retrieved a plush white terry bath sheet from the chaise nearest him and knotted it around his hips.

"Better?" he asked.

Another shiver, this one meant to be a nod. "Anything on Michael St. Gerard?" she asked.

"Nothing, which was exactly what I expected."

Temple couldn't hide her disappointment. Her voice actually cracked as she said, "I don't understand."

"There's no evidence he exists beyond the night of March fifth. The credit card he used was only activated that one time. Michael St. Gerard is an alias, and the man using it knows how to disappear. That will make him very hard to find."

He undid a corner of the bath sheet and lifted it to his face to catch the water dripping from his hair. With a roll of his head, he patted down his neck and shoulders.

"I'm sorry," he said. "Was there something else?"

"Well, just that June was acting strangely today. She insists that the island isn't safe and she warned me about snakes."

"June is dramatic," he said dismissively. "Sometimes too dramatic for her own good."

Apparently he wasn't concerned, although Temple questioned why he'd put up with such bizarre behavior in an employee. Her chest was still tight with disappointment over the news about St. Gerard, but at the same time, she was aware of a reluctant fascination with what Mark was doing. She'd meant to ask what his next move was, but considering the slippage of his bath sheet, she thought better of the question. There was a widening gap between the ends of the terry material that drew her eye like a magnet. He was discreetly trying to blot himself off, but to her overworked imagination, it had become a towel dance.

Unbelievable. She couldn't focus on anything but catching glimpses of his—

"I *really* should let you change," she said.

"Give me fifteen minutes," he told her. "I'll meet you in my private gym. It's adjacent to my office. There's a connecting door."

"Sure," Temple said. "Your private— Sure."

A private gym in a seventeenth-century castle? Temple's goal was to get herself back to the elevator without any further embarrassment. Once there she had no idea where she was going, but it wasn't to a private anything.

SIXTEEN

"Mind like water."

Temple echoed the phrase she'd come across in Mark's book the day before. It came to her now as she stood on the cliffs overlooking the ocean. The Pacific was indigo blue with pools of black, and as shiny as a skating rink. But there was motion beneath the surface. She could sense the powerful bottom swells, and they were lulling her into a strangely receptive state.

She'd come outside to clear her head, but she had never imagined how hypnotic the water could be from this vantage point. She hadn't been satisfied with the observation deck. She'd come down the steps to the cliffs, wanting to be closer to the deep currents, the whispering waves.

"Mind like water . . . mind like the moon."

Temple lifted her head at the sound of his voice. Mark had walked up behind her, but she hadn't heard his footsteps. Either she was entranced or he was that quiet.

She turned. "What does it mean?"

She stared at him searchingly. She was hungry for information about things it seemed only he could explain. The swimming pool was forgotten, but she didn't fail to notice that he was dressed all in black. He'd slipped on iridescent nylon workout pants and a jacket over a black tank. It made him look like part of the night sky, as dark and luminous as if he'd come from somewhere beyond.

"It means whatever you want it to mean," he said.

She couldn't allow him to be elusive. "What do *you* want it to mean?"

He slid his hands into the pockets of his pants and shrugged. "There's no way to tell you, but maybe I can show you. Are you up for that Aikido lesson?"

She nodded, thinking they would go back inside, to his private gym. But he had something else in mind.

"What did you feel when you were looking at the ocean just now?" he asked.

"Feel? I don't know."

"Look again."

He wanted her to return to her trance. And Temple wanted that, too. Below them was a cove of black glass water on which the moon's reflection sat like a silvery discus. But what struck her as she stared at it wasn't a feeling. It was the awareness that she was gazing into an enormous mirror. And that she was no longer cold.

"I want to be . . . a part of it," she said slowly.

"And where do you feel that? What part of your body?"

She touched her throat, not sure why, except that it was difficult to swallow.

"There?"

"Yes." A heartbeat jumped beneath her fingertips.

"Imagine a mind as calm as the surface of that water," he said. "A mind that can reflect with perfect precision whatever image it encounters. Now look at the moon in the sky, how it illuminates everything equally."

Her head dropped back and the light entered her eyes.

"If your mind were that quiet, that bright, that encompassing, you would never be taken by surprise."

"Why not?" she asked.

"You would see things before they happened."

"Clairvoyance?"

"No. Focus. With no clouds, no distractions."

Temple stared at the water. "Is that possible?"

"More than possible, if you believe that perception is ninety percent of reality."

She would not have picked a number that high, but she had always believed people created their own reality to some extent. Now she wasn't sure. It felt as if someone else were creating hers.

"Settle your thoughts and let your energy pool at the base of your throat," he told her. "Concentrate on that point, and you will begin to achieve emptiness."

She could already feel it happening. Tension was draining through her, seeping out like a mist and evaporating in the air. It was a hot, thin red vapor. And when it was gone, her body was blue, like the water. Indigo.

"Why would I want to be empty?" she asked.

"So that you can be filled . . . with whatever you need."

As Temple contemplated the water, an image took hold of her. She imagined herself an arrow, penetrating the full moon exactly at its center. Compelled, she moved toward the edge of the cliff and watched the slender shaft disappear through the bull's-eye. She could feel herself being drawn through with it, becoming a part of it.

The earth shifted beneath her feet, but she took no notice. Rocks broke loose and scattered, tumbling down the face of the cliff. She kicked off her tennis shoes for better traction, and kept inching closer to the rim.

"What are you doing?" Mark asked.

"I don't know. . . ." She'd never had a sensation like that

before, never felt as if she were in two places at once, *everywhere* at once. She had seen the arrow arc against the night sky. Yet she was the arrow. There was no conscious thought process involved. Still, it was more like watching someone dive than doing it—

"Temple!"

She heard him shout, but he could have been calling out anyone's name. She couldn't concentrate on anything but the brilliant circle and the perfection of entering it. There were no more cliffs, no air, no thirty-foot drop to the water. Everything was coalescing. It was all one silver sphere. The ocean rose to meet her. And the next thing she knew she was in flight.

Diving, sailing off the cliff, an arrow of pure moonlight.

It was surreal. Unreal. It couldn't be happening.

He'd asked her what she felt. But she couldn't feel anything—not wind, not cold, not the wall of icy water as she hit it. Someone else had just dived off the cliff. Those were Temple's thoughts as her body penetrated the black depths and sliced downward. She came within touching distance of the rocky bottom, curved into a turn, and shot back up, a fish.

She didn't truly understand what she'd done until she resurfaced seconds later, gasping. Her lungs were a vacuum, drawing on the air like bellows. She'd never been a good swimmer and had suffered with a recurring nightmare of drowning since childhood. *She wasn't a swimmer.* Yet there was hardly a ripple in the silver surrounding her as she tread water, and only the slightest of wakes as she began to stroke toward shore.

It was when she reached dry land that she became clumsy again. Mark was on the beach as she waded in. He watched her come out of the water, her thin cotton T-shirt and shorts pasted to her body like wet tissue. Every vulnerability was revealed, including the heartbeat in her throat. She was naked, dazed.

He came forward and draped his coat around her. Then he produced her shoes, sat her down on some driftwood, and helped her get them on. It made her feel like a child when he relaced and tied them. The child she'd never been. It was an awkward thing, that feeling. She wanted to reject it, but she didn't have the fight in her to reject anything.

After he'd zipped her into the jacket, they walked back in silence. Neither broke the strange mood until they'd reached the steps that scaled the bluffs, and then it was Mark who spoke.

"There might have been rocks, Temple, shallows."

"It was safe." That was true in some mysterious way, she realized. "I knew it was safe."

"Nevertheless, don't ever do it again."

He stayed slightly behind her as they climbed the steps, probably in case she should fall. It was a steep climb, and Temple was breathing heavily by the time they reached the landing. The air burned as it washed in and out of her lungs.

There'd been a power outage when she dived. All sensation had been cut off. Now it was flooding back. The breeze was ice against her bare legs, and her feet were as heavy as bricks. The smell of salt water clung to her hair and clothing. She could even taste it in her mouth.

The island was a noisy place at night, she'd just realized. The deep silence had been replaced by great commotion. Crickets and frogs chirruped like birds. Moths buzzed around the landing's lamplight, and the darting fireflies were airborne sparks from some invisible torch.

A paved walking path led back to the big house. At the place where it forked toward the bridge that led to her cottage, she turned to him, and saw that he was watching her. The look in his eyes made her stomach go hollow.

"You were right," she said. "I changed. For a moment, I did. Everything did. What happened?"

"You," he said softly. "You happened."

Their gazes connected, and just that quickly some irresistible force was involved. Temple wanted to reject this sensation, too. She wanted to badly, but she couldn't. It was a magnetic attraction that felt strong enough to reverse the poles. With a look he had penetrated all her defenses, just as the moonlight had, entering through her eyes and electrifying her senses. Grasping her soul.

She began to walk toward him. The volume of his jacket had swallowed her up, but she fought one of her hands free. It hovered in midair until he caught hold of it, and gave her a sharp tug. Temple had never known such tumbling warmth.

She all but fell into his arms.

And he all but ravished her with his mouth.

Within seconds they were both wet from her drenched body, and her lips were damp and steamy from his kiss. Adrenaline poured through her. There were tiny starbursts behind her closed lids, but she barely knew what happened it had been so fast and wild. She'd almost missed the moment, like the dive.

She wanted to kiss him again, slowly. She wanted their mouths to touch and cling, their bodies to connect like lightning. She wanted to know if his eyes had been open or closed when he kissed her. Desperately she wanted that.

"What *is* happening to me?" she asked him.

She meant the kiss, but he didn't seem to realize it. He studied her as if searching for a way to explain her to herself.

"You've discovered an ability to transcend self-imposed limits," he told her. "It exists in all of us. But for you the Aikido masters have a name. They would call you a mystic."

Temple could not comprehend that. She was the most

pragmatic, rock-solid person she knew. But the awareness in his expression was familiar. It said there were many mysteries she hadn't yet solved, and maybe one she hadn't even discovered, herself.

"A mystic." She searched his features. "And what would *you* call me?"

He stepped back, took up the hem of her dripping T-shirt, and pretended to ring it out. "I'm not sure we're ready to go there yet. Maybe you should take a hot shower and go to bed, pri—"

She'd thought he was going to call her princess. She waited, hardly daring to blink, but there was only silence as he investigated the one frivolous aspect of her appearance, a dimple in the hollow of her right cheek, first with his eyes and then with a feather brush of his lips.

"There's a little dent here," he murmured. "Have an accident?"

She couldn't think how to answer him, but it turned out to be unnecessary. He'd already changed the mood. "Will you be all right?" he wanted to know. "I could send June over to help you with the bath, although I can't guarantee her state of mind."

"I'll be fine." The breeze nipped at her bare legs, and suddenly the prospect of a hot, steamy soak sounded wonderful. She didn't want to think about anything, except to concentrate on that point at the base of her throat, empty her mind, and relax.

"I *will*," she said, noticing that he didn't seem convinced. She gave him a smile that said good night, Mr. Challis. The body language was unmistakable, but as she turned toward the cottage, she realized she'd just had a very close call.

Kissing him again, she thought, *that* would have been the accident.

• • •

Temple wandered the mill cottage in the man's white dress shirt she'd found in the closet. Her first act had been to find some tape and seal off the pinholes where she suspected the cameras of being hidden. She didn't want Mark watching while she obsessed about him.

Now she unbuttoned the cuffs of the shift, shook down the extra-long sleeves, and began to roll them up, wondering if it was his. She brought the crisp white material to her nose to catch scent of the man, and realized that he wouldn't provide second-hand clothing to the type of client he dealt with.

She had wanted it to be his.

You happened, he'd told her. *Mystic,* he'd called her.

The adrenaline had burned off, and she was shaky, but that hardly explained the storm gathering inside her. It didn't explain anything. She'd warned herself about the emotional danger, but who would have thought one kiss could do so much damage. She ought to be declared a natural disaster.

He'd had some hot tea sent over from Wings. The graceful wooden-and-glass infuser sat on a bamboo tray on the trunk table. Temple had sipped the mild lemon-laced brew from a small iron cup with no handle, but she had no appetite for anything, and the buttery smell of the sliced pound cake had put her off. It seemed she was either ravenous or listless.

She paced, sat by the blaze, absently touched herself through the shirt. And felt a need to be touched that flamed within her like the fire. She longed to love and be loved. To hold and be held. To be safe. To trust. For once. Just for once, to trust.

She was lonely, she and this body she didn't understand, she and this baby, whose very existence was an enigma to her.

Who was she? Whose body was this? Whose child?

Temple Banning didn't dive off cliffs and hear eerie music and wake up in strange places, pregnant by men she'd

never heard of. No wonder she hadn't been able to make a
decision about the pregnancy. It still didn't seem possible
that she was pregnant, no matter what the tests said.

Nothing she did led to answers. Only more questions. A
woman who could barely swim a stroke had dived from a
cliff. It felt as if that had happened to someone else, unless . . . she *was* someone else. But that was absurd. She'd
lost twelve hours, not her entire life.

More than anything she wanted to know the identity of
Michael St. Gerard and what he meant to her. It didn't make
any sense that she'd loved and forgotten him. She'd been
waiting for love like that all her life . . . consuming, soul-
burning love that swept you up in the wings of Icarus and
carried you too close to the sun.

Frustration took her to the cottage's closet, where she
knelt and began to go through her briefcase, looking for
something to distract her, a book maybe. Her work was
there, including all the notes for the cologne campaign,
which instantly took her back to a time when life made sense
and she was dealing with tangible problems that could be
solved, not these tumbling emotions and nightmarish fantasies of pursuit.

She could feel her estrangement from the real world, and
it made her acutely homesick. Her gray fleece jacket hung
on a hook on the back of the closet door. Temple caught the
stale mix of gasoline and smoke from the night of the explosion as she rummaged through the pockets in search of the
nautilus shell. It was where she'd left it, thank God. To have
lost it now would be like cutting a taproot to the past.

Ssshhh now, don't be afraid . . . ssshhhh.

She didn't need to listen, just to know it was there.

She left the shell in its hiding place and returned to the
living room. Her head felt heavy and her eyelids had begun
to burn. She sank onto the daybed, dreaming of sleep. But
when it didn't come immediately, she curled up on her side

and stared at the fire, dwelling in its lambent dance of the veils, and letting herself be hypnotized by the undulating flames.

She wanted to be hypnotized. . . .

Wanted that . . .

Almost immediately things began to melt and run together. Her sense of time. Her sense of herself. She could feel her eyelids drooping and her thoughts taking on the quality of a liquid. She was being drawn into the rippling blue inferno, but at the same time, she could see her body there on the bed, melting, turning to gold. . . .

Her shirt had fallen open, and she was lying on her back, her skin exposed to the heat of the glowing hearth.

Where do you feel it?

She touched her throat. But she felt it everywhere. Her senses sparked like the fireflies on the path, although she resisted the impulse to touch herself anywhere else. It would burn her up. She could set fires with her fingertips.

It was everywhere.

Something told her to close her eyes, and they sank shut immediately. Her lids were so hot and heavy, she wasn't sure she could ever get them open again.

From the darkness she listened to the hiss of the flames until she could hear nothing else. But as the roar of the hearth bathed her in its blue glow, she felt another kind of sensation come over her. Something had touched her. It could have been a hand, but it wasn't hers.

The breeze that curled around her ankle and snaked over her calf was so silky-soft she couldn't tell if it was hot or cold. A fluttering breath stole across her belly and over her breasts, but Temple still couldn't imagine what it was. Veils, feathers, gossamer snowflakes, none of them was soft enough. Her skin had never experienced anything this light. It was weightless.

She was left wondering, waiting for the next touch. And

when it came, it startled a sound out of her. One of her nipples was being traced with the whisper of a circle, and Temple's drawn-in breath was as hushed as the sensation.

When she opened her eyes, she saw it wasn't a man touching her. It was a butterfly. It had lit on her breast and was exquisitely perched on the tingling bud, as if she were a flower it had come to pollinate.

Temple could hardly believe it. Seduced by a butterfly?

She was entranced until she felt movement elsewhere, a slithering sensation that traveled up her leg, over her hip, and into the flat bowl of her belly. She looked down.

An emerald snake with carbon-black eyes zigzagged over quivering pink flesh. Her flesh. The tongue flicked out searchingly as it approached her breast and glided to a stop.

Yellow eyes blinked. Nothing moved. Even the butterfly's fragile wings were frozen in flight. Fear rose out of Temple in a red mist, as vibrant as the tension that had drained through her earlier. But inexplicably, once the mist had evaporated, she felt nothing. The fear and revulsion were gone. Her only reaction was a strange, numbing fascination with the fate of the two exquisite creatures.

This must be a dream, she told herself. Otherwise she would be shrieking. Somewhere a heartbeat clapped like thunder. A small voice cried for help, and yet there was nothing Temple could do. The thought that took hold of her, held her stunned and transfixed, was that she was watching a dance, perhaps of death, but one as natural as the cycle of life.

The forked tongue darted evily.

The slick green spine rippled like it had been touched with electric current.

Seconds ticked by, blurring into minutes.

The cry for help echoed in Temple's ears, but she wouldn't let herself listen. She had just begun to believe it wouldn't happen. This *was* a dream and the images were being controlled by her own subconscious. That's why she wasn't afraid. She was in control, and therefore nothing bad could happen.

She had just begun to believe that when the snake reared up. There was no warning but a hiss, a terrible, terrible hiss. Fangs gleamed, dripping with poison. And it struck like a whip being cracked, too fast for anything to stop it, too fast for anything to escape it.

A soft rumbling rattled the cottage's wall's. Temple stirred, wondering if the storm had blown up again. It sounded like someone was pounding on the door, she thought groggily. It was dark enough to be midnight, but the glowing clock on the mantel said it was just ten P.M.

A chill hung in the air, damp and penetrating.

She sat up and shuddered, realizing she'd fallen asleep without covering herself. A patchwork quilt was draped over the footrail. She grabbed it and wrapped herself up. The fire had burned down, and it was freezing in the cabin, but nothing could compare to the icy apprehension she felt.

The pit of her stomach was tight with foreboding, and she didn't understand why at first. But then she remembered the snake, the dream. She didn't want to get out of the bed, but the rumbling noises had grown louder. It was probably nothing more than the waterfall outside her window, but it sounded like thunder. Or drums.

Wrapped tight in the quilt, she made her way to the front windows and looked out at the mansion on the cliffs. Music, she realized. It was drums. Thundering drums. It was cymbals, brass, and strings. The din coming from Wings was loud enough to shake the old house's foundation.

The moon was primordial ice. Temple had never seen anything so bright. It eclipsed the stars as she made her way across the creaky wooden bridge and up the pathway to the house. There hadn't been time to dress. She'd bundled herself in a raincoat from the closet and slipped on her loafers.

The pathway branched to the observation deck and the side entrance, but Temple went straight to the front portico, where the double doors had been flung open and music was pouring out as if the castle were an opera house.

Temple was surprised to find no one around. If there really was round-the-clock security on the island, as Mark had told her, she would have thought this racket would bring the guards running. She went through several rooms before she realized the noise was coming from the main salon. There didn't seem to be anyone in the room as she descended the steps, but the music pulsed from a black lacquered cabinet near the grand piano. Its splayed doors revealed an array of sophisticated stereo equipment.

It *was* opera, she realized, aware of the lyrics for the first time. They were Italian, and Temple wasn't at all proficient, but she was able to make out a line sung with piercing emotion about a woman dying of a broken heart. What caught her attention was the word *butterfly* laced throughout the piece.

The stereo's flashing digital display bewildered her. There had to be a volume adjustment somewhere among the dials, knobs, and levers. Finally a plus and minus sign caught her eye, and she held the button down until the deafening noise dropped off.

She couldn't find the power knob, but the volume was down, and the cabinet had stopped vibrating. That would have to do for now. It was hard to imagine opera as an assault on the senses, but it had blocked out everything, including the sound she heard as she stepped back from the cabinet. Someone was crying. The choked sobs were heartrending.

Temple turned and saw a woman collapsed at the foot of the stairway. Temple hadn't seen her only because she'd been focused on the stereo. It was June, the housekeeper, and she was draped over her knees, her arms stretched out in front of her as if she were reaching for something. The position reminded Temple of yoga, except that June was weeping inconsolably.

Temple approached her cautiously. "June? What is it?"

A shudder racked the housekeeper's frail body.

"Are you hurt?" Temple asked as she knelt next to her. "Should I get Mr. Challis?"

June shook her head and mumbled something Temple couldn't understand. The sobbing eased as she drew in a breath and fought to gather herself together. It wasn't clear whether she was embarrassed to have been discovered, but Temple was reluctant to probe any further.

Gradually the shaking eased, and June sat up, but she wouldn't look at Temple. "He's gone to the mainland." Bitterly she added, "He won't be back until tomorrow evening."

Temple was surprised. Mark hadn't mentioned anything about leaving that night when they were together, but she didn't want to question June about it now. The housekeeper was struggling to get to her feet, and she clearly needed a hand. Temple steadied her and helped her to the nearest couch. Once she had June settled, she poured her a small glass of sherry.

"If there's anything I can do," Temple told her, "please don't hesitate to ask, even if it's just to talk—"

June nodded, but her hands were shaking so badly she couldn't get the sherry to her mouth. "It's my daughter," she said.

Temple took the drink and set it on the table. "Something's happened to your daughter?"

"I lost her several years ago in a boating accident. She drowned." June got that much out and looked up at Temple for the first time. Her fierce dark eyes blazed with emotion. With agony. "Tonight was the anniversary of her death."

"I'm so sorry." Temple wished there was something she could do, but June's demeanor still forbade it, even a comforting touch. Her thin body was locked tight with emotion, and Temple wondered if she would survive its release.

"The music," Temple said, making an effort to change the subject, "was it something your daughter liked?"

June nodded. "The opera, *Madame Butterfly.*"

Temple knew the story better than the music. It was a tragic fable about a young, beautiful geisha called Butterfly, married in a sham ceremony to an American officer, whom she fell deeply in love with. Unaware that Butterfly was pregnant, the officer left for the States, only to return years later with a "real" wife. Butterfly agreed to relinquish custody of their child, but in the wrenching final scene, she bid her small son good-bye, blindfolded him, and took her own life with a ceremonial dagger.

"Lorraine had a beautiful voice," June said wistfully. "She could sing Butterfly's part, every word of it, in Italian."

"Was she a singer by profession?" Temple asked.

"No, but I wish she had been." Now June picked up the sherry and drank from it. Her mouth had formed a hard line that reminded Temple of the angry woman she'd encountered before tonight, and her body language hadn't changed. She didn't want to be intruded upon.

By that time the music had caught Temple's attention. It played so softly she had to strain to hear it. The rippling runs and silvery glissandos reminded her of a butterfly in flight, and as she listened, she thought about the exquisite creature in her dream and the trophy mounted in Mark's office.

She would have dismissed it as a coincidence, but the timing felt too disturbing. June might know about the trophy, she realized, but as she considered the idea of asking, she heard something eerily familiar and raised her head. The opera had reclaimed her attention.

"Oh, my God, no," she breathed. She was glad she hadn't left the recamier. Otherwise she would have been in a shaking heap on the floor like June. This was it, the music! It was the same melody she'd heard that night in the honeymoon suite . . . and again in Mark Challis's office.

SEVENTEEN

His objective couldn't sleep. It was two A.M. and she'd been turning restlessly in her bed since midnight. Perhaps even longer, but that was when Mark had lost the battle with his dark and disorderly impulses, set aside his case notes, and switched on the laptop.

She was already in bed when he tuned in, already tangled in soft moonlit sheets and pensively resting her chin on the pillow she clutched to her breasts. He'd had violent thoughts about that pillow. It was in his way. Not only of what he wanted to see, of where he wanted to be.

On her. *In* her.

He had an insane desire to be the object clutched in those fragile white arms and lying on those lovely naked breasts. He wanted to smell her scent and feel her flesh dissolve under his hot, plundering weight. Her legs, her sex, all of it clutching at him the way her arms did, yielding everything. Melting like warm sweet cream while he took her.

Thinking about that pillow was giving him a hard-on.

Christ, he was sick. A sick man.

He, who was used to exercising total control over himself and others, whose pulse had been flatlined for years and who would probably have been pronounced clinically dead with his eyes open, now had high-frequency current for vital signs. The woman was shock therapy. She was restraints and electrodes. And he hated every fucking volt.

He'd made an executive decision. After they'd come back from the storm, he'd turned the video surveillance of Temple Banning over to his security chief. It was a first for Mark. But then so was she. He'd always handled every aspect of a case himself, but his objectivity was at stake, and probably that was the least of it, so he'd delegated.

It had felt like a shrewd move until a few hours ago, when images of her began to plague him. They'd been triggered by a call from his security chief on the island, reporting that music was blaring from the big house and Temple was on her way up there. Mark had told him to keep an eye on the situation, but not to intervene unless absolutely necessary.

June was legendary for her emotional outbursts. She'd broken windows and smashed the china more than once, but Mark knew what drove her to act out, and he had his own personal reasons for tolerating her behavior. His security staff kept a close watch on her activities, as did Mark himself. He'd never thought of her as truly dangerous, but the first rule of security was never to take anything for granted.

He was the one dangerous tonight.

He could see Temple Banning as if she were poised in front of him—the lithe, curious nude, cupping her breast and gazing at herself in the glass. The mystic cliff diver, who could barely swim a stroke, according to his research.

As long as he was watching her on the screen of his mind, he'd told himself, he might as well be doing it for real. Maybe that would kill the urge. So far it had killed nothing except his appetite for anything else in life but this. Ravishing her with his eyes and his restless, predatory mind.

She thought she'd cut him off. She'd found several of the camera sites and taped them. Mark almost wished she'd gotten them all. Chair springs groaned softly as he settled back. They echoed the sound in his throat. Maybe Temple Banning would like to save him, maybe she'd like to bestow her grace upon Mark Challis and forgive him for the sins he was about to commit. Against her. Against himself. Maybe even humanity.

Suddenly the light in her room flashed on.

Mark's head snapped up. He'd been lost in his own thoughts and hadn't noticed that she was getting out of bed. She was wearing a gown, but he could see through it, and his imagination hadn't done her justice. It never did. He wouldn't have thought a woman could be both slender *and* luscious, but she was. He wondered if that was what pregnancy did. Plump the breasts until they hung like tree fruit. Round a butt until it looked tart and juicy enough to make your teeth hurt.

He flexed his hand, and a tendon popped.

Why don't you just grab hold of a live wire, Challis? he thought sardonically.

Now she was sitting on the bathroom countertop, her feet in a sinkful of water. The misty cotton nightie had drifted up her legs and was tucked into her lap, between her thighs. She looked like a wistful girl as she rested her chin on her knees, and he wondered what she was going to do. A moment later she picked up a pink lady's razor.

Mark had rarely seen anything more graceful than the way she proceeded to shave her legs. Her body tilted over pointed toes and her fingers played the razor like a violin bow. Her strokes were long and deft up the calf, slow and delicate around the ankle bone, then light and quick over the shin. Too quick.

The razor turned on edge and she nicked herself.

A gasp rose, and Mark winced with her.

God, he could feel the sting. The sharpness of it reverberated even after she'd turned off the water and searched through the medicine cabinet for a bandage. It stayed with him after she'd gone back to bed and resumed her restless tossing.

It was too dark to see her anymore. She'd shut the blinds or the moon had moved, but the room was a cloak, protecting her from his hungry, angry gaze. All he could pick up was sounds—the rustle of bedsheets and her sighs of frustration.

He was about to turn off the computer when he noticed the play of shadows across the screen. Either the level of light had increased or his eyes had adjusted enough so that he could see her moving, shifting positions. And her breathing had changed, too. It was soft, rushing. She drew up her legs, and he heard a tiny, throaty cry. It opened inside him like a fresh wound, that sound. It could only mean one thing, and he was riveted to the screen.

He watched her head come off the pillow and imagined her spine arching in the darkness, imagined the intense pleasure that must be coursing through her . . . and how like pain it could feel.

There was so damn little difference—it was all pain.

He spun around in the chair and faced the deep, starred night, letting it envelope him. When you were used to hearing nothing, a whisper could be deafening. She had nicked him, too. Only he couldn't seem to stop bleeding.

He lost track of time after that. But when he turned back to his desk the first thing he did was reach down and yank the plug from the floor socket. After that he forced his thoughts back to the cases on his desk, *force* being the operative word.

Fortunately he had updates on both, including hers. St.

Gerard was a ghost, as it turned out. He never existed, according to the investigator. The trail began and ended with the phony credit card, and he hadn't resurfaced since, except once, to leave a message on Temple's machine.

None of that surprised Mark, but he'd hoped for more from his new man. Still, he knew what the trainee was up against. In the investigative business, a ghost was someone living under a false identity, and although Mark had not revealed it to anyone, including Temple, he had reason to know that St. Gerard was exactly that, a ghost.

He'd debated how much to tell her and how much to hold back, but the answer evaded him, and he couldn't afford a misstep. There was too much at risk. He distracted himself with the serial-assault case, curious about the status of the investigation. Mark had not been able to get his hands on any of the women's medical files, but the most recent police report said that each of them had visited a walk-in women's clinic seeking gynecological care prior to the assault.

Mark thought about that. His client, Diane Bradley, had told him she went because of missed periods and was prescribed female hormones. According to the report, the other two women had gone for pregnancy tests, and one had been positive, the other negative. There was no obvious correlation there, although that in itself wasn't enough reason for the police to declare the crimes unrelated. Mark could see "serial" written all over this one. It was one of those cases where the missing car keys were sitting on the bureau top, just waiting for someone to spot them.

"A women's clinic," he murmured, making a note to give Dan Llewelyn a call. Llewelyn had always been less a doctor than a visionary, and his input would be interesting at least. But that could wait. It was late, and Mark had no burning need to talk with him tonight. He had no burning need to talk with anyone, but maybe that was because of the sound echoing in his head . . . a tiny cry, ripped from a pregnant woman's throat.

"Everything looks good, Temple," Dan Llewelyn pronounced, pulling the stethoscope from around his neck. "I've got the blood and urine samples, just to be sure, but otherwise, you're exactly where you should be for this stage."

He rolled the instrument up and dropped it in his black bag, the very picture of a country doctor making a house call. Wispy hair and eyebrows, mostly gone gray, added to the image. There was an intriguing complexity to the man, to be sure, perhaps even a streak of shyness, Temple decided. But it was the easy warmth in his smile that made her smile back, despite the anxiety she was feeling.

"You're taking your vitamins, I presume," he murmured while he busied himself, gathering up his medical gear.

Temple nodded, though he couldn't see her. He obviously wanted to give her some privacy, although the exam had only been a partial one, requiring her to do nothing more than unbutton her cardigan.

She'd been surprised to discover that Wings actually had a medical examining room in the basement, next to the pool pavilion. And according to Dr. Llewelyn, Mark had once employed a full-time registered nurse, in case his clients needed medical care while they were on the island.

June, who was more icily intense than ever that morning, had told Temple at breakfast that Llewelyn was coming. She'd directed her to the room, and Temple had actually searched the small, surgically clean area for surveillance cameras while she was waiting for the doctor.

She had decided to tell Llewelyn everything, but didn't know where to start, it was all so bizarre. The last thing she wanted was for him to think of her as a hysterical patient, who needed reassurance more than she needed to be taken seriously. She was stranded in a high-security compound, which meant that someone from the outside might be her only source of help. If he didn't understand or believe her, she didn't know where else to go.

She hadn't realized how shaky she was until she began to do up her sweater. Apparently he hadn't noticed, either, but now he set down his bag and stared at her.

"Temple, is there something wrong?"

She was still sitting on the examining table, her feet hanging off the side. She told him there was, and he encouraged her to talk about it.

"I don't know how much Mark has told you about why I'm on this island," she said. She didn't know any other way to deal with it than to come right to the point. "But it's for my own safety, according to him. Some frightening things have happened, and it's possible that someone is trying to kill me. In fact Mark thinks it's more than possible."

The doctor's frothy eyebrows shifted. A tall, thin man, more bones than flesh, he settled back against the countertop to listen.

He was probably one of those doctors who'd heard everything, Temple thought, sensing that he might already be skeptical. She did her best to explain in a calm and rational way about the honeymoon suite, the missing twelve hours, and Michael St. Gerard. She kept expecting him to react, or to stop her and ask if she was all right, but his medical training served him well. He was interested but impassive, even as she went on to explain about the attempts on her life.

"That was how I came to be under Mark's care," she said, "but now I'm starting to have suspicions—about him."

"But if you suspect that someone's trying to kill you, surely you can't think that's Mark."

"Oh, no, it's the pregnancy." She was almost relieved. No wonder he looked a bit wary. She hadn't made herself clear. "That night in the honeymoon suite, I heard someone whispering to me, a man. The voice was vaguely familiar, although I have no idea who it was. And there was music that I didn't recognize at the time, but I do now."

"And you have reason to think this man was Mark? What about Michael St. Gerard? Wasn't that the name on the marriage certificate?"

She slid forward on the table's padded vinyl surface. "St. Gerard has disappeared, if he ever existed. The point is I've heard that music three times, once in the suite, once in Mark Challis's office, and now here on the island. It's from *Madame Butterfly*, but I didn't realize that until last night."

"What happened last night?"

She told him about being awakened by the music and finding June collapsed in the main salon. "She said it was the anniversary of her daughter, Lorraine's, death, and the opera had been Lorraine's favorite."

"But what does that have to do with Mark?"

"I don't know, but it was the same music, I'm cer—"

The look on his face brought Temple up short. He was no longer impassive. His expression was shadowed with concern as he abandoned his position of neutrality and came over to her.

"You were about to say you're certain of that." He studied her searchingly. "But there's something I don't understand. The music could turn out to be coincidental, and even if it doesn't, it's your only link to Mark. How does that prove he fathered your child?"

"I don't have proof, but there are ways to get it, tests that could be done."

"Are you asking me to run DNA tests? I couldn't possibly do that without Mark's knowledge. And think what you're suggesting, Temple. You say you might have been drugged at the time. That's a serious accusation. It's very grave."

Temple could feel herself go uncomfortably warm. Her earlobes burned, and a line of heat ringed her throat. He made it sound as if she'd branded Mark a rapist, and she'd never thought of it in those terms. She was pregnant, and her only clue was the music. Llewelyn was right about that. She just wanted to know who and why.

The doctor had gone silent, as if he were debating whether or not to speak his mind. "Listen," he said at last, "I don't want you to think I'm questioning you, or that you shouldn't have turned to me for help. I want to get to the bottom of this, too. And I do want to help you, Temple. But I have the sense that you're dealing with a lot of inner confusion about your feelings for Mark, and even about the baby, am I right?"

That wasn't something Temple had wanted to get into. She looked away, and heard the table creak softly as he joined her.

"Temple, I'm not criticizing you. If you *were* certain of your feelings, I'd be worried. What else could you be but bewildered and frightened, considering what you've been through? Someone's trying to harm you, and you're at the mercy of a man like Mark Challis. Or at least it must seem like that. He can be a scary character."

The understatement of the decade, Temple thought.

He touched her hand, as if trying to be sure she was listening. "But what's his motive? Have you ever asked yourself that? Why would he ever do such a thing?"

"I can't imagine," she answered honestly.

"Exactly," he chimed in. "I've known him since he was a kid. I know his father, and they're both honorable men. There's no love lost between them, I admit. You could even say they've been enemies since Mark refused to take over the family business concerns, but the Challis men are proud. They have deep roots in the community and the country. They're empire builders. Not scoundrels or thieves."

The heat had crept up her throat and settled in her face, like burn marks, she was sure. "Then why do I keep hearing that music and having these thoughts? I'm not imagining it, Doctor. There's something wrong, and I'm afraid Mark's involved."

The room's fluorescent lighting illuminated the thoughtful lines and furrows of his face. It also lit the bracing blue of his eyes. Such contrast in one face, Temple thought. It might have had more to do with her need to think of him as a doctor and a healer than anything else, but she could feel his compassion, too. She could even smell the soap he'd used on his hands. It was some pungent combination of lemon and borax.

"I don't have an answer for you," he admitted. "But I can tell you this. Mark Challis would never do anything to harm you, I *am* certain of that. He's much too involved."

"Involved?" Instinctively her heart began to race.

"*Involved*, Temple. I've never seen a man so determined to protect a woman. He didn't need to bring you to this island. He could have parked you in a hotel or a convalescent care facility with a guard at the door. The way I see it, he'll stop at nothing to keep you safe."

His smile was quick, ironic. "The way I see it, the man can't help himself."

Temple was tempted to pretend she didn't know what he was talking about, although she understood perfectly. *Helplessness* she understood. She was already on an intimate basis with the condition. When she'd come back from Wings last night, after the ordeal with June, she hadn't been able to sleep. But had she spent the time analyzing her desperate situation and what to do about it? Had she thought about salvaging what was left of her life, her career? Had she thought about Ivy?

No, of course not. Her mind had drifted down the river on a raft called Mark Challis, and her hand had drifted down her body to the place that wanted him most.

God, she had been helpless then.

Llewelyn rose from the table and went back to packing his medical bag. "Maybe the problem is that you're involved, too?" he wondered aloud.

Temple could have denied it, but what was the point? Emotion had turned her breath into a sharp sigh. "And how would that explain my suspicions about him?"

"It would it you *wanted* it to be the same music. Think about it."

She didn't have to. He was suggesting that she suspected Mark because she wanted him to be the father. And this wasn't the first time that uncomfortable notion had struck her.

"This is embarrassing," she said under her breath.

He seemed to be packing and repacking his bag. He was giving her time, and when finally he did look up, he crooked an eyebrow, commiserating with her.

"If I thought you were in danger from Mark Challis, I would tell you," he said. "You believe that, don't you? I wouldn't allow you to stay here."

Temple nodded. Perhaps she did believe him.

"Wait a minute." He rifled through the bag one last time and produced a business card. "I'm going to leave you a couple of phone numbers. The first one's my cell phone, the other's my pager, and I want you to call if you have any more concerns, night or day."

Temple took the card and was grateful, more so than she could express. As he reached for his bag, she said, "I don't suppose there's any possibility that I'm not pregnant? That it might be a virus or something?"

"A virus?" He looked her up and down and laughed.

"Do they ever come back?" she asked quickly. It was the question she'd intended for Susan Gilchrist. "The one I caught ten years ago, could it resurface?"

"I suppose it's possible, although the process isn't fully understood. Some viral groups are known to be latent, like

AIDS and herpes. But if we're talking about your average, everyday flu strains, the answer is no. The body's immune system is plenty strong enough to keep them in check, assuming you've been exposed and have the antibodies."

Temple finished buttoning her sweater and slipped off the table. She'd never told him the details of that March night in the honeymoon suite, but he was familiar with her medical history. She would have thought he remembered her bout with the plague, but possibly not.

"I'm talking about Z190, Dr. Llewelyn. It's a highly virulent, highly contagious agent that ultimately attacks the nervous system. Do you think a virus like that could be induced by say, stress, to cause memory loss, even amnesia?"

"I've been practicing medicine too long to rule anything out, and viruses do have the advantage of being as close to immortal as anything God ever created. Theoretically they can stay dormant forever. But the odds of a virus to which you're already immune resurfacing are pretty slim, Temple."

He studied her searchingly. "I wasn't aware that we were having memory problems. Are we?"

"Oh, I guess not," she said after a moment. "I guess we're pregnant, then."

"Good. That's settled."

He smiled and so did she. This time he did pick up his bag and was heading toward the door when Temple noticed a prescription bottle rolling across the floor.

"Wait," she called to him. She knelt and corralled it for him, observing that the greenish capsules reminded her of the multivitamins he'd given her.

"Ah, my lost cause," he said, dropping the bottle into his bag. "It's an herbal compound I developed to protect against miscarriage, but I can't seem to get anyone's attention."

"Why is that?" she asked.

"In a word, money. The medical community is heavily influenced by drug-industry funds these days, and this compound is easy and cheap to make. It's also being prosely-tized by a maverick—me."

His gentle "country doctor" quality made it difficult to think of him as a foe of the establishment, but she had heard Mark call him a visionary.

"They're apparently terrified by the all-natural ingredi-ents," he added. "There's a little black cohosh, a little cramp bark, some evening primrose, and a blend of natural proges-terones that I call Progest."

"And they object to that?"

"Anything that isn't made by some pharmaceutical giant is snake oil to them," he told her. "They rush to approve dan-gerous weight-loss drugs, but they block natural com-pounds, force them into rigorous testing, and then reject them because they don't have enough 'science' behind them."

"That must be frustrating."

"It is, especially since my studies indicate that there are no side effects, no contraindications or drug interactions. It's far safer and more effective than anything currently on the market, but I can't budge the FDA. I've been trying to get it into clinical trials for years, and I just got word they turned me down again."

"Oh, I'm *sorry*," she said.

He shook off her sympathy, but there was something in his manner that told her this rejection had been devastating. She could feel his frustration, even though it was clear he was trying to hide it.

He zipped the bag with an angry sigh. "Blind fools," he muttered. "One of these days they'll regret their stupidity."

Temple sensed the depth of his outrage. She had the im-pression that he'd always been something of a trailblazer, forced to deal with drones and often mired in the red tape of medical and federal bureaucracy. Years of that had to be painful, especially if the medicine really could save lives.

"I don't suppose it does anything for pregnant women with amnesia?" she asked, hoping to boost his spirits a little.

"I'll have to work on that," he said with a wary grin. "And now if you'll excuse me, I have an appointment with a helicopter." He gave her an official-looking salute, picked up his bag, and this time he actually left.

EIGHTEEN

Susan Gilchrist was on her office phone before it rang.
That's how tight her reflexes were these days. She probably
had the motor-nerve response of a trained arm wrestler.

"Susan Gilchrist," she said briskly.

"Susan! Get your butt up here, and see what I've got."

It was Brian Rice, and Susan was used to his shenanigans
by now. He probably had a three-eyed rat or some other
freaky lab accident to show her. A fair percentage of the research nerds were arrested adolescents, she'd discovered,
and she was just as glad it wasn't her thing.

"Where are you?" she asked.

"The maximum containment lab, Level Four. Where I
live, silly."

Level Four was where the most virulent infectious agents
were stored and analyzed, and Susan hated going in there.
To breathe the air was to die. The space suits made her
claustrophobic, and she didn't want to be on a respirator at
age fifty from the chemical baths.

"Sorry, Brian, I'm all tied up here."

His voice dropped to a whisper. "Susan, I've got it on the screen, and it's the most beautiful thing I've ever seen."

"Calista Flockhart nude, right?"

"Behave, woman! I've isolated the virus. It's Agent Z190, and not just Z190, but the original strain."

He whooped so loudly she had to hold the phone away from her ear and still she could hear him.

"Do you know what this means? *Do* you?"

Susan wanted to laugh. Of course, she knew what it meant. She'd been waiting ten years for this opportunity.

"C'mere, you little monkey," Eddie Baker chased after a dead geranium branch with his clippers, wincing as it got away and he amputated a fuzzy green sprout instead. At least he hadn't snipped one of the coral blossoms. That would have brought tears to his eyes.

He popped his lower lip and cooled himself off with a gust of air. *"Phfffft."* But it wasn't a moment later he was using his cap to wipe his brow. Hot today.

Guns and roses, he thought. Funny that a man could find gratification in two such opposite things. The rock group he could take or leave. Too many tattoos. But the real thing, guns, they were a man's security. And roses, they were his purity. Eddie'd always thought of them in that way. He couldn't imagine anything more pure than a delicate white rosebud, swaddled in green and gently unfurling its heart to the world.

Gardening wasn't one of his official duties at Wings, but the groundskeeper didn't seem to mind if he helped out, and Eddie had a feel for it. He liked watching the plants grow and flourish, worried about their welfare, and stole time from his other responsibilities to check on them. He even enjoyed the weeding.

But today it was hot. Too hot for March. He was the

newest employee at Wings. He hadn't been here six months yet, but it was long enough to know that island nights could be foggy and damp, even in the summer, and the days were often swept by chilly sea breezes. Still and sultry weather like this was unusual. Eddie hadn't felt a whisper of air all morning.

He sat back on his haunches and tugged at the collar of his sweatshirt, cooling his neck. He'd slept badly last night. Her infernal music had kept him up again, but he'd known better than to investigate. Everybody did. June was unpredictable when she got on one of her crying jags. She could even be violent, and Eddie had the bruises to prove it. He'd tried to stop her once and got in the way of a pot she was swinging.

He'd been hearing whispers about bad blood between her and the Challis family since he arrived, although he hadn't yet gleaned all the details. It had something to do with the death of her daughter, which June blamed on the old man, and maybe the son, too. It was widely believed among the household staff that June hated Jonathan so much she'd put a curse on him.

Eddie settled back to view his handiwork and pronounced it "Pretty damn spectacular." He'd created a border for the front flower beds, and it looked as if someone had splashed bright coral paint over a forest green canvas. Apparently June hadn't cursed the geraniums. They were thriving. But the family patriarch hadn't fared so well. The great Jonathan Challis was knocking at death's door, although that was a well-kept secret from the world.

Eddie, however, knew it for a fact. Circumstances had inadvertently put him in a loop of information to which supposedly only a handful of the country's highest and mightiest were privy, including a few government mucketymucks.

Eddie was on the island under orders and was simply awaiting his instructions, but meanwhile he'd overheard scuttlebutt about a top-secret contingency plan to handle the news of the old man's demise, when it happened. There was actually fear of a stock-market crash. That was how powerful a figure Jonathan was.

But not powerful enough to elude the Grim Reaper, Eddie acknowledged with a certain sense of cosmic justice. Every little guy had to take some satisfaction in knowing that the big guys couldn't buy their way out of everything, although Challis had given it a valiant try. The old man's condition had sounded like some new antibiotic-resistant form of TB, although that was mostly an educated guess on Eddie's part.

The diagnosis was as closely guarded a secret as Challis's prognosis. But Eddie had been a medic in Vietnam and a lab technician at the CDC. He knew something about life-and-death odds. And if what he suspected was true, he was betting on the housekeeper's curse.

He pushed to his feet with a grunt and brushed dirt off his jeans. Falcons were flying over the house that had been named for them, their black wings outstretched against the sun like the images in medieval heraldry. It looked like some kind of omen, the birds circling overhead that way, especially with the house so still and silent now.

Lull after the storm, he thought. The place had sounded like it was coming down last night. Eddie had endured bombing raids in Nam that made less commotion. He didn't sleep in the house, but that hadn't made any difference.

Eventually Wings had gone quiet, but Eddie's mind had not. He hadn't been able to sleep, so he'd pulled on his jeans and gone out for a walk, and over the sounds of the sea and the swish of falcon wings, he'd picked up other noises.

In fact he'd been stopped in his tracks by the gasp of pleasure he'd heard coming from inside the mill cottage. Ms. Banning didn't even have the window open, and he'd heard her sharp little moans. It had taken him a moment to figure out that she was all by herself in there. And then he'd been startled, real embarrassed.

The island was as rife with eerie noises as the Challis family was with secrets. The big house bellowed with pain, the mill cottage gasped with pleasure, and even the tower made its own hauntingly muted music. Eddie took some pride in the fact that he, the outsider, might be the only one who knew what all of those noises really meant.

Temple stood in the shower, drenching herself in the icy-cold, needling spray. It was a painful wakeup call, but out of that cleansing, sobering act had come what felt like her first rational decision in some time. She was not going to confront Mark with her suspicions. As real as her fears were, Llewelyn was right. She still had no proof. And if her attraction to Mark was so obvious that Llewelyn could see it, then she needed to reexamine her motives anyway. It didn't seem possible, but maybe she was acting on some hidden impulse.

As she turned in the bracing water, she made an attempt to distract herself by reviewing what she'd done that morning. After her appointment with Llewelyn, she'd gone to Mark's office and tried to call Ivy. Her little sister had been in a class, so Temple had left word that she would call back, and then she'd checked her voice mail at home and picked up messages from Donald and Dr. Gilchrist.

Gilchrist had left her cell phone number, and both had sounded anxious to speak with her, but Temple hadn't returned either call yet. She needed to talk to Mark first. He'd questioned her about Donald, and she wasn't sure why. She didn't want to do anything to impede Mark's investigation.

She stepped out of the tub, dripping, and grabbed a thick white bath sheet from a heated rack. But she couldn't seem to get dry no matter how vigorously she rubbed and patted herself down. It was the humidity, she realized. The entire cottage felt stuffy. What she was needed was some fresh air.

In the bedroom closet she found a long, floaty skirt in white tissue linen and a delicately cropped matching sweater. The outfit fit perfectly and was light enough for the warm weather. She'd shampooed her hair in the shower, but had left it damp, and as she walked out the door and into the sunshine, the warm breezes felt wonderful. They buoyed her clothing as well as her auburn locks.

Eddie was toiling away on one of the rock gardens as she crossed the wooden bridge. She called his name and waved, but he just blushed and ducked his head, pulling the bill of his cap down over his eyes. Temple let it go. She'd probably caught him talking to his plants or something.

All she wanted to do was walk, and not in any particular direction, but a glance back at the creek gave her an idea. She loved its mossy, ferny banks and bright, gurgling noises. It looked so cool and refreshing, maybe she'd just kick off her shoes and go for a wade instead of a walk.

It turned out to be one of her better ideas.

The water was deliciously icy and cooled her off instantly. The problem was her skirt. It fell nearly to her ankles, and there was too much of it to pick up and carry, Southern belle–style. About all she could do was gather it up in front of her and tie it into a bulky knot, which made normal strides difficult, but left her hands free.

As it turned out, she needed them for balance.

She started cautiously, staying close to the bank, but before very long, she was navigating near the center of the stream, where the water ran as deep as three or four feet in places, and the rocks were smooth and slick. The occasional miniature waterfalls required the agility of a gymnast. Temple had never thought of herself as particularly graceful, but she drifted with the current and congratulated herself on not having fallen yet. The worst she'd done was get her skirt wet.

Once she had the knack of it, she was able to appreciate

the lovely wooded valley the stream traversed. There were groves of flowering fruit trees, full-crowned island oak, crimson patches of California poppy, and cresting waves of blue sage. Peregrine had its own little fertile crescent, and Temple seemed to have discovered it.

She must be heading toward the interior, but there wasn't a sign of the security measures Mark had mentioned. Other than the morning she flew in and Mark's personal surveillance of her, she'd seen no evidence of security anywhere. It made her wonder how safe the island actually was and whether she should be concerned.

An island fox peeked at her from behind a tree stump, startling her. He was a beautiful little thing with a silky gray coat and a great plumed tail. She wanted to stop for a closer look, but the currents were too strong. They tugged at her ankles, and a patch of moss sent her splashing before she could catch her balance.

She expected the fox to be gone when she looked up, but he'd strolled out into the open and was staring at her, as if he couldn't imagine why a human was trying to act like a fish. Temple had the feeling he would have eaten out of her hand, but she had nothing to offer him and the creek was too wide and fast to cross at that point, so she left him sitting on the shore and went on her way.

Charmed by woodsy beauty and the nesting birds, she was probably no more than a quarter-mile downstream when she began to wonder how far into the island she actually was. She would have turned and gone back, but the silvery stream was as irresistible as the river she'd fantasized about last night. There were moments when it appeared to ribbon off into infinity, and that was having the same magnetic effect on her as the house did.

She was being seduced. First the glass doors of his office in the city, then Wings, and now this, a stream. Everything she associated with him pulled at her, enticing her to enter some mysterious realm, and promising great revelations if she did.

She'd already answered the siren's call with her decision to come to the island. She'd dived from the cliffs and given in to a powerful erotic urge in the dead of night, things she'd never done before. She was answering today, but her explorations only seemed to bring more questions. She never reached the truth, and it was impossible to know how to calculate the danger.

Ankle deep in white foam, she wondered if she should go on. She'd hit some baby rapids, but it was the time that concerned her. The sun had moved in the sky and the air had cooled significantly, which meant she'd been gone awhile, possibly hours. Her hair had dried in the mild air, and that would have taken an hour at least.

The island's music surrounded her. The swish of leaves overhead and the rush of water at her feet reminded her of the whispering nautilus. But there was another sound, faint, yet oddly sinister. She could hear the iridescence of chimes, ringing madly in the breezes. She turned toward the house, but realized that it came from downstream, the direction she was going.

Wind chimes? she wondered. He'd told her the center of the island was off-limits, and she'd imagined some kind of electronic surveillance system, perhaps even underground with banks of computers and glowing terrain maps. Not the kind of place where you'd expect to find wind chimes.

A glint of light hurt her eyes. It bounced off a large stone alongside the stream, and Temple realized there was something engraved on it. It almost looked like a headstone, but she could only get close enough to see the name Challis and the date, 1990. That in particular caught her because it was the year she was in Zaire.

Suddenly Temple's heart bucked and she whirled as if under attack. A shadow pitched the area into darkness, and the thrashing blades of a helicopter brought her head up. It hovered above her like a roaring, bloated monster. Someone had spotted her, Temple realized, and they were in pursuit. There was no way to know if it was one of Mark's helicopters, but that could hardly have terrified her any less.

Temple stood frozen in the water, lashed by the wind. The powerful blades created a hurricane force that held her in place and nearly tore the thin clothing off her body. The knot had fallen out of her skirt and the material was hanging in the water, heavy and wet. It tangled in her legs, hobbling her when she tried to move.

The chopper circled and dropped low. Temple ducked her head, terrified it would cut her to pieces. As the barrage continued, she could smell gasoline and feel the heat of its engines. Something was about to explode again, she knew. Everything was going to explode.

She struggled toward the bank and heard a voice yelling at her through a bullhorn. He was telling her to turn around and go back immediately, ordering her to turn around and go back. Temple was so rattled she couldn't think. Did he mean go back into the water?

That was when she decided to run.

She unbuttoned the heavy skirt, left it in the stream and began to make her way toward shore. When she had something solid under her feet, she would figure out which way to go. There were places to hide, even if only briefly. The area was thick with trees that would conceal her and give her some time to decide what to do.

She fell once, and was soaking wet when she got to shore.

The helicopter was still circling, and Temple went immediately to the cover of a huge oak. She wrung the water from her sweater and searched for an escape route. There was a grove of island cherry trees close enough to get to, but as she prepared herself to make the dash, a man stepped into her line of sight. A rustling sound alerted her to another one behind her, and in seconds they were everywhere. Guards, armed guards.

Temple was surrounded.

She backed against the tree and saw another one. Striding toward them, with the sun against his back, was Mark Challis. He was coming from upstream and nothing about the way he looked calmed Temple's heart rate this time.

NINETEEN

꧁ꕥ꧂

Mark's shouts resounded with banked fury as he ordered his men to disperse and signaled the helicopter to leave. That done, he turned to Temple with questions flaming in his dark eyes.

"What are you doing out here?"

"Just taking a walk." She was dizzy from the blood roaring in her ears, but she'd begun to understand. He thought she'd intentionally defied his warning to stay away from the interior.

A painful shudder cut through her. It was nerves, but he must have thought she was cold because he pulled off his leather jacket as if to give it to her.

"I don't need that," she said.

"Like hell you don't. You're blue."

She wouldn't let him get close enough to put it over her shoulders. Instead she plucked the jacket out of his hands and did the best she could to tie it around her waist and cover her legs.

"Are you all right?"

It was a low, savage question. If words had been fire, Temple would have ignited like kindling. But she was angry herself.

"I guess it could have been worse," she said accusingly. "You could have used floodlights and attack dogs. Or your men could have opened fire with their automatic weapons."

"My pilot saw someone in the creek, and I told him to check it out. What in hell were you doing in the water, Temple?"

"I was wading."

"Wading?" He was incredulous. "Christ, woman, haven't you heard a damn word I've said? I had to kidnap you to get you to this island. Now you're leaping from cliffs and wandering off where you're not supposed to. There's a drop-off just beyond those rapids and you could have drowned."

He was frightened, she realized. A flash of insight told her what all the anger was about. He was frightened for her. That mollified her slightly, but it still astonished her that he was berating her like she was a child, that he treated her like a child to the point of sitting her down and tying her shoes. She may have needed the help that night. But she didn't today.

"I was taking a *walk*," she said, "a harmless walk."

She didn't know how to deal with a man who was determined to take care of her, think for her, breathe for her, as he himself had put it. And if she'd ever liked it at all, even a little bit, she regretted that misguided impulse. He was grossly overprotective. She wasn't prepared to say it was intentional, but everything he did chipped away at her ability to take care of herself. There was no quicker way to cripple someone and make them completely dependent on you.

"I'm going back to the cottage," she said.

"I've got the jeep. It's just up the path."

"I'd rather walk!"

"You're not walking!"

By then Temple was already on her way. There was still enough adrenaline buzzing around in her veins to make her dangerous, and she needed to work it off. But his hands surprised her. They spun her around and locked on her arms. His expression surprised her even more. His eyes were still angry, but they were lit with that same dark, burning tenderness she didn't understand.

"Dammit, Temple—"

Embers, his gaze. Embers flaring in the night. Temple could feel her own anger melting, and knew, as surely as she knew anything, that this man would be the death of her. No one else but him.

"We've been over this before," he said. "It's my job to protect you, and if that means protecting you from yourself, so be it. One of us has to exercise good judgment."

"I was wading in a stream, Mark. How is that bad judgment?"

"It is if I say it is. As long as you're here, you follow my orders, just like everyone else. There is no slack in this rope, Temple. There can't be."

"How long then? How long will I be here?" *Why are you keeping me prisoner?* That was the question she wanted to ask.

"Until I know you're safe."

"No, I can't do that. I can't live like this."

There was something he wanted to say, but he stopped himself. She could see the impulse move through him and catch in the wires of his jaw.

He released a sigh and his grip on her arms gentled. "Someone has threatened your life, Temple, but that doesn't seem to frighten you. I'm trying to keep you safe, and apparently that does frighten you. Would you please tell me what's wrong with that equation? Because I can't do the math."

She averted her gaze and his hands dropped away. But she could still see him, dark and burning. Possessed of eyes that could reach inside and control you. Possessed of a sensuality that could make you touch yourself in the night.

And she wished he would kiss her again.

Dr. Dan Llewelyn was a weary man. He'd routinely put in twenty-hour days since his medical school marathon in the seventies, but the fatigue he suffered tonight wasn't physical. He'd never bothered much with sleep. His work had always fueled him, but what drove him even more than the need to make good his Hippocratic oath was a desire to open wide the boundaries of traditional medicine—to the natural remedy as opposed to the designer one, even to the so-called mumbo jumbo of the mind-body connection. That goal had earned him the label of maverick. And a man could only fight and lose so many moral battles before it began to wear on his spirit.

Maybe it wasn't his destiny to change the face of modern medicine, even a little. Maybe he was the rebel and the zealot he'd been called.

Tonight his study was low lit to match his mood. And his comfortably worn leather chair felt like a support system as much as an old friend. Normally he would already be composing a fiery rebuttal and formulating a new plan of attack against his nemeses at the FDA, but no words came to mind except those of capitulation. He was beginning to wonder what he'd been fighting for all these years. And why it had seemed worth the effort.

His wife's voice came to him from down the hallway.

"Dan, honey? Dinner's on the table in ten minutes sharp, okay."

"Try and stop me," he called back, glad he hadn't told her about this latest setback. She had enough to deal with in her alliance with a mad scientist like him without having to share his every disappointment—and there had been many. Somehow she'd never let any of it get her down, even the obsessive-compulsive work habits that would have sent most women screaming.

He should have been cooking dinner for her. But that wasn't the way their marriage worked. Dan Llewelyn sacrificed himself for medicine, and Maggie Llewelyn sacrificed herself for Dan. He owed her for that. His eyes misted up as he though about how much he owed her.

"Sharp, Danny!"

She bugged him because he was notorious for forgetting things only moments after he'd agreed to do them, including eating. He couldn't count the times she'd brought hot food to the den or the lab and stayed until he finished it, knowing otherwise it would sit on a countertop, grow cold, and eventually end up in the "toxic materials" bin, uneaten.

They'd shared big dreams in the early years, he and Maggie. He'd been trumpeted as a visionary and nominated for a Nobel for his work in infertility. But he'd fallen out of favor. A little too "progressive" for the bottom-line medical orthodoxy, who didn't appreciate his irreverence toward their sacred cows.

Now he was routinely overlooked for such prestigious plums, and federal funding sources had long ago dried up. There was private funding available, but that had only intensified his battles with the feds, who didn't trust the "quality" of privately funded studies.

His eyes went to the bottle of capsules on his desk, a simple natural compound that could so cheaply and effortlessly improve the quality of life and, in many cases, save it. He had Temple Banning on the compound, although she didn't know it. Any woman under that much stress needed extra protection.

Bastards, he thought, they had finally worn him down. That was what hurt. Not that they won, but that they'd won by default. He had always believed he would go down fighting.

It was time to join Maggie, according to his watch. But if he showed up at the table promptly, she would probably have been suspicious. His bone-thin one hundred sixty-five pounds felt heavy as he leaned across the desk and picked up a pencil to jot a reminder on his desk calendar.

Mark Challis had left him a message about the Amnesia Assaults. Apparently one of the three victims had shown up in Mark's office, and he'd agreed to take her case, either because of some similarity to Temple Banning's case, or because Mark felt the police were on the wrong track. It seemed he wanted to pick Dan's brains.

He circled Mark's name several times, aware that he had concerns about the man, although he'd been careful not to convey that to Temple Banning. Mark was altogether too consumed by the situation with his young "client." He seemed to be losing his objectivity, and Temple, who was clearly in a vulnerable state, was acting like a woman in love.

Dan feared that Mark wanted the woman totally under his control. Dan didn't understand why an elaborate island refuge was necessary. Based on what he knew about the place and its secrets, Peregrine might even be dangerous. He'd tried to tell Mark that, but Mark had been adamant.

Dan had been a friend of the Challis family for years, through most of their tragedies, in fact. Long enough to know that Mark and his father had feuded incessantly, but it was the death of his mother and younger brother, Will, that had changed Mark, turned him ice cold. His work in intelligence had contributed, too. He was different after that. Scary different.

"Dan!"

"On my way, babe!" Dan rose from the chair, thinking that perhaps he had better initiate a little investigation of his own. Temple Banning wasn't the only one who had begun to question Mark Challis's motives.

It was the perfect antidote to insomnia. Instead of tossing and turning, Temple had decided to curl up on the daybed with a book. She'd borrowed *Innate Power* from Mark's library and was fascinated with the concept of physical space.

"Pay attention to what gives you power," the author advised. "It can be an object, a time of day, or a weather condition, anything at all. Often it's a place."

Wings came to mind as Temple read on, but the castle didn't quite fit the description of a "power place," which was supposed to fill you with a sense of centeredness and peace the moment you entered. She'd felt the house's pull, its echoes and ghostly voices, but there was too much unresolved there.

She set the book down and listened to the music blaring from the mansion again tonight. It had started only moments ago, and based on what happened last night, she'd known there was little she could do. But she couldn't just sit here, either.

Maybe it was a disease, this need of hers to fix things that were broken, but she had to go. She'd left a warm sweater and jeans hanging over the brass banister, just in case. And moments later she was on her way out the door. She made her way down the steps carefully, letting her eyes adjust, and by the time she'd reached the bridge she felt like a part of the night.

The raw salty winds bit at her nose and cheeks. They chilled the breath trapped in her throat. Her attention was fixed on the house as she crossed the bridge, but she was so attuned to the darkness that she caught sight of someone slipping through the trees, apparently on their way to the inner island.

She tracked the shadowy form with her eyes, thinking it

was June or perhaps one of the security guards. Temple was torn. She instinctively wanted to know who it was and where they were going. The impulse was strong, but it would force her to go into the forbidden zone again, and the nightmare with Mark and his security force still played heavily in her mind.

It hit her suddenly that the music had dropped off in volume. She had to strain to hear it now. Halted at the foot of the bridge, she came to a decision and felt her senses quicken. Felt everything quicken with exquisite dread. She wasn't going to the house. She was going after the shadow.

The looming blackness swallowed her up as she made her way down the slope and into the trees. Huge ironwoods and island oaks blocked what moonlight there was, making headway slow. But as she tested and felt her way through the undergrowth, she found the trail that ran parallel to the creek. She'd discovered it when Mark drove her back in the jeep yesterday.

God, she would be dead if he caught her this time.

Suddenly she sighted an odd glow in the darkness ahead. It reminded her of a signal beacon, although it didn't flash. It grew steadily brighter as she struck out on the pebbled path, curious where it would take her. The music was nothing more than a distant drone. But every now and then she could hear the soft swish of falcon wings and catch glimpses of their darker-than-night wingspread.

Eventually she rounded a curve and came to a halt. Before her lay a beguiling, breathtaking scene. The rest of the path was lit by candles. Brilliant against their velvet blue backdrop, the votives seemed to go on forever, ribboning off into the vault-like interior of the island.

Nothing could be seen but candlefire and darkness.

Temple hesitated, wondering what she should do. What lay ahead appeared to be an even more heavily wooded valley. The black forest, she thought, only half facetiously. This was like something out of a classic gothic novel. It was impossible to make out details because of the glare, but the sparkling trail she'd taken looked as if it were about to enter a tunnel of wild, endless night.

It made her think of the nautilus's chambers and what it would be like to explore them. She could even hear their soft whisperings, but realized it was the hushed voices of the creek water, which was still gurgling alongside the trail.

Everything seemed to be talking to her, calling to her. Wasn't that what happened to crazy people? They heard voices?

Led by the flames, she ventured farther and finally came upon a clearing where the stream emptied into an enormous lily pond, afloat with tiny fires. More candles, seemingly hundreds of them, bobbed on the surface. It was one of the loveliest sights Temple had ever seen.

Enormous island oaks, the largest Temple had encountered since she arrived, draped the area with their branches, and an ornamental structure that resembled a ceremonial teahouse sat on a tiny island in the center of the pond. It was connected to the grassy bank by a red bridge.

Movement caught her eye, and Temple was astonished to see not June or a security guard, but Mark Challis cross the bridge and go into the house. He was the shadowy figure.

The dread resurfaced, unbidden. And now Temple understood the feeling. Despite the beauty, something was wrong here. She had no idea what it was, but she could feel it in her gut. Frozen with curiosity, she waited for Mark to come out, hoping to get some clue what it all meant. He'd told her the area was off limits for security reasons. Obviously that was a lie. Yes, something was wrong.

Shivering in the icy night air, Temple listened to the whistle of raptor wings overhead and heard the soft eerie cries echoing in the night. It felt as if she was faced with something outside her experience and would never understand.

Or if she could grasp it, she would never feel the same way about Mark Challis.

Something cold and smooth slid over her foot. Temple swallowed a scream as she watched it slither away, melting into the darkness. A snake? She'd been warned about them. It couldn't be a cobra, but that was what flashed into her mind. And just as swiftly she was imagining them everywhere, swaying from the branches of the trees, poised to strike. She imagined him, devoid of emotion, empty inside. Lethal.

Candles flared as she turned and ran back down the path.

June was there as she entered the house. The housekeeper was standing in the foyer, fully dressed, as if she'd been expecting Temple. And even though the music was still playing, the opera she'd said was her daughter's favorite, there were no tears in her eyes tonight.

"Who lives in the center of the island?" Temple asked.

June went pale with shock. Clearly Temple didn't have to explain what she'd seen. June knew about the teahouse and the bridge. She knew about the candles and the lily pond. And of course, she knew about the snakes.

"Bastard," June whispered. "He goes to see *her*—"

"Who do you mean?" Temple asked the question again, but the housekeeper wouldn't answer her. June rushed away, whispering that one word, "Bastard!" And Temple was grateful to have her gone. She was certain of only one thing. She didn't want to know what June meant. What any of it meant.

He goes to see her.

It was a backhand to her face, those words. Somewhere inside her a defenseless child had just been viciously slapped. She'd really never been able to deny the attraction to Mark. It was there from the first, but this. This terrible, annihilating pain. She didn't know what that meant, why anyone should hurt like this.

Love didn't hurt like this, did it? Because if it did, then she had never been in love in her life. If it did, then love could destroy a heart as easily as save one . . . and hers was dying.

TWENTY

It was morning, and Temple had barely slept. It hadn't seemed worth the effort to try, so she'd spent the night in a creaky old rocker, wrapped in a quilt, listening to the water splash through the mill wheel outside her window. Sadly it couldn't elicit the feeling of peace it once had. There was no peace to be found in Temple Banning.

The thought of Mark with another woman brought lacerating pain. It cut like broken glass. There was nothing to do but lie back in the chair and hold herself, one arm criss-crossed over her chest, a hand cupping her shoulder. Such dreadful hurting she didn't know how to breathe in its presence.

As the light rose, she forced herself to get up, too, knowing it was the right thing. Her stomach was growling, and she had to eat, whether she had any appetite or not. There were responsibilities that went with her condition, and even though she wasn't aware of having come to any conscious decision about what to do, she seemed to be feeling them strongly.

Remembering the baby brought an unexpected wave of pain. Even that hurt? she marveled. There didn't seem to be any escape from the ways she could be reminded of Mark Challis.

Crazy, but she thought of this baby as his.

She did. And that must be why it hurt so badly.

Get dressed, she told herself. Have breakfast. Soothe your stomach with food, pray it eases the heartache, and go about the motions of a normal existence. Later, when these feelings subside, you'll decide what to do.

Temple was aware of a sense of déjà vu as she walked into Wings a short time later. She was becoming familiar with the eerie stillness that permeated the house most of the time. And perhaps unknowingly, June contributed to that feeling. She wasn't waiting for Temple in the foyer this time, but when Temple entered the kitchen, the housekeeper was there, and she looked up expectantly.

"Are you all right?" June asked, setting down the silver tray she'd been polishing. "You look pale. You're shaking."

Temple protested that she was fine, just tired and hungry.

"Sit down then, and I'll get you something to eat."

June insisted that Temple make herself comfortable at the kitchen's center island while she put something together. Temple thanked her, watching with mild surprise as June hustled about, warming up a steaming bowl of rich, raisiny bread pudding and brewing a pot of herbal tea that she said was good for expectant mothers.

Temple was appreciative, but it was difficult to know what to expect from June, and the sudden friendliness was out of character. Still it was better than icy hostility, and given Temple's state of mind, she was glad for something as basic as the comfort of a warm kitchen.

Moments later June was pouring a hot, honeyed cup of tea

and setting a generous serving of crusty, golden brown pudding in front of her. The housekeeper even hovered a bit as Temple ate, which forced Temple to be a good soldier and dig in as if she had a hearty appetite.

The pudding was actually delicious, but there was only one thing on Temple's mind as she spooned it into her mouth. While June went on about how easy the recipe was to make, the warming spring weather, and other things of no consequence, Temple struggled with how to ask about the woman.

June's reaction last night had told her that the housekeeper knew who the woman was and what she meant to Mark. The only thing stopping Temple was her own dread of what she might hear. June could have more devastation in store, and Temple didn't know if she could handle that. She didn't even know how to bring the subject up.

She also had some concerns about being overheard. Her brush with the island's security force had left a lasting impression. But by the time she'd finished her tea, her need to know the truth, no matter what it was, had won out. She picked up the breakfast dishes and walked over to the sink, where June stood.

"Is there somewhere we can safely talk?"

Temple asked the question under her breath, and June glanced around as if she shared Temple's concerns about surveillance cameras. She gestured toward the butler's pantry.

Dutch doors led to a small, well-stocked closet off the kitchen. Temple had thought of looking for signs of surveillance, but they were barely inside the pantry's walls before June did something startling. She clutched at Temple's hand and told her she had to get off the island.

"You're not safe here," the housekeeper warned in a voice that hissed of lurking dangers. Her dark eyes burned high with some emotion Temple didn't understand.

"Please believe me," she said, overriding Temple's attempt to speak. "You should leave as soon as you can. If you don't, you'll never be allowed to go, you and the baby."

"What do you mean I'm not safe?"

"I can't tell you without endangering myself." Her voice cracked if she were fighting tears. "Just go now. Leave! Do it while Mr. Challis is gone to the mainland."

The housekeeper wouldn't explain what she meant beyond that, although Temple begged her. She couldn't make a decision unless she knew what there was to be afraid of. And if June was still distraught over her daughter, she might be acting irrationally. But no matter what Temple said, June kept insisting that Temple had to leave. There was no reasoning with her. She even told her how, in guarded whispers.

"There's a skiff hidden in an old boathouse on the far side of the island." She pulled a little notebook and pencil from her apron pocket and drew Temple a quick, clumsy map.

"Here," she said, tucking the directions into Temple's hand. "You should go now, this morning, while the tide is low and the winds are down."

Even if Temple had known how to sail, she couldn't imagine evading the island's security force. It would be far too dangerous, but June's warning had touched into her own fears of being a virtual prisoner here. There was no way off the island without help, but there might be a way to calm the housekeeper's mind and ease her own at the same time.

"Call Dr. Llewelyn for me, would you?" she said. "Tell him I'm not feeling well, in case the phones aren't safe. He already knows I have some concerns about staying here. If he believes I'm in danger, he'll help, I'm sure."

A door slammed, and June cut her off with a look that said someone had entered the kitchen. Temple immediately went quiet, her heart pounding as June left to see who it was. She could hear a man's voice, but it wasn't Mark. It sounded like Eddie, the handyman.

Apparently he hadn't come for breakfast. Temple cracked the door slightly and heard him asking June when Mr. Challis would be back. June seemed reluctant to answer, and Eddie began to shuffle and apologize. All he wanted, he explained, was to let Mr. Challis know that ventilation system in the tower needed some repairs.

As Temple waited for them to be finished, she made the very difficult decision that it was time to leave the island. Whether she was in danger or not, she was going. And once she got back to the mainland, she would go straight to the police and report the attempts on her life. Let the authorities solve the crime. She no longer cared about finding St. Gerard. She just wanted her life back.

The pain made him think of a Frankenstein monster being shocked to life. Absurd, but that was what he experienced when the wires connected and the electricity forked through him. It was like life being forced into his body, and there was pain with every aching jolt. He felt that now, watching her plan her escape.

What would he do? he wondered.

What would he do if she escaped?

She would have more to fear from him than from anyone else on earth, because he would never stop searching. He would tear the planet apart.

June had gone too far this time, he thought, watching the housekeeper scribble down a map and thrust it into Temple's hands. She was the instigator, feeding Temple's fears and urging her to risk her life to escape. It was as crazy as it was dangerous, but Mark had suspected June might try something like this, so he'd decided to monitor her work areas. He'd excused June's erratic behavior for years, but he couldn't excuse this. She'd gone too far.

Temple's face was ashen. Her gray eyes were bright with fear. But they harbored another emotion, too, one he could have recognized in the dark he was so familiar with it. There was only one pool of pain, and you quickly learned to recognize the other swimmers. She was going under.

Another jolt of electricity rocked him. It sent the chair skittering backward as he got up. This was the danger, he thought. This brutal vulnerability. It was pain that made people killers, not hatred, and she kept unknowingly inflicting new wounds.

As if the old ones weren't bad enough, he thought grimly.

She was wearing a pair of slim denim jeans and a T-shirt that clung to her breasts. There might have been a slight swell to her waistline, or was he imagining it? Pregnancy was a turnoff for some men, or so he'd heard. He should have been that lucky. He found her more beautiful knowing what was happening to her body.

He glanced out the window, searching for his own reflection. The movie monster sought love to make him human. What did Mark Challis seek? Refuge, probably, like some mortally wounded animal in search of a hiding place. But that was where he'd lived all his life, in hiding. This agony, it was what he feared, and craved. It was life. And nothing else could fulfill him, not after this.

Maybe it wasn't all that complicated, living. Maybe all he needed was a moment in her arms, a moment of ecstasy inside her. For a deaf man heaven was hearing one poignant chord of music. He would drown in a symphony after so many years of silence. But he couldn't let himself have that, either. He'd already intruded too profoundly in her life, more than she knew. He'd taken what wasn't his, more than his share. And because of that he couldn't have her, ever.

But God, how could he let her go?

Candlefire and shadow people.

Temple was haunted by the images. Well into the night she sat at the window, staring out at the creek. She watched, aware of her fragile emotional state, and knowing what she might see could have the power to destroy her. Her heart wouldn't allow her to do anything else. She couldn't not watch, even if what she saw was him, slipping through the darkness on his way to see *her*.

The only other place Temple's eyes strayed that night was to the clock on the mantel. As the hands crept toward midnight, she grew unbearably restless. Her intention was to be gone from the island by tomorrow. There were so many reasons to walk away from all this and never look back, but she had to know the truth before she left.

The nautilus shell lay hidden in the soft folds of her jumper skirt, where she'd left it. She'd found the blue denim jumper among the loaner clothes. It had looked so easy and comfortable, she'd slipped it on over one of her T-shirts.

She'd picked up the shell for comfort, too, as well as for any wisdom it might impart. And then she'd studiously avoided it. Perhaps she was afraid it would tell her how foolish she was being. Now she picked it up and cupped its familiar contours in the cradle of her palm. As she held it to her ear, the silence startled her. No sound came from the shell's inner chambers. There was nothing, not even the whispering *sshhh*.

She pressed the opening closer, thinking it was her state of mind, not the shell. It had to be, she told herself, aware of the cold dread that had invaded her chest cavity. She covered her other ear, blocking out any noise that could interfere. But it wasn't until she closed her eyes that she heard the faint tinkling of bells. Wind chimes, she thought. It sounded like the wind chimes she'd heard coming from the teahouse.

She left the shell on the table and rose from the chair. It was still rocking as she went out the door.

There were no candles on the path tonight. The way was dark, but the stream guided her with its mysterious music, and she would have known the direction anyway. It was etched in her psyche like a map. There were shadows everywhere. At times she thought she was being followed, but when she looked behind her, there was nothing there.

Somewhere above her raptors took flight. Cool air whistled smoothly beneath their searching wings. But Temple's senses were attuned for the sound of wind chimes, and as she rounded the turn that led to the lily pond, she heard wave after wave of bell-like tinkling. Several crystalline chimes hung from the eaves of the teahouse, their music silvering the air.

Without the glare of candles, she could see the graceful wood-shake house more clearly in the moonlight. Its deck was perched on stilts over the water and shaded by awnings of golden matchstick bamboo.

"He's there," she breathed. Light glowed through the translucent sliding door panels. Someone was inside.

Temple wasn't sure how she got from the path to the doors of the house. She had to have crossed the red bridge and climbed the steps to the deck. But all she could see as she rapped on the door was him as he opened it, and the woman behind him.

That would be the death blow, she knew. Seeing him like that would put her out of her misery. It would answer her questions and release her from whatever hold he had on her. She would not die of this severing pain, she would turn and walk away from it. She would be free.

That was why she'd come here, she realized. To finish it.

The honeyed glow of rice paper danced before her eyes as she waited. The chimes had quieted and the night had grown still, enclosing her like a curtain. The air was now as silent as her shell had been. Again, Temple wondered if it was her, in some state of limbo and tuning things out.

She knocked again, harder. It sounded as if she was pounding, but still no one answered. The door didn't have a conventional latch, and it wasn't locked, Temple discovered as she applied some pressure to the frame, and it gave.

The interior was a room as spare as a monastery. It was lit with pungent juniper candles, but nearly bare of furniture, except for a woven covering of seagrass on the floor, mats made of sweet-smelling rice straw, and an arrangement of floor cushions. It was truly a traditional teahouse, she realized.

Hardly daring to breathe, she stepped inside and saw that she was alone in the room. There was a large alcove to her left, apparently designed to serve as a kitchen, where water simmered in a black kettle with a handle that curled above it like an incomplete circle. In another smaller corner across the room sat a splendid bouquet of pink cherry blossoms, set off by scrolls of delicate calligraphy.

To her left was an odd shrinelike area where tiers of votive candles flickered and incense wafted from delicate bowls of latticed metal. The centerpiece was a framed picture of an exquisitely lovely young woman. Her eyes sparkled like precious onyx, and her hair fell to her shoulders in a feathery curve, glossy black and shivering with highlights. But it was her wistful expression that captured Temple.

Of course he was in love with her, Temple thought. Who could resist her?

If she'd thought she could silence the pain with this visit, she'd been wrong. It ignited like fire. Each individual candle was burning her, hundreds of them.

She backed to the door. But as she whirled to leave, she collided with another human body. Raw shock nearly toppled her. It was Mark Challis, and Temple had no idea how long he'd been standing there, but the darkness in his expression frightened her. The snake was out of its basket. The cobra had uncoiled.

"Temple? What the hell—"

He'd already taken her by the arm and propelled her out the door before he finished the statement. She wasn't given time to do anything, including answer him. But Temple was angry, too, and she demanded to know why he lied.

"You said this area was off-limits for security reasons!"

"It is off-limits." He pulled her with him toward the bridge, but she resisted. Struggling to free her wrist, she heard something whine sharply past her ear a second before it caught Mark in the shoulder. A bullet. He'd been hit and the sound of the punctured flesh was terrible.

Blood flew everywhere, spattering Temple.

He released her hand, and she let out a gasp, tumbling backward. She was unable to stop herself. Nothing could have stopped her fall. The slippery rocks at the edge of the pond spun her off her feet and threw her into the water.

The shock of it numbed her. The water was icy, but she could barely feel the cold as she sank to the bottom. Her arms flailed, seeking purchase, but the only thing that made contact was her head. It struck a large rock as she plummeted.

TWENTY-ONE

"Princess, please—"

Temple came to shivering in a man's arms. Her body was deeply chilled, but her senses responded to his gentle tone. He was smoothing her face and arms, whispering into her hair. It was difficult to hear what he was saying, but he seemed to be begging her to be all right, and the low, husky pitch of his voice tugged at a knot of longing inside her.

Her whole life she'd waited for someone to talk to her like this, she realized. Maybe all she'd ever wanted was to feel loved and cared for.

She tried to speak, but it came out unformed, a half-moaned need.

"That's my girl," he said, whispering, whispering, like her shell. "Stay with me, Temple."

Her eyelids were heavy, but it was Mark she saw through her misted vision, and his expression astonished her. There were tears caught in his eyelashes. She had never seen so much tragic beauty in one man's face. She was devastated by it. And desperate to understand.

It was as if he was losing the thing he loved most in life.

His lips brushed over her cheek, and she rose up to catch his mouth with hers. He groaned in surprise, and they clung that way, touching only there. Joined by an arc of light. It felt like the sweetest, wildest, most impulsive thing she'd ever done with a man. She was trembling so deep within that she could barely speak.

"Please," she implored. Now she was begging him. Whatever he was offering, she had to have it. She wanted to feel it all through her, the dark burning tenderness.

"Please, I need you."

Mark didn't know how to answer her. The catch in her voice aroused a quick, hard shudder. He couldn't feel the pain of his shoulder. Another kind of agony had completely consumed him, but he couldn't let himself make love with her. He'd fought that battle and come up a loser. He'd taken too much from her. He couldn't take this, too, her first time.

"Sshhh, you bumped your head," he told her soothingly. "You're going to be fine, but you need to rest."

She fell back with a sigh and lay there, breathing softly.

He thought she'd settled down enough that he could withdraw and let her rest. But when he slid his arm from beneath her, she let out a tiny cry of alarm. Mark was rocked by it. He'd never heard such naked longing. He gathered her close, struggling not to hurt her, but feeling helpless. He didn't know what else to do but hold her and try to calm her. *It was all he ever wanted to do.*

Their wet clothes were in a heap by the teahouse door. It was where he'd undressed her after carrying her inside. He'd found blankets to wrap her in and then he'd torn off his own clothes, stopped the bleeding from his shoulder wound, and dressed it. Fortunately the bullet had gone straight through the fleshy part of his shoulder and made a clean exit.

There hadn't been time to go after the sniper. He couldn't do that and take care of Temple. But he'd called his security chief, whom he trusted implicitly, and asked him to pick two men and scour the island.

After that he'd taken some of the codeine he carried for pain, wrapped himself in blankets, and lay down next to Temple. He'd had nothing more in mind than keeping her warm and safe, but somehow she'd found her way through the layers of material to the muscles of his arm and she was drowsily stroking them and murmuring things he couldn't understand. But God, they sounded as gentle and sexy as anything he'd ever heard.

He knew she wasn't trying to be sexy, but the more basic parts of his anatomy didn't give a damn about her motives. Everything was tightening except the liquid pleasure in the pit of his stomach.

She found his chest next, those petting hands of hers, and then his belly. His shoulder had begun to throb from holding her, but when her hand dropped between his legs, when she grasped him there with her cool fingers, all physical pain was gone. It was the wound inside him that broke open. He had to have her or die of it.

Instinct drove him from that point on. Her scent and her textures were maddening. They teased his senses. His needs were dark and primal. And yet they were transcendent, too. It felt as if some blinding light had hit him, as if he could fly.

Temple was reduced to a moment of incoherence as he gathered her naked body to his. Their mouths caught again and clung. Their hips knocked sweetly, and their legs entangled.

But the sound that groaned from inside him was regret as he tore himself from her lips. "Temple, we can't do this," he whispered. "You're a virgin."

"A pregnant virgin," she agreed.

"Two reasons not to—"

"Two reasons we must, Mark. If I'm having a baby, then I want the full experience. I want to have a man, too. And the only man I want is you."

She hadn't said that. She must be delirious from the blow.

He rose up and drew the blankets away to look at her blossoming body. He smoothed a palm over her belly and gazed achingly at her luscious breasts. Their fullness cried out to be touched and loved. Her parted legs cried out for that, too.

She saw how dreadfully hard he was, how knotted up and needful of a soft, wet, welcoming woman to ease his pain. She saw that he could melt into her like rain into a river, like a river into the ocean. Sex could melt into sex. Life could melt into life.

She came up, trembling a little as she presented him with a breast. And just in case there was any chance he misunderstood her intentions, she cupped it lightly in her palm, a goddess offering a sacrifice.

"We can't, Temple—"

"We *must*, Mark."

His lips drew gently on her nipple, and Temple felt her womb contract. She dropped back and brought him to her lips, whimpering. He answered with a snarl and scooped her up, wanting it his way, kissing her hard, so hard their teeth clicked and their sounds of joy burbled up like spring-water. This was joy, this hard, wet, grinding need.

She gasped as they joined. Her first man. Him, only him. And in the heat of physical sensation she was swept by a purely emotional one. Swept by a wave of raw vulnerability. Of soul sighs and the exquisite sense of feeling your heart open to someone, along with your body. Shyly. So shyly.

Neither of them could stop. Temple was immersed in the beauty, he by an agony of wanting that couldn't be distinguished from ecstasy. Barriers fell away until there was nothing but light. And Temple was reduced again. Emptied.

Only as she drifted in his arms afterward, did she remember the gunshot—and ask him about it.

Someone had tried to kill him. Or was it her?

"You're safe. Nothing else matters." Mark bent as if he'd spotted something of unusual interest on Temple's face. And then he casually faked her out by kissing the bridge of her nose.

The cobra strikes again, she thought, smiling.

"I didn't hurt you, did I?" he asked.

"No, my nose is fine."

"I meant the *rest* of you."

"The rest of me is fine, too, thanks." A sigh welled up from some sweet place within her. "There wasn't any pain, none at all." She hadn't actually expected that there would be, but she hadn't expected such ravishing pleasure, either. She wasn't sure why people did anything else other than make love.

"You're the one who's hurt," she said, touching his heavily bandaged shoulder. "Do you have any idea who shot at you? Or why? Or do you think it was me they were after?"

He put a finger to her lips, gently halting the questions.

"I'd rather know," she said, sensing his hesitance. "Not knowing is worse. It makes my mind run."

Apparently he found some humor in that statement.

"We wouldn't want that, would we," he said with a trace of irony. "The truth is I don't know who they were after. I suspect the sniper was someone who lived here on the island, possibly even a member of my security staff. I've got three men combing the area."

It felt as if she should be frightened, but Temple couldn't work up the energy. Maybe it was the head wound. Or the sex, but she couldn't remember ever feeling this safe, as if she were in the hands of a guardian angel. If this was after-glow, she thought, someone ought to set up a concession and sell it. It felt as if nothing could ever happen to her as long as she was here, with Mark Challis.

She shifted in the cradle of his arms, trying to find a comfortable position. The seagrass smelled as sweet as freshly cut hay, but it provided very little cushioning against the wooden floor. She thought better of rolling to her side when she saw how little blanket there was available. Most of it was caught in the tangle of their legs. There was also the problem of her head. It hurt whenever she moved.

She touched a large, very tender spot behind her ear.

"You landed pretty hard," he said. "It may be sore for a while, but you'll be fine."

She gave him a skeptical look. "Are you sure?"

"Part of my training at the 'school for spooks' was a crash course in emergency medicine. I could run my own little hospital with what I know. So yes, I'm sure, and you would be wise to heed the doctor's advice in this case."

"Which is . . . ?"

His voice went husky, and not very doctorlike at all. "Kiss me again, patient."

An impulse ached inside Temple. The thrill of lifting up and catching his mouth with hers was still cut into the tracery of her nervous system. She wanted that thrill again, but her head felt as if it might not make the trip with her. And she had to wait for him to come to her.

Worth it, she thought as he grasped her chin with his fingers and curved his mouth to hers. He moved and moaned until the fit was perfect, and then he shifted above her, deepening the kiss. His tongue played at the crease of her lips, a long, hot thing that wanted her helpless. And when finally he did slip it in and go deep, soul deep, Temple made a sweet noise of her own.

It was a mating call vibrating like a violin string in the

back of her throat. He answered with one of his own, but this was not an echo of their physical joining, it was a prelude to more sex, with the promise of something deeper, wilder.

He was already hardening against the swell of her thigh, which allowed her to feel every growing, demanding inch of him. But Temple fended him off with her fingertips. She pressed them gently to his chin when he bent to kiss her again.

"I can't," she said, "not just yet."

"I did hurt you, then?"

"No, no—of course not." She smiled, wondering if he could see the sudden pensiveness in her expressive. It had nothing to do with the physical aspects of their lovemaking. This was something else entirely. It was the picture in this very room where they'd just made love, the candlelit shrine. It wasn't a sniper or a bullet that frightened her, she realized. It was a woman. It was the thought of him loving someone else.

How did she ask? And why hadn't he told her yet?

"This house is very unusual," she said quietly. "Is it yours?"

"My father had it built for my mother."

His head barely moved as he spoke, and his voice had lost some of its strength. Strong clues that this was not a subject he wanted to dwell on, but Temple had tortured herself over the woman in the photograph. She had to know who that exquisite creature was.

"Who lives here now?" she asked. "The teapot was simmering when I came in, and the flowers are fresh."

"No one has lived here for years, not since my mother died."

Had he lifted his head to glance at the low table where the photograph sat? Temple couldn't be sure. "Your mother . . . is she the woman in the picture?"

Yes, he was looking at the photograph. He seemed to be

studying it. But when Temple followed his gaze, she could see nothing beyond the amber glow of a candle flame, reflected in the glass.

"Lorraine Challis," he said, "daughter of June, wife of Jonathan, mother of Mark and William. This teahouse was her refuge and, probably, her prison cell."

"Your mother, then." Temple tried not to show her reaction, but she was dizzy with relief. It took some concentration to get her other questions out. "Daughter of June. Do you mean the housekeeper?"

"Yes." His smile was faintly bitter. "She's my grandmother, although I'm sure she'd prefer that weren't the case. June is Eurasian, from French aristocrats on her father's side and a long line of Aikido masters on her mother's. June also married a Frenchman, and then left him because of his infidelities and came to the States while she was pregnant with my mother. . . ."

Temple had the sense as he talked that he knew every detail of his family history, well beyond what most people normally did, unless they'd researched it.

"June had a little family money from her mother," he said, "but not enough to sustain her and a child, and when this country proved to be a disappointment, she started saving money to go back to Sapporo, to her mother's side of the family, where she'd visited as a child. She worked as a housekeeper and trained my mother in those skills, which was how my mother and father eventually met."

"June worked for your father?"

"No, June had gone back to Sapporo by then. My mother was eighteen and working at the estate of a business associate. Jonathan was lost the moment he saw her. The two of them fell so instantly and deeply in love, they defied both their families, as kind of Eastern-Western Romeo and Juliet.

His mother was Eurasian. That was the elusive quality Temple had discerned in his features but not been able to define. You could look forever and not catch what was different about the hard elegance of his face, the long, cool contours. The optical illusion wasn't a shadowy character flaw. It was part of who he was, inbred in the proud, mysterious countenance. He was the product of years of an exotically mixed ancestry that had nearly vanished with Mark.

"Their families banished them when they married," he explained, "which only seemed to bind them closer. I sometimes think they would have had a happy life together if they hadn't had children. As it turned out, they had profound differences on how males should be raised in this culture. And my mother, as delicate as she looked, came from people of strong mettle. She was determined that both her sons be not only exposed to, but educated in, the warrior side of their Asian ancestry."

Temple had rolled to her hip and was gingerly resting her head on her arm as she listened to him, utterly rapt. He feathered her lashes with his knuckles, and his smile was full of sudden tenderness.

"Go on," she implored, "tell me what happened."

"Will and I were the only blood family Jonathan had left, and he was terrified of losing us. He ordered my mother never to speak of her ancestry in our presence, her own children. He'd built a billion-dollar software industry. That was his legacy, and he was afraid his only heirs would be lured away by the romance of kung fu fighting and great adventures in the Orient."

"And he was right, wasn't he?"

"He was, yes. My mother's secret defiance, and only real happiness, was enthralling my brother and me with tales of her forbears' exploits. We were both desperate to train under her uncle, a revered master who lived in Sapporo. Of course, Jonathan wouldn't allow it, but my mother had quietly reconciled with her family, and she made arrangements to send us anyway. When Jonathan found out, he was outraged.

He'd cut himself off from his family for her. He couldn't believe she would betray him like that or expose his sons to such risk."

Mark released a breath. "Jonathan Challis appointed himself judge and jury. He found his wife unfit and banished her to this island."

"My God," Temple breathed. "Just like feudal England."

"Just like that," he said. "But by cutting off all contact, he punished himself as much as the rest of us. He never stopped loving her, and the guilt of separating her from her children nearly destroyed him. He brought her mother over from Japan, and then he had the tea garden and house built, all in an attempt to keep his exiled wife happy."

"Did you ever see her again?" Temple asked.

It was the wrong question. He looked away, but not quickly enough to hide the emotion that clouded his expression. Grief was not easy to conceal, even for a man like him, and his defenses were down. She didn't want them to go back up. She was just beginning to see through the smoke and mirrors of her own fantasies and learn who Mark Challis was.

"Let me get you some floor cushions," he said, easing his arm out from under her. He rescued one of the blankets and knotted it around his waist. "You look miserable."

Not nearly as miserable as you, she thought. But she smiled and thanked him when he brought over several of the purple *zabutons* to shore up her aching head and make her more comfortable. She noticed a little blood on the neatly wrapped gauze that covered his shoulder wound. He'd been favoring that arm but didn't seem to be in pain.

The cobra temperament? she wondered.

His next offer was to make her some tea.

She was glad she'd accepted when he returned with a tray of implements, including the simmering iron pot, bamboo canisters, ladles, and scoops, and deftly performed a short

version of the elaborate four-hundred-year-old tea ceremony. It was considered a metaphor for life by devotees, he
told her, and, if correctly performed by a tea master, was believed to help one find one's inner joy.

Temple thought that she had already found hers, but tea
was always nice, and Mark did seem to know what he was
doing.

He poured boiling water from the pot into a cooling basin.
"To let it calm," he explained, and then he ladled it into a
bronze bowl, called a *cha-wan*, where the delicate green
powder that he'd scooped from the canister was waiting.
Temple had never smelled anything so lovely and sweetly
pungent as the fragrance that arose from the *cha-wan* as the
brew steeped.

Moments later Mark presented her with a ceremonial
bowl of pale green tea, mysteriously suggested that she turn
the bowl twice clockwise, and watched quietly while she
sipped. Focused on the still-swirling liquid, Temple became
more alert to her surroundings. The incense curling from the
metal pots smelled of ginger and sandalwood, and the wind
chimes pinged like diamond drops. She was especially
aware of her tea master, who seemed to meditate over his
own cup and looked strangely monklike in his seminaked
state.

"You asked if I ever saw my mother again."

Temple put down her bowl, startled that he'd spoken.

"And I just realized I never did," he said. "I never actually
saw her alive, but I was able to communicate with her
through June. And I talked to her the day she died."

His voice had a removed quality to it, and Temple sensed
that he'd had to find a way to detach in order to go on with
this painful biography of his. There was nothing she could
do or say, she realized. The wisest course was to listen and
let him deal with it in his own way.

"My mother called me that morning at the house on the

mainland, and I knew something was wrong because she'd never done that. June had always made the calls for her. She told me she'd found a skiff, and she was going to use it to escape the island. I begged her not to do it. I even threatened to tell my father, and that seemed to terrify her."

Temple knew what it was like having to parent your own parents. She'd grown up with the task, although she'd never faced anything like this.

"It was the only way I knew how to stop her," Mark explained. His head was slightly bowed. "But what a terrible mistake that was. It sent her into a panic, and she drowned trying to get away before my father could stop her."

"Oh . . . how terrible." Temple remembered his stricken expression the day of the storm when he'd seen the sunken boat. Now she wondered if that could have been the one his mother used. And perhaps the gravestone by the stream was where Lorraine Challis was buried.

He'd already picked up Temple's bowl and the rest of the tea things and was taking them back into the kitchen. One of the bamboo scoops fell off and hit the rice straw matting, but he didn't notice. And Temple didn't move.

"June has held me responsible from that day forward," he said as he set the tray down on the countertop, "and in a way I am. She's the one who turned this house into a shrine to my mother, and she threatened to put a curse on the Challis family if I ever spoke my mother's name or came here. I told her I didn't believe in curses."

Temple had the feeling he was going to say he'd changed his mind about that, but he was silent.

"It's June who lights the candles, isn't it?" she asked. "And plays that music." Her head throbbed, but she forced herself to sit up, pulling a covering around her. "It's your mother's favorite opera, *Madame Butterfly*."

"Favorite?" He turned around, but he didn't seem to understand. "I think the opera may have reminded my mother of her situation—a beautiful young geisha trapped in a sham marriage with an American, who deserts her, and ultimately takes their child away from her."

All Temple could remember was her shock the night she'd been awakened by it. Was it all opera or just all Puccini that sounded like the mystery music she'd heard in the honeymoon suite? The question still confounded her. And it was the only one she couldn't bring herself to ask.

Mark came back with Temple to the mill house that night. He didn't want to leave her alone until he was assured that the island's security had been restored.

They slept together in her small brass bed by the fireplace and they were never not touching. Even during those moments when they drifted off and lost all conscious awareness of each other, it seemed that their bodies were drawn by some kind of physical need that was as urgent as anything Temple had ever known.

It was painful unless they were touching. Painful when they were touching. She'd never known that a man could shake and sigh and be as naked as a woman. She'd never known a woman could be as racked with carnal needs as a man. Or that for one night or one moment, they could be the same physical body, the same heart.

She was awash in the glory of that discovery.

He was her clock. She had no sense of time, except when he woke her to hold her again, and taste her lips, and press himself into her body, whichever way she was curled.

Cradled in the curve of his warmth, she heard him whisper, "If you could have anything you want, what would it be?"

"This," she said. "I want nothing to change."

Tears wet her eyes. There was something of destiny here. She couldn't speak of love, but she was thinking of it, and she sensed that he was, too.

Those were the thoughts in her head as she drifted off to sleep, her back to his front, two bodies, one being. Swimming deep. From outside her window, the musical rush of the waterfall spoke to her like the whisperings of her nautilus shell. It seemed to be telling her that she had found what she'd always been searching for. That this was it, this wondrous sense of completion.

When she woke in the night, she heard him talking to someone, and realized he was on his cell phone.

"Mark?"

She reached for him and he came to her immediately. "I have to go," he said. "That was security. They haven't found the sniper, and I think I know why, but I'll need to make a trip to the mainland."

"Why?" She gathered the sheet around her and sat up.

"Temple, there isn't time to explain, and I don't have the answers yet. Just trust me that you're not in any immediate danger, I'm certain of that. My security chief is taking over my watch until I get back. He won't intrude. You'll never see him, but you'll be safe."

"Mark, please tell me what's going on."

He didn't respond, just continued with his instructions. "Stay here in the cottage until I return. You're to go nowhere, confide in no one, trust no one. Do you understand?"

"No, Mark—"

"No one but me, Temple," he said as he bent to kiss her one last time. "Trust no one but me."

She sensed something in his voice that frightened her. "Mark, please, tell me what's going on."

But all he would say was "Wait for me here, and you'll be safe."

Temple didn't try to stop him. She couldn't move for the shock rolling through her, because his last words, harsh and aching, as he disappeared through the door were "I love you."

"Miss Banning, wake up—"

It wasn't the hushed voice that woke her. It was the hands that were shaking her. Temple was sunk in the deepest sleep imaginable. Fatigue had taken possession of every cell of her being after Mark left. And now someone was trying to pommel her back to consciousness.

Submerged in the quilt, she vaguely recognized the man's voice, but it wasn't Mark.

"Wake up," he urged. "There's someone here to see you. He says it's important. He's outside."

The message began to register in Temple's groggy brain. She struggled to clear her head and get herself to a sitting position. He must be talking about Mark.

"What's wrong?" she asked, startled to see Eddie Baker crouched beside her bed, as if he were trying to hide from something.

Eddie put a finger to his lips, warning Temple not to talk. "Somebody might be listening, ma'am," he told her in whispers. "You need to get yourself dressed quick and come outside."

If fear could have been poured from a pitcher, Temple had just taken a gulp. She wrapped a sheet around her nakedness, dragged herself from bed, and quickly got dressed.

TWENTY-TWO

The man waiting outside to see Temple was Dr. Dan Llewelyn. A look of world-weary consternation creased his deeply lined face as he stood on her front porch. Temple sensed his mood as she came out the door, but when he saw her he rearranged the concern into a smile and took her outstretched hand.

"Dr. Llewelyn?" She made no effort to hide her surprise.

"June told me you weren't feeling well," he explained. "I came as quickly as I could."

"Oh, that, I—"

Temple hesitated. She picked up a warning in his eyes and the barely discernible shake of his head. He was trying to tell her something. That he didn't want her to talk? That confused her until she realized he must think they were under surveillance. Eddie had said the same thing.

"So . . . what's the problem?" Llewelyn asked, and then added, "the *symptoms* you've been having. Tell me about them."

There weren't any symptoms, but he wanted her to

come up with some, she realized. He urged her with a nod of his head to play along with him. Apparently he really was concerned about being overheard, and there was a good chance they would be. Mark had told her before he left that his security chief would be taking over, but that Temple would never see him, which meant the video cameras were on.

Still, Temple didn't understand why that was a problem. Mark had also told her he trusted his security chief implicitly and that she would be safe. She wondered if it was possible that the doctor knew about the sniper incident. Perhaps Mark had talked to Llewelyn himself and asked him to come here.

Questions were beginning to crowd in on Temple's thoughts, but she was reluctant to ask any of them. She wasn't sure what Llewelyn's concerns were, or what she should and shouldn't say.

"Is it the dizziness?" Llewelyn prompted. "The morning sickness again?"

Temple felt cool air against the back of her neck. She looked around to see that the handyman had slipped behind her, stolen down the porch steps, and disappeared.

What was going on?

"Any nausea?" Llewelyn pressed.

"Yes, morning sickness. I've been feeling queasy."

"Why don't we go for a walk in the gardens," he suggested. "It's a beautiful, sunny morning, and the fresh air might be all you need. If not, I can give you some tablets that will settle your stomach, and be perfectly safe for the baby, of course."

"All right . . ." But Temple's heart had begun to pound. Mark had told her not to leave the cabin. He'd said it repeatedly, and he'd told her to trust no one but him.

Llewelyn had moved to the stairs. Temple didn't pick up urgency in his expression as much as gravity, which made her wonder if he had something to tell her about her condition and wanted to reveal it in confidence.

"Would you like my jacket?" he asked. "There might be a slight chill in the air."

"I'm fine, thanks." She'd put on the first things she could find—a T-shirt, cardigan sweater, and jeans.

"After you." He gestured for her to lead the way down the steps, and Temple didn't know what to do. Surely Mark hadn't meant not to trust the doctor. He'd taken her to Llewelyn in the first place. They were family friends.

Temple could see Wings looming in the foreground, framed by a cloudless sapphire sky. It was probably midmorning by the slant of the sun, but there was no sign of anyone about.

"Where's June?" she asked.

He shook his head as if to say he didn't know. "I thought it better to come straight here."

Temple wasn't sure what she was waiting for, a sign perhaps, something to tell her it was safe. One of her tennis shoes had come untied and as she knelt down, she heard herself saying, "I've never seen the east garden. I've heard it's lovely."

"I'll take you."

Dizziness nearly tipped her over when she tried to stand. Llewelyn caught her hand, steadying her as he helped her to her feet, and then somehow they started down the steps that way, hands still clasped. The gesture stirred an odd, sad awareness in Temple. He seemed to be concerned that she might fall, and it made her think of the fathering she'd never had.

The east garden was lush with greenery, fat buds, and a few tender new blooms. The sun was honey warm. Still Temple shivered as the first breezes hit her. It wasn't from lack of clothing. The chill she felt came from the coldness that lay dormant inside her. It was fear, lying in wait.

They stopped near an arbor made of delicate green trellises that were dripping with pale yellow climbing roses. Temple gave in to an impulse and picked a bud that was just beginning to frill with color. Within the arbor's veil of flowers was a marble birdbath and fountain, surrounded by antique verdigris benches.

"I'm really all right," she told the doctor, wanting to ease his mind if his concerns were about her health. "I did ask June to call you, but it was to calm her fears more than mine. She seems to think I'm being held hostage on the island, and if I don't escape, I'll never leave alive. She won't tell me why she believes that, but—"

June's prediction had nearly come true last night, Temple realized with a start. Both she and Mark were lucky to have escaped the sniper situation with their lives.

"June's a bit eccentric," she said, aware that the rose she'd picked was twisted in her fingers.

"Eccentric, perhaps, but I'm afraid I have to agree with her this time."

Temple stared at him, waiting for an explanation. The direct sun was growing hot, and he touched her elbow, guiding her into the shade of the trellises. They sat on one of the benches, and he grew somber, as if preparing himself.

In the short time Temple had known him, he had become one of the few stable elements in her world. He'd talked her out of her unreasonable fears before, and she wanted that again. She wanted reassurance, not this gloomy visage he'd taken on.

"I have reason to believe you *are* in danger here, Temple," he said at last. "And not just you, the baby, too. I want you to consider coming back to the mainland with me."

"The baby? What do you mean?"

He told her that he'd done some investigating since his

last visit, and what he'd discovered was serious enough to make him think her suspicions about Mark were correct.

"It's worse than serious, Temple. I honestly don't know how to tell you."

She'd broken off a piece of the flower stem. "Dr. Llewelyn, you have to tell me now. I'll be more frightened if you don't."

He patted her hand as if to quiet her, but Temple could feel the unsteadiness in his touch.

"Yes, of course I will," he said. "There's nothing else I can do at this point. My obligation to tell you is as imperative as your right to know. But with the technical jargon involved, it may not be easy to follow."

"Please," she urged. "If I don't understand, I'll stop you."

He nodded, obviously torn, yet driven by some sense of responsibility to her and perhaps the oath he'd taken. Temple wasn't the only one who had something at stake in this, she realized. Dan Llewelyn had come here to warn her, despite the cost to his long relationship with Mark and the powerful Challis family.

Odd how she was torn between wanting to reassure him and wanting to silence him. She was afraid of what he was going to tell her.

"I doubt the lay public is aware of it," he said, "but the first successful transplant operation did more than revolutionize medicine. It also created a rampant black market for vital organs—viable kidneys, hearts, livers, even human corneas, are in short supply—and great demand. Ironically, every time medical science makes great advances, the demand seems to increase and in some ways it grows more frightening and perverse."

He hesitated again, perhaps wondering if there was any way to prepare her for the rest of it.

"I'm fine," she said. "Go on."

His exhalation was not laughter, but pain. "Forgive me,

but I wish *I* were fine. I wish there were some way to make what I have to tell you fine. But since I can't do that—" He bent his head and rubbed at his heavy eyebrows. "Let me get to the point.

"Medical science is in revolt again. The new biotechnology is embroiled in great and terrifying things—gene therapy, germ-line genetic manipulation, cloning, and designer human beings. It's hard to grasp, even for me, a doctor. And the ethical implications are staggering. Still, I've always believed that it's more dangerous to postpone revolutionary research out of fear than it is to forge on, especially when the future benefits are great. Always believed that, strongly. It's been the cornerstone of my career. Only now . . . I don't know."

Temple was silent, unable to do much more than try not to mutilate the flower she held. And listen dumbly.

"With each new frontier," he said, "the black markets proliferate. God knows what will happen when gene therapy is perfected. Right now, there's an operation under way to supply the research labs vying to develop billion-dollar drugs and vaccines."

"Supply them with vital organs?"

"No, with stem cells, cord blood, and possibly even the antibodies of pregnant women."

Temple's knees bumped his. "You aren't suggesting that Mark is involved in a black-market operation? You can't be suggesting that."

"No, no, that's inconceivable. But he has a very personal stake in this. His father is dying of the same virus that killed your parents."

She stared at him, stunned once again to dumb silence, yet knowing exactly what he was going to say next. *The virus you survived.*

He took the mangled flower from her hands. "Your case was written up in a medical journal, Temple. The authors couldn't do much more than theorize why your immune system produced antibodies against Agent Z190, or how, for that matter. But they did discover that another group of victims produced antibodies, too. None of them survived, but they outlived the others by weeks, even months.

"I'm talking about the pregnant women."

Temple had no formal medical background herself, but it felt as if she'd spent as much time memorizing the anatomy and physiology texts as Donald had, studying with him through school, his internship, and residency. She'd even helped him with the plans to start his small, family practice, and learned a great deal in the process, more than enough to understand what Llewelyn had just implied.

In a voice far calmer than she felt, she said, "I now have the viral antibodies, plus the immune response associated with pregnancy? Is that it?"

"Exactly, and if the antibodies are still viable and the virus hasn't mutated, then you're the next thing to a living, breathing vaccine."

"But that's me, not the baby." Temple had turned into a cold, fact-gathering machine.

"Not necessarily. Your antibodies can only provide passive immunization, which is temporary. For lasting protection, a vaccine that includes an altered form of the virus would have to be developed. Stem cells are the most effective medium for culturing the virus. And they can also be used to generate new immune systems for the victims."

"Dear God," she breathed. "What are you saying?"

"Agent Z190 destroys organs, Temple."

Temple knew what it did. Her parents were gone by the time she got to the hospital, but she'd been quarantined with the dying before they brought her back to the States. She'd seen the devastation. The virus crippled the heart, the lungs. It invaded the nervous system and the brain. Still, she couldn't let it in, not the full horror of what he was suggesting.

"Stem cells, what are they exactly?"

"Theoretically they can divide and become any cell type—bone, muscle, or nerve—and ultimately any new organ. But there's only one source of such powerful cells, and that's the baby itself. The umbilical cord also teems with stem cells, but they're more specialized, and somewhat more limited in what tissues they can generate."

He was saying that what the cord couldn't provide, the baby would. Her child would be a backup in case the needed tissue couldn't be harvested from the umbilical cells.

Was that *really* what he was saying? Something inside Temple had gone numb. There was no tone in her voice when she spoke, no inflection. "How do you know all this?"

"I am a doctor, Temple, a researcher. But the truth is, I hired an investigator."

He drew an envelope from his jacket and handed it to her. Temple stared at it, at him, but he wouldn't look at her.

The envelope could have been a monthly bill or a solicitation to join a record club. She felt very little more emotion than that as she opened it and pulled out the two documents inside. The numbness had invaded every part of her being as she studied a newspaper article and a copy of a prescription slip for a tranquilizer.

The prescription was made out to a June St. Gerard. Temple recognized the surname, but other than that, it didn't register as significant. The article did, however. It was the piece Annette wrote about Mark Challis, the very same one, except that it was intact. There was a photograph with this one, and Temple recognized the man in it.

She touched the bench's cold metal arm, steadying herself as she struggled to understand what the picture meant. The article was about Mark Challis, but the man she was

looking at couldn't be Mark, although there was a certain
resemblance. This man had a moustache and long wavy
black hair to his shoulders. He looked more like the
stranger in the snapshot Annette had shown her, the man
in deep shadow who was supposed to have been standing
at the bar the night they were celebrating Annette's birthday.

"Who is he?" she asked, aware of the computer software
that could alter photographs with a few deft brush strokes.
They could even add or remove people and change the backdrop.

"It's a picture of Mark taken during his military intelligence career. He did some undercover work in those days,
and used an assortment of personas, including the name
St. Gerard, which came from his mother's side of the family.
Her maiden name was Lorraine St. Gerard."

And his grandmother was June St. Gerard.

"Does June know about all this?" she asked.

"I doubt anyone but Mark Challis knows all of it," he
said.

Temple went quiet while Llewelyn explained that he'd
been called in by Jonathan Challis to treat June after her
daughter drowned. June had been so distraught, Llewelyn
had prescribed Miltown, a powerful tranquilizer and an-
tipsychotic, but he hadn't realized there was a connection
between June's surname and the man Temple described as
Michael St. Gerard until the investigator he hired pointed it
out to him.

Temple wasn't sure she understood it yet. "So there was
never any marriage? The honeymoon suite, the license, the
phone message, and the letters, it was all a lie?"

"It was a way to get you here, to keep you here, and make
sure you didn't do anything rash, like end your pregnancy."

"Stop—stop, please!" She turned away, her brain
whirring, trying to make sense of something that was so to-

tally unthinkable. Her head might spin off like a top if he said anything else.

Llewelyn went quiet, too, obviously aware that she was in crisis. After a moment he said, "Temple, please come with me. I want to get you off this island. We'll go straight to the police, if you want. Or if you're not ready for that, we'll find a safe place for you to stay until we can figure out what's best."

"Wait!" she demanded in a soft, anguished voice. "Just tell me one thing. Is this his baby? Is it Mark's?"

"I would guess that it is, Temple. Any risk of rejection is greatly reduced if Mark is the father."

She began to shake her head, to hold herself. She could feel the ground shifting under her feet, the sky going dark, swooping down on her like a huge black peregrine.

"No, he could never do that. He couldn't."

"His father is dying."

"But you know him." She was angry now. Ready to kill the messenger. "You know Mark Challis. He's not that kind of man, and even if he were, he hates his father. You told me that yourself. Why would he try to save a man he despises?"

"I don't know," Llewelyn admitted.

"Then maybe you're wrong. You could be wrong about this."

"I'm not wrong. And even if I were, you couldn't and shouldn't risk it."

She shook her head. "I can't go back with you. They'll never let me off this island. Mark's chief of security has taken over while Mark's gone."

"I spoke with the security chief. I told him you were ill and I might have to take you back with me. I came over on a chartered helicopter, and it's sitting on the helipad now, waiting for us. Temple, this might be your only chance to get off the island."

"You think he'd let me go? Without Mark's okay?"

"I said I was concerned about complications with the pregnancy, and to allay any suspicions, I suggested he contact Mark. Fortunately Mark wasn't answering his pager, but even if he had been, Mark has no choice but to trust my medical judgment on this, Temple. It wouldn't be difficult to convince him you needed care you couldn't get on the island."

He rose heavily from the bench. "There's just one other thing."

Temple shook her head. She couldn't deal with anything else, but Llewelyn went on anyway.

"I think Jonathan Challis is hidden somewhere on this island, and if the CDC knew what he had, they would quarantine the entire island immediately. Their concern would be for protecting others, not Jonathan, and he would almost certainly die. That's why Mark brought him out here."

"Am I at risk? Is the baby?"

"You're at risk of being trapped on this island, just like June said. You're not at risk of contracting the virus. Unless it's mutated drastically, you're still immune."

Temple walked out of the arbor into the sunlight. She needed to feel the elements and know that she was alive. Maybe the sun's pounding heat could revive her stunned heart, maybe it could start the blood flowing in her veins. It seemed incomprehensible that someone carrying life could feel as if they were dead.

It is incomprehensible that he could do this. Sacrifice his own child? She would never believe it.

It felt like Temple must have stood in the sun a very long time. Her skin was fiery hot and there were tears streaming down her cheeks when she turned back to Dan Llewelyn. The look on her face must have told him what he needed to know because he nodded, and then he bent his head, bowed by some terrible emotion.

• • •

It was the moaning that brought Temple back to the clock tower to investigate. The sound of it had left a distinct impression. Breathy. Intimate. She'd actually wondered if there could be some kind of love tryst going on in the upper floors. But then June had materialized and told her the place was unsafe.

What *wasn't* unsafe? Temple wondered. Her own body was a chem lab for the "new frontier," as Dr. Llewelyn had called it.

Fortunately, the mansion had been quiet when she slipped inside the front doors moments ago. She couldn't afford to be caught this time. Llewelyn had mentioned that Jonathan Challis was somewhere on the island, and this was the first place that had come to Temple's mind. It was one of the reasons she'd decided not to go back with the doctor. That and the simple fact that she couldn't go.

She had to know for herself if Mark had done things she didn't believe him capable of. Dan Llewelyn may have wanted to save her the pain, but no one could do that for you. No one could be born, die, or hurt for you. No one could love for you, either. And no one could tell you that your love had been brutally betrayed.

She wasn't going to confront him. There wouldn't be any accusations. Because of what had happened between them, she believed that she would know the moment she saw him. There were no more masks or optical illusions to hide behind. They were both naked. And she would know.

Meanwhile he'd asked her to stay here and wait for him. He'd told her he loved her in a voice so harsh with emotion it had made her ache. And in her heart she'd answered. A promise had been made. Unspoken, but a promise nonetheless.

The morning he'd brought her to the island, he'd said there came a time when you had to trust someone. She didn't remember the exact words, but she knew it wasn't

Mark she was choosing to trust. It wasn't even Dan Llewelyn. It was the mysterious whispering that spoke from somewhere inside her. It was the shell and the stream and all of the music that guided her without her understanding how.

It was only now, at this very moment, as she entered the chalk-white interior of the medieval tower, that she wondered if she'd done the right thing. The octagonal structure had seemed ethereal before, even a heavenly staircase. Now it was stark and forbidding. If anything Llewelyn said was true, then she was exposing herself and the baby to a terrible risk. But she had come this far.

No one was waiting for her on the landing as she climbed the first flight of stairs. And the sound she heard was not a moan, but an odd rustling squeak, like Saran Wrap being ripped away from something. There was also a soft background noise that reminded her of respiration, as if the entire tower was an iron lung, breathing for its inhabitants.

The rustling grew louder as she climbed the second flight, and by the time she reached the top, it had begun to sound like someone was wheezing, perhaps even choking. The landing led to a door, and Temple didn't bother to knock. She opened it and entered a narrow anteroom that looked as if it had been made into a temporary bedroom.

A man's robe was draped over the only chair, and there were magazines and other odds and ends on the table next to the bed. Someone clearly slept here and Temple would have investigated if a second door hadn't caught her attention. It gave the appearance of a bank vault, and the panel of numbers on the wall next to it looked like a combination lock.

The rustling, moaning noises issued from what seemed to be a generator, and the overhead piping told her it was running some kind of elaborate ventilation system that served the interior room. Temple was going in. She just didn't know how she was getting in.

She tried some obvious number sequence with no success then remembered that the most likely combinations were personal numbers that people could remember. Not expecting anything, she tapped out the date it all started—the lost night of March fifth. The door didn't budge. She'd memorized Mark's phone number on the mainland and the one here at the house, but neither worked. She didn't know the date of his birth, so she punched in hers, aware that it was futile, and then she tried that day's date.

The vault door slid open, and Temple entered an air lock. When the hissing stopped and the air had been exchanged, the next door opened, and Temple stood on the threshold in disbelief. A huge plastic bubble hovered in the middle of a large semicircular room full of medical equipment. This was what was breathing, she realized, the bubble. The respiratory sounds must be coming from an air-filtration system. She'd been quarantined herself and recognized it as an isolation tent.

There was someone inside, she saw, drawing closer, a man in a hospital bed, hooked up to what looked like life support. The squeaking she'd heard might have been his hand, but only if the sound had come through the ventilation system. He'd gripped a section of the tent and was yanking at it, as though he wanted out.

Virtually certain she'd found Jonathan Challis, she moved closer still and saw why he was struggling. A section of his breathing tube had come apart, and he wasn't getting any oxygen. He was choking. The tent had built-in safety gloves that could be used to treat the patient from outside, but Temple didn't know how to operate them, and there was no time. Her concern about entering the tent was for the life she was carrying. If this was Jonathan, he was enclosed not for his own protection, but so that he couldn't contaminate others.

She prayed the virus hadn't mutated as she ripped through an opening made of an air-tight Velcro-like material. Once inside, she reconnected the tubing and waited anxiously to see if she'd done it correctly, and if his breathing would return to normal. He was pale and thin, but he didn't look like the virus victims in Zaire.

Their bodies and faces had been encrusted with sores, and they'd had the gaunt, emaciated look of corpses. Most of them had lived no more than seventy-two hours before they were eaten alive by Z190. This man was seriously ill, but Temple had the feeling he'd been hanging on for much longer than seventy-two hours.

His struggling ceased almost immediately, and he began to breathe easier. Temple was weak with relief. She hadn't realized how frightened she was. Her hands were dripping, and she was trembling inside. She needed to sit down a moment, but whoever was taking care of him had to be told what happened.

She was getting ready to leave when she saw his lids flutter open. His eyes were unfocused, searching the tent, and then he saw her. Perhaps what shocked her was his resemblance to Mark. It wasn't the dark eyes. It was the way he used them, the holding power.

"Who are you?" he whispered, searching her features. "Are you the one? My son found you, yes?"

His son. That could only mean he was Jonathan Challis. And the questions he was asking made her fear that Mark could have done what Llewelyn said. Temple felt the strength draining out of her. She wasn't at all certain she had enough left to walk.

He tried to lift his head off the pillow but fell back. "Don't let them do this," he said. "I'm ready to go. I want to go. Save yourself. Save the child."

Temple backed to the door of the tent, staring at him in shock. The horror she felt left her unable to move. She had no strength left at all, nothing left. If there was such a thing as emotional death, they would find her that way, crumpled at the foot of Jonathan Challis's bed.

June was at the sink chopping vegetables when Temple entered the kitchen. Temple made it to the center island, where she steadied herself against a bar stool. She had to tell someone about Jonathan Challis's condition. He'd sounded as if he wanted to die, and she was afraid the breathing tube might have been an attempt to take his own life.

"The man in the tower room needs help," she said. "Someone should check on him immediately."

June turned, the knife still glinting in her hand. A flash of silvery light seared its way into Temple's consciousness. She released the chair and stepped back, frightened by the woman's strange, bright stare.

"What were you doing in the tower room?"

"June, he needs help," Temple pleaded. She rushed to explain that Jonathan was choking and what she'd done.

The housekeeper left the knife on the counter, much to Temple's relief, and went to the kitchen wall phone. She picked up the receiver, tapped out some numbers, and hung up without speaking.

A pager, Temple realized, despite her numbing exhaustion. Mark's? No, there must be a staff member on call who cared for Challis, probably whoever slept in the anteroom. She also saw that her news had come as no surprise to June. She knew all about Jonathan Challis.

She'd put a curse on him, according to Mark.

Had June disconnected the breathing tube?

A drumming noise caught Temple's attention. June had left the tap on full blast and the water was running hard.

Temple was compelled to go to the sink herself and turn it

off. It felt crucial that the pounding noise be silenced, but she didn't move. No one moved. The housekeeper remained by the phone. And the water streamed.

"Is something wrong?" Temple got out.

"I've taken care of it," June said coldly. "You can go."

"Go? What do you mean?"

"Get out of my kitchen. Can't you see I'm busy."

Temple shook her head in confusion. This was insanity. June had been begging Temple to save herself, and now she was wielding knives and throwing her out of the kitchen. It was impossible to tell friends from enemies on this island, not that June had ever been a friend.

I'm calling Dan Llewelyn, Temple thought. I'm getting off this island today. She drew a breath and touched the countertop to ward off her dizziness as she came around it. The phone was only a short distance, but June was blocking her way.

"I need to make a call," Temple said as the housekeeper stepped in front of her.

June's expression was fierce. "Mr. Challis has been trying to reach you," she informed Temple. "Security contacted him and said you were ill, that Dr. Llewelyn was taking you to the mainland."

"No, I didn't go. It was morning sickness, that's all. I'm fine now. What did you tell Mark when he called?"

"That I thought you were still sleeping."

Thank God, Temple thought. That might give her some time. It would depend on what June told him when he called next, and who else could hear this conversation. The noise from the running water should have blocked their voices, she realized.

"Actually, I am going back to the mill house for a nap," Temple said. "If Mark calls again, would you tell him I'm fine, that I'm just resting?"

"I'll tell him you're fine, and there's no need for him to cut short his business," June snapped. "Now go!"

Temple nodded and gradually realized that she was holding herself, that she was freezing cold. There was no way to know whether June was simply doing her job and imparting information or if she'd just attempted to warn Temple.

No way to know anything, Temple thought, except that she had to get to a phone.

TWENTY-THREE

Temple's laser pointer projected a tiny dot of red into the black vault of the night. She had no idea if the device's four-hundred-yard range was enough to signal a boat hovering offshore. All she'd ever used it for were her pitch sessions at Blue Sky. But a flashlight would surely have been picked up by security, so the pointer was her only hope.

She was crouched on the clifftop, shivering in her gray sweats and trying to conserve body heat as much as to avoid being seen. The water below wasn't whispering tonight. It rumbled and rattled, bursting as it hit the rocks. The moon wasn't lying on the water like a jewel. It was in a million pieces.

She'd found a phone in the pool pavilion that didn't seem likely to be bugged and had used it to call Llewelyn. He'd agreed that a second helicopter trip, especially at night, would invite suspicion, and had suggested a pontoon boat that could hover offshore undetected.

The problem was getting out to it. Temple would either

have to use the skiff or swim, and she wasn't familiar enough with the island to be sure she could find the skiff, or that it was sailable. That left swimming, which she couldn't begin to imagine, despite the fact that she'd done it before. She'd even dived off these cliffs. God, she would drown.

If you believe that perception is ninety percent of reality.

Salt spray burned her face. A wave hit the rocks below, and the wind picked up the droplets and flung them up at her like pebbles. These were the same cliffs where she'd been transformed into an arrow of light. She wanted to laugh that was such a ludicrous thought.

It would be over soon, she told herself. When she got to the mainland, she would go to the police. She would tell them everything, and it would be like lifting the weight of the world. She shuddered with relief at the thought. All she wanted was a moment of sanity, safety.

A low rumbling growl brought her out of her reflections. She searched the black horizon, seeing movement everywhere. The water was choppy, and she couldn't tell whether she'd heard the noise of a motor or of waves.

She turned the pointer on blink mode, and the red dot began to pulsate. Seconds later a blip of white caught her eye. And another. The tiny flashing light confirmed that her signal had been picked up. The boat was out there.

Temple began to strip off her sweat suit. A tennis shoe popped out of her hand and went tumbling down the rocks. She glanced around to make sure she hadn't given herself away, and then disposed of the rest of her clothing the same way, over the side. Thundering waves hid the splashes.

That done she crept to the edge of the cliffs, shivering in her shorts and top. A sick fear filled her at the sight of the dark turbulence below. She couldn't do it. It was some other woman who'd been transformed. This was Temple Banning, an earthbound realist who didn't believe in mystical forces.

She could do it. *She already had done it.*

All she had to do was get to the beach. Instead of taking
the lighted stairway, she melted into the shadows alongside
the steps and groped her way down. The water was paralyz-
ingly cold, but the flashing light guided her, and adrenaline
drove her in deeper.

What if it wasn't Llewelyn's boat out there?

That thought hit her as the ocean floor dropped away and
she was forced to swim. She floundered and struck out, with
no way of knowing what she was heading into. Mark had
beefed up his security measures. He could have ordered a
shore patrol.

Temple kicked hard. She churned water like the wheel in
the stream, but the waves were too much. Buffeted by dark,
powerful swells, she fought not to get sucked under, but her
ankles kept tangling in something slimy. She was dropped
into trenches walled with black water, and one of them
crashed over her with such force, it swirled her under, into
the slime.

She was aware of nothing after that but thundering darkness and choking salt, until she was caught by powerful
arms and dragged bodily out of the sea. She knew immediately that it was Llewelyn's man. He was wearing the
hooded black wet suit of a saboteur, and as soon as he had
Temple in the boat, he wrapped her in a blanket and fired up
the outboard.

She dropped back against the side, gasping, grateful.

The island filled her line of sight. A dramatic black land
mass, looming like the primordial mountain peak it had once
been. She hadn't realized they were so close, but then he'd
probably had to come in to get her.

It felt as if the peak could reach out and snatch her back.
Only when the boat had turned and was racing toward the
mainland would Temple be able to relax. They were still
dealing with heavy swells, and the driver struggled to control the lightweight craft. But finally he brought it around.

At last he was headed the right way, and the island began to disappear from sight.

The soft roar of the engine filled Temple's senses.

They were moving. Relief washed over her, and the shaking noise she made was like laughter. But moments later as she glanced back and saw how much the land had receded, she felt another emotion flare inside her. It was sadness, burning like a candle flame. She'd escaped something, but she was leaving something, too, and she couldn't sort those things out in her mind.

She was aware of the ocean roaring and somewhere in the distance, a lonely voice crying, "Mark, Mark!"

A shadow crossed the moon and she realized there were birds flying overhead. Gulls, she supposed, but from the wingspread, it could have been falcons. That was what she'd heard, their cries.

A short time later a helicopter passed them on its way to the island, and Temple knew that it was him.

"Mark, Mark!" the birds cried softly.

The minivan pulled through the gated driveway of an old, California Spanish–style home. It was a spacious and meandering multilevel design, similar to the estates that graced Sunset and other fabled southland drives. However, this one had fallen into some disrepair. The iron gate was rusting, and the gold stucco walls were water-stained. But Temple knew this must be Dan Llewelyn's home, and water stains were the least of her concerns. She was overjoyed to be there.

"This is it, ma'am," the driver said. He leaned over Temple and opened the door for her. It was the same man who'd picked her up in the boat. He hadn't yet changed out of his wet suit, although he'd pulled off the hood, revealing youthful features and hair that was probably surfer blond when it was dry.

Temple was still wrapped in the blanket he'd given her.

She slid from her high perch to the ground, shouldered the van door shut, and stepped away from the car as it pulled around the drive and left. The chill of clay tiles nipped at her bare soles as she checked out the small courtyard. There was a covered entry and arched double doors, one of which swung open almost as soon as she'd pressed the bell.

"Thank God," Dan Llewelyn said when he saw her. "Are you all right?" He held out his arms, and Temple couldn't contain herself. She walked straight into them, choking a sob as he embraced her, blanket and all.

They hugged like old friends, like reunited family, and in some ways, that was how it felt. She'd known him only a short time, but the extreme circumstances had created a bond.

He took her to the kitchen, where she told him about Jonathan and the isolation tent. Ever the doctor, Llewelyn got his bag, checked her vital signs, and insisted on taking some blood, just to be sure she hadn't been infected. He also went through a list of symptoms that could have signaled problems for the baby. She hadn't experienced any of them, fortunately, despite everything she'd been through.

Satisfied at last that she was all right, he put on water for tea and warmed some buttermilk biscuits in the microwave. Temple's mouth watered at the smells, especially when he brought the biscuits to the kitchen table, heaped in a basket with butter and honey. Next he set mugs of hot tea on woven wood placemats and offered Temple a napkin with a trailing ivy border that matched the Dutch door's curtains.

It was a small, cheery kitchen, with stainless-steel accents everywhere, which she imagined were the doctor's touch.

The tea was plain old Lipton, and Temple was glad to have something so normal. She breathed in the steam, took a sip, and sighed. "Good," she murmured.

His smile turned serious. "Where is Mark?" he asked.

She told him about seeing Mark's helicopter pass over on its way to the island. "Do you think he'll come here?"

"He might, but I don't think we have to worry tonight. He probably won't discover you're gone until tomorrow."

Llewelyn settled back in the chair and rested a moccasined foot on his knee. The khakis and blue broadcloth shirt he wore hung on his frame, making Temple wonder if he lived the ascetic life she imagined. His long fingers curled around the mug, and he lifted it up occasionally but never drank.

"He'll know tonight that I'm gone," she said, wondering how she was going to explain. "Mark was trying to reach me on the island all day. June intercepted his calls, so I never actually spoke with him."

"Will she tell him where you've gone?"

"She doesn't know, and even if she should guess, I don't think she would volunteer any information to Mark, do you?"

"June's hatred knows no bounds where the Challis family is concerned," Llewelyn agreed. "If she could shoot a gun, Mark would be dead."

Temple was startled. "Someone did shoot at Mark, last night—" She hesitated because it seemed like years ago. "He was hit in the shoulder, but we both thought the bullet was meant for me."

"Hit? My God! Is he all right?"

"Yes, I think so." She was going to have to tell Llewelyn everything, she realized. "I didn't mention it before. It didn't seem relevant, but Mark and I, we— Well, we were together last night. That's how I know he'll go to the mill house looking for me. When he left he told me to wait there for him."

If the doctor was surprised at her news, he didn't let on.

"I think you'll be safe enough here," he said. "The house is old, but it has a state-of-the-art security system, and the

Neighborhood Watch group employs a private firm that patrols all night long. I'll tell them to keep an eye on this place."

"Maybe I should stay somewhere else," she said, aware that she could be endangering him.

"Is that what you want?"

"No, honestly, I don't." It felt safe here, and she didn't want to let go of that feeling. "But it might be less risky for everyone concerned if I went to the police and filed a report, then found a hotel somewhere."

Llewelyn rose and came around the table, perhaps to make his point. "I'll take you down to the station first thing tomorrow. As for tonight, everything will be fine. You're not going to a strange hotel room, Temple. Do you hear me? You're staying here."

"Yes . . . all right." Overwhelmed with emotion, she bent her head and rested it against her knuckles. The conversation about Mark had exhausted her.

"Thank you," she said, hoping Llewelyn could hear her because she couldn't look at him. It was all welling up inside her, the confusion, the despair. The enormity of what Mark had done was almost beyond her comprehension. She was heartsick over the things he'd said, the promises he made. He was the one who'd convinced her she had to trust someone. And after all those years of being afraid to believe in anyone but herself, she had done it. She'd trusted.

"How about a shower and something hot to eat?" the doctor suggested. "Does soup and a sandwich sound good? I could bring a tray to your room once you're settled."

Temple had no appetite left, but she gave him a quick nod, then looked up with a smile. He deserved that much. It would do her good to eat, and it would make him feel better.

She needed to get up and do something, make herself useful. Her clothes were nearly dry, so she left the blanket on the chair, picked up her teacup, and took it to the sink. There was a bulletin board tacked to the end of some maple cabinets. On it were pictures of the doctor and a vibrant, smiling woman who looked about his age.

"Is this your wife?" Temple asked, hoping she wasn't prying.

His voice immediately softened. "Yes, that's Maggie. She's away this weekend, but if she were here in this room, she would insist that you stay, too. You'd like her, I'm sure."

Temple imagined she would. Maggie looked solid and earthbound like Temple, and she was probably the perfect match for her brainy, philosophical husband. But something else had already caught Temple's eye, a pink phone message from Susan Gilchrist.

Temple turned to Llewelyn, whose mind had wandered somewhere else by the pensive look on his face.

"Do you know Susan Gilchrist?" she asked him.

He glanced up. "I do, yes. I used to work with her once, years ago. She's probably out here investigating something for the CDC. I haven't had a chance to return her call."

"She was the investigator on my case," Temple told him.

Now that Temple was out of hiding, she couldn't see any reason not to talk to Gilchrist. She was curious about what the doctor wanted, but something told her to wait. Temple needed some time to recover and put the pieces back together.

"Do me a favor," she said to Llewelyn. "Don't mention I'm here when you call her back. I had a message from her, too, but I'd like to talk to the police before I speak with anyone else . . . except Ivy," she said, remembering her little sister with a jolt. "I really should call my sister tonight."

The doctor checked his watch. "It's late, nearly midnight. Sure you wouldn't rather wait until tomorrow? You probably want a hot shower and a good night's sleep."

"A good night's sleep—" She laughed. "What is that?"

Her room turned out to be a small suite with a sunken tub,

and Temple could hardly imagine anything more relaxing. Every muscle in her body ached at the thought of the hot, soothing water. He offered to leave a tray of food outside the door so that she could get ready for bed undisturbed.

"If you wake up later or need anything," he said, "I'll be up. I have some work to do in my office. It's at the end of the hallway parallel to this one."

She thanked him sincerely, knowing that he probably intended to stay up and work anyway, whether or not she was there. But he must have understood how it reassured her to know there would be a night watch, awake and on guard, so that she could rest easy.

It sounded like someone was telling secrets in her ear. Temple didn't know if she was awake or dreaming the breathy sounds, but the whispers were compellingly familiar. It couldn't be the nautilus shell. She hadn't brought it with her. There'd been no way to bring any of her belongings.

The murmuring went on for several moments as she lay there, and finally she threw back the quilt and got out of bed, wishing she had a robe. At least her gown was warm. She'd found it in the bathroom with the towels, a long cotton V-neck lounger made out of soft gray fleece. She imagined it was one of Maggie's.

"Midnight?" There was a clock on the bedside table, but the time made no sense. Temple hadn't noticed the clock when she went to bed, but that must have been close to an hour ago, and Llewelyn had said it was midnight when they were in the kitchen. Apparently one of the timepieces was wrong. She put it off to that and went in search of his office.

The sound grew more distinct in the hallway where she found his office. The light was on, but he wasn't there, and while she debated waiting for him to return, she noticed that the whispering seemed to be coming from a doorway farther down the hall. It sounded less like people's voices and more like curtains rustling in the breeze. Or a ventilation system, she realized.

The door opened on a stairway lit by recessed lighting, and the basement Temple descended to reminded her of the chemistry labs she'd taken in high school, except that this was far more sophisticated. Everything was walled off by glass, except for the vaultlike door directly in front of her.

Temple's instant impression was one of déjà vu. But hard on its heels came denial. This couldn't be. She'd seen this door before. It was almost identical to the one she'd discovered in the tower at Wings. It even had the same panel of buttons.

Within mere seconds the eerie familiarity she felt had escalated into a dread so complete, she could smell it in her nostrils, along with the lab's pungent disinfectant. All she had to do was look to know there was something godawful inside that door.

TWENTY-FOUR

Temple tried the combination that got her inside Jonathan Challis's containment unit. Her fingers were flying so fast, she had to start over several times, but even when she was certain she had typed every number correctly, the door didn't open.

She took a mental step back, trying to stop her racing hands, her racing heart. Obviously she didn't have the right sequence, and the possible permutations were infinite. Lightning was not going to strike twice, and maybe it was just as well. Dan Llewelyn could explain this, she told herself. There was a reason he had a containment unit in his basement. It probably wasn't unusual for medical researchers to do work that required extreme safety measures.

She tried one through five, forward and backward. Neither worked, but suddenly it struck her what was wrong. She had typed in yesterday's date. It was after midnight, and she had to change it by one day. One digit.

The seal popped as she hit the last button. The door rolled

open soundlessly. But as she peered into the stark white room, it felt as if someone had jammed an elbow into her chest. This was déjà vu. She could have been staring at Jonathan Challis's isolation tent. But it wasn't Jonathan inside, she saw immediately. He had looked as if he had a fighting chance. This poor creature, whoever she was, had none.

Temple recognized the woman's death rattle wheeze, the blotched, fever-burned skin and dazed, blind-eyed stare for what it was. The death throes of an Agent Z190 victim. In Zaire Temple had witnessed the dying being carried off day and night, stretcher after stretcher. They would be admitted with a cough, and a day or two later they were gone, ravaged by a microscopic time bomb with the power to explode their cells from the inside out. That was how quick and lethal the virus was.

A stainless-steel holder hung on the wall. It held a medical chart that would tell Temple who the woman was and if she had the virus, although Temple had little doubt about that. She carried with her a mental scrapbook of Z190's effects. They were snapshots she would have lit a match to if she could.

The label on the folder said MARGARET LLEWELYN.

There wasn't time to read the chart. Temple never got the file open. As she stared at the name and realized who the dying woman was, she heard the hiss of the door's air lock.

"I see you've met my wife."

Dan Llewelyn was wearing protective gear, a mask, gown, booties, and rubber gloves, and the sight filled Temple with apprehension. She was dealing with a total unknown. The man, not the disease. His wife had Z190, but it was Llewelyn who was dangerous to Temple. She knew that instinctively.

"Why did you bring me here?" she asked, voicing the second question that came to her mind. The first was unthinkable. His wife was dying, and he'd mentioned things like stem cells and cord blood on the island. Did he want the baby?

"Are you the one who's been trying to kill me?" she blurted, perhaps as much to divert him as to get more information. She didn't know what she was dealing with. Her only plan was to learn as much about his intentions as she could.

The mask muffled his voice, making it sound strangely muted and calm. "Kill you? No, I need you alive, Temple. If it weren't for you, Jonathan Challis would be dead."

So it was Llewelyn. The realization hit her with a wrenching mix of hope and despair. It seemed the doctor himself was doing everything he'd accused Mark of doing. But if that was true, then it was possible Mark was a scapegoat, that he knew nothing about any of this.

"You *are* a human vaccine," he went on. "I've been treating Jonathan with a method called passive immunization. He has the original strain of Z190, the same one you contracted, and your blood has the antibodies he needs to survive."

She had no idea why he was volunteering the information, but it was clear now why he'd taken what seemed like copious amounts of blood every time he'd examined her, including tonight. What puzzled her was why Jonathan Challis had clearly responded and Maggie Llewelyn hadn't. Surely the doctor was treating his own wife with the antibodies, too.

"How long has your wife been sick?" she asked.

She had to call upon all of her reserves of strength to stay calm as Llewelyn approached her and took the file from her hand. She moved out of his way as he produced a pen from somewhere and began to make notes, apparently on his wife's progress. His detachment was unnerving. And his voice seemed unnaturally even as he described the accident that had put his wife in a plastic bubble, fighting for her life.

"She was contaminated less than forty-eight hours ago," he said. "Maggie was assisting me down here in the lab, and neither one of us saw the perforation in her suit, although I hold myself totally responsible," he admitted. "She has no formal medical training, but I couldn't trust anyone else, not at this stage. The competition for viral cures is ferocious since the onset of AIDS, and there's always the risk of having your life's work stolen or sabotaged."

His life's work? It sounded as if he was talking about a vaccine. Temple searched for any sign of his true emotional state. He was trained to deal with crises, but this was his wife. He'd exposed her to a deadly disease, and she was clearly terminal. He should have been showing the strain in some way, and yet his voice was full of resolve, his manner calm and doctorly.

That frightened her more, she realized. That and his seeming desire to tell her everything.

"I've got a serum in the experimental stages," he said, "but unfortunately Z190 has a nasty habit of mutating its surface antigens, and it's tricky to grow in a tissue culture. Maggie joked that the virus had attention deficit disorder. Just when you thought you had its attention, a bright light came along."

A serum, of course, Temple thought. Something to save Challis and now, his wife. A vaccine was made up of the killed or altered virus and injected to stimulate antibodies that would fight off the live virus, if the host became infected. If the host already was infected, an antiviral serum or drug was necessary.

"That kind of research costs a fortune," Temple said. "Where are you getting the money?"

He acted surprised that she didn't know. "The Will Chal-

lis Foundation is funding it. Everything I told you about
Mark is true. He's determined to save his father, but if this
research leads to something marketable, the Challis family
will probably end up the globe's first trillionaires."

Temple's hopes plummeted. As she stared at the doctor
and at the whispering tent that housed his wife, the bewildering chain of events that had led to this moment began to
make some sense. Obviously there was a lot she didn't
know, like how Will Challis figured into it, if he did. But
she'd just caught a glimpse of the design behind it all. And
what a frightening, fiendish design it was.

"Why am I pregnant?" she asked him. "Is it just the antibodies, or does it have something to do with your research? Is this about molecular bioengineering? Am I one
of your lab animals, doctor? *Have you done something to
the baby?*"

He glanced over his shoulder, and all she could see were
his eyes, but he seemed stricken at the suggestion.

"God, no," he said, "it's nothing like that. Perhaps I didn't
make it clear that you have an extraordinary immune system, Temple. It produces an abundance of what we call NK
cells, natural killer cells that target viral invaders. Scientists
all over the world have been trying to synthesize that kind of
reaction in their laboratories, much as they did with human
interferons for cancer. But meanwhile Jonathan Challis is
dying."

"But I was infected years ago. How did Jonathan catch
it?"

"The same way Maggie did, right here in this lab."

"Do you mean recently?"

"A little under twelve weeks ago."

"I don't understand," she said, watching him make nota-
tions of his wife's vital signs and her temperature. "Why
would Jonathan have been in your lab?"

He hesitated in his examination, staring at his struggling

wife as he spoke. "Apparently you weren't aware that Will Challis died of Agent Z190 ten years ago, in the same outbreak you survived."

"No, I wasn't." Temple went silent, listening as Llewelyn explained that Will was in his twenties at the time, and Jonathan had just promoted him to vice president of international sales. Will had been traveling the globe on behalf of Challis Technologies, but he was in Zaire on a goodwill mission.

"Jonathan tried to get him out of that death trap where you were quarantined," Llewelyn said. "He probably bribed every official in the country, but no amount of money could buy off Agent Z190. Will was dead in a matter of days, like everyone else, and Jonathan Challis had a new mission in life, to eradicate the virus. That's when he came to me."

Llewelyn's voice had taken on the droning quality of someone regressed by a hypnotist. Temple had to move closer to hear him explain that in his earlier days he'd worked for the CDC, developing the vaccine that earned him a Nobel nomination. But Llewelyn had fallen out of grace and was in desperate need of financial support by the time Jonathan approached him and offered to lavishly fund him in his other research if he would work on a Z190 cure.

"At first it was pure missionary zeal on Jonathan's part," he said, "but he was a capitalist at heart, and when he got a whiff of the potential windfall profits in drugs, his motivation changed. As I got closer to a viable serum, he insisted on suiting up and coming into the lab. He wanted to see how his money was being spent, I suppose, but he was also obsessed with beating the virus. It was personal."

Brought down by his own profit motive, Temple thought, Jonathan Challis had not beaten Z190. The way it looked to her, the virus was winning.

"How was he infected?" she asked.

"A blunder, a stupid blunder, on his part. He made the mistake of handling one of the infected lab animals, despite my repeated warnings, and he was bitten. Jonathan didn't follow orders well. If I hadn't immediately inoculated him with the serum, he would have been dead within days."

How lucky for the both of you, Temple thought. But she couldn't allow herself the luxury of sarcasm. She couldn't let anything affect her judgment at this stage, even her growing outrage. There was too much she still didn't understand.

"If you had the serum, why did you need me?"

"Because the serum wasn't there. It bought him some time before it became ineffective, but that's all. And your antibodies did the same. He was still being devoured, just more slowly. The virus had become a chronic killer instead of an acute one. That's when I went back to square one and discovered that the only other victims who showed resistance to Z190 were the pregnant women. They all had a marked enhancement of both proliferative and cytotoxic T-cell antiviral immune response after being infected . . . so the next option, the *only* option as I saw it, was to experiment with the pregnancy-enhanced immune response."

So Temple Banning was impregnated without her consent and against her will solely for the purpose of saving a dying billionaire's life. *God, no, it was nothing like that.* Dan Llewelyn's words, and Temple would never understand how a doctor could have said them. She clearly was one of his lab animals, too, and it was a gross misuse of power and money.

"You should have come to me," she told him, "*asked* for my consent."

He negotiated a half-turn, curious. "And you would have agreed to become pregnant? Why? For money?"

There isn't enough money, she thought. She would never have done it, and that was his point.

"What do you want with me now?" She regarded him with quiet defiance. It was time to bring this atrocity to an end, and Temple was ready to face the worst, if that's what it took to have it over. Given what he'd already done, she imagined him capable of anything.

Maggie Llewelyn's chart banged against the bottom of its holder. Temple flinched as Llewelyn turned and came toward her. She braced herself to fend him off and felt a dizzying surge of adrenaline. But there was another examining table in the room that she hadn't noticed, and next to it, another holder. That was his next destination. He walked past her and pulled out the folders, three of them.

"I need more time" was his answer. "This latest batch of the serum inactivates most strains, and I've also got a vaccine in the works. I've already tested the vaccine, Temple. Admittedly it was a small study, but there was only one subject who developed symptoms, and her case was mild at most."

She had no idea what he was talking about. "What do you mean study, subjects?"

"I've conducted preliminary tests on humans. Successful tests—" He held up the files. There were three in all, each folder marked with a different woman's name, and as Temple took them, she saw that he intended to wait while she read his notes.

"Do you understand what that means, Temple? I'm almost there."

His handwriting was a barely legible scrawl, but from what Temple could make out he'd inoculated three different women with the vaccine, or whatever it was, and then he'd actually infected them with the virus and kept them under observation to see if they developed symptoms.

"All of these women survived?" she asked.

"Yes, yes! They're fine, all three."

She was curious to know where he'd found his volunteers, but there was a more imperative question that had to be asked.

"You must have tried the serum on your wife. What happened?"

The whispering tent drew his attention. He went there and studied the dying woman. "Maggie—"

Grief made him haggard right before Temple's eyes. He swayed as if he might collapse. But as he caught himself and shook off the reaction, his expression gradually returned to one of detachment. Or was it denial? she wondered. Now he was the doctor studying the patient. Still, he obviously loved his wife, and that might be Temple's only chance.

"I don't know what happened," he said. "She hasn't responded to the serum. I'm running an IV, and I've inoculated her with your antibodies. That was a few hours ago, and she's due for another shot. I just need a little more time."

He turned to Temple. "I need your help. We *can* save her, you and I. We can save millions."

Temple nodded, hoping to pacify him. She had no idea what kind of help he had in mind, but there was one more question she had to ask. One more terrifying question.

"Do you know what strain Maggie has?"

He shook his head, dismissing her question. "It's possible the virus has mutated again. . . ."

That was all Temple heard. If Maggie had a mutated form, then it was entirely possible that Temple's antibodies couldn't help her, and that Maggie could kill Temple. One rip in that tent and Temple was infected, and if there'd already been contamination in the room, it was too late anyway.

If she understood that, why didn't Llewelyn? Everything he said sounded rational, she realized with a bolt of insight. But the man was insane. Totally insane.

She drew back, but instead of panicking, she could feel herself calming, emptying of fear. She wondered if it was shock. Llewelyn was eerily delusional, and his profound state of denial seemed to have sucked all the gravity from the room. But this felt like something else. Her psyche was dealing with the situation by growing still and alert. It felt like the power Mark had spoken of.

What she remembered was the moonlight, and Mark telling her that if her mind was that lucid and all-encompassing, she would never be caught off guard. She would be able to see what happened before it occurred. Temple couldn't imagine possessing such powers of concentration, but something had already changed.

Mind like water . . . mind like the moon.

Llewelyn had pulled off his face mask. He'd gone over to talk to his wife, and he was telling her that everything was going to be all right. But Temple saw his movements as if they were in slow motion. Even his speech seemed delayed.

The life support equipment had been affected, too. She could see the heart monitor. Maggie Llewelyn's vital signs were recorded on a digital display, and Temple watched the blip crawl to the top of its arc and hover there. The woman's heart had all but stopped.

"Help me, please!"

Someone had cried out for help. Temple heard the plea, but she didn't know where it had come from. No one had spoken. She'd been watching Llewelyn, and he was whispering to his wife, barely moving his lips.

Temple felt the first flutters of panic, and edged back toward the door. Maybe she was crazy, too. She never took her eyes off the doctor, thinking she might risk this strange ability to alter his movements if she did. She hadn't stopped time, or even slowed it down. It felt as if time had expanded, but she couldn't begin to comprehend how that had happened. Or how long it would last.

This was the feeling she'd had on the cliffs the night she dived, but had deserted her when she swam out to the boat. She palmed her stomach and felt a shiver of apprehension, perhaps even of wonder. She had no idea why it had come back unless she was in shock and her nervous system was insulating her against any more trauma. It might even have something to do with the baby, she realized. The maternal instinct. Her conscious thoughts were grasping for answers, blocking her intuition. The only thing anchoring her now were feelings, and it felt as if the pregnancy itself had given her power.

For you the Aikido masters have a name. They would call you a mystic.

No, that was crazy, she thought. She was as crazy as Llewelyn.

There was a panel of buttons against the wall by the door. She prayed it wasn't a different combination to exit the room, because that was her only chance. Reasoning with Llewelyn was useless. She knew intuitively that nothing she said would have any impact on him. He was on a mission and her pregnant body was a part of his arsenal, perhaps even his secret weapon. Her rights, her freedom, meant nothing to him. She wasn't a person. He could barely remember that his wife was a person.

Today's date, she reminded herself.

The door gave off a little hiss as Temple finished the combination, and Llewelyn looked around. His eyes narrowed with a terrifying light as he saw her, but what Temple read in his expression surprised her. It was shock and disbelief, even pain.

"Oh, no," he whispered, shaking his head. "Oh no, Temple, I can't let you go. There are millions of lives at stake, don't you understand that? An outbreak of Z190 in the developed world could wipe out entire populations. Haven't you grasped what's at stake? Of all people, I thought I could trust you. You lost your parents to the virus. It killed hundreds and you were the only one to survive. Your life was saved, and you have an obligation to your fellow man. You owe a debt—"

"Help me, please."

Someone was pleading for help. Temple could hear it as clearly as if the caller was standing next to her. It wasn't inside her head. But who? Llewelyn? His wife?

The doctor was coming toward her, lumbering like a stick-figure giant. Temple could easily have evaded him if there'd been anywhere to go. She kept pushing buttons, but nothing happened. Either she was using the wrong combination or the door was as slow to respond as everything else.

His pace was lethargic, but his grip was paralyzing as he hauled her up and away from the door. He was on top of her, wrestling her back into the room when Maggie Llewelyn began to flail at the tent. "No! Dan, no!" she croaked.

As the doctor turned, Temple saw it happen, a split-second in the arc of motion when his body was off-balance. One of his feet had left the floor, and the other was on its edge. She pushed him hard, and he swayed in midair like a tree about to fall. She heaved again, and he went down.

It could never have happened at any other time than that moment she realized. He was too big a man, lean but tall. Only someone massively built could have sent him to the floor with a push.

The door had crept open a crack, but not enough for Temple to slip through. Llewelyn was still on the floor and coming up on all fours. He had begun to tear off his protective gear and Temple didn't know what that meant. She didn't know what to do.

For you the Aikido masters have a name. . . .

Perception is ninety percent of reality.
Perception. Reality.

Mark's words were flooding into her mind now. Either the door was jammed or everything that was happening was a function of her altered perception. Nothing was moving normally but her. The only way to get through the opening was to change form, she realized, to become water and flow. Was that possible? She had become an arrow once.

She could hear what sounded like bones cracking as she forced her arm through the opening. There was no experience of pain, but she was wedged in, unable to move. Llewelyn was on his feet, and she had trapped herself.

Embrace your enemy without hatred and you can use his energy.

"Help me, please," Temple whispered as the doctor came toward her. *Help me, please.* It was her? Her mind had been telling her to call out those words?

She implored him with her eyes, and Llewelyn hesitated. His face contorted with the sudden anguish of a man who has been given a glimpse of the devastation he's caused, the impossible choice he faces.

"I can't," he whispered. "She'll die! Maggie will die."

Reality returned with a crash. Suddenly everything was rushing, racing. Time and space were on a collision course. Llewelyn was thundering toward her, and Temple struggled to force her way through the opening. If he tried to drag her away from the door this time, she might lose an arm.

The night her car had exploded she'd been battered senseless with noise, the roar of death. Tonight the noise was inside her. Her mind was screaming and the doctor's shouts were reverberating, but only one faint sound registered. The tiny beep of monitors had become one continuous hum. It was the life support system. Maggie Llewelyn had flatlined.

Dan Llewelyn heard it, too. He whirled toward the tent and staggered as if he were going down again. "No, Maggie, please!"

The words sounded as if they were being ripped out of him against his will. He appeared to be frozen, unable to move, and Temple knew this was her only chance. She heaved against the jammed door, forcing it with the strength of her shoulders and back. When she felt it give, she butted hard.

Embrace your enemy, she thought, aware that the door was her enemy now. She'd forced her shoulder through, but there still wasn't enough room. Limp with exhaustion, she stopped struggling. She gave in utterly to her helplessness, and every fiber of her being seemed to sigh at once. She admitted defeat, and relief washed through her in a wave. It simply carried her away, and she was loose now, pliable. Her body had liquefied, or the space had widened. She didn't know which, but somehow she slipped through the opening and was free.

She had trouble catching her footing on the other side and had to concentrate hard on moving normally. Life was constant balance between struggle and surrender, she realized, and she was only beginning to understand the transforming power of the latter. As she headed for the second set of doors, she could hear Dan Llewelyn's struggle, his broken pleas. He was begging Maggie to come back, to forgive him. He was begging God to help him. *Help me, please.*

Mark pulled into the driveway of Dan Llewelyn's house, geared the BMW into park, and left the car running.

"Dan!" he called as he sprinted toward the entrance. He mashed the doorbell, then jammed down both lever handles at once. The double doors weren't locked, and he plowed through them into the living room.

Dan was nowhere to be found, and neither was Maggie.

Mark was halfway down the hall to the kitchen when his brain registered a familiar sound. It was the dry, hollow crack of metal against bone. Next came the pain, a blinding flash of red that filled his skull and shot out through his eyes.

Someone had come up behind him.

Mark dropped to his knees, staggered by the violence of the blow. He fell forward and caught himself with his hands. Bile washed up from his belly, but he choked it back. There was another blow coming, and this one would kill him. His instincts were fouled by fear, but he knew that much.

He sank to his elbows, rolled to his back and saw Eddie Baker, his handyman, above him with an M-16. The automatic weapon could kill Mark twenty times over, and Eddie was unquestionably an assassin. Mark could see the cold purpose in his eyes.

Mark lashed out to kick the barrel away, and the gun discharged. Pain seared his skull, and his vision blurred red. Blood splattered everywhere. The world was painted in it, but Mark didn't know what had happened until he saw Eddie's ghoulish smile.

Temple was headed for Ventura. She'd found a car in the doctor's garage with a key in the ignition. Typical of someone like Dan Llewelyn, she thought, to care so little about his possessions that he would leave the key in the car and risk having the car stolen, rather than chance misplacing the key.

Her first impulse had been to hit the gas and drive. She'd picked streets at random, with no purpose other than to be a moving target while she mapped out where she might hide.

She was still wearing the long gown and needed some clothes, but Mark would probably check her apartment, and she couldn't go to the police in this condition. She needed to clear her head and figure out what she was going to tell them.

A motel seemed the only solution until she remembered Annette's condo. Her friend had given her a key, and she'd also hidden one in the fuse box. If the place hadn't been rented or sold, Temple might be able to stay here.

Annette's condo seemed unnaturally quiet when Temple let herself in. But maybe that was because Temple could so vividly remember the romantic music and the movies of tormented love. Her sense of loss was immediate, aching. The Phantom cutout, incongruous as it was, brought tears to her eyes, and Temple wondered if she would be able to stay in this place, surrounded by reminders of her friend.

She felt on the brink of collapse but knew she couldn't let that happen. She had to hold it together a little longer, for reasons that totally escaped her now. There were clues scattered about that told her someone had been in the condo recently. That day's newspaper sat unread on the living room coffee table, and there was mail on the kitchen table, mostly advertisements and a few bills, all unopened.

They could have been picked up by a neighbor or a relative, Temple reasoned. It didn't necessarily mean the place was occupied, and she had nowhere else to go. At least the condo was familiar and more welcoming than a dingy motel room. And she needed the rest. It hurt when she walked, it hurt everywhere.

Moments later, with a sense of relief and Annette's teapot heating on the stove, Temple went to the bedroom to take a quick shower and borrow something to wear.

The gray cotton gown was in a heap on the bathroom floor and she was about to turn on the shower when she heard the front door open. A robe hung on a hook near the stall. She grabbed it and slipped out of sight, preparing herself for anything.

Her mind flashed a terrifying image of Dan Llewelyn. But it was another man who walked in the door, whirled, and stared into the blade of the butcher knife Temple had brought with her into the bathroom. He was even more terrifying than Llewelyn. It was Mark Challis, and he was drenched in blood, dripping.

"Temple?" he said. "Thank God—"

"What happened to you?" She held him off with the knife.

"Eddie Baker jumped me with an M-16."

"Eddie? Why?"

"I hired him on Llewelyn's recommendation as Jonathan's nurse, but he turned out to be a spy and an assassin. He's the one who shot at me, probably on Llewelyn's orders. I was struggling with him for the gun when it discharged and killed him."

Eddie Baker was dead? Temple didn't know whether to believe Mark or not. Why would Llewelyn want Mark assassinated? They were working together.

"Stay away!" She flashed the knife as he started toward her. She would have cut him, and he knew it. She was frightened enough to kill him.

"I want the truth," she said, "all of it—" A low twist of pain made her catch her breath, but still she held him off. "I know about your father, I know about everything, but I want to hear it from you."

"I'll tell you whatever you want to know, but not now. Something's wrong," he said.

She winced and leaned against the wall. This pain was bad, so sharp she nearly blacked out.

Mark moved, and she lashed out reflexively. "No!"

"Temple, let me help," he pleaded, gripping his hand. She'd caught him in the web of his thumb and forefinger, and blood was oozing from the wound.

A door slammed and Temple realized someone else was in the condo. Mark signalled her to be quiet, but Temple had little choice. She was too dizzy to stand on her own. Leaning heavily against the wall, she gripped the knife, expecting the worst.

"Who's there?" a woman's voice called out.

A moment later she appeared in the doorway, a startled pixie with spiky black bangs and a ponytail.

Temple barely noticed as Mark took the knife away from her.

"Annette?" she whispered, and slid to the floor in a faint.

TWENTY-FIVE

&ref;

She *wasn't* dead. Temple had opened her eyes in a strange hospital room with that one thought crowding out all the others in her head. Annette Dalton was not dead.

Temple still didn't know if it was true. And the tiny dynamo of a nurse, who'd just taken Temple's vital signs and was now arranging bouquets of get-well flowers, didn't seem to know what Temple was talking about when she asked about Annette.

The nurse knew about Mark, though. Her smile turned alert and slightly conspiratorial when she explained to Temple that a Mr. Mark Challis was the one who'd brought her in, that he was also responsible for all the lovely flowers and that the poor soul had been pacing the halls of the hospital all night, waiting for reports on Temple's condition.

"What exactly is my condition?" Temple asked, sensing the nurse would love to know more about the "Mr. Mark Challis" situation. For Temple's part, she could hardly deal with knowing the flowers were from him. Any mention of

Mark brought confusion and turmoil, and yet there was no way to avoid dealing with him. If any of what Dan Llewelyn said was true, Temple would have to brave the labyrinthine web of lies and deceit that Mark had woven. But at least this time she would be a smarter fly.

"Mother and baby are doing fine," the nurse said cheerily. "I can't tell you much more than that, but the doctor who treated you will be by on rounds later this morning, and he'll answer any questions you have. Meanwhile, there's an official visitor here to see you."

The nurse's eyes darted to the door and back. Her voice dropped to a whisper. "She's from the CDC."

Susan Gilchrist turned out to be the official visitor, and Temple wasn't at all sure what to expect as she entered the room. The thirtyish doctor hadn't changed all that much in the ten years since she'd been a fledgling member of the team that investigated the Zaire outbreak.

She still had the striking blue eyes and the smile that managed professional distance as well as warmth, which was no mean feat. Her gray flannel pantsuit was stylishly tailored, and if anything she was even more trim, efficient, and professional in her demeanor. Temple found it rather ironic that she'd had fleeting thoughts of Gilchrist as a suspect in the attempts on her life. Temple could see her running the CDC someday.

"How are you?" Gilchrist said, extending her hand as she approached Temple's bed. "You've been through hell from what I've heard. Are you up to talking?"

"What is it you've heard?" Temple asked. She was genuinely curious what the doctor knew of her ordeal, but she'd learned to be wary. It was sad that her own attempt to be more trusting had left her less so.

Gilchrist lifted a briefcase-like tote off her shoulder and set it on the floor. "Dan Llewelyn woke me with a phone call at my hotel last night and told me what he'd done. What a

nightmare that must have been for you, Temple. I'm sorry
you had to go through it, but it's over now."

She added softly, "And he's beyond hurting anyone."

"What happened?" Temple asked.

"When I got to his place, I found him sealed in the isolation tent, lying beside his wife. He was unconscious, and his
wife was already gone. There was a note, signed by him,
asking us not to revive either one of them. And he confessed
to everything."

If Temple felt relief, she was also deeply saddened by the
thought of how they'd died. And even more so for the
tragedy of such a rare gift gone wrong. Llewelyn was a visionary blinded by his own lack of insight.

"He had a dream of saving millions but couldn't save his
own wife," Temple said. "I think that's what destroyed
him."

"Exactly," Gilchrist agreed. "He weighed a few lives ver-
sus millions and saw it as the cost of waging war against the
virus, friendly fire, if you will. But when his wife got sick,
he began to understand that the cost of even one life is in-
calculable when it's someone you love. You can't weigh it
against millions, because love doesn't understand numbers."

Temple was surprised to hear Susan Gilchrist's voice
break. She seemed to be struggling with some emotion.

"Were you and Dan Llewelyn good friends?" Temple
asked.

The doctor shook her head. "If anything we were com-
petitors. Llewelyn was a consultant to the CDC when I
started there, but he was terminated shortly after the Zaire
outbreak. He was accused of taking a vial of infected blood
from the lab. It was never proven, but it ruined his credibil-
ity, especially since there were rumors that he had unlimited
private funding to develop a vaccine on his own."

The Will Challis Foundation, Temple thought.

Gilchrist's mouth tightened over a smile. "It's frightening

what people will do when their dreams are in reach, how they'll bargain with the devil, go to *any* lengths. Maybe this situation has brought that home like nothing else could. I should probably be grateful to Dan Llewelyn."

Temple was beginning to wonder what devil Susan Gilchrist had been bargaining with. "Did you have a dream in reach, too?" she asked.

The doctor's blue eyes narrowed as she took Temple's measure, perhaps deciding how candid she should be.

"Very perceptive," she admitted with some irony. "Actually, you're looking at the woman who was supposed to have saved L.A. County from the plague. I probably shouldn't be admitting this to anyone but my priest, but when I got the HMO's call for help, I kept it to myself. The outbreak sounded uncannily like Z190, and I'd been waiting ten years for another shot at that virus. I wanted to be the one to contain it, isolate the strain, maybe even come up with a vaccine.

"That was my dream, and suddenly it was in reach."

She took a long breath. "Luckily I came to my senses before anything irreparable happened. It really defeats the purpose of being a hero, doesn't it, if you have to lie, cheat, and steal to get there."

Temple had begun to think that one day Susan Gilchrist might be a very good head of the CDC. "You left an urgent message for me," she said, curious.

Gilchrist was obviously a little embarrassed. "That was in response to your message mentioning Z190. It sounded like you knew something about the outbreak, and I wanted to get to you before anyone else did."

"My call had nothing to do with an outbreak," Temple hastened to assure her. "I didn't know there'd been one."

"That's because it never hit the media, and thank God it didn't. There would have been a frenzy if the press had found out that one of the patients was also an Amnesia Assault victim."

Temple still had no idea what Gilchrist meant, and as it turned out the Z190 outbreak was just one of many things that Temple Banning didn't know about. She'd had no access to news on the island anyway, so she'd heard nothing for days, and certainly not the strange happenings the CDC doctor proceeded to describe.

When Gilchrist mentioned Dan Llewelyn's confession, Temple had assumed Llewelyn revealed the master plan that involved keeping Jonathan alive and impregnating Temple in order to do it. But Gilchrist seemed to know nothing about that. She described a totally different scenario to Temple, one even more bizarre.

"I've spoken with your Mark Challis," Gilchrist said, "the man who brought you to the hospital last night. He's had Llewelyn under investigation and believes he was behind the serial crimes the press are calling the 'Amnesia Assaults.'"

Temple hadn't heard of them, either, but she immediately identified. Her episode of amnesia had begun to feel like an assault. And she hadn't missed Gilchrist's reference to *her* Mark Challis.

"Challis discovered that Llewelyn was on staff at three different walk-in clinics under falsified credentials," Gilchrist explained. "He picked clinics that needed doctors and were lax about checking. If they questioned him, he simply went to another one. Apparently he had no trouble finding subjects for his own 'personal' clinical trials."

"I read their files," Temple said, just now realizing what Llewelyn had shown her. "He gave them the vaccine and then injected them with the virus, right?"

"Exactly. He picked women who lived isolated lives and would be unlikely to spread the virus, but it was still insanely risky. He inoculated them with the vaccine at the clinic, and then he waited long enough to let it take effect before he abducted them and injected them with the original strain of Agent Z190."

The doctor's slight shudder told Temple how heinous she considered the crime. As an epidemic intelligence officer, she routinely dealt with the devastation caused by outbreaks, but it was bugs causing havoc with humans, not the other way around.

"His files said he kept them under observation," Temple pointed out, "to see if they developed symptoms."

Sunshine beamed through the room's one small window. The partially opened blinds created a pattern of slats on the far wall. Ironically they reminded Temple of the striped patterns she'd always found so reassuringly simple and beautiful. Sadly they reminded her of another life, one she would never be able to reclaim, she realized. Not after all this.

"That was where the amnesia came in," Gilchrist was saying. "They were given a substance similar to Rohypnol, the date rape drug, but untraceable in the bloodstream. Llewelyn's intention was to keep them unconscious long enough to make sure they weren't developing symptoms, and then return them to the real world in a way that it looked as if they'd been sexually assaulted by some nut playing doctor. Obviously that was to throw suspicion off what he'd really done."

The room was warm and Gilchrist had slipped off her suit jacket, but seemed to have forgotten she was still holding it, crumpled in her fist.

"Apparently he didn't follow up after that," she said, "because one of the women actually developed symptoms. It was a mild case, but she passed the virus on to her secret lover, a college professor, who hadn't been vaccinated, of course, and he died of it just after passing it on to his pregnant wife, who survived. That's when I was called in."

Temple went cold inside. "Z190 may have mutated, and I

may have been exposed to the new strain last night. I was in the isolation unit with Maggie."

"You're fine." The doctor moved quickly to reassure her. "The new strain isn't airborne, we know that much. Also, it incubates in hours, and you're not even sniffling. But I've sent a blood sample to Atlanta for analysis, just to be sure."

Temple was wearing a generic hospital gown that pulled like a straitjacket when she tried to sit up. "Do you think I'll be able to leave soon?"

"That's not my call, Temple. I'm here to let you know that the outbreak is contained. The young woman who developed symptoms has been isolated and should make a full recovery, and Dan Llewelyn's home has been quarantined. But the police will want to talk to you about Llewelyn. The LAPD wants to close the Amnesia Assaults case, and you're officially considered the fourth victim."

"Really?" Temple reminded herself that Susan Gilchrist didn't know about Llewelyn's attempt to keep Jonathan Challis alive. Apparently Llewelyn had implicated only himself in his confession, and that must be why Gilchrist had assumed Temple was one of his victims. She was, of course, but in a much larger sense.

I could tell her everything right now, Temple realized. I could ruin Mark Challis. I could put him in jail and his father in the grave. I hold the cards. I have the power now.

She stared at the wall, at the lines of sun and shadow that could have been prison stripes, and her mind snagged on a stick that had nothing to do with power and ruination. It had to do with love. I need to call Ivy, she thought. I want to hear my sister's voice. There was nothing else safe to think about, and it was the only thing in life that actually mattered to Temple Banning at that moment.

Temple was packed and nearly ready to go when Mark appeared in the hospital room doorway. Not that she actually had anything to pack. She'd cajoled one of the female obstetrics residents out of a pair of ripped jeans, a tie-dyed T-shirt, and some Birkenstocks, but only after promising to return the treasured outfit or forfeit the first-born she was carrying.

The intern couldn't have known how painful a joke that was.

Especially now, Temple thought. It had looked like she might be able to slip out without seeing him, return home to her cardboard boxes, and try to forget for a little while that Mark Challis existed.

But when she glanced up, there he was, the man whose fiery tenderness had shattered her life. *Shattered her heart.* And left her with no defense except one.

"It is Mark? Or is it Michael?" she asked coldly. "I don't know what to call you."

"Mark." He said it softly, as if the sound of his own name was more than he could stomach.

Whatever fire had ignited his eyes was burning somewhere inside him now. It was burning him up. His head was bowed and he was slowly being consumed by an emotional firestorm, but Temple could do nothing. She felt nothing. That was the only defense he'd left her.

She was probably staring, but she'd never seen him disheveled before. He looked as if he hadn't slept in days. His hair was a tousled mess. His tie hung lopsided, and a dark growth shadowed his jawline.

He looked like hell. Beautiful hell. Poetic hell.

And she had to stop thinking like that.

"This was in the cottage." He held up her duffel bag as if it could buy him entry into her room.

"You can leave it there, by the door."

"I thought you might want this, too," he said, pulling a book from the bag. It was *Innate Power,* the one she'd borrowed.

"Leave it on the duffel," she said.

But he ventured into the room as far as the bed and set it there. He couldn't possibly have known that the book may have saved her life. But he seemed to understand that it was too important a possession to be left so far away.

The stick that had snagged on thoughts of Ivy was now caught in Temple's throat. It was scraping her raw.

"Thanks," she said.

"Temple, I need you to let me explain—"

No, she didn't want that. She'd already endured two confessions. "Just tell me it's not true," she said, rivaling his voice for softness. "Tell me that Dan Llewelyn lied about you."

The weary shake of his head killed all her hopes.

"If only I could," Mark admitted. "God, how I wish I could. But the truth is I've been funding Llewelyn since my father got ill. I wanted him to find a cure, but I had no idea what he was capable of."

"But you knew how he intended to use me and you allowed that. You made it possible."

"Temple—" His voice caught on her name, as if he already knew it was futile but couldn't stop himself. "I'm not here to ask for your forgiveness. I don't have the right. But I can't leave without telling you the truth, all of it. At least then you might understand what I did and why I did it."

"And why *did* you do it?" she burst out, hating him for making her ask. She didn't want to know!

"Because I couldn't let anyone else *die*."

His savage declaration cut through her anguish.

Temple didn't know what he meant by anyone else, unless it was his mother. He was a teenager when she drowned and he'd probably carried the guilt all his life. Crushing guilt, she was sure. But that didn't justify what he'd done.

"You *hated* your father," she said. "How could you go to those lengths to save a man you hate?"

"It didn't matter how I felt about Jonathan. I couldn't let him die, not that way. Not after what happened to Will."

"Your brother? The one who died in Zaire?" Llewelyn had told her about Will, and she asked the question without rancor, but Mark had already shut her out. He didn't want her to see what was happening to him, Temple realized. His head was twisted away, his neck muscles jutting.

"Christ," he breathed, fighting to control whatever violence was going on inside him. "I'm sorry. I'm just so fucking sorry."

He was locked up in some prison, locked up for so long that Temple thought he was going to slam open the cell door and walk out of the room. She should have told him to do that, to leave and keep going. She didn't want to hear about his brother. She didn't care about Mark Challis's pain. If he hurt she was glad.

But again his voice broke through her struggle. It was raw, like trees in the winter, stripped down to the bark.

"I got there too late," he said, still facing away. "The virus had already eaten Will alive. It had turned him into something I didn't recognize as my brother. He was a strong, proud kid, and it stole every shred of his dignity."

His jaw caught, worked. "He was strangling on his own vomit and covered in excrement, but he was in isolation, and I couldn't touch him, not even to clean him up. I don't think he heard a word I said after the first day, but the night he died, he was lucid for a moment, and he asked me to take care of our father.

" 'He has nothing left, Mark, nothing but you.' That's what Will kept telling me."

He looked around, stared at Temple with blazing eyes.

She didn't know what to do. The hospital had given her a toiletries kit because she'd arrived with nothing. She hadn't intended to take it with her, but now she picked it up off the stainless-steel tray and zipped it shut. She was desperately sorry about his brother, but that didn't give him the right to willfully alter the course of some innocent bystander's life.

"Did you ever consider the cost to me?" she asked him. "Nothing is ever going to be the same. I'm pregnant, I've probably lost my job."

He let out a defeated sigh. "This may speak volumes about how little men understand these things, but I was hoping you might come to love the baby, that you might want to keep it . . . or let me have it. As for the job, you haven't lost anything. I created it. I created Blue Sky."

"What?" She'd thought she was beyond surprises.

"I needed a way to bring you into my life."

"But an entire company?" she whispered. "All of those people? The accounts, you fabricated it all?"

"The company is real and so are the accounts. What you accomplished for Blue Sky was real, too. As for the employees, there were only two who knew, Annette and Sonia David, the president."

"Who is Annette?" Temple asked. "An actress? One of your investigators?"

"She wanted to be an actress once, but ended up a reporter instead. I hired her and trained her as an investigator when I went private. Sonia was one of her acting friends from the old days."

"And what about the amnesia? I must have been drugged the night it happened."

He didn't want to answer her questions. Regret and resistance were etched into his expression. *Don't make me do this,* he was saying.

"Was I, Mark? Was I drugged?"

Finally a nod. "That was Shirley, your apartment manager. It was in the food she gave you."

An icy dread had crept into Temple's breathing. This wasn't anything as innocuous as a spider's web. It was a conspiracy beyond her wildest dreams. She'd been locked in before she ever left Houston.

"What about the elevator accident and the explosion? The attempts on my life?"

"That was my own stupidity. I wanted you where I could protect you. Maybe I didn't trust Llewelyn. God knows I shouldn't have. But you proved to be a tough case, Temple. Once you decided you didn't need my help, there was virtually nothing I could do to convince you."

Temple wanted to cry. She could hardly swallow back the constriction in her throat. "God, how I wish you'd told me it wasn't true. That none of it was true."

She turned away and the room went quiet.

His voice reached out to her, harsh, aching. "It isn't true that I ever meant to hurt you, Temple, however ludicrous that sounds now. And it isn't true that I wouldn't do anything to change it if I could, *anything.*"

"Don't ask me to forgive you. I can't forgive you."

"I'm not asking that."

Her heart was breaking. How could that be? It was already in pieces. "And don't ask me to trust you, ever. There is no way a relationship could ever be based on lies and deceit."

"Could it be based on a man's blundering attempts to make amends to the only thing in life he loves . . . to you, Temple . . . and to the baby?"

She shook her head, refusing to let him suggest such things. They were impossible. And she couldn't look at him. That was impossible, too. Not at those blazingly painful eyes.

"No, it can't, Mark. You lost the right to be part of my life when you took it out of my hands."

"Temple—"

"I could have put you in prison. The police questioned me, and I told them nothing, but please don't think I did it for you. I don't want to be part of a trial. I don't want to have to testify against you and be forced to relive this nightmare."

"Prison would have been a gift compared to this, Temple. I would rather you had done that than lose you. God, I would rather my own father have died."

She turned to him, and the tears began to flood. "Me, too," she said, a sob anguishing in her throat. "Me, too, Mark. Isn't that terrible? How do you base a relationship on that?"

He went silent then, as if stunned by some realization.

"Jesus," he whispered after a moment, his voice barely discernible. "I've done exactly what he did. I've destroyed the thing I loved. My father destroyed my mother with his obsession to control her, and now I've destroyed you. I've destroyed *us*. I vowed not to be like him and look at me. I'm worse. I knew what he did, and I did it anyway. God— God, forgive me."

His entire being changed as he finally realized that too much damage had been done. It was futile. The hope burned out of his eyes and his powerful frame seemed to sway. He was lost. He didn't know what to do next. He was as helpless to save this as he had been his mother and brother. The only thing in life he'd been able to salvage was the thing he hated. And he would have to live with that terrible truth the rest of his life.

"All right," he said on a dying breath. "I'll do whatever you ask. I'll stay out of your lives. You don't even have to tell the child I exist . . ." He hesitated, his jaw knotting as he made one last request. "But let me do something. Let me take care of your expenses at least."

She turned away this time, unable to look at him any longer. It tore at her that she might be inflicting pain. No matter what he'd done, it tore at her. But this was not a time to save anyone but herself. It was a time to struggle with the impulse that had always made her put others first. It was her needs that counted now, the baby's. Nothing else.

"No, don't pay for anything," she said. "Don't *do* anything. Just keep your promise. Stay out of our lives."

Some time later she heard him go. And her heart broke again. It splintered into so many shards of sorrow she knew they would never be found.

TWENTY-SIX

THREE MONTHS LATER . . .

"I ate the whole jar?" Temple rummaged through the top shelf of her refrigerator, searching for the jumbo jar of roasted jalapeños she'd bought just yesterday. She was making a turkey sandwich to take out on the front porch, and it wouldn't be the same without some of the tart, tangy little peppers.

Lately she'd taken to wanting jalapeños with everything. She'd tried them on her toast and peanut butter that morning and then minced some for tunafish. But when she'd toyed with the idea of sprinkling peppers on rocky road ice cream, she'd known her doctor was right. This was a craving. Her first.

Moments later she was sitting on the front porch steps in the waning sunlight, nibbling her sandwich and wondering if life could get any quieter than the one she was living since she'd returned to Houston. Her days consisted of managing a friendly little neighborhood bookstore that was walking distance from the two-bedroom patio house she'd taken, and fussing over the vegetable patch she had growing on her patio in big black tubs.

The second bedroom was for Ivy, who'd come home during spring break, albeit somewhat reluctantly, and who couldn't have been more nonchalant about the news of Temple's pregnancy. Ivy's twenty-one-year-old needle was stuck on important things.

"Everyone's going out to Padre Island!" she'd lamented so incessantly that Temple had finally bought her an inner tube, a ticket to the resort area, and driven her to the bus station.

A swallow fluttered from the sky and landed on the walkway in front of Temple. Watching it search for food, she realized her tunic top was a bowl of bread crumbs from the sandwich. She flapped the black-and-white striped cotton and created a little snowstorm, which brought more swallows, dropping like stealth bombers from the neighbor's elm trees. She tossed more crumbs from the plate, and thought about the crisis that had led her to put on a tunic top this morning.

She hadn't been able to zip her jeans. The slide had jammed and it had hit her like a thunderbolt that she was pregnant, irrevocably with child. But she had never made a conscious decision to keep the baby. She'd walked the bedroom floor in her unfastened pants, and finally realized what she was afraid of. She, the mega-responsible one, was terrified of the responsibilities of parenthood. She had no idea whether or not she would be a good mother—and that was unthinkable, given her childhood. She couldn't raise a child with anything other than total commitment. It had to be with her whole heart.

Some time later that morning, after having worn a path in her bedroom carpet, she'd shucked the jeans, put on the roomy striped tunic and black tights she was wearing now, and realized that, given what they'd been through together, this baby *was* her heart. Her whole heart.

I hope it likes jalapeños, she thought, smiling as she picked up the sandwich plate and rose to her feet. Maybe she ought to try growing the peppers. She'd never expected to be in the gardening mode again after having been the care-taker of her parents' macramé jungle of philodendrons for so many years. But the conservatory at Wings had made her re-alize how deeply responsive she was to living, growing things, and she had decided to try plants that would feed her body as well as her soul.

She'd started with the easy stuff, but her tomatoes, cu-cumbers, zucchini, and carrots were coming along beauti-fully. The green beans were a little shy, but Temple was optimistic.

And she had some hope for her own future, too.

There were days now—or was it hours?—when she hardly thought about Mark Challis, when his striking fea-tures didn't stand out in her mind like sunlight on water. She took it as a sign of progress, although she was still haunted by what had happened on the island. So far he'd honored his promise. He hadn't tried to contact her, but she had received phone messages from Annette Dalton. The latest one had come in earlier today. Annette had spoken of important news. She'd begged Temple to call, and although Temple hadn't done it, she'd thought about it all morning.

Temple headed back to the kitchen, plate in hand, know-ing she would pass the kitchen wall phone on her way to the sink. She swished some water over the china, dropped it in the rack to dry, and wondered if she would make it out of the room without returning the call.

The answer to that was no. Temple's hyper-responsible nature wouldn't allow her it ignore "important news."

"Annette?" she said the moment the other woman picked up the phone. "This is Temple Banning."

She was touched by her friend's surprised gasp, and by the emotion in her voice.

"Oh, Temple, I'm so glad you called back! I never got a chance to apologize. I know there's nothing I can say that will make it right, but I wanted you to know how deeply sorry I am for what happened. I could just kill myself—Oops, sorry, bad choice of words."

Temple smiled inwardly at Annette's exuberance, even at expressing regret. She graciously accepted the apology but was still wary of resuming the friendship. Fortunately Annette had another reason for calling. She wanted Temple to know that Jonathan Challis had been undergoing a new and highly experimental treatment, developed in the CDC labs. They'd been working on a serum for Z190 as long as Dan Llewelyn had, and it was actually Dan Llewelyn's formulas that had helped them perfect their own.

"The prognosis is good," Annette said, "and of course everyone's grateful to you for helping keep Jonathan stable until the serum was ready."

Temple had actually gone down to the local Red Cross and donated blood, which they'd shipped to the clinic where Jonathan was being treated. She was grateful to know that it was over now, because his condition had been weighing heavily on her mind, and she was genuinely relieved. Now that his life was no longer dependent on her or her unborn child in any way, there was nothing left to tie Temple to the Challis family, or to Mark. She was free of that burden and could get on with her life.

"I thought you might also like to know about June," Annette said. "Mark arranged for her to leave the island and to get grief therapy. She never really recovered from her daughter's death, but she has a resilient spirit, and she's doing well. Mark also found her a house in Thousand Oaks, and they've even worked out some of their differences. Actually it's him I'm concerned about—"

"Thank you, Annette." Temple cut her off perhaps too quickly, but she didn't want to hear about Mark. Still, as she wished Annette well and hung up the phone, she knew what it must feel like to lose a vital part of yourself. The concern about Jonathan had weighed on her, but it had also been an artery that kept her connected. And now that it was gone, she felt an odd mix of loss and confusion, as if she'd reached a crossroads, but didn't know if she'd chosen the right direction.

She touched her newly rounded belly, feeling very much alone as she stood at the kitchen counter, wondering what the future could possibly have in store. And when she would finally be at peace with the choices she'd made.

The next several weeks passed uneventfully for Temple and her unborn charge. There were no more calls from Annette, and Temple settled into a routine that involved tending to her bookstore and to her garden. As she entered her fifth month, there were moments when it felt as if she could be happy with nothing more than that, working at a bookstore and raising a garden and a child in a quiet neighborhood among good people. If not happy, then content.

But as the days began to shorten, and fall approached, she was aware of something different in the air, almost sinister. She wanted to write it off to the weather, to hormones, to anything but the threat she sensed. She actually had the feeling of someone hovering at the periphery of her life and watching her.

She told herself it was a holdover from her ordeal, a form of delayed stress. But one morning she made the discovery that it was none of those things. The weather was unusually chilly, so she decided to drive, and as she passed the store on her way to the parking lot in back, she saw him at the entrance, peering in through the etched glass panels. But by the time she'd parked and walked around front, the frail white-haired man was gone.

He was the one who'd been watching her. Temple sensed that strongly. If he'd been younger or tougher looking, she might have summoned the police to her peaceful little street. As it was she'd watched the entrance all day, jumped whenever the door opened, and stepped outside several times for a look around.

That evening she arrived home to an open front door, a breezy apartment, and the man in question sitting in her living room. He looked startlingly familiar, but Temple wasn't certain of his identity until he began to talk about his son.

"I'm worried about Mark," Jonathan Challis said, without any preamble whatsoever. "He's holed up out there on that godforsaken island and nobody can get him off it. He refuses to talk to me, but then he always has, damn idiot."

He put on a good show of being gruff, but Temple could see the grief seared into his dark gaze, and it reminded her of Mark. Money had not saved Jonathan Challis from losses beyond what most people could bear.

"I can't help you," she told him firmly. "And you had no right to break into my house. No amount of wealth entitles you to break laws and bully people."

By the look on his face it was clear that not too many people had ever called Jonathan Challis a bully. He struggled to stand, and she could see how weakened and ill he still was.

"Your door wasn't locked," he said. "And I didn't feel well enough to stand outside waiting for you."

He took a couple of shaky steps toward her, and Temple found herself hurrying over to steady him.

He thanked her with brusque pride but held her off with a look, just the way his son was able to do.

"I've never thought my money entitled me to anything anyone didn't want to sell me," he said, "and most people are happy enough to do that. I know it won't keep Mark alive. Only you can do that."

"This is blackmail," Temple said, struggling against the rush of emotion she felt. "You're blackmailing me, and if this is how you treat people, I can see why Mark won't have anything to do with you."

"Blackmailing you?" He stared at her in some confusion. "I don't know what the hell you're talking about, but if I thought it would work, I'd do it. I already owe you my life, Miss Temple. All I'm asking is a little compassion and understanding. Mark won't listen to anyone but you."

Miss Temple? Did he think her first name was Shirley? If he hadn't been so blustery and overbearing, she might have found his old-fashioned ways endearing. This was not the Jonathan Challis she'd imagined. Not at all.

"Is Mark sick?" she asked.

"Sick, no, except for his soul. He could pass a physical tomorrow, but I doubt he'll live out the year."

"What do you mean?"

"I said he's dying. What don't you understand about that?"

He dismissed her confusion with a shake of his head, moved closer, and began to speak in a conspiratorial whisper, as if he was certain someone was listening in. Maybe God, Temple thought with some irony.

"You can't *ever* tell him I came here," he instructed her firmly. "Mark would have my head if he knew what I was about to say. He's got too much pride for his own good, that one. He'll go to the grave before he'll tell you what he did . . . and God, I'm afraid he might."

"What he did?" Temple echoed.

Jonathan wet his lips, as if reconsidering, then lifted his chin enough to peer down his nose at her. Talk about pride, Temple thought.

"He saved your life. My son saved your life. Or maybe you already knew about that."

Temple had no idea what he was talking about.

"In Zaire, at the hospital. He got there too late for Will, but when he came across you, lying in your isolation unit, he thought he'd seen a vision. It made him think of some fairy tale—the princess in her deathlike trance. Like Sleeping Beauty, I think he said. You were lying in some moonlit corridor, and he could see you weren't sick like the rest of them, but he was convinced you'd die from the substandard care, which is probably true."

"Mark saw me? In Zaire?"

"That's what I said, didn't I? I think he was in love with you at first sight. He said something about a soft white aura, like it was a religious experience. I know that sounds crazy, but it's true. He was probably distraught over Will and hurting like hell, but Mark couldn't let himself feel those things—pain, loss, *love,* especially that, so he put his energies into getting you out. I still don't know how he did it. The place was under government quarantine and barricaded by military troops. I couldn't even get Will's body back."

Temple didn't know what to say. That must be why she thought she'd heard his voice before, whispering to her, calling her princess. Now she understood the tenderness, the tears.

"That's what's killing him now," Jonathan said. "That he saved you only to have to betray you in that way. Imagine being faced with the choice of using someone you love to save someone you hate. I think that must have been the ultimate sacrifice for a man like Mark, and it's destroying him. He could never tell you any of this, but I can. *I have to.* So, please, hear me now, while I've still got the strength."

He attempted to steady himself against her walnut coffee table and failed. Temple started toward him and felt the stopping power of his fierce gaze all over again. He would not accept her help, not in that way.

By the time he'd settled himself on the chair arm, he could barely speak for the effort, but his conviction was unmistakable.

"If you have any feeling left for him, then I'm asking you to go there," he said. "You don't have to stay. You don't ever have to see him again if that's your choice, but go there, Miss Temple, please. And forgive him, if you can. Do it for me or for the baby, not because Mark deserves it . . . because he can't live without it."

Long after Jonathan Challis was gone, Temple wandered the house and thought about what Mark had done. And said . . .

I didn't want anyone else to die.

It forced her to ponder what extremes people would go to to save their loved ones. She'd never been put in that position, thank God, but she did know that had Ivy contracted the fever, she would have done anything to save her life, including become pregnant.

Sometimes people did bad things for good reasons. She remembered thinking that when she discovered Mark had her under surveillance. She'd been ready to condemn him out of hand for not telling her, until she realized that she was lying to Ivy to protect her. When it came to blood ties, there weren't any rules, she realized. We simply followed our hearts and did what we had to, as long as no one got hurt.

But there was the hitch. Mark had hurt her. He'd stolen her life away from her, changed it forever. No one and nothing else could have kept Jonathan alive but her, so Mark had exercised what to him must have felt like his only option.

That was a line she didn't believe she could have crossed, but she was learning not to judge what she didn't understand. Perhaps the deep conflict Mark felt toward his father had made it more imperative. It was wrenching to lose someone you both loved and hated because there was no closure. Only what you would have said and done, if you'd had the chance. Temple gave out a sigh. She didn't have an answer, but she knew forgiveness was the key, if she could find her way to the door. She also knew if she did forgive him, it would be for herself, not for him.

At some point in her reflections, she realized she hadn't eaten and that all the pacing had left her starving. There was leftover pizza in the fridge, so she heated a piece in the microwave and took the bubbling wedge outside with her. She fed the swallows so often they were coming right up on the porch with her now. She hadn't had one perch on her hand yet, but that would happen, she imagined, and then the rest would see it was safe.

One of them had hopped up to the step she sat on and was staring longingly at the morsels in her cupped palm. She understood the bird's reluctance to trust, even though it was being tempted with something it wanted very badly. She understood that impulse well.

Still, her life was good, not the one she'd planned, but it was exactly what she needed right now. And when the bookstore was no longer challenging, she might well go back to advertising, perhaps even start her own little agency.

She took a bite of the pizza, felt the baby kick, and smiled. The little one doesn't like pizza *or* jalapeños? Temple pulled off a string of melted mozzarella and made do with that.

Inexplicable as it seemed, maybe in the greater scheme of things, Mark hadn't actually hurt her. Maybe he'd given her something. She'd been able to move past her fears and accept the responsibility that comes from love rather than guilt or obligation. She really wanted to love and care for this child. It wasn't a burden. It was a blessing.

There was a part of her that wanted to forgive him, that was ready to be relieved of a heavy burden and start new, and a part of her that didn't. It was safer this way. She was surrounded by bunkers of safety. But an even larger question loomed in her mind. If she were to forgive him, where did it go from there? Could there ever be more? Could she ever give her heart to Mark Challis again?

The island looked virtually uninhabited as Temple flew over in the helicopter she'd chartered. It was a fairly rickety machine, and the pilot hadn't looked entirely sober, but Temple had been in a desperate hurry, and nothing else was available.

"Could you find somewhere closer to the house to land than the helipad?" she shouted at him.

He nodded, although she suspected he hadn't heard a word.

To her relief he started down over a barren patch of land next to the road that led to the mansion. She would be able to walk that distance, she realized, even with her extra weight.

There was no sign of June or anyone on the household staff as Temple entered Wings. The magnificent old place had clearly not been cleaned or maintained in some time, and she immediately picked up a sense of abandonment and disorder, even distress. It was bizarre how the house telegraphed itself, and how she was able to pick up its signals.

She rushed through rooms that looked as if they hadn't been lived in for months, and when she got to his office, she found it empty, too. She didn't know where his bedroom was, and as her thoughts scattered, racing to the pool, to the tower, another idea came to her.

The path to the teahouse felt like miles. She tried to pace herself but was breathless as she climbed the steps. The rice panel doors were gaping open, and Temple could see without stepping inside that this place was empty, too. The furniture had been cleaned out. There was nothing but straw matting on the floor, and emptiness.

Her disappointment was piercing. It was despair. She had thought that certainly he would be here. The idea had come to her with such clarity it felt like the force she'd learned to heed on this very island, her own intuition.

She turned to go, but picked up a whispering sound that nearly stopped her heart.

Ssshh now, don't be afraid. . . .

Her shell. The nautilus. She hadn't seen it since she left the island, and she'd assumed it was lost forever, a symbol of the emotional cost of her experience. Now she looked around and half expected to see it materialize in front of her eyes.

Ssssshhhh . . .

It wasn't the wind chimes. There was no wind. It wasn't the stream or the tree leaves. This wasn't nature's music, it was the soul's.

And it was coming from inside the house, she realized.

She remembered the smells of fragrant tea and the sounds of naked longing as she stepped over the threshold. The desolation of the place made her ache. How much more painful to remember the richness when you were surrounded by barrenness. The contrast was stark.

Ssssshhhhhhhh . . .

The sound pulled her around, and she saw him standing by doors that opened onto a side deck. He was looking out, with his back to her, but his head was tilted, and it looked as if his hand was cupped to his ear and he was listening to something, her shell.

She was afraid for him to turn around. He looked thinner and his hair was long and glossy. She didn't want to see his face. She knew the bones would be edged like razors, and the eyes would have a thrust that could impale her.

Jonathan had said he was dying, and that was how he

looked. She didn't know how to see Mark that way. It would kill her, too.

Finally she was able to form a question.

"What are you doing here?" she asked him.

His head jerked up, but he didn't turn. "I've been here ever since you left."

"Why?"

"Because this is where we made love."

If she could have touched his voice, her knuckles would have bled. It had the raw scrape of sandpaper. She had come here for the same reason he had. Her intuition hadn't failed her, but now she wished it would tell her what to say.

Sssssshhh . . .

Finally she whispered, "You kept my shell?"

"I wanted something of you close to me. I should have returned it, but I found that I couldn't."

His spine was so stiff it looked like one more degree of arc would shatter him.

"Can you tell me what you heard?" she asked. She had waited a lifetime to know what the whispers meant. Maybe he knew.

Her question turned him around, and Temple saw the devastation with her own eyes. He looked so gaunt and desolate she wanted to run to him. He obviously still believed he was the cause of everything that had happened, all the loss, all the pain.

"Impossible hope." He looked past her, remembering. "It sounded like that. Impossible hope."

She didn't want to think it was that. "Are you sure?"

He nodded wearily. "What else would there be? What else is there? The sound of redemption, whatever that is?"

"Why not?"

"Because some things are beyond it."

"Nothing is beyond forgiving, Mark."

When he met her gaze, she knew what impossible hope

looked like. After a moment he walked over and gave her the shell.

"Tell me what *you* hear," he said.

She palmed the treasured shell and thought about it a moment. "It always reminded me of a mother hushing her child and telling her everything would be all right. Ssshh, don't be afraid . . . ssshh, you're not alone."

His jaw flexed painfully, but he nodded with understanding.

"I never had that," she said, "but I hope and pray I can give that feeling to my child . . . our child."

He looked at her pregnant body, and his eyes sparkled with pain. Abruptly he turned away, and the rigidity that had held him together seemed to shatter into a million crystalline pieces. He made a massive effort to fight the tremor that shook him, so much so that his shoulders hitched uncontrollably.

Temple watched him in quiet desperation. This was the strongest man she'd ever known, but he was bowed and broken at thoughts of his own child, the child he'd agreed never to see again. If she could do nothing else, she had to help him find the way to forgiveness.

"Mark," she said, "please look at me. Please."

It was some time before he could do it.

"You're not responsible for anything that's happened," she told him. "Except this."

She touched her belly and watched him flinch.

He looked as if someone had struck him, but Temple wasn't through. "I expect you to do your part, Mark, to be a good father, to love this baby, to—"

She never got the last demand out of her mouth. He had turned and he was looking at her for some sign that it was all right to come near her. Their locked gazes brought him a step or two closer, and then she let out a helpless sound, a sweet sound. It was little more than a whimper, but he was there before she could think about whether or not she'd done the right thing, letting such nakedness escape. He was there, gathering her into his arms, wetting her hair with his tears, and calling her by the name he'd given her that night. "Princess," he said, "I love you. I have *always* loved you."

Temple closed her eyes and rested her forehead on his shoulder. She allowed herself to be held, but she didn't hug him back at first.

I can forgive him, but can I ever again give him my heart?

That was the question that had brought her here, and until this very moment Temple hadn't realized how deeply her feelings ran. She had never let herself. Now it swelled inside her with enough force to burst the seams of her heart. She hadn't shown him the way to forgiveness. They would find it together.

Her hands caught at his waist, and she hugged him hard.

She did love Mark Challis, despite everything. And what greater power than that, she wondered. Than love.

FOUR MONTHS LATER . . .

Temple laughed joyously as she rested in her hospital bed, cradling a seven-pound bundle in her arms. The baby had just finished nursing, and much bubbling, smacking, and cooing could still be heard.

"Did you hear that?" she asked Mark, pretending to be thunderstruck. "I think she just said ga-ga."

"Quite a vocabulary on that girl." Mark sat on the bed at Temple's side, the proud father of her bright-eyed baby girl and her very own passionately devoted husband. They'd been married just two months ago, in a small ceremony on the cliffs of Peregrine Island, with the waves crashing below and the falcons swooping overhead.

"Time to take her home?" Mark lifted the little bubble blower from Temple's arms.

Temple adjusted her nursing bra, drew her gown back on,

and carefully slipped out of bed. "I was ready yesterday," she assured him, "right after the delivery."

Moments later Temple was in a wheelchair, holding the baby and waiting for an orderly to come roll her out. Mark had her bags together and was giving the room a last-minute check when the hospital door opened.

Their visitor was probably the last person either one of them had expected to see here. Jonathan Challis had entered the room, looking slightly less frail than the night Temple found him in her house.

Temple whispered his name in surprise, ready to welcome him into the fold. But Mark went rigid at the sight of his father.

It was a visible reaction, and Temple braced herself for the confrontation. She hadn't seen Jonathan since that evening in Houston, and she knew Mark hadn't seen him in years. Father and son still weren't speaking. They were both too stubborn, but it was unthinkable to Temple that these two grown men had not reconciled.

"Mark," she said under her breath.

She told him with her eyes what she expected and what he must do. And then she handed him their newborn.

Mark took his daughter gingerly, clutching her to his chest. When he looked up at his father, the room crackled with tension. Finally Mark drew in a deep breath and crossed the room to the older man. He offered his cargo to a startled, emotion-choked Jonathan.

"Just in time to meet your granddaughter," was Mark's softly spoken flag of truce.